CAROL ARENS
A Yuletide Proposal

Two classic historical stories

QUILLS: A YULETIDE PROPOSAL © 2023 by Harlequin Books S.A.

THE VISCOUNT'S YULETIDE BRIDE
© 2020 by Carol Arens
Australian Copyright 2020
New Zealand Copyright 2020

First Published 2020
Second Australian Paperback Edition 2023
ISBN 978 1 867 29826 7

THE VISCOUNT'S CHRISTMAS PROPOSAL
© 2021 by Carol Arens
Australian Copyright 2021
New Zealand Copyright 2021

First Published 2021
Second Australian Paperback Edition 2023
ISBN 978 1 867 29826 7

Published by
Quills
An imprint of Harlequin Enterprises (Australia) Pty Limited
(ABN 47 001 180 918), a subsidiary of HarperCollins
Publishers Australia Pty Limited (ABN 36 009 913 517)
Level 19, 201 Elizabeth Street
SYDNEY NSW 2000
AUSTRALIA

MIX
Paper | Supporting
responsible forestry
FSC® C001695

® and ™ (apart from those relating to FSC®) are trademarks of Harlequin Enterprises (Australia) Pty Limited or its corporate affiliates. Trademarks indicated with ® are registered in Australia, New Zealand and in other countries. Contact admin_legal@Harlequin.ca for details.

Printed and bound in Australia by McPherson's Printing Group

CONTENTS

Books by Carol Arens

Harlequin Historical

Dreaming of a Western Christmas
"Snowbound with the Cowboy"
Western Christmas Proposals
"The Sheriff's Christmas Proposal"
The Cowboy's Cinderella
Western Christmas Brides
"A Kiss from the Cowboy"
The Rancher's Inconvenient Bride
A Ranch to Call Home
A Texas Christmas Reunion
The Earl's American Heiress
Rescued by the Viscount's Ring
The Making of Baron Haversmere
The Viscount's Yuletide Bride
To Wed a Wallflower
A Victorian Family Christmas
"A Kiss Under the Mistletoe"
The Viscount's Christmas Proposal

Visit the Author Profile page
at millsandboon.com.au for more titles.

THE VISCOUNT'S
YULETIDE BRIDE

Carol Arens delights in tossing fictional characters into hot water, watching them steam and then giving them a happily-ever-after. When she is not writing, she enjoys spending time with her family, beach camping or lounging about a mountain cabin. At home, she enjoys playing with her grandchildren and gardening. During rare spare moments, you will find her snuggled up with a good book. Carol enjoys hearing from readers at carolarens@yahoo.com or on Facebook.

Author Note

This is a poem written by my eleven-year-old granddaughter, Brielle Iaccino, in response to something we would never have dreamed possible...social distancing. She wrote this one night before bedtime and I would like to share it with you because..."out of the mouths of babes"...

"In a day or two"

In a day or two we will cheer
A trembling world will be calm
We will reunite
The gates will open
We will sing with joy
I'll give you a hug
You'll give it back
We will be happy
And we shall hold hands
And Laugh
And Play
In a day or two
I will see you.

Coming to the end of a very trying and unusual year, I suspect that we all need a bit of Christmas cheer. I hope Felicia and Isaiah's story brings you a smile. I wish you all the hope, the joy and the love the season can bring.

"In a day or two we will cheer."

Wishing you the very best,
Carol and Brielle

To Brandon Matthew Iaccino.

My smart, thoughtful and generous grandson.
You are awesome and I love you.

Chapter One

⚭⚭⚭⚭⚭

Scarsfeld Manor—November 15, 1889

The letter in Isaiah Elphalet Maxwell's hand stung like a ball of ice—or perhaps it burned as if he crushed a live flame.

He stared out of the conservatory windows watching his young half-sister play on the shore of Lake Windermere, his heart feeling as if it were being crushed between his boot heel and a stone.

Abigail leapt, twirled in the air, then presented a deep curtsy to her cat, Eloise.

How could he not smile at her antics? Even with the letter crushed in his trembling fist, how could he not?

Eight-year-old Lady Abigail Elizabeth Turner was the one bright spot in his rather bleak home. In his life, really.

She was his, by blood and by right.

Ever since that rainy night eight years ago when his butler carried a dripping, screeching bundle into the parlour followed by a harried-looking fellow who turned out to be his late stepfather's lawyer, Isaiah's life had not been the same.

Half-brother—yes, he was that to Abigail—but father, too. He was the one to have cared for her, loved and nurtured her all her life. In spite of the fact that he had been only twenty-two at the time, no natural father could have been more devoted.

Spinning about, he stalked towards the fireplace, flung the missive into the flames, then returned to the window.

The wind was rising, dancing through the tree tops and scattering the last of the autumn leaves across the ground.

Naturally, Abigail did not appear to mind the cool bluster in the least. She chased the brightly hued foliage about, stomping and laughing. Her tortoiseshell cat frolicked about her skirt, swatting the lace hem.

It was time to call her inside. While it was not likely that a weakened branch would crack, fall and strike her, it could not be discounted out of hand.

Experience had taught him that he could not be too watchful when it came to keeping a child safe. An unlocked door on a freezing night had taught him that lesson.

Besides, even from here he could see the nanny shivering in her coat while stomping her feet as if that might somehow warm her.

Coming out on to the terrace, he stood for a moment bearing the cold in order to gaze at the lake. Wide and long, it resembled a frigid blue ribbon cutting the land.

Isaiah looked down the gentle slope leading to the shore. He waved his arm to get his sister's attention. Wind caught the lapels of his coat and flapped them about.

Truly, he disliked this time of year. Hopefully it would

not snow any time soon. The further they went into autumn and winter without it, the better it would be for everyone.

Seeing his signal to come inside, Abigail scooped up her cat and dashed up the stone steps. Out of breath, she wrapped her slender arms about his ribs and pressed her ear against his heart.

'Will it snow, Isaiah?' She hopped up and down, which made the cat wriggle out of her arms and leap inside the open door of the conservatory.

Well, lack of snow would be better for most people, but clearly not his little sister.

The nanny, her shoulders hunched, hurried past, following the cat.

'If it does, at least we will remain properly inside the manor as sensible people should,' she muttered in passing.

It did not seem to matter that he was Viscount Scarsfeld—the ninth one, in fact—nor that his social position outranked hers. Miss Shirls spoke her mind.

On that night when Abigail had arrived the woman had been summoned from her duties in the kitchen. With a bottle of warm milk in hand, she took the screeching baby. Before the bottle was fully suckled, Miss Shirls appointed herself nursemaid. He had allowed it since he'd had no one else. As it turned out, the transition from kitchen to nursery had worked well for Miss Shirls and for him.

Miss Shirls had been devoted to his sister every day since. He supposed it was fair and just to overlook her familiarity. Status notwithstanding, the nanny did feel as though she was family.

As family went it was only he and Abigail. If Miss Shirls placed herself with them, he did not mind in the least.

'I want to play outdoors in the snow! I shall build half a dozen snowmen and snow cats. Will you help me, Isaiah?'

He kissed the top of her head where her hat had fallen off. Her blonde curls smelled like cold, fresh air. Could one actually smell happiness? If so, he smelled that on her, too.

Making sure Abigail grew up happy was what mattered most to Isaiah. He would do whatever was needed to keep her from the loneliness he had suffered in childhood.

As long as he drew a breath she would know every day that she was cherished.

No matter that he had tossed the letter from his late stepfather's brother into the flames, the words remained seared on his fingers, burned into his brain.

He read them over in his mind. He did not wish to, but could not seem to help it, no matter how he tried.

Greetings, Lord Scarsfeld,
My wife and I hope all is well with you as we approach
Christmas time—a holiday we have been negligent
in celebrating with you and our dear niece Abigail.'

Their 'dear niece Abigail' whom they had never set eyes upon.

We will, however, make amends for it this year. We
do appreciate that you have taken on the burden of
raising her. We are forever grateful.

As if they had just due to be grateful for anything.

But now the time has come for my wife and I to lift
that burden.

Abigail had never been, nor would she ever be, a burden to be lifted.

> *It seems only right and appropriate, since you remain unmarried and my lovely Diana has yet to bless us with a child of our own, that our niece should be raised at Penfield. I trust this is agreeable.*
>
> *Please look forward to our arrival on the fifteenth of December.*
> *With kind regards,*
> *Penfield*

Why would Penfield decide this now? In all of Abigail's eight years they had not visited or asked for her to visit them. A rare letter was all she had received from the Earl and Countess of Penfield.

The best he could make of it was that they had given up hope of having a child of their own and had now set their sights upon his sister. Perhaps they thought London could offer advantages that a quiet life here could not.

'You look like thunder, Isaiah.' Abigail slashed her slim brows at him in censure. 'It is no wonder people think you are forbidding.'

'Who thinks it?'

'Nearly everyone. You ought to smile upon occasion so they do not think you so imperious.'

'Imperious?'

'Or crusty.'

'Crusty!' He was only thirty years old and years away from being crusty!

'Do you think I'm crusty?' Please let her not.

'I know you are not. You can be great fun when you want

to be and you have the kindest soul of anyone. Although you do your best to hide it.'

'Why would I?'

'It is the very question I ask.'

'You seem older than eight years.'

'And you seem grumpier than you are.'

He did have a reputation for being glum—even surly—he had heard some whisper that sentiment. People did not seek his company unless it was necessary. Which was fine since he preferred to avoid what was to him the false merriment of social gatherings, where at every turn young ladies and their mothers vied for his attention—for his title, more to the point.

On the occasions where he had to attend a function, presenting the darker side of his nature had given him a buffer of sorts.

His distant behaviour did keep him isolated from society for the most part, but it did not overly trouble him. He was rather satisfied with the way things were. Quiet, orderly, predictable—it was how he liked his life.

'What would you do if you were me? To make people think I'm not crusty?'

'Smile more, of course. Perhaps laugh out loud. And put a Christmas tree in the parlour.'

A Christmas tree! He had not put up one of those since he was a child—and, no, even for Abigail he could not do it.

'I never knew you wanted one.'

'Everyone does, you know. Ribbons on the stairway and bows on the mantel can only bring so much Christmas cheer. As much as I enjoy the Yule log, I'm eight years old now and it is past time I had a tree.'

'This is the first time you've brought up the subject.'

'And it will not be the last. I've seen them in town, how lovely they are. In all the books people sing carols while gathered about them…and while eating sugar plums! What must Father Christmas think? Asking him to come into a home with no tree is rather disrespectful.'

Perhaps he ought to try to set aside his bitter resentment of Christmas trees. It was probably unreasonable to tie his crushed childhood to them. It was not a tree's fault that his stepfather had been a beast, or that his mother had chosen him and cast off her small son.

He ought to be reasonable about it—yet he found he could not. He would give his sister anything—anything but that symbol of his deepest grief.

'Would you rather live somewhere else, Abigail? Somewhere that can offer you more?' Of course she was far too young to make such a choice, but given the letter from her uncle, he did need to know.

He clasped her small hand and led her into the conservatory. She clung tight to him and remained oddly silent.

Once inside he unbuttoned her coat and slid it off her.

'Are you sending me away?' she asked, her voice small and quavering.

'No! Never—why would you think it?'

'Some girls are sent away. They have to go to boarding school and learn to be proper ladies. Is it why you have not yet hired a governess to teach me?'

'Abigail, I would never send you anywhere you do not wish to go. I promise I will not.' Her relieved smile showed off the gap of a missing tooth. Her customary blue-eyed sparkle returned.

Isaiah's throat tightened when the ghost of their mother

skittered across her face. Their mother when she was young, before she married Palmer Turner, Fifth Earl of Penfield.

'But it is true that you are growing up quicker than your cat can dash after a mouse. I can see you getting taller by the hour. You will need someone to teach you to be a lady. There is more to it than one would guess.'

'Someone who will live here with us?' Once again she looked suspiciously at him. 'A governess, or a tutor?'

'I was thinking more of a female relative.'

'Lady Penfield is the only one. I believe she will not leave Penfield.'

'I must marry. It is past time that I did.' His sister's mouth popped into a perfectly surprised circle. 'How would you feel about that?'

Having a wife could only go in his favour when Lord and Lady Penfield came. He must do whatever he could to dissuade the Earl and the Countess from taking Abigail. If the issue went to court, he would lose. A married earl would be given custody over a crusty unwed viscount by any judge.

'I'd feel a lot of things about it. But you know you must make an effort to smile at a wife or she will not be happy here.'

'What I want to know is if you will be happy.'

'It would be rather like having a mother in a sister. Yes, I would like that. But—will you love me less when you love her, too?'

'Nothing in this world could make me love you less. Besides, it is not required to love one's wife. There are happy marriages founded on friendship.'

'If you truly thought so, you would have married by now.'

Or if his mother had found a scrap of happiness in her

second marriage, he might have a more hopeful outlook on the prospect.

'Honestly, Abigail, are you really only eight years old?'

'I'm an eight-year-old girl, which makes all the difference. Were I a boy, all I would want to do is climb things and run about making mischief. You have seen the stableman's son?'

'I am forever grateful to have a sister. But do I have your approval?'

'You do, just as long as the lady approves of cats.'

London—early December, 1889

It did not appear that it was going to snow while Felicia snipped branches. Given that the clouds dotting the sky were no more than wispy puffs, it was not likely to drizzle either.

To her mind it might as well be spring in the garden of Cliverton House, with birds singing and flowers budding.

It was enough to make a holly-gatherer weep.

Christmas was supposed to be crisp and lovely.

Pausing with the clipper blades poised over a branch, she did have to admit that it was crisp and lovely. At the same time she had to remind herself that it was not in the spirit of the season to be imagining spring.

At least her fingers were chilled, her nose red with the lovely nip in the air. There was even a cup of hot cocoa close at hand, spewing fragrant steam into the garden.

Perhaps it would not snow or rain, but she carried on snipping evergreen branches with a smile. After all, Christmas was coming regardless if it arrived white and frigid or green and mild.

All things considered the weather did not really matter.

Christmas was the most wonderful time of the year no matter the circumstances.

Her sisters, Cornelia and Ginny, grumbled that it was far too early to celebrate it. Of course they were not the ones to be named Felicia Merry.

Names were important. It was Felicia's belief, and her late mother's as well, that names had meaning, they were not simply fetching titles. Mama had often pointed out that was the reason why no one named their sons Beelzebub or the daughters Jezebel.

Funny how thinking of her mother made her smile and weep all in one tender emotion.

Time and again, she had found Mama's name theory to be true.

In Felicia's case it certainly was. As her name suggested, she nearly always saw the bright side of things.

'Happy times.' Mama had been fond of telling her what her name meant, of how she and father had thought and prayed upon it before naming her.

'Happy times' also described Christmas and so she had no problem whatsoever beginning to celebrate this early.

Cornelia could be excused for having her mind on other things than Christmas. She had recently become engaged to a very suitable earl. No doubt Mother and Father were gazing down and feeling very proud of their eldest child.

Ginny might come outside to join her once she put down her journal and put on her spectacles.

Spectacles she did not really need for seeing clearly. Her younger sister, by one year only, was an irresistible beauty and Felicia knew she donned them in an attempt to keep the young swains at bay.

Indeed, with her sunny curls and eyes the lavender-blue shade of a harebell blossom, she was quite sought after.

A situation which did not please her sister at all. Poor Ginny was as shy and as timid as a newborn fawn.

With the solicitor meeting with Peter in the study at the moment, Ginny would not come down without wearing her big, black glasses. Like every other man, the fellow was smitten with her.

From above, Mother and Father were probably congratulating themselves on naming her Virginia to ensure that she did not fall headlong over every gentleman wanting to woo her with flattery.

At least Mother and Father need fear nothing of the kind where Felicia was concerned. She was neither pretty nor petite. She quite towered over her sisters. To her knowledge she had never turned a man's head. There were occasional suitors, but they were half-hearted wooers, being more interested in what Father's title had to offer them than in her. For most of them it took no more than half an hour of being looked down upon—or having to gaze up at her—to send them searching for a more fetching lady.

An overly tall, red-haired and green-eyed woman was no one's first choice.

After three Seasons with no offer of marriage, she was quite firmly on the shelf. In another year she would become positively dusty.

Which was not a horrid thing. No, not really.

Surely a woman could lead a satisfactory life without a husband to dictate how merry she could feel, especially at Christmas? Living at Cliverton House with her sisters and her cousin, Peter, who was now Cliverton in Father's stead, was a satisfactory existence.

She tried not to think of how this would all change once her sisters married and once her cousin took a wife—and, really, at thirty years old it was time he did. Everything was bound to change then. It was mortifying to see herself being dependent upon her cousin and his future wife's good will for every little thing.

'Lady Cliverton, I would like a new bonnet, if it is not too much trouble,' she mumbled, imaging she might one day say such a thing.

Still, for the moment she was the unattached cousin of Viscount Cliverton and she was, for the greater part, free to act as she pleased.

For instance, when she decided to decorate the parlour on the first day of December no one forbade it. While it was true that they considered her actions a wee bit eager, no one prevented her from draping holly over the fireplace mantel and red ribbons on the banister.

A husband might stay her hand, douse her joy. Not all men were enthusiastic about celebrating Christmas. She was better off unwed than being bound to a cheerless man.

Was she not?

As it was now, she was free to trim greenery with no grumpy fellow to cast a frown.

She could sing carols while she did it.

'"I saw three ships come sailing in, on Christmas Day, on Christmas Day. I saw three ships come sailing in on Christmas Day in the morning."'

It did feel glorious to sing. There were few things she loved more.

She went up on her toes to snip a branch that her sisters would not be able to reach. They would be forced to summon a gardener to do it. Even Peter would have to stretch on his toes to manage.

"'And what was in those ships all three, On Christmas Day on Christmas Day—'"

'Screeching cats.' Peter's voice, so unexpected, nearly made her drop the shears.

'Take this,' she said and handed him the branch she had just cut.

Her cousin often made jest of her singing voice. It was difficult to take offence since she knew he stated the obvious with affection.

Sadly, in spite of the fact that she adored singing, she could not carry a tune.

'You do realise that by Christmas Day these will be dried out?'

'In the event, I will simply cut more.'

Peter might be her cousin, but he felt more like a brother. After the death of Felicia's aunt and uncle, he had come to live at Cliverton House so they had been raised together.

Father had made no secret of the fact that he was delighted to have his heir presumptive under his roof. Felicia always felt that Mother and Father had loved their nephew with the same affection they bore their own children.

Love was the abiding spirit at Cliverton. Even more so with Christmas so close at hand. Why, already she imagined the house scented with evergreen branches.

'It is a nice morning, Felicia. Will you sit in the sunshine with me for a moment?'

For all that he called this a nice morning, his expression appeared drawn.

'It is lovely, even though it is not my first choice for weather this time of year.'

Peter cleared his throat, tugged at his cravat while she sat down beside him on the garden bench. He looked rather as though he was sitting on a drawing pin.

'Choice is a thing we do not always have, wouldn't you agree?'

Why was his mouth drawn tight? It did not appear that he was about to break into a smile at the pleasure of spending a few moments with her.

'Yes, of course,' she said. 'There are times when we must muddle through, regardless of circumstances.'

'I hope this is something you believe and not a mere platitude.'

'I'm beginning to feel that I hope I believe it, too.' She suspected this was not simply an idle conversation on a pleasant day.

A movement on the steps caught her attention—Ginny standing on the porch, wringing her hands in front of her and looking like spoiled milk.

Clearly Felicia needed to hurry with the Christmas decorating. Something was going to need muddling through. A bit of cheer would only help.

'Yes, well you might. Felicia, the solicitor has brought—news.'

'Are we to assume it is not good news?'

One only needed to look at Ginny, her glasses clenched in her fist, to know it was true.

'You had best tell me what the problem is before I imagine the worst.' As clearly Ginny had already done.

'Viscount Scarsfeld is requesting a bride.'

Chapter Two

Scarsfeld!

'Surely not!'

After all this time?

'I thought he had forgotten about us,' Cornelia declared.

Felicia's insides whirled in confusion.

'We all assumed he did not wish to marry.' Ginny hurried down the garden steps, her hand clutched in a fist over her heart.

Cornelia rushed out of the door, following close behind.

'He gave every indication of it when last we saw him at Lady Newton's ball,' her older sister stated, nodding as if she remembered the occasion of meeting him as though it had been last week.

The fact of it was, Lady Newton's ball had been three years ago when Felicia and Ginny were freshly come out.

'Perhaps he does not wish it. Men often wed even without wishing to,' Cornelia added to her thought.

'Peter, are you certain he is asking for one of us?'

'I'm sorry but, yes. The Viscount has sent along a letter which his solicitor says he discovered among his mother's belongings when she died eight years ago. It is a letter which both his mother and yours wrote together expressing their fondest wishes that "Sweet little Isaiah should one day wed one of the darling Penneyjons girls."'

'But he is not sweet!' Ginny's eyebrows slashed a frown over eyes creased in worry. 'Why, as I recall it, he did not smile at anyone at the ball, nor did he ask anyone to dance.'

'Perhaps he was simply out of sorts for some reason or another,' Felicia pointed out because it only seemed fair to do so.

'I would think you would be less charitable with regard to the man,' Cornelia said. 'You are the one he blanked, after all.'

'I hardly remember that.' Truly, she had been ignored by so many gentlemen over the last three years that she barely recalled the moment. And who could blame him for it? She had been a blushing debutante while he had been a mature, experienced man.

The only reason she had approached him was because she remembered how Mama always spoke so fondly of him and his mother.

Felicia had been too young to remember Mama's friend, but Mama had told many stories of them growing up together as close as sisters.

She did not need to read the letter as proof of how much Mama wished for one of her girls to wed Juliette Scarsfeld's son. Until Mama and Father passed away ten years ago in a carriage accident, she had listened to Mama tell of her cherished dreams.

Until this moment that was all they had ever been.

When Lord Scarsfeld had been pointed out to her at the ball she had stared in awe at the man because of Mama, imagining how pleased she would have been to introduce her girls to him and to begin matchmaking.

Yes, his gaze had passed over her without even engaging her eye, but it had not really stung. The fact that he also blanked Ginny made her feel oddly better about the experience.

'The letter is not binding, you understand,' Peter explained.

'Perhaps not, but we all know how Mama longed for just this,' Cornelia said.

'Surely she would not expect us to go through with it after all this time,' Ginny said, unable to cover the hiccup in her voice.

Cornelia sighed, lifting her shoulders in apparent resignation of what had befallen them. As well she might since she was betrothed and safely unavailable. 'A marriage between our families would honour her memory as nothing else would.'

It was true, yet it was a rather drastic way to do so.

'I am saddened to read that Mama's friend has passed away.' Cornelia shook her head, the expression in her bright blue eyes dimmed. 'I recall that she and her little boy used to visit. But only until she remarried.'

'We need not wonder how her son turned out. We saw his sullen nature for ourselves,' Ginny said with a shudder she made no attempt to suppress.

'Which of my sisters has he asked for, Peter?' Cornelia tapped her fingers on the waist to her gown, looking more curious than alarmed. As well she might, being safely removed from the choosing.

A profound silence settled over the garden.

It was as if even the breeze held its breath waiting for the answer.

Oh, but surely it could not be Ginny! She was far too timid for a man like him—or, more accurately, the one they recalled him to be. Although, of course, shy and timid girls were required to marry as well as anyone else was.

But if on the odd chance he did remember them, it would be Ginny he chose. Any man would.

'Who has he chosen, Peter?' Felicia had to ask because the tense silence could not go on. It was as if an axe were poised over them and the sooner it fell, the sooner the situation could be muddled through.

Please do not let it be Ginny, she prayed silently. Her sister was not much of a muddler. She was as likely to plunge headlong into despair as anything else.

'Yes, well...apparently he has left the choice up to us... or you, rather.' Peter glanced between her and Ginny.

'We will take our time and make a decision,' Felicia announced, taking Ginny's hand and squeezing it. 'Nothing needs to be settled in the moment.'

For all that she wanted to jump in and martyr herself for her sister's sake, she could not quite gather her legs for the leap.

Peter stood up, walked a few steps along the garden path. When he spotted a small stone, he kicked it hard into a tree trunk.

'Unfortunately,' he muttered without looking up, 'there is no time. Lord Scarsfeld is requesting that one of you come to Windermere with all haste.'

When Peter did turn he was staring at Felicia, not Ginny.

Of course, everyone would assume she would be the one

to fill the role. Even she understood this would be her one chance to get a husband given that Lord Scarsfeld was not particular about whom he wed. His only requirement was for her to be a Penneyjons.

Perhaps he wished to fulfil his mother's wishes as much as she wished to fulfil Mama's.

Oh, she could nearly feel her mother's giddiness from above. Although Mama had passed away before Felicia's Season began, she surely noticed, in whatever way the dearly departed had of noticing, that their middle daughter would not find a husband on her own.

Some might say she should be grateful for the chance to wed.

Spinsterhood was a humiliating state and one to be avoided at all costs.

Felicia would argue that, so far, it was not at all horrid.

But it would not be long before she would watch her sisters and her cousin wed. She would see them bringing babies into the family, watch their joy overflow the house, while she sat in a chair and knitted her nieces and nephews socks.

'Perhaps he is not so wretched,' Ginny said with a fragile smile, now that she was not the one likely to have to make the choice. 'I do recall Mother telling the story of how adorable little Isaiah was and how he used to lead you about by the hand when you were learning to walk—and how you laughed and laughed.'

'Yes!' Cornelia clapped her hands. 'I had nearly forgotten! Mama said you used crawl after him, wailing when he let go of your hand.'

Perhaps, but what had that to do with anything now? Felicia scarcely recalled what the man looked like three years ago, let alone any memory of crawling after him as a baby.

Those were Mama's cherished memories, not hers. Oh, but she did cherish her mother. Even now, after all this time and with the mysterious distance which separated the mortal and the immortal, she wanted to please her mother.

Yes, it would honour Mama to fulfil her dearest wish, but there was more to it. She would also honour her mother by watching out for Ginny. Felicia believed her sister would not thrive being married to a man like Viscount Scarsfeld.

Felicia stood up, yanked the folds of her skirt into order. 'Very well. I will travel north to meet him.'

'I will go along.' Ginny bravely lifted her chin, offering up her life to fate—and her sister. 'It is only right. Perhaps we did misunderstand him, or he might have changed.'

It was probably fair to allow the man to choose between Felicia and her sister.

Certainly it was, yet, given the choice, he would pick Ginny.

Which would leave Felicia free of obligation—and laden with guilt for ever.

'I feel that it would be unkind of you to risk my one chance to have a husband, Ginny. You are pretty. You will have your choice of a dozen proposals to accept whenever you wish to.'

Peter opened his mouth, but Felicia shushed him by slashing a sidelong frown.

'Please give me my chance to meet Lord Scarsfeld. If he rejects me, then you may have a chance with him.'

Saying those words brought her up short. He might well reject her. He had overlooked her at Lady Newton's ball.

It was one thing to be passed over at a social gathering, quite another to be rejected as a bride.

The humiliation would be crushing.

'He will not turn you away, Felicia,' Peter said softly as if reading her mind. 'I'm given to understand that he requires a wife in all haste. If you agree to this, you will become Lady Scarsfeld within a fortnight.'

Muddle through, muddle through, she repeated the mantra in her mind a dozen times while stating out loud, 'How lovely. What a grand adventure it will be.'

The lie was worthwhile if only to see Ginny's face take on a bit of colour.

And perhaps the words held an ounce of truth. One's attitude towards a situation often made it a blessing or a curse.

How many times had she stood beside Cornelia while they watched a glowering sky? Her sister would grumble about the horrid weather coming while Felicia looked at up in anticipation of rain tapping merrily on her umbrella?

She would muddle through this and do her best to keep a smile about it.

Standing in the centre of the parlour, Isaiah turned in a circle, judging the room with a critical eye. How would a stranger view it? The stranger he was going to wed, in fact?

It was a welcoming space for all its size, in his estimation. Wood-panelled walls gleamed with polish. A large rug in shades of red and gold warmed the floor in front of a fireplace so huge that the flames cast the entire room in a cosy glow.

The banisters of the wide staircase which he had played upon as a child rose to a landing where a trio of stained-glass windows cast reflections of red, blue and green on the floor.

Even now he could see a crack in one of panes. When he was four years old he had thought it would be a fine thing to toss a ball at the window in the hopes of it breaking a hole in it large enough for a bird to fly inside.

Mother had laughed, ruffled his hair and assured him all was well. A week later she purchased a pair of budgerigars. She never did repair the window, claiming it gave the house character.

He shook his head, nipping the inside of his lip. It was better not to think of those times. In the end the sweet memories turned bitter.

Left to his own inclinations the house would be a grey, sombre place. It was for Abigail's sake he kept the fireplaces cheerfully snapping, colourful paintings on the walls and flowers or whatever greenery was to be found this time of year in vases all over the mansion.

He would do anything to make sure his sister knew she was loved and appreciated.

Which included marrying a stranger if that was what it took to keep her with him.

It had been ten days since he had had word from Lord Cliverton that his daughter would fulfil the wish of their mothers and wed him.

Circumstances prevented all the typical celebrations involved in arranging a wedding.

Would Miss Penneyjons mind it so much? It was not as if they were celebrating their love—or even their friendship.

The one and only thing he felt for her was gratitude. He could not appreciate her beauty since he had no idea what she looked like. Nor could he admire her wit. For all he knew she was dull—or she might be bright and charming. The only knowledge he had of her was a vague memory of holding a tiny hand, of a screeching baby crawling madly after him—and that her name was Felicia, which he would not have recalled on his own, but the names of all the Penneyjons daughters were in the letter he had found among his mother's belongings.

The only thing that mattered in the end was that Miss Penneyjons had consented, although he was left wondering why. Was the woman as desperate to be wed as he was?

Whatever her motivation, he would welcome her. One of the reasons Lord Penfield had given for wanting custody of Abigail was that Isaiah was not married.

In a few days he would be. The Earl's argument in that area would be crushed.

If the reason they wanted Abigail had to do with them having no child of their own, there was nothing he could do about that.

But damn it all! His sister was happy living here. He would not have her ripped away from Scarsfeld as he had been.

Isaiah had no wish to marry, but clearly, if he had any hope of Abigail remaining with him, he must.

It would have been right to travel to London and offer Miss Penneyjons a proper proposal, but time would not allow for it.

Time was precisely what he needed more of. It was important for the Earl and the Countess to witness an easy rapport between Isaiah and his bride.

As it was, he feared she would barely have time to settle in, let alone portray an image of contentment.

Settle in, yes—but settled in where? Not the master's

chamber, certainly. It was one thing to ask the woman to be his wife, but quite another to expect she would be willing to become his lover.

Perhaps in time—once they became acquainted and—

'You look more dour than usual, my lord,' Miss Shirls commented as she hurried past him with a stack of books she must be carrying to his sister's quarters. She paused to frown at him. 'No doubt it has to do with your hasty decision to take a stranger as a bride.'

Thankfully she said so under her breath. While Miss Shirls felt free to speak to him this way, she did not feel the rest of staff had the same privilege.

'As it happens, I am wondering what to do with her.'

'Surely not!' The nanny did not blush when she turned back with a wink.

'Where to put her.' Oddly enough, despite having a reputation as the harshest man in Windermere and beyond, he blushed rather easily.

'If there is to be no heir, then I would suggest your late mother's room.'

With a nod she was off to deliver the books to Abigail.

The Viscountess's chamber did make the most sense since Miss Penneyjons would be Viscountess Scarsfeld within a matter of days.

So be it, then. He mounted the steps towards the third-storey rooms. It had been a very long time since he had entered his late mother's chamber.

The staff saw to its care regularly, but they did not suffer the attack of grief that was sure to overtake him the instant he opened that door.

Not grief for her death, although he did grieve that, but because it was where so much joy had lived—and perished.

There had been a time when his mother was his whole world—a time when he had been hers.

He opened the door slowly. Nothing was the same as it had been when he was seven years old. Everything that had belonged to his mother had been replaced long ago. He had no wish to keep his home a museum.

But still, she was there: standing in the doorway, laughing while she gazed at him; then later weeping; and in the end staring at him from the nursery doorway, blank and silent.

Worse than the weeping and the silence was the distance. On that last day, Christmas Eve, when she had stood in his doorway just as he was now standing in hers, there had been no emotion in her eyes. He might have been a neighbour's child for all there was left between them.

Perhaps having a new Lady Scarsfeld residing in the chamber was for the best. It could hardly be worse, at least.

Of all the things he wondered about where Felicia Penneyjons was concerned, the most important was how she would get along with Abigail.

It was crucial that she did, he thought while closing the door and turning his back on the room and its ghosts. He hoped Lord and Lady Penfield would think twice about ripping apart a loving family.

The opposite was true as well. If Miss Penneyjons and Abigail did not suit, they could feel justified in taking her.

Standing alone in the hallway, he considered what Abigail had said about smiling—how he ought to do it more often.

All right, then. He lifted his cheeks, but wondered if his teeth ought to show or not. The gesture, offered for show, felt awkward.

Suddenly the door across the hallway opened. Miss Shirls

stepped out of the room with a different load of books in her arms.

'Are you going to attack me, my lord?'

There was his answer. No teeth. A socially motivated smile must be presented with his lips closed.

Felicia's sisters asked to accompany her and Peter to Scarsfeld. She turned them down. They did not really want to go, but felt guilty for her having to face 'Sir Gloomy' alone.

That was what they had taken to calling Lord Scarsfeld: Sir Gloomy, or, at times, Lord Scowl.

It wasn't fair, of course. None of them had ever had a conversation with the man. He might have a perfectly lovely disposition for all they knew. They had only seen him, as an adult, that one time and perhaps there had been a reason for his moodiness.

Gazing out the train window, Felicia watched pastureland appear and then drift away with an occasional cow or sheep to return her gaze.

Shifting her gaze to Peter seated on the plush crimson bench across from her, she was so nervous it felt as though bees buzzed about inside her. When they were ten minutes away from Windermere Station, she had no fear that her cousin was suffering any anxiety.

His head nodded towards his chest while he blissfully snored.

If only she could feel such calm. Of course her cousin was going to go home next week to carry on with his life.

With a mental shake, she reminded herself that she was also going to carry on with her life. She did not know precisely what that life would be like, but she had no option but to carry on with it.

Not unless she wanted to let her family down and ignore her mother's wishes. Not unless she wanted Ginny to come in her stead.

And especially if she did not wish to become the pitiful Penneyjons spinster, cooing over everyone's children but her own.

There had been times when she thought she might manage life that way, but now that this new path had opened she wondered if she had been forcing herself to think it because she had no choice about it.

Looking for the bright side of things and all that.

Of course she could be doing the same thing now. Feeling she had no choice in the marriage, was she now looking for the best in it?

Perhaps she was one who just muddled through whatever life presented. She did have to wonder if muddling was a step short of being fulfilled.

At least Windermere was reported to be an exceptionally lovely village. Indeed, beyond the train window everything looked properly cold and grey for this time of year. The glass felt frigid when she pressed her fingers against it.

Peter had been all for going immediately to Scarsfeld as soon as they stepped off the train. Felicia wanted to spend a night in town before heading to the estate and she held firm to it. One did not toss a fish into new aquarium water and hope for it to survive. No, indeed, it needed a few hours to acclimatise.

She fully intended on taking a day to acclimatise, to tour Windermere, get used to the sights, sounds and people.

After that she would proceed to the estate which was said to be only a few miles north of town.

A place where, she had heard, it was not uncommon for snow to cover the ground at Christmas.

While Peter continued to snore, Felicia wondered about Scarsfeld. What was it like? Cheerful? Glum? Had anyone begun to decorate for the swift approach of Christmas?

Perhaps not. If Lord Scarsfeld actually was a gloomy scowler, he might not think to do it.

A part of her hoped he had not. Decorating her new home would help her bond with it, make her feel as if she had a place and a purpose.

Yes! A purpose was exactly what she needed.

Lord Scarsfeld had not revealed why he needed to marry in such a hurry, but she assumed she played a rather large part in whatever it was. There was bound to be some sort of purpose involved in her role as Lady Scarsfeld.

Whatever it turned out to be it had to far outshine a spinster's purpose which was, to her mind, providing an object of pity, becoming an example for young ladies not to follow—that and knitting endless pairs of extra socks for nieces and nephews.

One by one her fellow passengers began to stretch and stand in anticipation of arriving at the station.

The whistle shrilled. Felicia reached across and jiggled Peter's shoulder. He blinked, glancing about fuzzy-eyed.

'Do you wonder,' she asked while rising and shrugging into her coat, 'if I might have been sent here for a reason?'

She buttoned up, then attached her hat to her hair. The weather did look rather foreboding.

'You know you have. To get married and honour your mother's wishes. And to make a life for yourself, Felicia.'

Peter stood, peered out the window and fastened his coat. 'It looks like a beast of a day.'

'There is that, of course—for Mama. But it is what you said about starting a new life...' It was funny how she thrilled to the idea and at the same time recoiled from it. It was a distinctly unsettling feeling. 'There must be some sort of purpose for me in it that I am not yet aware of.'

'To make a bear purr? Knowing you, you might have it in mind to encourage Lord Scarsfeld to amend his sullen ways.'

'An unknown purpose can be a mysterious thing, so perhaps that is it. But we do not know for certain that the Viscount is sullen.'

'If he is and anyone can bring him round, it is you.'

Maybe. But if he was the man her sisters feared him to be it would be a difficult task, even for someone named Felicia.

'Look, Peter!' She bent to peer out of the window. 'Isn't Windermere beautiful?'

When she straightened, Peter was staring at her. A deep frown cut his brow.

'I pray that you will be happy here, Felicia. If you are not, I will come straight away and fetch you home.'

She kissed his cheek, half-tempted to return to London this instant.

But only half. A part of her did wonder what life would be like as Viscountess Scarsfeld. Less than a fortnight ago she had seen her future as one where her heart dried out and she became an object of charity.

The truth was, she wanted to give charity, not be the object of it.

'I'll arrange for our bags to be delivered to the hotel,' Peter said while helping her down the train steps.

Felicia ought to be used to the stares by now. Being nearly six feet tall when every other female was so much shorter and having hair so red it would make her velvet hat look as though it might catch fire—well, she did not go unnoticed.

Not that she blamed people for taking a second glance at her. Honestly, Felicia would stare at herself if she saw herself strolling along the other side of the street.

What, she could only wonder, would her fiancé's first reaction to her be? It would be nice if he were not taken aback. In the end it hardly mattered. The pair of them were to be wed, bound by vows for the rest of their lives.

'I wonder why,' she murmured.

'I would prefer not to carry them on my back.'

'Oh, naturally not. But, Peter, why is it so urgent for Lord Scarsfeld to marry, is what I wonder…and wonder. In fact, I have not ceased to dwell on it.'

'All of us have been.' It was true. The Viscount's motives had been discussed for hours on end at Cliverton. 'But I meant what I told you. If you are unhappy, I will come for you.'

'Thank you. Just knowing you will makes this easier. But for all we know he is as pleasant as the star on top of a Christmas tree.'

Or the lump of coal in the bottom of a stocking, was what her cousin's expression answered.

'It was a very long time ago that you encountered him and no doubt he was simply in an ill humour,' Peter said, but she well knew he did not mean it.

Still, she took courage from the white lie because the braver the words, the braver the face, and the easier it was to smile.

'I will meet you at the hotel at half past the hour.' She

nodded at the picturesque inn across the road nestled among a grove of bare trees and backed by the blue water of Lake Windermere. 'I see the sweetest gown in the dressmaker's window. Perhaps it can be altered to fit me. I would feel more at ease meeting the Viscount wearing something new.'

Her cousin shifted his gaze to the dress shop and nodded. 'That shade of green suits you. It looks like Christmas.'

Indeed, that was why it had caught her eye. Not only was it the colour of a fresh evergreen, but there were tiny red beads adorning the hem, neckline and ruffled sleeves. The snowflake-hued sash at the waist made it the most cheerful gown she had ever seen.

She would look like a proper peppermint stick—but ever so subtly.

In the end, purchasing the gown took longer than she expected. Peter was no doubt beginning to worry about her.

Coming out of the shop, she sniffed the cold air. The mingled scents of chimney smoke, baked goods from the café next to the dress shop and evergreen trees made her smile.

Lifting her skirts to cross the road, she had a favourable feeling about her future.

She hoped it continued once she met Isaiah Maxwell.

A noise caught her attention. She cocked her head, listening.

Someone was weeping. It sounded like a child, a young girl, perhaps.

This could hardly be ignored. Felicia let go of her skirt and hurriedly followed the sound along a pathway between the dress shop and the café.

Oh, dear—just there, standing under a tree and gazing up, was a tearful little girl.

Not weeping helplessly, as it had first sounded, but rather in frustration.

'Eloise!' The little girl shook her gloved finger at a cat peering down from a branch. 'Come down at once or I shall leave you to find your own way home!'

Her words were brave, but the tone in which she spoke them indicted her dismay.

'Hello,' Felicia said softly so as not to startle either the girl or her cat. 'I think perhaps I can reach her.'

'Oh, I do hope you can.' The little girl swiped her eyes with her sleeve. 'The silly thing leapt from my basket to go exploring.'

'As a cat will. The ones I have back at home are crafty wee creatures.' Felicia stepped to the base of the tree, slowly lifting her arms, but the cat climbed casually beyond her reach.

'I suppose I will have to summon my brother to climb the tree,' the child muttered with a resigned-looking shrug. Sable lashes narrowed over blue eyes. She shoved a straggling lock of honey-hued hair back under her hat.

'He will not be happy about your antics, mark my word.' She shifted her gaze from the cat, who had paused just out of reach to leisurely groom her tail, to Felicia. 'He told me not to bring her to town, but I did it anyway. Now look what has become of her!'

'He won't be angry, I hope.' She was as unfamiliar with the little boy as she was with the girl who stared at her pet in equal parts worry and annoyance, but she supposed the boy might be upset, given that his wise advice had not been heeded.

'He won't want to be distracted from his errand in order to climb a tree and fetch her down. I do imagine he will be unhappy. My brother is rather accomplished at appearing glum.'

'Let's not trouble him then. I'll climb the tree.'

'Oh, but you mustn't! Not in your skirt. It's far too dangerous. It could tangle and—'

All the more reason it should be Felicia to do it. Little boys were at enough peril on flat ground.

'I'll be right as rain. You need not worry.' Felicia glanced about to make sure they were hidden from view. Satisfied, she bundled up yards of skirt and petticoat, then secured the wad into her waistband as best she could manage. 'I was once adept at chasing cats up trees.'

Of course that had been years ago, but, really, how much could have changed?

'But your shoes? You will need to remove them if you have any hope of not falling.'

'Of course, I was about to do just that.'

She unbuttoned her travelling boots and set them at the base of the tree. Last time she had climbed a tree she had done it barefoot. When one was twelve years old, having unshod feet was acceptable.

The same could not be said for a nearly viscountess. Balancing on branches in stocking feet was sure to be risky, but she could not see any way to avoid it.

So, up she went, grasping rough bark with fingers, knees and toes. She had not made the second branch before she felt her stocking rip.

What a lucky thing no one was about because her big toe popped boldly into view.

No matter, she was nearly within reach of the cat. It would take but a second to grab it, tuck it into her skirt, then scurry down and put her boots back on.

Goodness gracious, but her feet were cold! Not as cold as her hands, though. They were so frigid she could barely feel what was under her fingertips.

A foot beyond her grasp the cat stared down, languidly swishing her tail.

Chapter Three

Isaiah placed the velvet box containing a wedding band in his pocket, pushing it down deep to be sure it was secure.

He could not recall ever having had such trouble making a purchase. One saw what one wanted and bought it, confident that one's choice was appropriate and pleased to be quickly finished.

This time was different—unsettling, to be honest. The ring was something his bride would wear all her life and he had no idea if she would even like it.

According to the jeweller any woman would adore the warm gold engraved with evergreen needles and dusted with tiny diamonds. Sadly Mr Thompson knew no more about Felicia Merry Penneyjons than Isaiah did.

He would have welcomed Abigail's advice, but she was not here. Mr Thompson had taken one look at Eloise popping out of the basket his sister carried and emitted a room-shattering sneeze.

With the jeweller's eyes growing red and itchy, there had

been no choice but to send his sister to their next stop, the dress shop.

With the wedding set for the day after next, time was of the utmost value. It was vexing to think that the cat might cost him some of it.

As young as she was, he did value his sister's opinion. Females, he had come to learn, had opinions on fashion at a very early age. Her advice on the ring would have been helpful.

He really did want to put his best foot forward for his bride. The woman deserved that respect.

He wondered if perhaps their paths had crossed at a social gathering in the past. It was possible for it to have happened. Now he wished he had paid more than passing courtesy to the ladies presented to him. Had he done that, he might have some idea of who his bride would be.

Stepping outside the jeweller's shop, he shivered. Everything indicated snow was on the way. He would need to hurry if he was to be home before it began to fall.

Hopefully it would not inconvenience Miss Penneyjons.

Isaiah hurried across the street and went inside the dress shop.

Abigail was not there. The shopkeeper shook her head, looking puzzled. Apparently his sister had not arrived.

That could not be! He had watched her cross the road and approach the shop door.

Dashing out of the shop, he pivoted on his heel. Where could she have got to? He felt his skin grow tight, pinched with worry. For all that he tried to smooth his frown before someone noticed, he could not.

Where was she?

Surely she had not become lost. She was familiar with

Windermere, every shop and eatery in the village, each street and alley. She knew everyone and they knew her. But she was only eight years old and tourists—strangers from all over—were common.

As if to reinforce his concern a man came out of the hotel, his expression grim. Isaiah reminded himself that just because the fellow scowled while he walked towards the dress shop did not mean it had to do with Abigail. It was unreasonable to think it did.

To say that he was overzealous in protecting his sister would be true, yet he could be no less. On her deathbed his mother had given Abigail to him, trusting that he would keep her safe.

He had failed once when he did not notice that she had toddled outside in a snowstorm. He would never be careless with her safety again.

As soon as he found her he would have a stern, brotherly word with her about caution.

While he thought about what words would best express discipline tempered by love, he heard a screech. It came from behind the dress shop.

Abigail!

On top of Abigail's cry came another. This one seemed to come from a woman.

Skidding on a spot of mud while rounding the corner of the building, he nearly went to his knees.

There was Abigail, her arms spread wide as if to catch a woman dangling from a tree limb. Even from here he could see the lady's grip slipping.

If she fell, both she and his sister would be injured.

'Stand away!' he shouted on the run.

Abigail jumped aside just in time to avoid being knocked over.

'Let go, miss! I'll catch you!' Feet flailing, she nearly smacked him in the head. As it was, she grazed his hat and sent it flying.

She glanced down, blinking at him with eyes the loveliest shade of green he had ever seen, for all that they were wide with consternation.

Biting her bottom lip, she shook her head fiercely. A lock of red hair lashed her nose. Even in the midst of the crisis he noted that it was softly lustred rather than blazing wildfire.

'You can trust me not to drop you.' Still, she hesitated. 'I promise I will not.'

'He is stronger than he looks,' Abigail explained.

In the next second the lady did tumble, but not, he thought, by choice.

He locked his arms when her weight fell on to him. She gave a small squeak, then stared at him in what could only be surprise.

'You see?' Abigail pointed out. 'Much stronger.'

'I do thank you, sir.'

This was no feather of a miss who would blow away in a breeze. In fact, she filled his arms in such a pleasantly solid fashion, he did not want to put her down.

But he ought to—her bloomers were showing and one long, lovely pink toe peeked out of a rip in her stocking.

'What—' barked a man's voice. Ah, it belonged to the scowling man he'd spotted coming out of the hotel. 'Unhand my cousin! What do you think you are about?'

He would have to, he supposed, the fellow had good reason to be outraged at what he saw.

Setting the lady to her feet, he found that they were of

a height, gazing at each other eye to eye. But she was not wearing boots. He imagined when she put them on he would have to adjust his gaze up an inch. The idea intrigued him.

Most women he met were wary of him, of his size and the stern image he tended to present without fully meaning to.

Quite contrary to what his sister had to say, he did not appear a weakling.

'No need to look so surly, Peter,' the lady said, her smile a flash of sunshine on this gloomy day. 'All is well. I was simply fetching the cat out of the tree and I slipped. This kind gentleman caught my fall.'

Eloise chose that moment to claw her way down the tree trunk. With her tail proudly lifted, she sailed across the grass to Abigail, purring and ready to be cooed over.

His sister scooped up the basket from the ground.

'You silly thing,' she gently admonished. Easing Eloise inside, she shut the lid.

This was Isaiah's own fault, he supposed, for not inspecting what she had in the basket when they left Scarsfeld.

'Abigail, did I not instruct you to leave the cat at home?' Perhaps this was best spoken of in private, but the woman might have been injured and he felt his sister ought to apologise. 'Offer your regrets and tell the lady you are sorry to have involved her in your reckless choice.'

'Oh, truly there is no need.' The woman's smile dimmed. 'No harm was done.'

'Your clothing has been torn. Lady Abigail will find a way to repay you.'

Glancing down, the lady blushed, yanked the hem out of her skirt and let it drop, securing her shapely pink toe from his view.

'Your brother?' she asked Abigail with an inquisitive-looking tilt of her chin.

'You see? It is true what I said.'

'I thought you were speaking of someone much smaller.' The lady shifted her glance to him, her frown settling more firmly into place. 'But I do see your point.'

What point?

'Tell the lady you regret having risked her safety and let's be on our way. I'm certain she would like to get out of the cold.'

She was not wearing shoes after all and her toe—dash it, he must put the somehow seductive image of it from his mind. He was to be wed and thoughts of a ripped stocking were not appropriate.

'I would.' The cousin shivered, hunching his shoulders against the nip in the air. 'The weather is a bit of a beast compared to what we left behind in London.'

'I regret that in helping me you were nearly injured.' Abigail cast him a frown, one which he was fairly certain she had learned from him. 'I also apologise for my brother's severe attitude. I will suffer no lasting harm from it, though. Nor will Eloise.'

As if she was suffering even an ounce of harm in the moment. He nearly huffed out loud.

'Naturally not. I'm sure…' In stooping to pick up her shoes, the woman glanced up at him. 'Goodness, I'm only grateful you were close by.'

If his bride was half as lovely as this lady, he would be a thankful man.

Of course, he did not require that his bride be a great beauty. He only prayed that she would be a charming woman who would dissuade Lord Penfield and Lady Penfield from upending Abigail's life.

He squatted, reached for his hat which had come to rest on the heel of her boot. As he gazed at her eye to eye, his stomach took the oddest turn.

An image flashed in his mind, but was gone before he could secure it.

In the instant she grabbed for her shoe, their hands collided. Her bare fingers looked flushed with warmth. He was grateful that he was wearing gloves because to feel the warmth of her skin would twist his belly even further.

He frowned before he could call the gesture back. What a cad he was for getting lost in the colour of her eyes when he ought to have been wondering what his intended's eyes looked like. The situation between him and his bride would be difficult as it was without his interest wandering.

'Have I injured you, sir?' she asked, her voice a horrified whisper.

His dashed frown! Scrubbing it from his face with an open palm, he sent her a smile of reassurance that she had not.

'Oh...' she gasped '...you have been hurt!'

'I have not. As my sister pointed out, I'm stronger than I look.'

The corner of her mouth quirked up. A merry green twinkle flashed in her eye. It was a lucky thing he was squatting because it nearly cut him off at the knees.

'Rest assured, sir, you do not look at all frail.'

He should not ask her name, but rather rise and carry on with purchasing a dress for his sister. The less he knew of this woman the better. As it was, he feared he would imagine her face in moments he ought not to. Which, given his circumstances, would be any moment at all.

'Come along before we freeze,' complained the lady's cousin.

'The weather is lovely, Peter, you simply need to adjust your attitude towards it.'

They were nearly knee to knee when she reached for the package she must have dropped when she went to Abigail's aid. Somehow it felt the most provocative position he had ever been in with a woman, which did not honestly make much sense.

'You'll make an icicle of me, Felicia. Let's be on our way.'

Felicia?

'Felicia?' Surely heaven was smiling upon him.

'Felicia Penneyjons,' she muttered, rising and casting a 'look' at Peter.

Isaiah came to his feet, feeling half-buoyant.

'I'm grateful to—pleased to, that is—meet you.' He took her hand, bent slightly over it. 'I am Lord Scarsfeld.'

'He's not an ogre, at least,' Felicia muttered to the bedroom at large while dressing for dinner—dinner with Lord Scarsfeld. In her mind, she was not ready to call him Isaiah.

'Not an ogre, perhaps, but as formidable as he was at Lady Newton's ball.'

It surprised her that she had not known him right away when he'd caught her tumbling from the tree. There had been a flash of familiarity, but given the situation she had suddenly landed in—and, well, to be honest, the exceptionally strong arms—she had been so distracted that she had not fully recognised him until he introduced himself.

Something else about the man remained the same. It came

to her in the moment she understood who he was. Lord Scarsfeld was still an amazingly handsome man.

She could not deny that looking into his eyes had made her heart flutter. In fact, she wondered if he noticed her fingers trembling a bit when she reached for her boots.

She walked to the mirror, twirled about. She did look like a peppermint stick, but subtly so that only she was likely to know it.

Of course, that was what she intended. While one might wish to feel like a peppermint stick inside, one also wished to appear sensible.

She stopped suddenly, her skirt twirling about her calves.

How sensible, she had to ask herself, was wedding a stranger known to have a less than cheerful disposition?

When it came to his sister he was abrupt, even overbearing. But young Lady Abigail had been unfazed by his attitude. She had said what she wished to her brother and about him. If he truly was the man he appeared to be, she would not be so comfortable—bossy, more than that—in his company.

Lord Scarsfeld did confuse her.

Fluffing her skirt, then smoothing her hair, she was determined to sort him out over dinner.

Lady Abigail needed no sorting. Even knowing the child for only a few moments, Felicia liked her immensely. No doubt as the child grew, she would prove equal to society's changes, to the progressive times she would be growing up in.

From what she could determine, her brother had been the one to raise her. In Felicia's opinion he had done an outstanding job.

In the beginning of all this—the summoning of a bride—

she had imagined herself playing the role of a martyr to her poor shy sister.

But now…well, having looked into those dramatic, amber-coloured eyes, she was not quite sure she was martyring herself after all. Truly, how many martyrs went to their doom all aflutter over a pair of shapely lips?

None she had ever heard of.

Peter's familiar rap tapped on the door, indicating it was time to go down to the dining room.

Perhaps the flutters had to do with nervousness as much as with a vision of masculine lips and captivating eyes.

Things could be a great deal worse.

Indeed, much worse. Flutters, for whatever their origin, were not a horrid fate. And for all her bravado about offering herself to duty, she had reserved the right to change her mind.

It did seem important to know his reasons for wanting to marry so suddenly after all this time before she committed to it.

Surely he must also have questions for her, such as why she had agreed so readily to the marriage?

She opened the door to find her cousin with a half-smile on his face.

'You are trying to hide the fact that you are worried,' she said, closing the door and taking his arm while they walked towards the stairs.

'Concerned only. You are taking a very big step.' Peter looked her over, at last settling his gaze on her face. 'I'm not sure the two of you will suit.'

'It does remain to be seen, but what we do know is that I am far better suited to Lord Scarsfeld than Ginny would be.'

'You can refuse. I'll take you home this instant.'

'The Viscount and I will dine together. At the end of it I will know if you need to take me home.'

'Very well.'

'And, Peter, I need you to sit at another table. I have questions for Lord Scarsfeld and I wonder if he will answer candidly with you sitting there looking as though you will pummel him at the least provocation.'

Peter huffed out a breath through half-parted lips. 'I'm your guardian. It is suitable for me to appear fierce.'

'You are also a gentleman. Surely you can appear so.'

'Yes, all right. But I will be close by. If you need me, raise your hand in the air, crook your finger and I will come.'

Isaiah would have married any woman and considered himself lucky. It was all for Abigail, after all. Whether the lady was a thistle or a rose, he had prepared himself not to care as long as she was willing to wed him.

Ah, but now, while standing to welcome Miss Penneyjons, watching her willow-like figure as she strode towards him on her cousin's arm, seeing her confident smile when she had every reason to be quaking in her slippers at the prospect of dining with the stranger she had agreed to marry, a stranger his own sister had labelled crusty, he could only admire her.

If she was uncomfortable with gazes shifting her way, she hid it well. Being as tall as she was, she did command attention.

Felicia Merry Penneyjons soaked up every bit of his. To his mind she looked like Christmas.

For an instant the swish of her green skirt, the red beading and white bow at her waist made her appear a walking peppermint stick. A long-dead whisper of Christmas joy echoed in his memory. He sucked in a shallow breath, held it, then snuffed out the feeling before it overwhelmed him.

Christmas joy, the anticipation of something wonderful on the way, all that had died when he was seven years old and his mother had gone away. Without a kiss or a smile, without even a word of farewell, she had vanished from his life.

'Thank you for joining me, Miss Penneyjons, Lord Cliverton.' He nodded in heartfelt welcome while a waiter pulled out a chair for his—his intended was what she was.

Peter shook his head when the waiter went to pull a chair out for him. 'I'll take a table by the window if one is available. The view of the lake is stunning.'

It was, or would be once the sun was shining on it. Being totally dark, the only interest the lake held were a few lights from the opposite shore shimmering through the drizzle.

Isaiah was glad for the empty place at his table. What he wanted was to get to know Felicia. It would be easier with only the two of them making conversation.

'The dining room is lovely,' she said, glancing about the space with a smile.

The woman had an uncommon smile, to be sure. It was pretty, but more than that it made him feel warm inside.

'I dine here often. The food is delicious and there is a beautiful view of the lake when the weather is clear.'

'Everyone does seem to be enjoying themselves.'

'It is cosy with the fireplace burning.'

Humph, if this start to their conversation were any more brittle it would crack.

To prove the point, it did. For a long uncomfortable moment they stared at everything but each other. The silence became embarrassing.

'Do you enjoy it?' she asked at last.

'I do. I find the lamb to be excellent and the wine superb. May I offer you a glass?'

'The rain, I mean. Do you enjoy it? And, yes, a splash of wine would be wonderful.'

'It is a nuisance,' he answered while pouring them each a modest glass. 'I enjoy rain best when it stops.'

For some reason his answer seemed to disappoint her, so he hurried on to another topic. 'My sister sends her thanks for helping to rescue her cat.'

That rallied her smile. 'It's been an awfully long time since I had occasion to climb a tree. But then I don't believe the cat needed rescuing after all. In the end she came down on her own terms.'

'Eloise does live on her own, feline terms, but she is as attached to my sister as Abigail is to her.'

'Your sister seems to be a sweet child and very intelligent to go with it.'

'She's only eight, if you can believe it.'

Silence felled the conversation once more, but this time he nearly saw thoughts swirling past her eyes. She had something she wanted to say, but did not know how to begin.

'Feel free to speak, Miss Penneyjons.'

'Yes, well… I must, mustn't I?' She took a long sip of wine. 'Do you remember us at all? I'm told you and your mother visited Cliverton upon occasion. Also, my sisters and I did encounter you at Lady Newton's ball three years ago.'

'I can't say that I recall meeting you at the ball.'

'I would not expect you to, of course. Ginny and I were only making our debut. A gentleman like you would naturally have his attention focused on the more sophisticated ladies in attendance.'

'May I tell you a secret?' He wanted to smile, but according to Miss Shirls the gesture might frighten her. 'My attention was not on any lady, not that night or on any other. I confess, I am not one for socialising. But there was something, now that I think of it. When you dropped from the tree I had a vague sense of recognising you, but I had no idea from where. Lady Newton's ball must have been it, then.'

'Yes, well, I do tend to be noticed.' She blushed with the confession and for some reason it went straight to his heart, which was odd. When it came to matters of the heart, his was quite dead. 'But, I wonder, do you have any memories of visiting Cliverton? I would not expect you to, really, since you would have been a young boy.'

'Not memories in the usual sense, but I do have a memory of a feeling. I recall a sense of having fun at Cliverton.'

Again, he was struck by her smile. He had to remind himself not to let it affect him in any more than a casual way.

Feeling anything deeper than friendship for anyone but Abigail was not something he was willing to risk. The past had taught him the folly of doing so.

'Well, I'm relieved to hear that.' She took a sip of wine, her lips smiling against the rim of the glass. 'The story that my mother used to tell was that when I was a baby I crawled about after you, wailing and screeching, until you relented and took my hand and helped teach me to walk.'

'Apparently I did a decent job of it. You appear to be agile on your feet. Truly, though, I wish I did remember. No doubt I found you adorable.'

She laughed quietly, pursing her lips in a smile. 'All babies are, of course.'

'For all that they demand every bit of your time and your heart.'

At last, they were speaking easily to one another. It was good to know they could carry on a conversation without tripping all over it.

'Miss Penneyjons, I want to say something—something that cannot be left unsaid.'

'Please Lord Scarsfeld, do speak freely with me. I feel it important that we should be frank with one another.'

'It is simply that I understand you must have given up a great deal in leaving London to come here. I do not take your decision lightly or for granted. You honour me by agreeing to become my wife.'

'Yes, well…in fact, I have yet to give formal approval of the arrangement.'

Had she not? For all that it made sense that she would be cautious, he felt half-sick, fearing she might refuse him. What was he to do if she did?

'What can I do to help you approve? If you have heard things about me, I assure you—'

'I do not pay attention to gossip, my lord. I see with my own eyes that you are not an ogr—' She waved her hand, as if shooing something away. A strand of silky-looking hair escaped confinement, brushing across her ever-so-subtle frown. 'I find it a more reliable habit to form one's own judgements rather than trust someone else's. I promise you that my decision will have nothing to do with anything others might have said about you.'

That was something, at least. The fearful thud of his heart began to ease, the twisting in his gut let up.

'What, then? How can I put your heart at ease?'

'It's my mind more than my heart, I suppose, but what I would like to know is why is it so urgent for you to marry quickly?'

What an uncommon young woman he was going to wed—at least he hoped he was. Some women would not have cared about that, only been content to learn the size, and importance, of his estate.

While he wondered how to begin, he listened to the sounds of silver on china, the quiet murmurs of fellow dinners and the steady tap of rain on the window. His future, and Abigail's, depended upon him presenting his case in the best way.

He was nearly certain she did not want to hear some trite declaration of how he had become weary of being single and that he yearned for the company of a wife. Or of how Scarsfeld needed a viscountess to make it a success in society.

Those reasons were untrue and she would know it.

'It is for Lady Abigail's sake. I must wed if I have any hope of keeping her with me.'

'May I ask why, my lord?'

'It is something you need to know, should you choose in my favour.' He drummed his fingers on the table once then forged ahead. 'My mother died giving birth to Abigail. I was estranged from her and knew nothing of her life, let alone that at forty years old she would— But eight years ago—I was twenty-two then—my late stepfather's solicitor brought Abigail to me in the middle of the night. She was only two days old.'

'It must have come as a horrible shock, finding out about your mother that way.'

'It was horrible. Yet, at the same time, there was Abigail, who is a great blessing.'

'Am I to understand that my purpose in marrying you will be to help you with her?'

'It is more complicated than that, Miss Penneyjons.' Every noise in the room blurred except the increasing tap of rain pelting the windows. 'My sister's uncle, my stepfather's brother, and his wife have decided that she will be better off in London with them. The reason I am in such a hurry to wed is that they are coming to visit for Christmas—they intend to take Abigail with when they leave. My hope is that if I am married they might think me more capable of raising her.'

No one knew any of this, not even the canny Miss Shirls. But Miss Penneyjons did deserve to understand the problem she would be stepping into by accepting his proposal.

'Abigail's uncle and aunt are rather high up in society. As a viscount I would have little chance in court against the Earl of Penfield. My only hope is that if I am respectably married, they will reconsider.'

'Penfield?'

'Are you acquainted with him?'

'No, not really, but being a Londoner I have heard of the Earl and the Countess. I have encountered them briefly in society, although I doubt they would know me. Truly, Lord Scarsfeld, I am very sorry to hear of your trouble. How does Abigail feel about it?'

'She doesn't know.' He scraped his hand across his chin, felt the freshly shaved stubble. 'I can't bring myself to tell her. I'll do whatever is needed to prevent it from happening, as your presence here is proof of.'

'I am taking what you told me to heart.'

'I throw myself upon your mercy,' he whispered and not in jest.

All of a sudden, from one breath to the next, the tapping on the window stopped, which probably meant the rain had turned to snow.

Dash it. He had hoped to make it home before it began to fall.

'Miserable snow,' he muttered. He could only hope that there were a pair of spare rooms to let here at the hotel. The last thing he wanted to do was force his carriage driver to get them home in the slippery mess.

'Surely you do not mean that? Will you escort me outside to see it?' Miss Penneyjons stood up. He suspected she was actually bouncing on the balls of her feet.

He signalled for the waiter to bring their coats. How could he possibly refuse her simple request when he was asking for her life?

In passing by her cousin's table the man looked up, smiling. 'You finally got your snow, Felicia.'

'Isn't it grand?' she answered her cousin, but she was looking at Isaiah.

Judging by her bright smile, she would not care that by going outdoors they would become cold and wet.

'You remind me of Abigail in your love of foul weather,' he pointed out.

'Foul or lovely, it's all in the perception. Snowfall is what it is. It can be miserable or lovely. For me, I choose lovely.'

She was lovely. That was all he could think while he escorted her on to the patio overlooking the lake.

Regrettably, the roof over the terrace kept snow from falling directly on them. Felicia dearly wanted to lift her face and feel icy fingers pat her cheeks, to open her mouth and catch a flake on her tongue.

Since Lord Scarsfeld clearly did not share her joy in being outside, she contented herself with trying to grab the flakes filtering in at them.

For all that she appeared to be having a merry time—appeared to be because she was—she was also deeply considering everything he had told her.

She was grateful he had not flattered her with promises of happy ever after or eventually having an undying love for her.

No, he had trusted her with the truth, confiding his secret. It was going to be a difficult thing to refuse him, if indeed she did.

'Do you wonder, my lord, why I decided to honour our mothers' wishes—to come here and consider your offer? It seems to me it would be important for you to know.'

'I will confess, I have not thought overmuch about it. I was so grateful that you agreed—I am ashamed of that now and I beg your forgiveness.'

'Well, you are in a distressing situation and facing it all on your own. I do forgive you because you ask, even though there is no need to be forgiven anything.'

Isaiah hunched his shoulders against the cold, clearly uncomfortable being out in the elements.

'But why did you come? There are three sisters, are there not? Were you the only one with the courage to face the ogre?'

'It had nothing to do with courage, at least for me. I've told you how I feel about gossip.'

'Why then?'

'Since you have been honest enough to give me the

truth I shall give you the same.' He might not like it, but it was what it was. 'Cornelia, my older sister, is already spoken for. Ginny, the youngest, is terribly shy to the point of being timid. You ought to have seen her face when the news came—oh, well, perhaps you would not have wanted to. She actually does believe gossip. In the event, that left me.'

She shrugged because he could not have failed to be disappointed in her size and her flaming hair. No doubt the thought of being bound to her for ever was daunting.

The only thing to do was to offer him another way out of his problem—because there was one.

'I think you would have been happy had it been Ginny in my place. She is petite and as pretty as a rose and—'

Ginny would be a bride he could be proud to have on his arm. Felicia would clearly be seen as someone Lord Scarsfeld had rescued from the dusty shelf.

'You remind me of a peppermint stick.' Since she could not tell for sure if he was smiling or grimacing, she was hard put to know what he meant by the comment.

'I have no idea if, in your mind, that is a good thing or a bad. I rather like that you think so, though. But there is more to my being here than that I was the only one who would suit. For the one thing, I am a traditional person at heart and feel it only right to respect our parents' wishes. More than that, though, as you surely noticed, I am solidly on the shelf, well on my way to spinsterhood.'

'And marrying me will save you from that?'

'Indeed. I sometimes thought I would not mind it so much. But the fact of it is, when your offer came I was relieved to have a way to avoid that fate.'

'And will you?' He arched a brow. The gesture made him look younger and somehow vulnerable. 'Avoid that fate?'

'Yes…and no.' It cut her to see him look so crestfallen. 'I think I have an idea which will help keep your sister with you, but not bind you to a lifelong marriage.'

To a woman no one else wanted to even dance with.

'It is what I offer you, Miss Penneyjons. My name and my home.'

'But you needn't. At least not for all time. Only until after Christmas and Abigail's aunt and uncle give up their pursuit.'

'For one thing, they might not give up their pursuit. Even if they do…' He shook his head slowly, looking grim. 'At the risk of you turning me down, I will not agree to a temporary marriage.'

He wouldn't? Something in the area of her heart went completely soft. She had offered him an annulment, but in her heart of hearts it was not what she wanted.

'Call me traditional if you like, as you said you were, but I believe marriage is not meant to be temporary, no matter if it is a love match or an arrangement. Vows will be spoken. To me they will be sacred. If you accept me, I offer you all that I have or will have. As far as providing Scarsfeld with an heir, I will not force that upon you. The choice in the degree of intimacy in our marriage will be yours to make.'

Her hair and her face must all look like one great flaming mess.

'You know that I cannot promise undying love—we have only just met.' He took her hand, squeezed her glove. Even through the fabric she felt the heat where they joined. 'What I can and do promise is my undying gratitude.'

Honesty from him was quite a bit more than she had hoped for. Until this afternoon her only hope had been that he would be a bearable man to spend time with.

Lord Scarsfeld, while seeming severe, was honest. Forthright in what he wanted and what he had to offer. In spite of his apparent inability to present a genuine smile, she thought she liked him more than she didn't. And she did genuinely like his sister and cared for her plight.

'There is something—' Isaiah dug about in the pocket of his coat. 'I want to show this to you. Abigail was supposed to help me choose it, but instead she got you stuck up a tree.'

Was that a quirk of a smile at one corner of his mouth?

If it was, she wanted to see more of it. She had the feeling a full grin would banish his vinegary expression at once and expose the man she hoped lived under the mask of severity.

'The truth is I volunteered to go up the tree. I hope you were not—'

While she blundered about saying she hoped he was not too harsh on his sister, he drew the lid off the small box he had taken from his pocket.

Inside was the prettiest gold band she had ever seen. Engraved evergreen branches imbedded with tiny diamonds that looked like a dusting of snow? Had he known her all her life he could have picked nothing she would appreciate more.

With her hand at her throat, she stared at it in silence while fighting a bout of tears.

For a woman who only weeks ago had been resigned to knitting socks in a rocking chair, this moment was overwhelming. To be proposed to with a beautiful ring—she could never have imagined such a thing would happen to her.

'If you don't like it, we can choose another together.'

'It is the most perfect ring I have ever seen.' She closed

the lid because looking at it one more moment would make her weep out loud.

'But you are turning me down?' He slid the box back in his pocket. 'It's all right, Felicia. I know I asked a great deal. I wish I could accept your offer of an annulment, but I cannot.'

'I didn't want one. I only thought it the right thing to do. And I am not turning you down.' She moved to swipe away a tear , but he caught her glove.

'Are you truly willing? It's not my intention to offer you a trap.'

'I'm a good bit more willing than I expected to be, if you want the truth.' If she did not wipe that tear, it would drip off her nose.

'We will face challenges, Felicia. You will more than I, but I promise to be the best man I can be.'

Saying that, he leaned forward, lifted his lips a scant inch and kissed the tear away.

Chapter Four

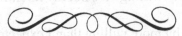

Sitting in the rented carriage, Felicia opened the window to let fresh cold air nip her face. She breathed in the scent of Lake Windermere, then took a deeper breath of fresh spruce which made her long for everything Christmas.

She was on her way to Scarsfeld, on her way to the rest of her life, whatever it turned out to be.

The fact that it did not involve long lonely hours in a rocker, clicking knitting needles and napping, told her she had chosen wisely in agreeing to wed Lord Scarsfeld.

More than that, the fact that she still felt his lips on her cheek hinted that she had made a very good—

'This is a mistake, Felicia. It sends a chill up my neck. We were in town only a short while and I heard people speaking ill of the man.'

'What kind of ill?'

'They say he is sullen and joyless. I do not think he will suit you.'

'Idle tongues… I am surprised you listened to them.'

Resigned to the fact that her happy moment of gazing out the window was at an end, she closed it and turned her attention to her cousin.

'You ought to look for good in all things, Peter.'

'That is exactly my point. You see it even when it ought not to be. I fear you see everything through rose-tinted spectacles.'

'Why is it that I feel somehow insulted?'

'Insulting you was not my intention, only to make you look at this situation clearly. You will not be happy with the man, in my opinion. You need a more cheerful fellow.'

'It is not your cheek he kissed,' she mumbled.

'What was that?'

'Never mind.' She doubted that Peter had deliberately cast doubt upon her ability to make a sound decision. Rose-tinted spectacles, indeed. 'Just because I choose to cast a positive light on people…and circumstances…does not limit my ability to make a sensible decision for my future.'

And for young Abigail's.

Let her cousin doubt her. She was not going to reveal Lord Scarsfeld's secrets. No matter how feather-witted her cousin thought her to be, she would remain silent on her intended's reasons for marrying.

'You accuse me of looking through rose-tinted spectacles while all the while you are wearing blinkers. The Viscount has made me a respectable proposal of marriage. My mother would have approved of it and so do I.'

'But why, for pity's sake?'

'Because one day you will marry, my sisters will, too. You will have children. I have no wish to be their burdensome maiden aunt.'

'Any one of us would be happy to take you into our homes.'

'I know that…but I would not be happy. I would wake up every morning wondering how much pity I could endure.' She reached across, squeezed Peter's hand. 'I only want what any other woman does.'

'I don't know any other woman who would want it with Lord Scarsfeld.'

'That is because they have not felt him kiss their cheek.' This time she said it plainly.

'What?' Peter's jaw fell open. In her mind she saw it hit his knees. It was not easy to withhold a giggle. 'He did that?'

'Indeed. It was quite sweet considering he is an ogre. I was crying and so he kissed the tear away.'

'He made you weep! And you have yet to say your vows! Now I know you are not thinking clearly.'

'I was weeping because he was truthful with me in his reasons for wishing to marry, which I will not share with you. And because he nearly smiled. I'm certain I saw the man beneath the frown in that moment.' And here she was, ready to weep again just remembering. 'But mostly he gave me something I never dared hope for—a heartfelt wedding proposal. And wait until you see my wedding ring. He chose it himself. Really, it could not be more perfect had I designed it. Honestly, Peter, I never dreamed a woman like me would ever have that moment.'

Her cousin blinked at her in silence. Of course he was a man and might not understand.

'And he did not have to stand on a stool to kiss my cheek.'

'There is that, I suppose. If you are certain… I support your decision.'

'Thank you.'

Her cousin was a very good man. He had been only twenty when he became Cliverton and took over the care of her and her sisters. It was no wonder he was protective of them. Playmates turned suddenly into girls to be watched over. It could not have been easy for him.

'Do you remember what we spoke about on the train?' she asked.

'Some of it.'

'The part about me having a purpose? I wonder if it is my purpose to bring happiness to Lord Scarsfeld's life?'

'I wonder if you might have just as easily found your purpose at home, but I did say I support you so I will not speak of it again.'

'No one at Cliverton really needs me. But here... I think perhaps they do.'

Because she had caught a glimpse of the man Lord Scarsfeld kept hidden, she hoped she could give him what he needed. And not only with regard to his sister's situation.

A challenge had been set before her and she felt a thrill at rising to it.

'And I said, if anyone could make the Viscount happy it would be you.'

'You see? I have not made a mistake. I am fulfilling a higher purpose.'

A rap tapped smartly on the roof. Peter rolled down the window and peered up at the driver.

'Scarsfeld Manor just ahead sir.'

Settling back, Peter crossed his arms over his chest, then simply stared at her.

'I pray that no one ever takes away your rose-tinted spectacles, Felicia. The world is a better place for you wearing them.'

She did not know about the world. She only hoped to make her new home a better place. That she would be able to help convince Lord and Lady Penfield that Lady Abigail was better off being brought up where she was.

Isaiah stared out of the conservatory windows, his attention on the half-mile view of the road leading to the estate. He had been doing this on and off all morning. Now that it was nearing one in the afternoon, it was more on than off.

Surely any moment he would see a hired carriage coming from the village. His offer to send the Scarsfeld coach to bring Felicia here had been rebuffed by her cousin.

No doubt it was because Lord Cliverton hoped Felicia would change her mind and return to London.

Watching the expanse of white where nothing moved except a half-hearted breeze plopping snow from tree branches, he wondered if she had changed her mind.

Looking back, he probably should not have kissed her cheek. Her tears were her own business and it had been forward of him to take them upon himself.

Of course, women's tears had always been a difficult thing for him to see. Ever since that Christmas morning when, before dawn, his mother had shaken him from sleep and, weeping, informed him they were going away to live in London with her new husband. Being as young as he was, he hadn't understood what it all meant—nor had he foreseen what was coming for him and his young, beautiful mother. The only question he really had had for her in the moment was how Father Christmas would find him.

He had often wondered over the years why his stepfather had chosen Christmas morning to rip them from home. Pure nastiness was all he had ever been able to come up with.

Try as he might, he had never been able to forget the

worst of that morning. In memory it was as horribly vivid as the moment it happened.

In passing the Christmas tree, he had caught sight of the small gift he had spent the autumn making. It was a necklace made from birch wood which the stableman had helped him create.

Wriggling free of his mother's grip, he ran to get it. A bony-fisted hand caught the collar of his nightshirt, yanked him off his feet, then hauled him towards the front door.

'You'll make us late.' His new stepfather had a stern voice that used to frighten him. 'And put away your snivelling, boy. Act like the Viscount you will become one day.'

His mother made an attempt to point out he was only a child, but her husband said something—he could not recall the words—only how hurtful they were and how his mother wept even harder.

Oddly, what stood out after everything had settled was how beautiful the tree looked in the dim light of the parlour. Even in the midst of his tragedy, it sparkled mockingly in the moonlight streaming in the window.

Shaking off visions of the past, he returned to watching the road, praying Felicia Penneyjons had not changed her mind.

If she had, what would he do? There was no time to find another bride. Besides, he liked Miss Penneyjons—had thoroughly enjoyed the slice of a moment his lips lingered on her cheek.

Closing his eyes, he prayed that Miss Penneyjons would keep her word, come to Scarsfeld and be his bride because no matter what, he was not going to allow his sister to be ripped from her home the way he had been.

'Amen,' he whispered, then opened his eyes.

And just there, turning on to the drive, was a carriage.

'Amen and thank you,' he whispered, rushing into the house and summoning the household to present a proper greeting to the future Lady Scarsfeld.

'It's not what I expected.' Peter's whisper was low enough that Felicia was confident the staff, lined up on either side of the hall, could not hear what he said.

'What did you expect?' she whispered back.

For Felicia's part, she had not thought to see the most appealing room she had ever entered.

It was elegant, but not in a stuffy way. With its walls and grand stairway polished so well the wood looked warm to the touch, with the cheerful rug in shades of orange, yellow and red, along with the huge stone fireplace that suffused everything in a welcome glow—well, she could only wonder if this room reflected a part of Lord Scarsfeld's character that he did not express.

'Something more severe, I suppose—more like him.'

'You do not know him well enough to make such a judgement.'

'I am about to—here he comes.'

Lord Scarsfeld strode into the room, young Lady Abigail walking beside him. They stood at the head of the line of servants.

Abigail tugged on her brother's sleeve, then whispered something in his ear. He grimaced, which made Abigail shake her head and frown.

With that, the pair of them made their way towards her and Peter. Luckily Abigail's smile was full of welcome because her brother's seemed rather pinched.

Which was understandable, Felicia thought. Proposing

marriage so suddenly to a stranger was a rash thing to do. But not, perhaps, as rash as accepting said stranger's offer.

No doubt her answering smile was pinched at the corners, too.

'Welcome to Scarsfeld, Miss Penneyjons.'

'You have a beautiful home,' she answered, then she nodded to her soon-to-be little sister. 'It is good to see you again, Lady Abigail. I trust your cat is faring well after her adventure in town?'

'She was in a bit of a mood from having been stuffed in the basket for so long, but she has recovered.' Evidently this was true since at that moment the cat was happily twining herself about the butler's ankles. 'Welcome to Scarsfeld, Miss Penneyjons. I hope you will be happy here with us.'

'How could I not be with a new sister to become acquainted with?'

She walked down the line of servants next to Lord Scarsfeld as he introduced her to the staff. She greeted each person, complimenting them on maintaining such a lovely house.

Having accepted their good wishes, she knew there was no going back now. Even before taking her vows, she had stepped into her role as mistress of Scarsfeld.

Funny that she was excited about it more than frightened.

Of course she had not been named Lady 'Woebegone' or Violet, as in shrinking.

And tomorrow she would become Lady Scarsfeld—Felicia Merry Scarsfeld, for better or for worse.

Teatime passed pleasantly enough with Isaiah's soon-to-be family, but now it was time to show off Scarsfeld to its new mistress.

He prayed she would like it. He had very little to offer her in this marriage other than this grand and lovely home, his title and his wealth. All things which some women would be contented with, but he suspected Miss Penneyjons wanted more.

What he could not give her was what a wife had a right to expect from her husband. The part of his soul capable of loving deeply was dead, killed by his mother, the one person who ought to have loved him most.

No woman he had ever met—other than Abigail—had been able to convince him that loving was worth the risk.

It might not be right, but friendship was all he had to offer his bride.

'May I show all of you the house?' he asked in order to be polite, but he hoped it would be him and Felicia, alone.

'I've seen it,' Abigail declared while picking up one of the special teacakes Cook had prepared for guests. Which meant she did not prepare them all that often. 'I'll take this one for my nanny, Miss Shirls. Maybe it will sweeten her and she will let me choose the book for our afternoon reading.'

Abigail skipped out of the room. Watching her go, Isaiah could not help but smile inside. He knew well that the scone would not last halfway up the stairs.

'My sister reads whatever she pleases as soon as Miss Shirls dozes off in her chair.'

Peter patted his stomach. 'Perhaps I will go exploring later. A doze sounds just the thing.' With that he stood, bent to kiss Felicia's cheek, then departed for one of the guest rooms.

'I would enjoy a tour.'

Felicia's voice startled Isaiah. Apparently he had lost himself, staring at the spot Peter so casually kissed. The previous night when Isaiah had kissed her cheek it had not been a casual gesture, done then forgotten. Oddly, it still lingered in his mind, had poked at his heart ever since.

While tender affections towards this woman were to be expected and completely appropriate up to a point, he reminded himself that the closest of attachments could be broken, leaving lives shattered.

Felicia had offered him a way to avoid risking heartache. No one would invest themselves in a temporary match.

Which did nothing to change the fact right was right and wrong was wrong: vows made were vows kept.

So here he was, showing Miss Penneyjons her new home. What he needed to keep in mind was that if a mother could leave her child, then—

It would be wise not to give Miss Penneyjons any more of himself than was required of a friendly marital union.

If he ended up losing Abigail, he would be shattered beyond bearing. To also risk such a thing with Miss Penneyjons? No, he could not.

'Shall we begin down below in the kitchen and work our way up?'

'The kitchen is one of my favourite places in a home. It is warm no matter the time of day or night and it always smells so good. Although, our cook in London does not like us underfoot and shoos us out.'

'You will be happy to know that Mrs Muldoon enjoys showing off her skills and does not mind being watched.'

He used to do that. As an adolescent he was hungry all the time. Mrs Muldoon let him sit on a kitchen stool while she fed him. She had also talked to him because she understood that he craved company as much as he craved food.

After visiting the kitchen, he took Felicia to the library, then the vast ballroom that was not used for anything.

'I'd like to know more about you, my lord, since we are about to undertake a task of great urgency.'

Urgency was an odd way to refer to being joined in marriage. Which did not mean it was incorrect.

He could not help feeling shamed. She was giving him so much—her life, in fact—and he was offering her marriage with no intention of giving her his heart.

'Have you lived here all your life?'

'Most of it. I was born here, but my father died when I was a few weeks old. Until I was four years old it was only Mother and me.'

An echo of long-vanished laughter washed over the ballroom, his babyish, his mother's joyful as she chased after him while he dashed madly about on his small German scooter.

'But when my mother remarried I went with her to live at Penfield. I was sent back after a few years. Lord Penfield decided Scarsfeld was where I belonged, given I was the Viscount. But I suspect he wanted to be rid of a child who was not his own. As young as I was, I knew he did not want to share my mother's attention with anyone.'

For many years this house and the servants who came and went had been his only family. These old walls, the only witness to the times he had frolicked with his mother, rolling on the floor while being tickled and cuddled—of the times he had fallen into sweet dreams snuggled on her lap.

Loss was a bitter thing and better not dwelt upon. He did his best not to think of those days. But they were there, lurking in the shadows of his mind. Especially now that he faced the threat of Abigail being ripped from her home—from him.

Ah, but here was his future, looking at him with her lips pressed and a frown dipping her brows.

'I imagine it sounds grim. The truth was, I missed Scarsfeld and was happy to be home.' It wasn't all of the truth, but he said so to put Felicia at ease. 'Come, let us go to the conservatory and you can tell me about your childhood.'

He led the way, listening to the rustle of her skirts as she followed.

'Life at Cliverton has always been noisy. You will recall that I have two sisters, but my parents also brought up Peter. My poor cousin, with three girls there was always someone crying over this or that, always yards of fabric draped everywhere because girls are in constant need of new dresses. Of course, there was far more laughter than tears, but naturally Peter, being the only boy, did not find it amusing. Being a big brother to three girls had to have put a strain on him.'

'I can imagine. I have only one and she is a challenge.'

'Yet she is the light of your life. I saw the way you smiled at her when she ran off with the teacake.'

'My sister was up to mischief. I did not smile.'

'Perhaps you did not in the normal way, with your lips. But I saw it in your eyes, Lord Scarsfeld. Your smile was as doting a one as I have ever seen.'

As far as he knew no one had ever looked close enough to see what lay beyond his habitual frown—to who he was underneath it. This pleased him—but it frightened him more.

'But you are correct, she is the light of my life. If I have any hope of keeping her, I will owe it to you.'

'Don't worry, Isaiah, when Lord and Lady Penfield come

they will see how happy Abigail is and they will not have the heart to disrupt her life.'

Hearing her use his given name caused something warm to roll through his chest—something odd and curious.

He opened the conservatory door. It was chilly in here, but not nearly as frigid as it was outside.

'We keep a fire going here at all hours,' he explained. 'Even though it is still chilly, I prefer to have Abigail play inside. It is much safer here than out there in the freezing temperatures.'

He watched Felicia walk to the window and touch the glass with her fingertips.

She was silent for so long—what was she thinking? That the view was forbidding at this time of year? That she disliked it?

'It is beautiful in the spring and summer,' he said.

'I imagine it is spectacular in autumn as well. But winter! It looks like a fairyland out there. I half expect to see a snow queen skating past, tapping the lake surface with her wand and turning it to ice ahead of her.'

Felicia spun about, her smile so bright and engaging that he half wondered if a snow queen might actually glide past.

'If one could step into a fantasy world, I rather think I would enjoy being a snow queen, all a-sparkle and glittering.'

'It would need to be a fantasy since the lake rarely freezes solid enough to be skated upon.'

She crooked her finger, beckoning him join her at the window.

'Come,' she said, standing so close that their shoulders nearly touched. 'You can be my snow king, King Snowfeld, mighty enough to freeze a volcano.'

She pointed to the furthest visible point of the lake. He ought to be looking where she directed, but her hand was so fair, her finger long, lovely and slender. He could look no further than that.

'Ah, there you are, covering the ice with such powerful speed that ice and sparks are flying from the blades of your skates. You are an impressive sight, to be sure. I'm not frightened of you, though. You and I often skate together and have the best time. Look, you just picked me up and sailed past this window. It looks as if I am flying, does it not?'

'I see us falling through the ice, never to be heard from again.' While he hated to burst her pretty scene, he was not a powerful snow king and if the lake did freeze, it would still be too dangerous to skate on.

'In the real world naturally one would not venture out on it.' She shrugged. It startled him to note that their shoulders were no longer nearly touching, but pressed together, arm to elbow. 'I'm sorry, I should have remembered that fantasy scenes are better indulged in with one's sisters. Peter was always driven to distraction when we tried to include him. It's only that the view from this room is incredibly beautiful. I got carried away and I apologise.'

The last thing she ought to be doing was apologising to him. A grateful man would have gone along with her little story, told her how holding her aloft made him feel as if he was flying with her.

'Yes, well—were I half the man as the King Snowfeld I… I would…twirl you about in a grand way…and—'

'It's all right, my lord. You need not play a game which goes against your nature. But it was kind of you to attempt it.'

'There is one thing I would do if I were Snow King.'

'Truly?' Somehow her smile made the world beyond the window seem less bleak. He had never seen a smile that could do that. 'What is it?'

'I would command you to call me Isaiah and to think of me as a friend.' He would have said husband, but that word implied an intimacy neither of them felt. A friendly husband was more what he was. 'An ally.'

'I will call you by your name as long as you return the favour and call me Felicia. And you are correct. We are allies in the cause of keeping Abigail at home.'

Allies, but she had not added friend. He could hardly blame her for leaving that word out. Friends had fun together. As far as he knew, the only one who considered him fun was Abigail.

'You have a very nice name, Isaiah. I shall enjoy using it. But do you have a middle name?'

'I do, but it is an odd one. Only a few people know it.' Because it was not only odd, it was downright strange. 'It is Elphalet.'

'Isaiah Elphalet.' She repeated it again. 'Do you know what it means?'

'It means that I keep it to myself.'

'Well, I thank you for sharing it with me. Did you know that names are meaningful? Have no fear, Isaiah, we shall get to the bottom of yours.'

Fear learning the meaning of his name? Of all the things he feared, that was not one he had ever considered.

However, he was beginning to fear the warm 'something' that stirred in his chest when he looked at her. He did fear that.

He had never allowed that depth of affection for anyone but his sister. He had never even allowed himself to fall in love.

It was safer not to, yet looking back over the lonely years made him feel as cold as if he had fallen into frigid Lake Windermere.

Chapter Five

It was not uncommon for a bride to be restless on the night before her wedding, even if it was a small, intimate affair like hers was bound to be, Felicia thought while coming out of the library in the wee hours with a book hugged to her chest.

For many brides it would be the anticipation of the wedding night keeping them restless. Apparently she had nothing to fear on that count.

That was something at least, was it not?

Walking from the cold dark library towards the kitchen, which was certain to be warm at any hour, she thought about what a puzzle her soon-to-be husband was.

Clearly he had been wounded by his childhood and deeply.

She had tested him earlier when he'd shown her the conservatory, inviting him to join her in the King Snowfeld game. She wanted to know how deeply his past had scarred him.

Her strategy had not revealed it quite yet, but at least he

had tried to join her in the fun. As awkward as the attempt had been, it had touched her because it indicated that he did care that she be content living at Scarsfeld.

And truly, she did want to be happy. In order for that to happen she needed to discover what her purpose here would be. There was Abigail's plight to be sure, but beyond that? Once the child's security was established, what was there for Felicia to do?

Surely it would become clear in time, would it not? For now she would keep her mind entertained by reading the book she had clutched to the lapels of her robe.

She needed something to keep her mind from entertaining sad thoughts—such as her sisters being unable to attend her wedding. For years they had played at it, dressing up in fancy clothing and marching down the aisle. Not once had they dreamed of doing it without one another.

But more than that, she missed Mama. Ten years ago when the accident had taken her parents, she, Peter and her sisters had needed to fight their way back from Hades. Poor Peter, he had borne the weight of it, becoming Cliverton at only twenty years old. But they had fought their way back and found new life—joyful life, as Mama and Papa would have wanted.

Well, now here she was on the eve of her wedding and she wanted her mother.

What she needed to remember was that she was doing exactly what Mama had wanted. Surely her mother was with her in whatever mysterious way she could be?

Maybe her book could provide her with some distraction.

At this quiet hour no one was in the kitchen, but the space was still warm. The scent of freshly baked bread lingered in the air.

She lit a small lamp and set it on the table top which formed something of an island in the middle of the room.

Tea would be lovely so she made a cup. Oh, and just there under a cloth were cakes left over from the previous day's afternoon tea.

She pulled over a chair and settled upon it. This was far more pleasant than pacing her chamber floor, feeling dizzy with all the emotions swirling inside her.

Opening the book of name meanings, she flipped the pages to the name 'Isaiah.'

Hmm… Apparently there were many ways to spell the name.

'I-S-A-I-A-H,' she spoke the letters aloud. This was how her intended spelled it. Of all the spellings she liked this one best.

Sipping tea and then nibbling a corner of the cake, she looked over the meanings of his name. There were a few to choose from, but they all came down to one.

'The Lord saves,' she read out loud, not sure how it applied to her Isaiah.

Oh. She dropped the cake in scrambling to keep hold of the teacup. Why had she referred to him as 'her Isaiah,' even in the privacy of her mind?

Because—well, it must be that he was about to become her husband and she his wife. The very nature of the union made them each other's.

She shook her head. She had thought of him as hers and no matter how long she stared at the cake she held in her fingers, trying to figure out why, she had done it, there was no changing the thought.

Elphalet. She redirected her attention to Isaiah's middle name.

'God has judged?' She set the teacup down, propped her chin in one hand then nibbled the cake. 'That hardly helps.'

'It would be quite unfortunate if one were found lacking,' came a voice from the shadowed doorway. 'What are you doing down here in the middle of the night?' Isaiah asked, stepping fully into the circle of lamplight.

What? She knew what she had been doing. But now? In this instant?

Well, she was staring at him, was what she was now doing. His hair was all—loose, the curls wild and tumbled looking. Not only that, the front of his robe gaped open and she caught a glimpse of his skin under the soft-looking flannel, skin that would normally go unseen. No doubt he expected to be alone this time of night.

What was she doing, indeed?

'I could not sleep so I decided to research the meaning of your name.'

He pulled a chair out and sat across from her.

'What did you discover?'

'That you are a mystery.' She broke the cake and gave half of it to him. 'Even a contradiction.'

'How so? And thank you.'

'Well, you see, we have "Isaiah." That means "The Lord saves." Which is lovely, but then it is complicated by Elpha-let. There we have "God has judged," and as you pointed out, that would be unfortunate if one were found lacking.'

'I suggest we should leave it at "God has judged merci-fully and saved." But tell me, Felicia, why are you so restless that you are in the kitchen at—' he glanced about '—what-ever time it is?'

'No doubt it is for the same reason that you are.' There was a crumb at the corner of his mouth. She wished it would fall off so that she would not have to resist the temptation to wipe it away. Had she been any other nearly bride she would have done it without a thought. 'Our wedding is tomorrow.'

'Are you now regretting it?'

For pity's sake! The crumb did fall, but it teetered on the lapel of his robe, right where the fabric crossed into a V shape. At this point it could either travel to his lap, or slip inside his robe and go—oh, never mind. She was not that kind of bride.

'I do not think so. Are you?'

'No, Felicia. I am not regretting it.' He reached across the table and covered her hand with his. What a warm and friendly gesture. 'I find you to be lovely and charming.'

He did?

She indicated the unkempt mass of her hair by lifting her brows towards it. She did not want to point to her head and lose the warm contact of his fingers.

'There is something I cannot help but wonder, Isaiah,' and it was not what his hand would feel like touching, oh, say her hair or her lips. 'I do wonder what you will want of me once your sister is secure here at home. What will my purpose at Scarsfeld be?'

'It can be whatever you choose it to be.'

'Honestly, Isaiah, that is rather vague. What does that even mean? I could swing about in the conservatory like a circus performer and you would not mind?'

'Perhaps I would mind that.'

What was that? She could not be certain in the dim light, but she thought, just perhaps, he smiled—with his mouth.

Was that to be her purpose? To make him smile? She had wondered about it, but really, that was a goal more than a purpose.

'Abigail will need you, of course. She has been too long without a woman to guide her. Miss Shirls is devoted to her, but she cannot guide her in the ways of proper society.'

All right, yes, she would enjoy helping Abigail, being a big sister to her. Not for social guidance only, which was important for a young lady, but also to show her how to have girlish fun. That was every bit as important and it was unlikely that she would learn it from her brother or her nanny.

Whereas Felicia excelled at having fun.

'Will you not hire a governess?'

'I intend to at the beginning of next year. But at the moment I am preoccupied with keeping my sister with me. If we succeed, then I will find a governess.'

'We will succeed. Never doubt it.'

It sounded a good thing to say even though she did have a rather strong dose of doubt. But right at this moment her purpose was to encourage him.

They were silent for a while. No doubt they were each trying to convince themselves that what she had just said was true.

'There is something about our marriage I must speak of—'

'Please do speak freely, Isaiah.'

He cleared his throat. 'As time goes by…when you get to know me and I you—you might find that you want—'

Good heavens! Isaiah Maxwell, the fearsome Lord Scarsfeld, was blushing. Even in the dim light she could clearly see the flush heating his cheeks.

'To give you an heir?' she supplied. No doubt she was blushing as furiously as he was.

What a pair they were. Her lungs hitched, a giggle escaping even though the subject they were discussing was a serious one. But really, the sight of two people blushing at each other on the night before their marriage was simply funny.

'Yes, but as I told you before, the choice is yours alone.'

'Is it really? I rather think it is a decision to be made by two people.'

'I only meant that—' She had to wonder if he noticed he was still holding her hand. Since she was enjoying the contact she would not point it out. 'As you have not had much choice in any of this, I feel you ought to have that one.'

'You are wrong in that, Isaiah. I did have a choice.' She turned her hand so that her fingers entwined with his. 'I made it and here I am.'

He closed his eyes, as if blinking, but left them closed for a long time. Then when he opened them, she thought—but of course she must be mistaken—that it was moisture he had been blinking away.

Lifting her hand, he drew it towards him, kissed her knuckles and then let go.

'There are no words to express my gratitude. Abigail would feel the same if she knew.'

'It is better that she does not know, I think. You made the right choice in not telling her. Why should she need to worry, especially with Christmas at hand?'

'It is good to have an ally. I can't recall ever having had one before.'

'Yes, well, you have never had a wife before. The very nature of the relationship calls for it.'

'I like you, Felicia.'

'I like you, too.'

'Is there anything I can say, any question you might have about tomorrow that I can answer to help you get some rest?'

'I do have one.' There she was, blushing again, but she really did want to know this one thing. Any bride would. 'Are you going to kiss me? After the vows are finished, do you plan to kiss me? If you don't want to, I understand, but—well—I just want to know what to expect.'

He stood up. The crumb fell into the robe. Where had it gone—never mind. She had been too forward already without adding that crumb to her sins.

'Would you welcome it if I did?'

The truth was the truth and there would be nothing to gain by denying it.

Her throat went tight and dry all of a sudden so her only answer was a jerky nod.

'Expect this, then.'

With that he leaned across kitchen table, bent and placed his lips on hers. The pressure was so light and brief that it might have been a hot breeze passing between them.

At ten in the morning on his wedding day, Isaiah stared at the grand stairway. From his position in front of the parlour window he had a clear view of the steps down which his bride would descend.

This wedding was not quite what he had imagined it would be—or, more correctly, the bride and his feelings about her were not what he imagined they would be.

At the start of his grand scheme, his fantasy wife was no more than a convenient means to an end. It had not mattered to him who she was. Either Felicia or Ginny—or any lady willing to come north and wed him at short notice— would have suited.

What a fool he had been to not understand that a wife would be more than a guest in his home.

Having known Felicia for little more than two days, he understood how wrong, how shallow, his thinking had been.

Clearly Felicia was not a lady to quietly take her place in the background of his life. He feared that she would become a flame to the brooding corners of his heart, lighting them one by one until he was as exposed, as broken as the little boy he had been when his mother had left him.

Somehow he could not shake the worry that even now Felicia might wish to flee from him—might reconsider her decision to wed him.

With everyone in their appointed places—the vicar on one side of him, Peter on the other and Miss Shirls standing next to the vicar's wife—Isaiah was the one who felt an odd urge to flee.

His heart pounded and, as unmanly as it seemed, his knees were nearly knocking.

Felicia ought to be coming down the stairs by now. It was ten minutes past the appointed time.

What if she really had changed her mind?

What if the kiss he had given her last night, as brief as it was, had displeased her? He hadn't meant to give it, but she was just so pretty sitting in the dim light of the kitchen, gazing up at him in expectation with that shy little smile on her face. Dash it, her lips had been glistening in the lamplight.

'If I were Miss Penneyjons, I would not come down.' Miss Shirls appeared suddenly at his elbow, glancing about the room and wagging her head. 'You, my lord, have made a mess of this.'

'I have no idea what you mean.' He did not since she could not be referring to last night. She could not mean his appearance since he was wearing his best suit and his boots were polished to a shine.

'Truly you do not? Where are the flowers? Where is the small orchestra for my lady to make her entrance to? Even a small wedding requires them.'

He heard the reverend clear his throat and saw him glance at the clock.

He vaguely recalled Miss Shirls mentioning those things were expected, but he had been distracted with all that was going on and not given frills their apparent importance.

He wished he had paid closer attention to her because now here he stood, feeling ashamed of his neglect.

He was not even a husband yet and already he had failed.

In a few more moments he was going to fail again.

Last night in the warm glow of the kitchen, in the warmer glow of Felicia's presence and talk of their future, he had promised to kiss his bride again—that the first one had been a mere foretaste of what was to come. At the time it had seemed right and natural.

But now? He could not be certain what the brief, light kiss had meant to her, but he did know what it meant to him.

Far too much. It had shaken him to the point that he began to feel things he did not want to feel, stirrings in his heart better left unstirred.

He greatly feared he could not kiss her again without giving a part of himself away that he had no wish to give.

Miss Shirls went back to her place beside the vicar's wife. They chatted quietly under their breaths.

Not so quietly that he could not catch a phrase or two. They wondered if he had even provided a bouquet of flowers for his bride to carry.

The ladies were about to discover he had not. No doubt they would conclude he would be a less than stellar husband.

He feared they were not wrong. But for a far more serious reason than failing to provide pretty decor.

Here he stood, on the verge of taking the most lovely of women to be his wife, yet had no intention of allowing her too deeply into his heart.

Guilt stabbed him right in the gut because, in spite of what Felicia believed, any man would be lucky to have her. Another man would have thought to give her flowers and music which would be a token of respect she deserved on her wedding day.

Another man could have given her not only respect, but deep affection. But his heart was damaged and so he could not offer her that, if, in fact, she even wanted his heart.

In spite of that—and the doubt and the nagging feeling that Felicia deserved better than anything he could give—it did not change the fact that Abigail's future might depend upon this marriage.

Isaiah watched the stairs, listening for the creak of footsteps from upstairs and wondering, again, if she had changed her mind.

How long was it proper to wait before sending someone up to see if she intended to come down?

As long as it took for the vicar to gather his wife and go home, was how long. He would not move from this spot until then.

Funny, he had never noticed how loud the clock ticked. It sounded like a drumbeat, more ominous than the wind whispering at the windowpane.

Abigail rushed into Felicia's chamber, out of breath.

'I found it!' She clutched a bouquet of holly and bright red berries tied up in red and white ribbons. 'It was not where my brother told me it would be, so I had to hunt high and low for it.'

'It is so beautiful. Perfect for a December wedding.' Felicia took the bouquet from her future sister.

'He made it himself, with his own hands.'

The maid who had helped her dress and styled her hair into lovely curls slapped her hand over her mouth, then spun towards the window.

Apparently the maid found the idea of Lord Scarsfeld doing such a thing as unlikely as Felicia did.

'He made a beautiful job of it,' Felicia said. 'I've never seen anything so pretty. How thoughtful it was for him to think of it.'

'Oh, my brother is often thoughtful.'

Hmm… Abigail's cheeks were flushed as if she had just run in from the cold. The stems of the holly felt chilled. There was no doubt about who the thoughtful one was.

Looking at Abigail's happy expression, knowing what she would do to save face for her brother—or perhaps to do what she could to please Felicia—she knew she was making the right choice in going down the stairs to wed a puzzle of a stranger.

Given what Isaiah was willing to do in order to protect his sister, he must have a loving heart. Felicia was convinced that there was more to him than the severe image he portrayed. Indeed, last night she'd had a glimpse of it—a taste of something she might want more of.

All right, she was ready for this.

She reached for Abigail's hand. Together they went out of the room and stood at the top of the stairs.

The sound of feet shuffling into place below made her heart slam against her ribs.

It was so very quiet down there, not a note of music to mark her descent down the stairs. Apparently the wind whistling about the house was to be her wedding march.

But wait—a voice came drifting from the parlour. Deep and masculine, it drifted up the stairs, the melody so very poignant.

'I forgot to tell you my brother has a wonderful voice.' Abigail squeezed her hand and they started down the steps.

This was her wedding march, sung by her groom. Truly, no orchestra would have sounded better.

All the dreaming is broken through,
Both what is done and undone I rue.
Nothing is steadfast, nothing is true
But your love for me and my love for you,
My dearest, dearest heart.

For all that the words did not fit their situation, they were beautiful and touching.

Peter, standing beside Isaiah, cast him a sidelong glance that clearly stated his opinion—singing a wedding march was an odd thing to do.

A woman who was probably the vicar's wife stifled a small gasp. Having attended countless weddings, she must think this irregular.

Well, Felicia thought it was a lovely gesture and she was the one being sung to.

When the winds are loud, when the winds are low,
When roses come, when roses go,
One thought, one feeling is all I know,
My dearest, dearest heart!

At least Miss Shirls dabbed her eyes, clearly touched by the tune and the tenderness in the singer's voice.

Isaiah began to sing the last verse, but stopped abruptly and thank goodness he did. She knew the song and at a point it became quite grim.

'Better to leave off with wind and roses,' he whispered, taking her hand from Abigail's and tucking her fingers into the crook of his arm. He tipped his head sideways, his breath skimming her hair. 'I'm sorry, I should have thought to make this better. "My dearest heart" was all I could come up with in the moment.'

The vicar opened his Bible, glanced back and forth between the bride and groom, then he nodded at Peter and Miss Shirls.

'Dearly beloved, we are gathered here in the sight of God to unite this man and this woman in holy matrimony...'

Yes, for better or for worse, here she stood, seconds from becoming Lady Scarsfeld.

If only her sisters were here, it would make this feel more like a proper wedding.

All of a sudden she felt utterly alone. She was becoming part of a family of people she did not even know and Peter was going back to London this afternoon.

She hung on tightly to Isaiah's arm to keep her fingers from trembling.

Of course he noticed. It must be why he covered her hand with his, giving it a bolstering squeeze. Had he smiled at her it would have put her at ease, but the corners of his mouth were pinched tight.

At least one person was smiling. Abigail grinned as merrily as a ray of sunshine bursting through a bank of storm clouds.

Felicia had to imagine that her mother was smiling, too. Mama's dream was about to come true.

Felicia looked into her groom's eyes when the vicar prompted her to say, 'I do.'

But did she? Was her dream about to come true?

She had made the decision two or three times already, but now it was for ever. Once the vow was uttered, it could not be renounced. All vows were important, but this one was sacred. One's reasons for repeating them had no bearing on their significance.

Searching her groom's eyes, Felicia looked for reassurance that she was doing the right thing, that the gold ring about to circle her finger was where it ought to be.

What she saw startled her, caught her breath and tripped her heart all over itself.

Felicia? His mouth moved, but his voice did not come out.

'Are you afraid of me, Isaiah?' How could he possibly be? And yet there was no denying what she could see.

The minister looked at them both, brows arched and no doubt wondering what was quietly passing between them.

He nodded. 'This—*you*—is not what I expected.'

'You have changed your mind.' Her stomach gave a sickening heave.

As rejections went this was a humiliating one. More painful than she could have imagined. It made the shame of standing alone at a ball while watching every other lady dance seem trivial.

Pressing her hand to her middle, she prayed for the strength to walk calmly from the room without creating a scene.

'I have not changed my mind. But I did not expect to

care who it was that I married—and now I find that I do care. And that scares me. Please Felicia, do not go back to London.'

How could she not believe him? His expression in the moment was completely unguarded. 'Here I am, Isaiah, and here I will stay.'

The vicar cleared his throat. 'Let us carry on. Felicia Merry Penneyjons, do you take this man to be your lawfully wedded husband?'

Isaiah took both of her hands in his and gripped them tight.

'Yes, I do.' She held his gaze hard, making the vow with her eyes as well as her words. A tremor passed through his fingers. Somehow the sensation raced up her arms, lodged in her heart and left it trembling.

'Isaiah Elphalet Maxwell, Viscount Scarsfeld, do you take Felicia Merry Pennyjons to be your lawfully wedded wife?'

'I do.'

'You may place the ring on your bride's hand,' the vicar instructed.

Isaiah held her fingers, slowly slipping the warm gold over her knuckles and into place.

'I now pronounce you man and wife.' The vicar closed his Bible.

There, it was done.

Someone sniffled—the vicar's wife, she thought, but did not turn her gaze to look.

Her attention was all for her new husband.

And he had promised her a kiss. The expectation of it had left her half-breathless all morning. If what he had given her last night had been only a foretaste, what would his genuine kiss be like?

Indeed, she was intrigued to explore this aspect of her marriage to Isaiah. He had left the direction it would take up to her, after all, and, to be honest, the images popping into her mind were fascinating.

Glancing about, she saw everyone grinning in anticipation of the happy sealing of the vows.

'You may kiss your bride, my lord,' the vicar stated.

'You may kiss your bride, my lord,' the vicar repeated, as if Isaiah had somehow forgotten.

No man with blood in his veins should need reminding. Not with his wife's cheeks flushing pink in expectation, her green eyes sparkling in happy expectation.

He had promised her a kiss. One that was more than the breath he had grazed her mouth with last night.

But this morning, in the cold light of day, he had promised himself he would not kiss her. It was true what he had admitted about her frightening him. It was all too easy to imagine losing his heart to her.

Unbearable heartache lay that way. Just the thought of possibly suffering another such loss as he had with his mother terrified him.

Yet with everyone looking on, what was he to do? A kiss was expected.

At his obvious hesitation, Felicia's smile sagged.

Someone tugged on his arm.

Abigail?

She pulled him down to whisper in his ear, 'I made her bouquet in your name, but you must do the kissing yourself.'

Of course he must—and yet he must not. The scents of a feast drifted in from the dining room. The wedding breakfast awaited.

The vicar frowned. Peter curled his fists. Miss Shirls shook her head, pursing her lips.

All right, then. With what he hoped was a smile, he placed his hands on Felicia's shoulders, drew her towards him.

He kissed her cheek.

A half-hearted cheer went up from those in the parlour. Also from a few of the servants who had gathered in doorways to watch the nuptials.

'Shall we go into the dining room, Lady Scarsfeld?'

His bride looked down at her hand, turned the gold band on her finger.

'I will freshen up and meet you in a few moments, Lord Scarsfeld.'

He deserved the distance she put between them by using his title. He only wondered if the kiss on her cheek had insulted her, or broken her heart.

While he watched her hurry out of the parlour, Miss Shirls marched up to him.

'That was not well done, my lord, especially if you intend to put an heir in the nursery.'

No doubt that was why the nanny assumed he had decided to marry, to get an heir. No one but Felicia knew the real reason for it.

But Miss Shirls was correct, the kiss had not been well done. Why had he not just given Felicia a formal peck on the lips?

Because he knew it would be impossible, was why not. He barely withheld a snort at the thought. There could never be a formal kiss between them, he feared.

There was something there—a draw, a small wavering

flame that, once kindled, would ignite in a blaze. A blaze that would consume him.

He had been consumed once before when love had walked away. He would not risk being left in ashes again.

Which did not change the fact that he had to try to make up for what he had done—or not done as the case was.

'I will meet you in the dining room, Miss Shirls.'

He had no idea how to set this straight with Felicia, only that he must find her and try to.

Several moments later he found her in the conservatory, standing at the window gazing out, her back straight and her arms crossed over her middle.

'It has been pointed out that I have behaved badly towards you.'

She spun about, her hand at her throat.

'You startled me, my lord.'

'I beg your pardon.' He strode forward. What could he possibly say to set things right?

'Surely there is no need.' She smiled at him, but it was easy to see the hurt behind the gesture. 'If it was Peter, he is very protective and—'

'It was Miss Shirls—and Abigail. But more than that, my own conscience.'

'I don't know why you would—'

'Of course you do, Felicia. You are simply trying to make me feel better about how I mishandled our wedding. I ought to have listened to my sister and her governess when they said there ought to be pretty decorations and music.'

'Well, we did manage without them. And here we are, Lord and Lady Scarsfeld, none the less.'

'None the less—you ought to have fond memories of your wedding day. I am sorry you do not have them.'

'That is not quite true. Your song for me was beautiful. Not many brides are serenaded by their grooms for their wedding march.'

'Had I given it more thought, I would have come up with something more cheerful. I should have and I apologise— for all of it.'

'Will you sing the end of the song for me?'

'Are you certain?' It was rather morbid.

'I would like to hear it, so, yes, please, do sing it.'

Just because he had a decent voice did not mean he enjoyed singing. He would not have done it for the ceremony had he not blundered in neglecting to plan music for her wedding march.

He cleared his throat, gazed out at the frigid vista beyond the window.

The time is weary, the year is old,
And the light of the lily burns close to the mould:
The grave is cruel, the grave is cold,
But the other side is the city of gold,
My dearest heart!
My darling, darling, my darling heart.

'There, you see, once one gets past the grim time there is the city of gold.'

Yes, in the song there was, but—

She touched him, her fingers pressing lightly on his heart. The wedding band caught a wink of sunlight streaking in the window and glowed warmly on her finger.

'May I speak freely, Isaiah?'

'Of course, we have already established that there should be candour between us.'

There was something about the way she said his name

that arrowed straight to his heart, but not in a way that made him feel vulnerable. No, it felt comfortable—familiar and strange all at once.

'I recognise that you fear me, although I cannot imagine why. I am not at all terrifying or judgemental. But one day I will know the reason because you will reveal it to me. I have confidence that you will come to trust me, Isaiah. Perhaps in time we will have our city of gold—just like the song says.'

She had far too much confidence in what he would reveal. He did not wish to even think about a past which had made him the bitter man he was today, let alone discuss it.

'I owe you something,' he said. 'I made you a promise and I did not keep it.'

She bit her bottom lip and, by it, silently told him that she knew he meant the kiss he had withheld.

Without a word, she spun about, started to walk away from him.

He caught her arm, halting her progress, but still she did not turn to look at him.

'Felicia?'

Placing his hands on her shoulders, he turned her to face him.

Still, she avoided his gaze and instead looked over his shoulder as if she found something fascinating happening on the lake. With one finger under her chin he turned her face until she could look nowhere but into his eyes.

'I will not be an obligation to be fulfilled,' she whispered, her eyes turning dark green with her frown. Firmly she removed his hand. 'Our guests are waiting. I will meet you in the dining room.'

In walking away, she brushed her cheek with the back

of her hand. From behind he could not see her tears, but he felt them. They sliced his heart as if with a dull knife.

Felicia, an obligation?

She had been that in the beginning, when she had only been an idea—a solution to a problem.

But the woman walking away from him was not that. Somehow she had seen him, had looked past his surly nature and glimpsed a golden city.

She could not know, nor did he dare reveal, that the reason he had not kissed her was because it would be so much more than a gesture. By indulging in the pleasure, he risked losing his heart.

So here he stood, the worst sort of cad. What kind of man let his wife suffer a broken heart so that he would not risk one for himself?

A miserable one. One who was a failure only moments into the marriage.

Chapter Six

Felicia sat straight-backed in the middle of the Viscountess's wide bed, feeling rather small. That was odd, she had never felt small.

Back at home her toes dangled off the mattress when she stretched out.

Back at home she was never lonely, either. There had always been the company of her younger sister in their cosy bedroom. Ginny snored and it was annoying, but she would take being sleepless thanks to her sister's noise over this silence.

'Not that I should expect—or even want anything different. I did not expect to make a love match.'

Indeed, the fact that she had made a match at all ought to be comfort enough.

'And it would be enough had you not teased me with that breathy little kiss,' she said to the man who was probably blissfully sleeping in the chamber across the hall from hers.

Honestly, she had held no hope of anything but friendship.

If only he had not kissed her and left the taste of his breath lingering in her mind. To be fair, it was not all his fault. If she had not brought the subject up, he never would have done so.

She had never tasted a man before, nor even got close enough to know the intimate smell of one. She had hugged her father and Peter many times, but that hardly counted.

A golden city, indeed. What had got into her, pushing Isaiah that way? She knew he was wounded. She had even threatened to discover why.

If he wanted her to know, he would reveal why without her nosing about. If he did not, it was none of her business.

'Unless it really is my calling to bring you happiness.'

Then again, it was presumptuous of her to imagine so, was it not?

'But on the other hand you summoned me here, married me.'

A wife did have a certain obligation to her husband. Felicia had grown up watching her mother guide her father along life's path.

For her effort, Mama never went without a kiss.

One of the stories that Mama had been fond of telling her girls was that she had made a love match, although she had not realised it until after the wedding night. By the dawn of their first day of marriage her parents were deliriously smitten with each other.

Clearly Felicia was not going to share her mother's lot. Isaiah had told her the decision about intimacy in their marriage was up to her, but she suspected it was not completely true. The man had shied away from giving her the courtesy of a wedding kiss and was unlikely to welcome her to his bed.

Hmm. What was there keeping her from putting that assumption to the test? His chamber door was no more than fifteen steps from hers.

All right, then. She yanked the blankets off her legs and shot out of bed.

In the eyes of the law she had every right to enter his room.

If she found him soundly sleeping, blissfully unmoved by his virgin bride being only steps away, she would trouble him no more over the issue.

One could not force affection. Loving feelings might sprout and grow, but they could never be coerced.

Shrugging into her robe, she walked towards the door in long determined steps. Somewhat determined, that was. It seemed the closer she got to reaching for her door knob, the less sure she was of going through with this little test.

What if he was awake and invited her to share his bed?

Taking such a step was something she would prefer to wait for, would she not?

Tonight her intention was only to discover if he might be willing, one day in the future, to take it.

She reached for the knob, turned it. It was not unreasonable to want to know such a thing—what course her life would take.

With a bolstering breath, she stepped into the hallway.

'Good evening, Felicia,' a deep voice rumbled from beside her—close beside her.

Spinning sideways, she found Isaiah, his shoulder leaning against the wall only feet from her doorway, his arms crossed over his chest and one bare foot leisurely propped over the other.

'What are you doing in the hallway?' she asked. 'It is awfully late.'

'I was on my way back from the—the kitchen—I heard you talking. I was just reassuring myself that all was well.'

'Oh… I was talking in my sleep, that's all.' What was it she had muttered aloud? 'I hope I did not embarrass myself by saying something nonsensical.'

Please let it have sounded nonsensical!

What on earth had she revealed? And now here she was, caught out.

'What are you doing out so late?' he asked, straightening away from the wall.

'Looking for something.'

That wretched kiss he had failed to deliver, was what. Staring at him in the dim hallway, all sleepy-eyed and dishevelled, she had to admit it had been her purpose in going to his room all along.

For all she had told herself she wanted some sort of revelation as to what her future held, she knew it had not been the whole reason.

She wanted that kiss—she wanted it now.

In theory she wanted it now. In the privacy of her mind she was indulging in it. Standing in the dim hall, she imagined him with his— Never mind that.

In reality, she was far too nervous to act on what she wanted.

'What are you missing?'

She could hardly let it be an earring or a shoe or anything that would cause the staff hours of useless searching.

'Dessert. I woke up hungry and am going to the kitchen to have some.'

'I'll go with you.'

'But you just came from there. I'm certain I can find my way to the kitchen and back. Scarsfeld is my home now, after all.'

'I only thought since we are both awake, we might spend the time together.'

She could hardly tell him that the more time she spent with him, the more she wanted what he owed her.

One thing was certain—she would never drag a kiss from him. Either he would give it on his own or she would not have it.

'You ought to get back to sleep. I'm sure your duties as Viscount make a high demand on your time.'

'The truth is, I have not yet been to sleep.'

He hadn't? Well, it was good that she had made her discovery without having to invade his sanctuary.

'Come along, then,' she said as boldly as if this had been her home all along and he newly come to it.

'Perhaps we are over-weary from little sleep last night and a busy day today.'

'They say it happens. But may I be honest about why I cannot sleep?'

'You know you can be, Felicia.'

He might not feel the same if he knew all that was tumbling about in her mind. For instance, last night it appeared he had little on under his robe. He would be scandalised to know where her mind was freely wandering. Were she not now a married woman, Felicia would be scandalised, too.

'I'm awake because I am lonely.' She could reveal this much truth. 'The only person in the world who I have known for more than a few days has gone home to London. No one here really knows me, nor do I know them. There has not been a moment of my life where I was more than calling distance from someone who knows me inside out, as I know them.'

'All the more reason for us to spend this time together.'

'There really is no need to go all the way to the kitchen. The house is cold and my chamber is right here, already warm.'

He looked past her shoulder. It was hard to read his expression in the dim light of the hallway. She sensed, though, that he saw things in the room which she did not.

Ghosts of the past? Of course he would have them.

Good? Bad? Both, no doubt, since life tended to be a mixture of blessings and trials.

'Since you are hungry, we will go to the kitchen.' He took a few steps towards the stairs.

Watching his purposeful stride, she reminded herself to keep patience with his somewhat imperious manner. He was the Viscount, after all, and accustomed to having everyone jump to do his bidding.

With Felicia's mother as an example to go by, this was not going to be easy. Mama was Papa's equal, his best friend and confidante.

When it came to marriage, Felicia wanted nothing less. Love match aside, she would not be under Lord Scarsfeld's thumb.

But for now, she rushed to catch him up. They'd had a pleasant time together last night and perhaps tonight would be the same.

'Why can't you sleep, Isaiah?'

'To tell you the truth, Felicia, I fear the same thing you do. Being lonely. Until Abigail came to me, I knew nothing else. And now that she might be taken away—I—'
He shook his head as if the words were too painful to be

uttered. 'What if our marriage is not enough to dissuade Lord and Lady Penfield? It is possible that they are determined to raise her in London and nothing I do will change their minds.'

'We will do our best to prevent that.'

Then, as if it were the most natural thing in the world, he caught her hand and held it as they walked towards the kitchen.

Coming into the welcoming space, breathing in the lingering scents of cinnamon and cloves, she sat on one of the chairs which Isaiah pulled up to the table in the centre of the room.

She watched him—well, his back and the way his muscles moved under the robe—while he prepared tea.

Brewing tea was not something a viscount typically knew how to do. She did admire him for not being above the task. Perhaps it was a result of the hours he had spent here with the cook when he was young.

'I wonder,' he murmured, his shoulders going suddenly still, 'if we are not as alone as we each feel at the moment.'

He must be right about that since she had not felt the sting of missing her family since Isaiah had taken her hand while escorting her to the kitchen.

'We do have each other in this—after all, we are allies united in our cause,' she said.

He carried two steaming cups to table, then sat on the chair beside her, not across as he had last night.

He lifted his cup as if to give a toast. She raised hers and china clinked.

'To our success, Felicia.'

And then he smiled. Truly and naturally smiled.

It was all she could do not to slip off the chair. She had waited, hoping to see this gesture, and it left her quite undone.

Also, he was fairly easy for her to read. The success he referred to was about the situation regarding Abigail—but not completely that.

Subtly, he was also referring to them—to their brand-new marriage.

No doubt he was trying to hide the thought from her, but how could he?

Wives knew things…even those new to the position did.

'To our success,' she answered, quite certain he was not aware of the way her heart flipped and fluttered.

Isaiah huddled into his coat while he walked towards the stable. Head down against the chill, he made his way briskly along the path leading from the manor, across a bridge and then a meadow to the large stone barn.

He needed to speak with the stableman. This time of year one could not be certain of when a heavy storm might occur. It would be wise to find what was needed, then make a trip to the village and lay in supplies, feed for the animals and food for people who lived at Scarsfeld.

Christmas gifts for Abigail, too. While he would not cut a Christmas tree and decorate it, he would provide the Yule log. There would be a large stack of presents set in front of the fireplace for his sister to open on Christmas morning.

After his meeting with the stableman, he would visit Mrs Muldoon in the kitchen. This afternoon he would take the carriage to Windermere and purchase all they needed.

Some gentlemen would distain the chore but Isaiah

wanted to make sure nothing was forgotten. Glancing back at the house, he spotted Abigail coming out of the conservatory followed closely by Felicia.

They appeared to be racing each other down the steps. The tinkle of laughter reached him across the distance.

He inhaled, intending to shout for them to go back inside, those steps were slippery. Before he could open his mouth, they were safely down and beginning a snowball fight.

Had he not needed to meet with the stableman, he might have joined in. Snowball fights were one of the things he and his sister enjoyed doing together.

As far as he was concerned, it was the one bright part of winter weather. That and remaining sensibly inside near a warm fire.

And soup. He greatly enjoyed the soups and stews Mrs Muldoon prepared in the cold weather.

What did Felicia enjoy? he wondered while entering the stable and relishing the warmth and the scent of wood smouldering in the stove. Whatever it was, he would do his best to indulge her in it.

He owed her more than he could ever repay.

But, no, even though he did, that was not the reason he wanted to make her happy.

Truthfully, it was because he enjoyed her company, found her easy smiles engaging.

Last night they had spent an hour over tea while she told him about her childhood. She shared the story of her parents' shocking deaths and how Peter had suddenly become Viscount, how being only a few years older than Felicia's older sister, he had stepped into the role of guardian and pulled them all through it.

During a lighter part of the conversation, she revealed

how she and her sisters enjoyed shopping. The three of them had a merry time purchasing hats and gowns, but more than that they enjoyed getting secret gifts for each other.

Since she took so much joy in shopping—an activity that he avoided when he could—he wondered if Felicia would like to accompany him to Windermere. She would be a big help when it came to picking out gifts for Abigail and the children of the staff, along with all the others living at Scarsfeld.

If she did come along, it would make it a pleasure instead of a chore.

'Good day, my lord.' The stableman, Mr Reeves, popped his head up from behind a stall gate. 'A storm's coming in, I feel it down in my bones.'

'Do they tell you when—your bones?'

'The closer it gets the more they ache, so in a way they do.'

'I'm going to Windermere for supplies. If there is to be a storm, we should buy extra goods.'

'I'll write a list and bring it up to the house.' Mr Reeves gave him a wrinkled smile. 'And congratulations on your marriage, sir. My wife tells me Lady Scarsfeld is a well-needed ray of light in the manor house. Ah, but I've let my tongue run amok again. Hilde will call me to task if she finds out.'

'She will not hear it from me, Mr Reeves. And you need not bother making a trip to the house. I'll come by for the list on my way out—in a couple of hours, I think.'

'I will see you then.'

Once back in the open air, he huddled deeper into his coat. The temperature was dropping quickly. Even though there was only a scattering of clouds in the bright blue sky, the sooner he made his trip to Windermere and returned, the better. Mr Reeves's bones were well known to be a reliable predictor of foul weather.

For all that Isaiah disliked inclement weather, he wondered if it might serve a purpose.

A blizzard would prevent train travel. Travel by coach would be even more unlikely.

With any luck Abigail's aunt and uncle would be delayed—for ever.

The thought was uncharitable, of course. Abigail should get to know her family. They might be good-hearted people. But given what their intentions were, he could not find it in his heart to wish them welcome.

He well remembered how it felt to be ripped away from home and he would not have that happen to his little sister. She was his to protect, his to nurture and love.

Now that Felicia was here Lord and Lady Penfield could not claim she lacked a woman's guidance.

It was clear to see, just in this short time, how well Abigail was taking to Felicia.

At first, it had taken him aback, seeing them together, laughing and talking about frills, books and the things girls loved.

All these years he'd assumed he was enough for Abigail, that the love he gave her was all she needed. Sending for Felicia had been for show, for an additional defence in keeping his sister where she belonged.

For as wrong as he had been in thinking Felicia could live here more a guest than a wife, he had also been that wrong about Abigail's needs.

Seeing the way she was with Felicia, so genuinely happy

to be with her—to have a sister of her own—his first, and selfish, emotion had been a brief but sharp stab of jealousy.

Since that stormy night when his sister had been delivered to him, he thought he had been all Abigail needed. What a shock it was to discover he was wrong in believing so.

More of a shock was how quickly his jealousy changed to gratitude. He was more than lucky to have wed the lady he had.

How things had changed from a week ago when his only requirement of a bride was that she be willing.

This afternoon he found himself looking for reasons to be in Felicia's company.

The trip to the village and then the shopping would take a few hours. After that he would take her to dinner.

Funny, he could not recall an afternoon he had looked forward to more than this one.

Felicia balanced three dolls in the crook of her arm while pointing to four more she wanted.

No one would be aware that her toes were tapping under her skirt but they were, propelled by 'Deck the Halls' and 'Jingle Bells,' which rang merrily in her mind.

Lady Scarsfeld had a purpose! Isaiah, having requested her help in purchasing a toy for each of the estate children, had given her one that suited very well.

She was skilled at shopping and apparently there was no budget to be held accountable to. Had funds been an issue surely he would have mentioned it?

Setting the dolls on the counter, she turned her attention to sailing boats.

'Lord Scarsfeld is being especially generous this

Christmas,' the proprietress of the shop commented with a great grin.

Felicia would know the truth of it when her husband returned from purchasing supplies for the stable.

While he had told her to buy whatever she needed, not all opinions were equal when it came to Christmas gift giving.

For instance, that one sweet-looking doll remaining on the shelf had eyes the most beautiful shade of brown and hair the colour of wheat. It would not be in the spirit of Christmas to leave it to gather dust when a child might be enjoying it.

Now that Felicia was Lady Scarsfeld some decisions were for her to make.

After she set a dozen sailing boats on the counter with the dolls, she went in search of balls, drums and books.

By the time Isaiah returned from taking care of his business, the counter would be buried under games, hats, scarves and whatever else she could think of which might make a child dance in delight on Christmas morning. Seeing the children happy would certainly make Felicia dance in delight.

The bell on the door jingled, announcing someone had come inside.

'Felicia?'

The moment of reckoning was upon her. She turned towards the door, her smile firmly in place.

Isaiah did look stunned, but to his credit recovered quickly.

'Abigail will be busy all year playing with all of—' he indicated the toys piled on the counter with a wave of his hand '—this. It was kind of you to go to the trouble.'

'Oh, indeed! But these are for the other children. Abigail's gifts are behind the counter.'

'Ought I to hire an extra carriage to cart all this home?'

Rather, yes. 'We have yet to visit the hat shop, so perhaps it would be wise.'

No doubt her husband was not used to shopping with a woman, especially at this most wonderful time of the year.

'And I imagine we will not leave Windermere without a trip to the sweet shop?' he asked. His dark brows slashed downwards, giving him a severe expression.

The woman behind the counter shuffled back a step, no doubt quaking at his brooding look.

What Felicia saw was something different. He was teasing rather than testy. Truly, the sparkle in those brown depths was clear to see if one cared to look closely enough. Because she did, it was all she could do not to hug him. Had the shopkeeper not been staring, open-mouthed, Felicia would have.

'I adore sweets. Thank you for suggesting it.'

He opened the shop door, standing to one side to let her pass. As she did, he caught her elbow.

'I would wager that you have never spent one dull Christmas in your life,' he whispered close to her ear.

'A wager you would win. And I do not intend for this to be the first, Isaiah.'

What was that? Yes, just there the corner of his mouth tipped—or quirked.

Not a smile, quite, but far from a scowl.

How would he react when she began to deck his halls tomorrow?

Chapter Seven

As it turned out, the stableman's bones proved to be correct again.

Wind howled through the streets of Windermere so ferociously that those sitting near the windows in the hotel lobby moved to the centre of the room.

'I am sorry, Lord Scarsfeld, but there is only one room available. So many people seeking shelter from the windstorm. Why, one gentleman has even rented the sofa in front of the fireplace.'

This would not do. It was one thing to spend quiet moments alone in the Scarsfeld kitchen with Felicia, but here at the hotel with one room having one bed—it would not suit.

'I will hire the chair beside the sofa,' he insisted.

'A private word, my lord?' Felicia tugged him away from the counter and led him a few steps beyond the clerk's hearing.

'You must share the room with me, Isaiah.'

Certainly not! He had promised her a choice. He would

not have one foisted upon her by sharing her room and then finding himself unable to keep his hands to himself.

He might appear to be as emotionally distant as a stone, but something was changing inside him and it was happening too quickly for his peace of mind.

'If the chair does not suit, I will stretch out on the floor.'

'I would not advise it. What will people think? Newly-wed and sleeping apart? If you intend to convince Lord and Lady Penfield that Abigail is better off with us, we must appear to be a contented, devoted family.'

'We shall begin when they arrive.'

She held his hand, smiled, then kissed his cheek. 'Perhaps you have not noticed everyone has been looking at us. If you do not go upstairs with me they will begin to talk. You know very well how easily gossip gets about. What is to say that Abigail's aunt and uncle will not hear of our coldness to each other?'

She was correct. Gossip did have a life of its own. His sudden marriage was bound to be a source of speculation as it was.

Keeping hold of her hand, he walked back to the desk.

'The room will do nicely.'

The receptionist did not ask if they had baggage to be brought up. No doubt he assumed that, like so many others, they were in town for the day and had become stranded by the weather.

Going up the stairs, Felicia's hand clutching his arm and having possession of a key to a room, he realised how very fortunate he was.

Had the wind risen an hour later they would have been caught out in it. They, the drivers and the poor beasts pulling the carriage would have been in peril.

It was no less than a tempest outside. Windows rattled in their frames, even paintings on the stairwell wall seemed to be vibrating.

'Here we are,' he said. Stopping in front of room six, he turned the key in the lock. 'I've spent the night in this room on occasion. It is comfortable.'

But cold. The fire had not yet been lit. And no wonder, the staff being so busy with people seeking shelter.

Felicia went in ahead of him. He closed the door, then knelt in front the hearth to build the fire.

Glancing over his shoulder, he watched her stroll about the room while removing her hat. She patted the bed as if testing it for softness. He wondered if she liked a mattress soft, or firm the way he did.

Flames ignited quickly in the tinder, but it might take time for the logs to catch fire.

He stood up, wiping his hands on his trousers.

'Shall I ask the kitchen to send something up? Dessert, perhaps, tea or coffee?'

'Tarts would be delightful—and a pot of good hot tea.'

He removed his coat, then placed it across the back of one of the two chairs in the room.

'Thank you for that, down in the lobby.' He rubbed his hands in front of the growing flames. 'I had not thought of presenting an image.'

After slipping off her coat and folding it neatly, Felicia set it on the other chair. Coming to stand beside him, she turned her palms towards the growing flames.

'I hope you do not take it amiss if I act overly familiar when the Penfields are present. The last thing I would wish is for my actions to offend you.'

'Probably not the last thing. The last would be having to say goodbye to Abigail.'

She was correct, yet at the same time he did not wish to offend Felicia, to have her think he was taking liberties.

Truth to tell, the thought of taking liberties in the guise of presenting a loving marriage to the Penfields had crossed his mind. Not just crossed, but lingered and presented images which a man set on keeping his heart to himself ought not to have.

'In the spirit of our cause, I will not take anything you do amiss.' She turned her hands to warm the backs. 'Besides, I like you. It should not be so difficult to portray feelings of friendship.'

An odd sensation buzzed in his belly. He was not used to having friends. Acquaintances who did not make demands of his heart, he had some of those, but the friendship Felicia spoke of was something else.

What her eyes told him was that what she had so casually called friendship might mean something more.

Surely she did not realise what her expression revealed.

A quiet rap sounded on the door.

'You may enter,' he announced.

A young maid, still a child really, stepped into the room.

'I've brought a pitcher of clean water and towels, Lord Scarsfeld.' She set them beside the washstand. 'My brother, Michael, is coming behind me bringing more wood for the fire. Shall I have a bath sent up, my lady?'

A what? In here? No, there was not a bit of privacy for such a thing. He would never survive watching Felicia bathe. Even though she was his wife and it would not be a sin—it felt very much as though it was.

'Please do not go to the trouble. I'm certain you have more to do than you can manage already,' Felicia answered.

Thank you, God.

Isaiah gave the girl a coin in thanks for offering to deliver the order for tarts and tea.

'Oh, one moment, miss!' Felicia opened her purse and plucked out two peppermint sticks. She gave one to the girl, then one to the boy who had had just finished stacking the wood beside the hearth. 'Have a very happy Christmas season.'

'Thank you, Lady Scarsfeld!' the children said as one.

They went out the door, their smiles shining as bright as the full moon coming into view through the window as it rose over the hills. The huge, bright orb cast shadows on the bed from a nearby tree. The spindly etchings lashed madly on the flowered quilt.

With the door shut and the two of them standing inches apart in front of the hearth, the room felt intensely intimate.

The bed in the room, to be precise.

In his mind it throbbed like a heartbeat.

Fondness for his wife was growing in a way he had not anticipated. She neatly threatened the iron safe in which he kept his heart safely stowed. Every time she smiled, each time she laughed, she spun the rusty lock. It was as if she knew the combination and was clicking the numbers in place one by one.

He feared that one day, without warning, the heavy iron door would squeal open and he would once again be left vulnerable.

Judging by the blush on her cheeks, she felt the pulsing bed in the same way he did.

'You are blushing, Isaiah.'

Curse it!

'No more than you are.'

Which was acceptable for a woman, but certainly not for a viscount who tried to portray himself as a man of cool emotions.

'It is rather funny, don't you think?' she asked.

'It would do my image irreparable harm if anyone were to discover my weakness.'

'I will not divulge it, but honestly, expressing one's emotions is a strength rather than a weakness.'

'Not for everyone.' Not for him.

'If you mean—'

A knock on the door cut her off and not a moment too soon. The last thing he wanted to hear was that she felt his stony demeanour could be redeemed. He did not want it to be redeemed. It was safe in the dark where no one could really see him.

A woman carrying a tray laden with teapot, cups and two tarts entered the room.

'Good evening, Lord Scarsfeld,' she said soberly. Then, smiling at Felicia, she added, 'Lady Scarsfeld, it was kind of you to give my children sweets. Your generosity is all they can speak of.'

'Peppermint and children are a natural combination,' Felicia answered. 'How many more children are here?'

'Four, my lady.'

Felicia cast him a glance that the cook would not see. Offer peppermint sticks to the others, it clearly said—demanded.

His bride could have made the offer herself, but was giving him the chance to appear congenial.

He walked to the wretched beating bed and withdrew four peppermint sticks from Felicia's stash.

'With your permission, of course,' he said to the cook.

'That is very kind of you, sir.' The woman looked at him as if she was surprised to find that he was.

No more surprised than he was since it was really Felicia who was the kind one.

The cook went out of the room, leaving behind a pair of exceedingly delicious-smelling pastries. Fragrant steam rose from the teapot. Simply breathing it in made the room feel warmer.

'You will make me out a saint,' he said while pouring a cup of tea.

He blurted the first thing to come to his mind because he did not wish to return to the conversation from before the cook knocked on the door.

It would not do for Felicia to continue probing his heart.

Sitting across from each other in the red, overstuffed chairs, they drank the tea and ate the tarts, mostly in silence. Their only comments had to do with the weather, which continued to grow worse for all that the moon continued to shine through the window and on to the blasted bed.

Isaiah could not recall ever having been more irritated with a piece of innocent furniture.

No doubt it was because his thoughts about that particular piece were not at all innocent. Not wicked, either, since he was married to the lady plucking a stray pie crumb from her bodice, then popping it into her mouth.

Anything he did to her would be—

He stood up. 'I'll go downstairs to the taproom and give you time to prepare for bed. You need not stay awake. I might be quite late.'

'As you wish, my lord.'

My lord? He had not known her long, but long enough to understand that in addressing him as such, she meant quite the opposite of what she said.

Surely she did not mean she wished for him to stay while she prepared for bed—or that he should join her in it? But if not, what was it that she did mean?

Dash it! He was taking his confusion and going down—

Glass exploded into the room.

Felicia shrieked and leapt from the chair.

Glittering in the moonlight, razor-like splinters of the window blew in on the wind, scattering them throughout the room. He caught Felicia up, wrapped his arms around her and spun her away from the shards.

'What was that?' she gasped, her breath warm where she buried her face against his neck.

'A tree went down. It broke the window. Look, there is a limb on the bed.'

Over the rush of wind blowing inside, he heard shouts of alarm coming from the rooms beside this one. Footsteps pounded on the stairs, some going up and some going down.

From what he could make of the shouts, the lobby windows had fared no better than this one had.

'Shall we go and spend the night downstairs?' She burrowed into him, seeking warmth.

'We are better off here. The fire is still going and we won't have to share it with a dozen other people.'

'The bed is unusable.'

'I have a plan.' He snatched his coat from the chair, shook it, then set it across her shoulders, giving it a tug under her chin. 'Here, Felicia, sit by the fire.'

She settled on the rug cross-legged while looking up at him. 'What are you going to do?'

'Make a tent. Will you be all right while I get it done?'

She nodded, but he could see that she was beginning to shiver with the icy air rushing inside.

As quickly as he could, he shook broken glass from the quilt and blankets. After that he dragged the chairs close to the fire and set them side by side. Draping the quilt over the chairs, he formed the back of the shelter.

Still he needed something to hold the blanket on the sides of the small tent to keep out the wind. And then something else to secure a blanket from the hearth mantel to form a roof that would funnel heat directly at them.

Ah, the curtain rod would work to anchor the blanket to the hearth if he wrapped and twisted it just so. The hall tree would hold up one wall of the shelter walls so he dragged it over.

Since the curtains were serving no purpose at the moment he placed them on top of the blankets.

What else? There was a large painting on the wall which would have to do to support the other makeshift wall.

In all he was satisfied with the tiny sanctuary, but one thing was needed. Protection from the cold floor.

He dragged the mattress off the frame and shoved it into the shelter. Then, after giving the pillows a good shake, he brought them over.

In all it took no more than ten minutes to build and would, in the end, be better than joining the grumbling, shivering people who would be gathering in the lobby.

'Why, Isaiah, I had no idea you had such a talent for construction.'

He settled shoulder to shoulder with her because there was room to do nothing else.

What he did not have to do was slip one arm around her shoulder and draw her against his side.

That action was required in the cause of shared warmth. Any man who allowed his wife to shiver when he could prevent it was not worthy of the name husband. He already felt unworthy of the title as it was.

'This is wonderful.' He knew she meant it because he thought she did not say things she did not mean. 'It's really warm and lovely in here. I nearly feel guilty being so cosy when other wives are not. I doubt all men have your talent for survival.'

'They would have, when they were young. It's what boys do, make tents and forts and the like.'

What the other wives would have was heat from their husband's bodies to keep them comfortable—more than simply an arm about the shoulder.

'It might be a long time before the wind stops and we can go home. What shall we do to pass the time?'

'You choose.' As long as it did not involve reclining on the mattress he would go along with it.

'All right, then. There is no going back on my choice.' Her smile looked rather satisfied so he wondered what he was in for. 'I choose that we sing.'

'Sing?' It could have been worse, he supposed. There were many popular tunes they could entertain themselves with.

'Yes, Christmas carols.'

'I don't know many.' And the ones he did know he didn't care for.

'Never fear, I know them all.' She tapped her lip with one finger. Surely she had no idea what that gesture was doing to him. Then again, she might since he was probably blushing like a fresh-faced boy.

'It won't be "I Saw Three Ships." Peter says I sound like screeching cats when I sing it.'

'Surely not!'

She shrugged, squinting her lovely green eyes.

'You will see. Let's sing "Silent Night." I'm sure you must know that one.'

He knew it, of course—had stopped singing it years ago. This carol had been one that his mother would sing to him on Christmas Eve when she tucked him into bed. During the innocent times, her sweet voice sent him gently off to sleep. Since it was difficult to remember the sweet time without the bitter, he no longer sang it.

Felicia was looking at him…into him as if she read the old heartache. 'But I think a longer one might be better. "The Twelve Days of Christmas"!'

'Have mercy,' he muttered.

'It is what I choose and we have a long night ahead of us.'

'"On the first day of Christmas, my true love gave to me a partridge in a pear tree…" Isaiah, you must sing along. We agreed on it.'

'"On the second day of Christmas…"' he sang along, thinking that Peter was correct about the quality of her voice. However, he could listen to it for hours if only to watch her face. She was aptly named Felicia Merry. He could not ever recall seeing a person take so much joy in an activity. Especially in one they did not excel at. '"My true love sent to me, two turtle doves and a partridge in a pear tree…"'

On the third day, the busy fellow added three French hens and, on the fourth, four calling birds.

"'On the fifth day of Christmas my true love sent to me, five g-o-o-l-d *r-i-i-ings*!'" Felicia drew this part out while wagging her hand and displaying her wedding band.

He went on singing, pretending he was unaware of the fact that he sat upon a mattress with his lawfully wedded wife.

Eight maids were now a-milking. His fingers twitched.

Ten lords were a-leaping and he wanted to leap...to take a risk.

When the twelve drummers were drumming, so was his heart...

The song was finished and so was he.

Out of breath, he whispered, 'Felicia.'

He touched her cheek with the backs of his fingers, felt her cheeks plump with her smile. Her skin was warm—softer than anything he had ever touched.

'I always keep my word, pay my debts.' Shifting his finger to her chin, he stroked the curve where there was the nearly imperceptible curve of a dimple.

He moved, closing the distance between their lips. She blocked his way with her fingertips. But then she pressed them to his mouth, her touch tender as they traced the curve of his bottom lip.

'I do not wish to be your debt.' She was not smiling. Her eyes held him—her captive—who could do nothing but surrender. 'I wish to be your wife.'

He kissed her fingers, then lowered them.

'You could never be a debt—not to any man, especially not to me.'

'There is the matter of sealing our vows with a kiss. That remains undone. So if you did mean them—'

'I did.'

And so he kissed her. Tenderly, respectfully, as befitted their friendship. But then she stopped, pulled away from the kiss, but still so close he felt the heat of her mouth puffing on his.

'Isaiah,' she breathed against his lips.

Then she kissed him. Heat swallowed him, sparks ignited in a kiss befitting of a marriage bed.

Which they were sitting upon.

One tumble backwards and—no, he did not dare.

Felicia ended the kiss, blinked wide and smiled.

'I've never been kissed before.' She was silent for a moment, leaving him to wonder if she had enjoyed it or had been horrified at how the match had been put to the flame searing them both. 'It was more wonderful than I imagined it would be.'

Her assessment of the kiss gratified him—rather a lot.

'I have been kissed, Felicia.' He stroked a lock of red hair which grazed the curve of her smile. 'And this was by far more wonderful than any of them.'

And exactly what did that mean? What course would their lives take from now on?

Since he could not take what he truly wanted of her and not keep his heart in the vault, he said, 'Lie down, Felicia, get some sleep. I'll keep the fire tended.'

Nodding she muttered, 'Tomorrow will be a busy day, I'm sure.'

She eased back on the mattress, gave him a small smile, then turned on her side, tucking the fingers of both hands under her cheek.

It looked rather as though she was praying.

While she drifted off into a dream, was she wondering the same thing he was?

What fire, exactly, would he be tending?

Chapter Eight

A woman kissed for the first time, especially at her ripe age, could hardly walk about the house in a romantic trance all day long.

For all that it felt lovely to be dancing on clouds, Felicia thought that she must find something productive to occupy her mind. After all, it was not as though her groom had given her a declaration of true, undying love.

No, and she would not have wished him to. Not yet—but at some point she thought she might wish it.

The kiss last night, for all that it had left her hot and breathless, had been no more than a road sign pointing the way. All she could do was follow the direction it indicated and see where it led to. Along the way she needed something to do.

Standing in the centre of the parlour, gazing around her, she knew what it was.

As luck would have it, Abigail came skipping into the room at that very moment, hugging her cat to her chest.

'Good morning, Sister,' Felicia greeted.

'And to you, Sister!' The child set the cat on the floor. 'You have other sisters, but you are my first and there are things I do not know.'

'Things such as?'

'Is it proper to greet you with a hug?'

'Very proper if it is what you wish to do.'

With a hop, Abigail leapt for her, wrapped her slender arms about Felicia's waist and held on tight.

'What do you think?' Felicia asked. 'Does this room need a Christmas tree?'

'Desperately. I've always thought the garlands and bows we put up seem rather sad without a tree.' Abigail twirled out of the hug. 'I've never had a tree.'

'Never?' This would not do!

'I told my brother it is rude to ask Father Christmas to come to a home without one.'

'How did he answer your valid point?'

'He didn't. He asked if I would rather live somewhere else, which I would not.'

If it was in Felicia's power to prevent such a horrible thing, she would.

'Let's go and find your brother and have him take us out to cut down a tree.' The wind was no longer blowing. It had stopped some time in the night while she was asleep. 'The sun is shining and it will be a grand adventure.'

'Isaiah is out for the day. He and the estate manager have gone out to see what damage the winds caused. It might be late by the time he gets home.'

'No matter. I only thought he might enjoy our outing.'

'We will still do it? Even without him?'

'Of course—just because we are girls does not mean

we cannot cut a Christmas tree. All we need is a saw and a sledge.'

'What a grand adventure! I'll get my coat.' Abigail ran, but stopped every ten steps to lift her arms and spin happily. 'Father Christmas is going to be so pleased to finally feel welcome this year!'

Within half an hour the two of them were bundled and pulling the sledge towards the woodlands. Not to be left behind, the cat rode along, sitting on the cover they would use for sliding the tree on to the sledge.

'There are so many to choose from,' Abigail said. 'How do we know which one is right?'

'We look for perfection in size and shape, then see if the tree tugs on our heartstrings.'

'I believe all of them are tugging on my heartstrings. Have you cut down many trees, Felicia?'

'This will be my first. In London we purchased them from Christmas tree sellers. All we ever needed do was to choose one and carry it home—well, we girls did the choosing. Peter and a strong lad from the tree lot carried it home. I imagine the process will be much the same out here, but the tree will be so much fresher.'

Entering a copse of cedar and spruce, they walked among the trees, pausing at each one to evaluate it.

Abigail asked a question of each of them. 'Are you my very first Christmas tree?' Then she waited quietly to see if it would answer.

Most did not, some whispered perhaps. But finally one stood out among the rest, very clearly giving the feeling that it was their tree. That it longed for nothing more in life than to be decorated, carolled around and to have Father Christmas admire it.

Felicia picked up the saw. She hoped she had the skill to fell a nine-foot tree. But how difficult could the back-and-forth motion really be?

She nearly wished the tree that called them had not been quite so tall, but only nearly. This one would look grand and lofty in the parlour.

It took a long time to finally cut it through the trunk, but when it fell they both danced about in the snow, cheering their accomplishment.

'We had better get this home.' Felicia glanced at the sky. Clouds were beginning to streak across it. They were only thin and wispy, but could change from fluffy to threatening in an instant.

The last thing Felicia wanted was for them to get caught out by the elements.

'Where are you, cat?' Abigail called. 'I didn't see her wander off, did you?'

'She was sitting on the sledge a moment ago.'

'Eloise!' Her little sister glanced about, her small hands on her waist. 'I should have made her stay home no matter how she batted at my skirt and meowed.'

'She is close by, I'm certain of it. Let's look for tracks.'

'Here are some, they go this way and then that and then—'

Abigail shrieked. A pair of red squirrels chattered.

A very large hawk swooped down from the sky, its target one unaware cat leaping playfully after leaves.

Abigail ran, waving her arms and shouting. Felicia picked up the saw, waving it about in hopes that a gleam of sunshine on metal would dissuade the bird of prey from its intended meal.

All at once, Abigail took a tumble into the snow. She yelped.

Felicia reached the cat before the bird did. It flapped its beautiful wings and, with a high-pitched cry, flew away.

Snatching up Eloise, she carried her back to where Abigail sat, hip deep in snow.

'What a bad girl you are, Eloise!' Abigail clutched her pet close to her heart while admonishing her.

'We had best be on our way,' Felicia reached a hand down to Abigail. 'The weather looks as though it might take a nasty turn sooner rather than later.'

'I think I may have twisted my ankle.'

'Is it terribly painful?'

'Not wickedly terrible, only mildly terrible.'

Luckily this was not the first time Felicia had been required to help a sister with an injured ankle.

'Here, then.' Felicia helped Abigail to stand. 'You hold on to your kitty and I will carry you to the sledge. There is a space between the branches where you should fit nicely.'

With the cat safe from the hawk and her little sister secure on the sledge, and all the while clouds growing ever darker on the horizon, Felicia was more than a little anxious to reach home.

Luckily it was not far. Coming out of the copse of trees she could see Scarsfeld Manor in the distance. She could not help but smile at the pretty mansion. Funny how only looking at it gave her a sense of warmth, of belonging.

Having lived her whole life at Cliverton, she did miss home very much. But she also found that she was beginning to feel at home here.

Perhaps it was because she sensed Scarsfeld was where she was meant to be—in this place and with these people. It was a comforting thought.

'My brother will not take it well that I have been injured.'

'Surely he will understand this was simply an accident.'

'He won't. Isaiah hovers over me, thinking every minute I will land in some sort of trouble.'

'He is your brother, after all. Even male cousins act that way.'

'I imagine so, but Isaiah is worse than most. You know that our mother sent me to him when I was a squalling infant—wailing and squalling is how he describes me in the moment he first took me from the lawyer.'

'Yes, I did know that. I'm very sorry that you lost your mother when you were so very young.'

'I did not know anything about that at the time, but then later I did feel the loss of having a mother. It is why Isaiah told me he married in such a hurry. So I would have a sister to help me grow rather than be sent off to a school for young ladies.'

That was not why, but Abigail would never hear the truth of it from Felicia's lips.

'I would not have gone, of course. I would run away before I did that.' Felicia glanced back at Abigail while she tugged the sledge. The child meant it.

'Well, here I am and you will not be going anywhere unless you wish to. But tell me, why will your brother be so distressed about your ankle? As far as injuries go it is a minor one. My sister, Ginny, sprained her ankle doing a pirouette in a pile of autumn leaves and was off her feet no more than a week.'

'He worries because of what happened when I was little.

I do not recall the event, but Isaiah tells me that once I toddled out of the house smack into a snowstorm and no one
noticed. He went into a rage at my nurse—not Miss Shirls,
she was on holiday at the time—for her negligence and tore
out of the house, thinking to find me dead. Of course I was
not, but I was sitting beside the lake, half-frozen through.'

'Your poor brother must have felt awful about it.'

'He let the nurse go on the spot without a recommenda-
tion. When Miss Shirls returned from holiday she was even
more outraged than Isaiah was.'

'It is understandable, is it not?'

'I suppose so, but, as protective as he is, I fear he will
not take the results of our adventure well.'

'We will simply have to make this the most beautiful
Christmas tree Father Christmas has ever seen. That should
take the edge off his temper.'

'It should.' Even without looking back at Abigail, she
knew her little sister did not believe it.

It was moments before sunset when Isaiah finally walked
in the back door of Scarsfeld.

He needed a bath, then a warm drink splashed with
whisky while he sat in a plush chair in front of the fireplace.

The storm that Mr Reeves had predicted was getting
closer and, according to him, it would be more wicked than
he first felt it would be.

Given that it was only the stableman's bones saying so,
perhaps it would not be really be apocalyptic in nature.

Walking towards the kitchen and the delicious smells
wafting out of it, he paused and heard—singing.

Felicia's merry voice, along with Abigail's and Miss
Shirls's, drifted out of the open parlour doors.

Standing in the hallway, he listened. While not in perfect harmony, there seemed to be a great deal of joy in the singing.

Perhaps Christmas carols were not so heartbreaking after all. If he could only get himself to live in the present as he ought to and not the past, he might even enjoy them.

What better time than now to attempt to adopt a more cheerful spirit?

Choosing levity over a bath, drink and cosy chair, he continued down the hallway.

He smelled it before he saw it.

It could not be—and yet—his chest ached with the need to breathe, his hands grew damp.

His reaction to a Christmas tree was extreme, he understood that. Yet there he stood, thrown back into the past, and there wasn't a thing he could do to prevent the tumble.

Memories assailed him before he ever set eyes on the blasted tree. Years fell away and, standing in the hallway, he did not hear happy voices in the parlour, but rather a rage of thunder—an echo of a blizzard crashing against the walls of Scarsfeld.

At first he had welcomed the storm because Mother would not end her visit tomorrow afternoon as she planned to. They would be mother and son, sharing the jolly times they used to before she married Lord Penfield.

For this one happy Christmas they would be as they had been before her marriage. Just him and Mama, loving each other so very deeply. No one would be more important to Mama today than he would be.

It was Christmas! He had decorated the tree, as far up as he could reach, with the special ornaments he and Mama always used. Each one had a story, each one cherished.

In the morning, while he unwrapped the gifts that Father Christmas would leave under the tree, she would tell him stories about his father. He knew from her that Papa had been wonderful, loving and the best man a son could ever hope to be descended from. He had always felt an ache listening to his mother's stories because, as wonderful as her recollections were, he had been a baby when Papa died and had no memories of his own.

But he did have memories of his stepfather, ones he wished he did not have.

But here it was, Christmas—everything should be right, but it was not. Even though Mama had come to visit without her husband, something felt wrong, wrong with Mama.

But he was only a child and trusted that Father Christmas, when he came, would make it all right. In the morning, good things would happen and he would no longer remember the way his mother had looked at him so oddly last night.

No doubt she had a stomach ache or something of the sort and that was why she did not sing him to sleep with 'Silent Night.' Or she probably had a headache and that was why she stood in his bedroom doorway, sober faced and making him feel that she did not know who he was.

It seemed to take a long time to fall asleep because Mama did not sing him the song. He must have, though, because he was awakened by the jingle of bells.

Father Christmas had come to make everything right!

He fell back asleep, but then sat up in bed before the sun rose, waiting under his blanket for Mama to come to him. Hand in hand they would rush into the parlour to see what magic Father Christmas had left behind.

He listened for her steps, for the rustle of her robe. He

sniffed, trying to catch the sweet scent that always surrounded her.

He waited and waited. When he could no longer wait, he got out of bed to find her. Perhaps last night's stomach ache or the headache had kept her in bed.

Rushing into the Viscountess's bedchamber, he found it empty.

'Mama?' He'd called her name over and over, but only silence answered.

It could only mean she would meet him in the parlour, of course, with the fireplace already ablaze—with gifts piled around the tree as high as his nose.

Only there was no fire, there were no gifts. There was no Mama.

As it turned out, the last he ever saw of her was standing in his bedroom door, gazing at him as if he were a stranger.

From that day to this, it had been, by far, the most horrible moment of his life. At the time he had not understood that Mama's husband was a jealous man or how very controlling he was.

He knew only one thing.

Love had died. Christmas had died.

And now, in this moment, the ghost of it called to him from the parlour.

He could not possibly go in. For all that he understood this was the present day, it felt wickedly like the past.

'Ah, there you are, my lord!' Mrs Muldoon stepped up beside him. 'I've a tray of cakes here. You are just in time to help us make merry.'

The cook all but propelled him into the room with her pointed elbow.

He felt no joy in this gathering. Years of heartache

grinned in the form of the tree, crushing his heart as if he were still a tender young child.

'Take it down,' he said.

Surely Felicia had not really heard those words, spoken coldly and anticipating no argument.

If Lord Scarsfeld expected there would not be one, he was greatly mistaken.

'I beg your pardon?' She turned about, deliberately taking her time. 'I am sure you are not referring to this beautiful Christmas tree which your sister and I spent the afternoon decorating.'

He stared at the lovely old ornaments as if they were about to leap from the tree and attack him.

'Take it down. Put the ornaments back in the attic.'

Clearly he was familiar with the decorations and held some animosity towards them.

'I will not.' Whatever his trouble with them was, she suspected it must have to do with something in his past.

As much as she disliked confrontation, she would not let whatever it was that had been done years ago to reach across the years and diminish Abigail's joy.

Her husband stared at her, quite obviously stunned at her refusal to do his bidding.

'Of course you will.' His brows lowered, giving him a dark, fierce expression. No doubt it was the very scowl that gave the impression of his being disagreeable. Which in the moment he was being. 'I am Scarsfeld, my word is final.'

Of all the ridiculous things she had ever heard spoken, this was near the top of the list. If her sisters could have heard it they would have giggled hysterically. Peter would have blinked in confusion.

'Perhaps when it comes to the staff, that is true.' From the corner of her eye Felicia noticed Miss Shirls cover her mouth to hide a—smile? 'But I am Lady Scarsfeld, by your own decree, might I remind you. I belong here now and I will have a Christmas tree—perhaps two of them.'

'You have no idea what—' All of a sudden his gaze shifted to Abigail sitting in a chair, her foot elevated and a bandage wrapped around it. 'What has happened?'

Wicked Christmas tree apparently forgotten, he rushed to Abigail, going down on one knee to inspect her foot.

'Have you been hurt?' he asked even though it was obvious she had been. 'How did this happen?'

'I've twisted my ankle for the first time ever!'

Felicia thought it might have been easier for Isaiah to accept Abigail's injury had she not appeared so proud of it.

'Running on the stairs? Sliding down the banister? I've told you not leap off the couch a thousand ti—'

'She was rescuing Eloise from becoming a hawk's lunch,' Felicia blurted out in order to halt Isaiah's recitation of the ways his sister might have disobeyed him.

'I caught my foot on a branch hidden under the snow. But you will be relieved to know that Eloise is safe.'

'You ventured outside in this weather?' Isaiah's face grew the shade of a freshly bleached sheet.

Given what he had been through in nearly losing his sister once, she understood how he might feel.

'We could hardly have cut down a Christmas tree inside the house,' Abigail pointed out.

A wise and valid point, in Felicia's opinion.

'You…' He spun on his knee, pinning his attention on Felicia. 'You took my sister outside with a great storm bearing down upon us to cut down this—'

He flicked his hand at the tree as if the beautiful thing was a mere weed to be scorned.

'I forbid you to take my sister anywhere without my consent.'

'I think,' Abigail declared, clearly unaffected by her brother's temper, 'she is my sister as much as you are my brother. Therefore I will accept her permission to be equal to your forbidding.'

Oh, dear. Her words had to have cut Isaiah deeply. After all, he was the one to have raised Abigail from infancy and given his life in the cause of seeing to her well-being. At a time when he might have been in London going to the gentleman's clubs, attending balls and seeking the companionship of fine ladies, he had been raising his baby sister.

For this, Felicia greatly respected him. A fact which had nothing to do with this Christmas tree.

'Isaiah…' Felicia touched his elbow, in a gentle attempt to lead him to a chair. 'Won't you sit for a moment, have some cake and look at our tree? See how beautiful it really is?'

'Take it down,' he muttered coldly, then jerked his arm out of her grip.

He stalked out of the room in long angry-looking strides. For pity's sake, it was a wonder that sparks were not flying from his boots.

'Do not take it to heart, Sister. I, for one, do not regret this tree,' Abigail stated, her smile bright and pleased. 'It is exquisite and I adore it.'

'What a pity we shall be forced to remove it.' Mrs Muldoon shook her head.

They would not remove it, of course. Abigail had as much right to be joyful over her first Christmas tree as her brother had to snarl over it.

'We will not remove one little ornament from it,' Felicia said with a determined nod. 'In time Lord Scarsfeld will adjust to having a Christmas tree, perhaps come to enjoy it even.'

'I hope that is true. It is a beautiful tree,' Mrs Muldoon said. 'May I say, my lady, how very grateful I am that you are here? For Abigail's sake and my lord's.'

She handed Abigail a cake, then bustled from the room.

In the moment, no words could have felt more encouraging. To know that she was appreciated was what she needed to hear.

Her spirits had sunk rather low all of a sudden.

Very clearly the favour of the one person who mattered so greatly to her was not shining upon her and there was very little she could do about it.

'Abigail,' she said, turning about with a false but bright smile. 'I think we need a few more decorations on this tree. What do you say we make some?'

For all that she did not show it, the child had to be discouraged by her brother's reaction to her first Christmas tree.

Because of it, it was imperative for Felicia to remain firmly in favour of having one.

'That sounds like a great deal of fun.' She frowned while saying so. 'I have never made a decoration. I hope I will not be a failure at it.'

'Do not worry, Sister. I've made a thousand of them and will show you every trick I know.'

If only she knew enough tricks to get her husband to accept the tree.

It broke her heart, something so beautiful going unappreciated. It was not to be borne that a symbol of Christmas that ought to be a joy was causing disharmony.

Just what she was to do about it, she could not imagine. Isaiah had suffered as a child and that suffering had formed who he was today for good or for ill.

She was not as foolish as to believe it was only ill. Far more of Isaiah was good than ill. Was he not dedicated to making sure his sister did not suffer the heartache of being ripped from home and family as he had been?

There was nothing she wanted more than to help him, to bring out the happier nature in him. However, she would not do it by yielding to unreasonable demands.

'I'll just dash outside and collect some pine cones,' she said. 'We will have a grand time of it, wrapping them in the red and green ribbons I bought in the village.'

'It's getting dark, Felicia. I can wait until tomorrow to do it.'

'Unless there really is a big storm on the way. We won't be able to get them once it is upon us. We will be house-bound with nothing to occupy us.'

Honestly, the thought of wild weather raging outside while remaining warm and cosy within was appealing.

Especially if she and her younger sister were creating Christmas ornaments together.

She was going to have those pine cones and some artful twigs as well. It was not horribly dark yet and she would take a lantern to gather them by.

It had grown completely dark by the time Felicia reached the grove of pines and spruce growing near the lake's edge. The copse was not far from the house, but it had taken more time than she had expected to find a cloth bag to put pine cones in and a lantern to light the way.

Stepping in among the trees, she glanced at the ground. It was still covered with the last snowfall, but she did see pine cones scattered here and there.

The moon, one moment shining brightly on the snow and the next blocked by heavy clouds, was no help in illuminating her quest.

She set the lantern on a rock. The circle of light exposed a small patch of ground where a dozen or so pine cones lay half buried.

It really was a magical setting—the snow aglitter in lamplight, the delicate etching of small animal tracks winding in and out of the circle of light. Beyond that, the great dark lake was being alternately lit and then hidden by the battle between moon and clouds.

Bending, she picked up pine cone after pine cone, placing the best in the bag and tossing less suitable ones over her shoulder.

Wind whooshed softly about. Bare branches overhead rustled, moaning and whispering to each other.

'Oh, aren't you the perfect one?' she whispered softly, not wishing to disrupt the beautiful solitude.

Glancing back at the house, seeing the windows merrily aglow in lamplight and smoke curling out of a dozen chimneys, she felt at peace.

Perhaps even at home.

The more she gazed at the stately manor, the more she felt she belonged here. She would not have thought it possible to form an attachment so quickly to a place.

There was a reason for that, of course, and it did not have to do with bricks and mortar. Rather, it had to do with the

cantankerous, handsome, and confused man who owned it.
Confused was the very word to describe him. Apparently,
because of his childhood scars—and they were horrible—
he felt he was incapable of love, yet he loved his sister quite
deeply. Which only went to show his heart was not dead,
but only in hiding.

Well, she would not allow him to hide from her! He might
never come to love her, but she would help him heal as best
she could.

She would not have believed it possible to form an attachment to her new husband so quickly, especially after
the way he had behaved towards an innocent tree.

But here she was, unable to get him out of her mind even
when she wanted to scold him as much as kiss him again.

She gave herself a mental shake. She had not come out
here to wool gather, but to gather pine cones.

From the moment when she had spoken her wedding
vows, she belonged to Scarsfeld and had a duty to see to
the well-being of everyone living here.

Which was wonderful because it gave her a purpose. In
the moment that purpose was to see that everyone living
here had a happy Christmas.

Decorations, both the making of them and the viewing
of them, added to the joy of the day.

She moved the lantern to another stone, then went to work
on the pine cones revealed in its circle of light.

The bag was becoming full and, rather than constantly
stooping to gather each cone, she duck-walked, dragging
her treasure behind her.

Oh, my! Just there beyond the circle of light she spotted
the rounded shape of the most perfect of them all. At least
it seemed so from here. But it was half-buried in snow and

greatly obscured in the dark shadow of a tree trunk so it was hard to know for certain.

Since it held a great deal of promise she could hardly pass it by without a look.

Deciding not to bother with the lantern, she duck-waddled towards it, keeping the hem of her skirt tucked into the crook of her arm.

It was terribly dark in this spot. It was all she could manage to keep sight of the most lovely and perfect decoration.

Now within reach, she grabbed for it.

What? It slid neatly away from her fingers!

That was unnatural and alarming.

The only explanation for that behaviour was an unseen slope. She had to have knocked it and sent it rolling to the right a few inches.

She reached for it again. This time she plucked it up, grinning at its great size.

'Lady Scarsfeld,' rumbled a deep voice which sounded as if it were hovering over her. 'What are you doing out here in the dark?'

Her gaze focused on a boot toe. So that was what had kicked her pine cone away. She glanced sharply up.

She was correct. The voice was hovering over her—right over her since Lord Scarsfeld was bent at the waist gazing down.

This was certainly a mortifying turn of events. Not that she had done anything to be ashamed of. It was more that she must have looked beyond awkward waddling about on her haunches.

And then to not even see him hiding in the shadows! He would think her careless of her safety now.

She stood up, waggling her bag. 'I am very clearly gathering pine cones.'

'In the dead of night?'

'It is only past seven.'

'Still, dark as pitch.'

Rather like his expression, she thought.

Felicia held the bag with both hands, pleased that her gathering had been successful enough to make it so heavy.

'Only when the moon is behind the clouds,' she correctly pointed out. 'And as you can see, I do have a lantern. Have you noticed how often you come upon me unawares? Pop right out of the shadows?'

Isaiah took the bag, relieving her of the weight, but then he tossed the bag aside. It came to rest with a dozen or more cones spilled on the snow.

'Have you no sense?' Darkness hid his expression, but she didn't need to see his face to know it would look judgemental, as in 'as her husband he knew best.'

One only had to see her work scattered over the ground to know this was not true.

'More sense than to toss aside a half-hour's work.' She jabbed her finger in the direction of bag. 'Why, I ought to—'

'Felicia!' He cupped her face in his cold hands. Apparently he had come after her in such haste he had neglected to put on gloves.

Who, she wondered, but refrained from saying so aloud, was the one lacking sense?

The moon slid out from behind a cloud. Oh, dear, it would be better had the cloud remained. She saw his expression now, flint being struck, sparks igniting his eyes. 'It might have been anyone standing behind the tree.'

She should not laugh at the thought of it. Really, she

should not, but how startled would that stranger have been to have his peaceful moment ruined by someone creeping up to snatch a pine cone near his boot?

'Is there someone in particular on the premises you feel I ought to be wary of?'

'Did it not occur to you that some bearish fellow from Windermere might wander on to the estate?'

'Or from the house?'

Honestly, it had been such a lovely evening until he had come to 'rescue' her from the peril of pine cones, shifting moonlight, and whispering breeze.

His hands fell abruptly away from her cheeks. Not a moment too soon since she had been considering biting his fingers—or kissing them.

'You mock me.'

'And you discredit my intelligence.'

Not to mention setting her insides reeling until she did not know up from down, laughable from serious.

'Could you not have done this tomorrow morning?' he asked while squatting to shove the spilled pine cones back into the bag.

'As I recall it, you disclosed that a storm was going to bury us alive. If Abigail and I have any hope of making it through the catastrophe, we will need a diversion.'

'We have plenty of kindling for the fire already set in store. But if you wish, you may toss these in as freely as you like.'

Burn her pine cones? She yanked on the bag.

'Have you never seen one wrapped in ribbons and hung on the—that is, hung about the room?' she asked in order to spin the conversation away from the hated Christmas tree. 'It is the prettiest—'

'In the future, you will not come outside after dark on your own. If you wish to brave the elements, you will request my company.'

He was not an easy man to divert. Given that, she would not attempt to. Better to lead with the truth.

'I would not have come out had you not frightened us with rumours of the looming weather and—'

'It is looming.'

'And because of your unpleasant attitude towards our Christmas tree, I felt something pleasant was in order.' She yanked on the bag again, but he held it fast in his strong hand. She would not be able to peel those long, manly, fingers off it even if she tried to loosen them one by one. Especially if she tried to, since she would completely lose her focus. 'In order to restore our happy mood.'

There, she was capable of being as frank as he was. She did not care to be, but she was well able.

'Peace will be restored once you have removed the wretched tree.'

'I imagine we are in for it, then, Lord Scarsfeld.'

He spun on his heel and strode towards the house, still in possession of her bag.

Marching along the path with long—and to her mind—arrogant strides, he did not glance back at her which could only mean he was confident that she would follow.

Which meant he was about to learn that she had more pride than to meekly trail after him.

Luckily, there was more than one path back towards the house. She spun about and walked in the opposite direction he took.

Peace indeed! She had no wish to bow meekly to the bear.

He was not the only one in residence whose wishes needed to be taken into account.

Only one, misguided person wanted the tree gone while a dozen others quite admired it.

'Felicia!' she heard him shout. He must have noticed she was not tagging obediently behind.

She would not give him the satisfaction of glancing his way. Instead, she ploughed along her own path, head down and determined. Because of that, she failed to see that it was blocked by a huge fallen limb and covered in a mound of snow.

There was no way around the object…or the humiliation.

With deliberate slowness, she picked her way back towards the trail Isaiah had taken.

Let him wait, shivering and probably cursing. There had been no need for him to come outside after her in the first place. Indeed, had he not, she would have been blissfully warm inside by now.

Curiously, the weather did seem uncomfortably cold all of a sudden, much more forbidding than when she had first come out.

However, now that she had set her course in motion, she must also suffer the nippy elements.

Drat it. She had suffered enough humiliation this evening as it was. She was not going to let her pride suffer further only because she was shivering—violently.

Oh, dear. Isaiah dropped her bag, came stalking back along the path.

She started to shiver. It was cold—but more than that the tremor had to do with the man stalking towards her. He was so very—and he made her feel—she was not frightened of him, so why was she shivering?

Now, standing nose to nose with her, he puffed steaming breath into her face, then he swooped her up into his arms and carried her towards the house.

'My pine cones!' she exclaimed directly into his ear as he marched past the bag on the ground.

Without setting her down, he bent and snagged the bag. He dropped it into her lap.

Oh…my…she had never been carried by a man before and it was a very interesting sensation. It made her belly tickle, her heart speed up.

Not only that, she was so close to his neck that she could smell the enticing scent of his skin.

And she wanted to kiss it.

'Do you intend to bite me, Lady Scarsfeld? Because if you do I promise, I will bite back.'

Would he? No, he would not bite, but nip perhaps, and how nice and warm would his lips feel against her throat?

She nudged his neck with her nose, but he only groaned. She felt his arms tighten about her as his lungs expanded.

Her anger faded. A heated and very curious longing to never get out of his arms rushed in to fill its place.

Which did not, by any means, change her mind about waging a battle to keep her Christmas tree or decorate these pine cones.

Indeed, for the sakes of everyone at Scarsfeld, she would carry on with her worthy purpose.

Chapter Nine

Staring at the Viscountess's chamber door, Isaiah wondered if he would ever have a proper night's sleep again.

Marriage was nothing like he imagined it would be, probably because he had not taken the time to imagine it. Wives, he had ignorantly assumed, were biddable souls with no desires greater than to be helpful and to please their husbands.

Such a supposition must have come from living a somewhat isolated life where the only two people to question his decisions aloud were his sister and Miss Shirls.

And now there was Felicia. What did one do with a woman who lacked common sense—who behaved in a way that put her safety at risk?

The first time he had met her she had been making wrong choices. She had been hanging from a tree, for pity's sake! Not only had she endangered herself, but Abigail as well.

If the memories haunting the Viscountess's chambers were not so painful, he would throw open the door, charge across the room and wake her and firmly explain what was, and what was not, acceptable behaviour.

But visiting old memories was not the only risk to be faced in the Viscountess's chamber. Felicia might be in bed—wearing something sheer. Or nothing at all.

He could not think of that if he was to deal with her behaviour.

What she had done earlier this evening was not acceptable. To venture out after dark was irresponsible. Anything might have happened to her.

What if she had hurt her ankle the way his sister had just done and no one had known she had gone out? The consequences might have been disastrous.

He had lived that horror once and would not do so again. It was only by God's merciful hand he had found Abigail that stormy night. Yes, six years had passed since then, but he had not fully recovered from the gut-twisting terror of what might have happened.

What if he had not looked up from his ledgers, listened to the still small voice prompting him to check on Abigail while she slept? He would never have known she'd wandered out. What if he had begun his search in the direction of the road instead of the lake?

She would not have survived. Years had passed since then but still, the sick fear he got whenever he thought of that time remained to haunt him.

Even though Abigail had survived, the 'what ifs' would not leave him alone. According to what fear suggested, history might change. He would not have checked on her and would have begun his search near the road.

Learning to put the past back where it belonged was not an easy thing for him.

What was going on in the moment was enough of a challenge.

Felicia probably thought badly of him. He had picked her up and hauled her back to the house. She would have had no way of knowing his reaction had been caused by fear more than anger.

If she thought him a beast, who would blame her? He had caused her to believe he would bite her.

If he could take that back, he would—except she had nudged him with her cold nose. He'd nearly dropped her right there and then. And if he had, he would have had to pick her up which might have involved leaning over her in a bed of snow. Which could have led him to behave in a way which would have melted the snow out from under them.

There was no denying there was something growing between him and his wife.

Before she had had the presumption to put up a Christmas tree in his house, they had been on course for a deep friendship. That could only be what it was, it was all he would allow it to be in spite of the way his temperature rose when he was within sniffing distance of her.

The tree! Even from downstairs he could smell the scent of it. To Felicia it was a pretty thing that brought only joy.

Perhaps because, unlike him, she had never lain beneath one shaking with cold and emotion.

The night his mother left he had come to the conclusion she was lost, alone in the snow and waiting for him to find her. Nothing else made any sense. The front door was not locked, so it stood to reason she had gone out—perhaps she had heard the bells like he had and gone out to see Father Christmas. Why would he not think it? He'd been only seven and it had made sense. He had hunted for her in the dark, with snow up to his knees for what seemed a long time. Defeated, he had come home, curled up under the branches of the Christmas tree. Mama was dead because he had failed to find her.

It was all he could think of that long-ago night while he cried and quaked under the decorated branches. Mama was dead. What else would keep her from being with him?

Hours later when the household began to go about their duties, they found him still weeping and shivering under the tree. After they had warmed him, drying what they could of his tears, they informed him his mother was not dead, but that her husband had come to fetch her in the night.

Although he was glad she was not dead, the news had crushed him. The person who used to love him no longer did.

Later that afternoon the butler helped him remove the decorations from the tree and pack them in a box.

The first he had seen of them since then was yesterday. It shamed him that the sight could devastate him after all these years.

He hid so many old fears behind a grim façade: unsettled by foul weather; too faint-hearted to enter his mother's chamber; dreading living alone again while at the same closing himself off to a woman who had vowed to remain with him for all time.

There was nothing he could do about the weather or about banishing the ghosts in his mother's bedchamber. But he could remove what had become the symbol of his mother's betrayal.

Before he could look too closely at the results of what he was about to do and what they would mean to anyone but him, he rushed downstairs.

Felicia would be disappointed. She was devoted to the tree and all its baubles. Abigail might be a bit distressed, but she had not had one in the past so it was unlikely she would be distraught over its loss.

Not to the degree he would be if the tree remained.

It was weak of him not to just bear having it. He understood that. None the less, it was coming down. They would make merry around the Yule log the same as they always had.

Felicia sensed something was wrong as soon as she was halfway down the stairs on her way to breakfast.

She paused, sniffed.

Her beautiful Christmas tree was gone! She felt the loss before she even rushed through the parlour entrance.

Not one needle of Abigail's perfect tree remained on the carpet.

Not only the child's perfect tree, but her only tree. One she had been injured in obtaining. Not that Abigail minded so much. The staff went above and beyond in pampering her.

Felicia stared at the bleak-looking corner of the room where the tree had reigned so cheerfully. She knew who the culprit was right off. Perhaps Isaiah was an elf, an imp or a puck. One thing he was not about to do was to get away with this bit of mischief. Surely he could put aside his dislike of the tree until after Christmas?

With luck she could have everything set to rights before Abigail came downstairs and discovered her brother's treachery.

'Mr Phillips?' she called. Having rushed past the butler a moment ago, she knew he was in the hallway. No doubt the poor fellow was anticipating her outraged reaction.

She put on a bright smile when he came into the parlour. This was no doing of his and she would not make him feel it was.

'Do you know where Lord Scarsfeld is, Mr Phillips?'

'He has gone to Windermere on business, my lady.'

'Good then. Do you know where he put the Christmas tree?'

'Indeed. He instructed me to deliver it to the woodpile, but as it turns out, Hemsworth and I only made it as far as the back courtyard.' He grinned while he spoke. 'Does my lady wish to have us bring it back inside?'

'I would be very grateful. And the ornaments?'

'Ah, Mrs Muldoon was to dispose of them. Somehow they ended back in the attic instead.'

'If you will be so kind as to bring everything back in here, I would appreciate it.'

Within half an hour the tree was restored to its rightful place. She began the process of placing the ornaments in the same places they had been, as best she could recall.

Mr Phillips was a help, grinning while giving advice.

'I apologise ahead of time for the temper Lord Scarsfeld will be in when he returns,' she said. 'I'll make certain he does not blame you for this.'

'My lord is a fair man, if I may say so. All of us in the

household have become accustomed to his scowls. We do not fear them.'

That was all well and good. She felt the same way about Isaiah.

Be that as it may, she was as adamantly determined to keep this tree as he was to dispose of it.

'Would you ask Miss Shirls to keep Abigail upstairs until I finish here? I would rather she did not know about this.'

The one and only reason Isaiah had married her was to protect Abigail.

She took that obligation to heart. If it meant protecting her from the not so lovely side of her brother's nature, so be it.

For all that Abigail held her own where Isaiah was concerned, this battle had to do with Christmas joy.

Now that she was lady of the manor, Felicia would do the fighting.

Isaiah's business in Windermere had gone on longer than he expected it to.

It would have been wise to spend the night at one of the inns in the village, but it was already beginning to snow and he did not wish to become stranded here.

The last thing he wanted was for Scarsfeld to have to deal with a crisis and for him to be away from home.

If the icy gusts pummelling his back on the ride home was an indication of things to come, he had made the correct choice.

The one bright spot in the weather was that, if it was as bad as people were expecting, the Penfields would be prevented from arriving at his front door.

* * *

After delivering his horse into the care of the stableman, Isaiah leaned into the wind and made his way to the house.

It was late and the staff had already retired to their rooms when he came inside. He was surprised to see fire glow spilling into the hall from the parlour.

Surprised and grateful. The journey back had left him half-frozen. It was beyond gratifying to be home.

Smiling in anticipation of warming himself before the flames, he strode into the parlour.

The breath he had been inhaling snagged in his throat, nearly choking him.

It was back! Unbelievably, the Christmas tree he had ordered sent to the woodpile, the ornaments he had consigned to the rubbish heap, were back!

Someone had disobeyed his orders. He did not have to waste time wondering who.

The pretty culprit slept upon a pile of quilts on the floor in front of the merrily mocking tree. Her knees were bent, the curve of her hip and her long limbs halfway under the branches.

Her long, exposed limbs! With her frilly sleeping gown rucked up over her knees, she still managed to appear a vision of innocence. Perhaps it was because of the way she tucked her fingers beneath her cheek in slumber.

It was hard to credit, but he found himself standing in front of a Christmas tree with a smile on his face.

Something was very off, he could not possibly be feeling anything tender in this moment—not in front of this symbol of ruin.

What was more, he had better not make the mistake of considering her his own, personal gift. For all that she resembled a tasty confection, the woman was a warrior. One who had declared war upon him.

For that was clearly what she had done. He could see it in his mind, how she must have smiled sweetly at his staff, convincing them to do her bidding instead of his.

Dash it! Just looking at her made him want to do her bidding instead of his. Not in this case, though. Were it anything but this bitter reminder of loss, he would gladly give her what she wanted.

'I'll go with you to gather pine cones,' he mumbled. 'I'll help you hang them from every rafter in the house, but I will not—'

Suddenly her eyes opened.

'Truly?' She sat up, blinking at him while she casually reached up to lift the strap of her gown back up to her shoulder. But it was a thin strap, a length of lace which still left her shoulders exposed, and the soft-looking skin of her neck and…and the—

He had to look away.

His wife wielded weapons he was helpless against.

'You defied me, Lady Scarsfeld.'

'You might say so.' She shrugged her shoulders. He was caught for a moment, wondering if her skin resembled satin or velvet. Whichever it was, the sight made his stomach flip. 'But then I might say that you undermined me and my position as Viscountess.'

She was correct. He had done that. He had been so set on getting rid of the tree, he had not considered that.

Even so…

'You do not understand.'

'You look cold, Isaiah. Go and warm yourself by the fire and tell me what it is that I do not understand.'

He did what she said because he was cold, but more than that he was also hot. He needed to put distance between himself and what she was barely wearing.

'Do you not have a robe?'

'Of course I do.'

If he had any doubt that she was using her feminine wiles against him, it vanished when she made no attempt to reach for it and cover herself.

She was waiting for him to speak, but he stared at her, struck mute and within a breath of surrendering, of laying bare the details of his sorry past. But he could not quite and so silence lay heavy between them.

She shattered it by saying, 'You will be relieved to know that Abigail never knew her tree went missing.'

'Do you think she will be terribly upset when she finds it gone in the morning?' Because he did intend to have it removed again.

Felicia's hair was loose. He just now noticed how one red strand curled at the spot on her throat where her pulse tapped in quick rhythm. A reminder that he had wondered about biting her there, in that very spot.

'She will not find it gone in the morning, so you need not worry that she will be anything but pleased.'

'My word is—'

'If you persist in this nonsense, your word will cause disappointment for everyone in this household. Do you honestly feel that one man's feelings are to be taken into account ahead of everyone else's?'

'Indeed, yes, if that man is the Viscount. And so far no one has complained about the lack of a tree in the house.' He cast a frown at an ornament he and his mother had fashioned when he was three years old.

Except for Abigail. She had asked for a tree.

'No one dared to,' Felicia said.

'Except you. You dare to.'

'Clearly someone must.'

'You risk a lot for the sake of that thing.'

'Not for the tree's sake alone, Husband. For your sake.'

Ah! Now he had her.

'If you mean what you say, then you will help me take it down.' Haul it outside and burn it along with every heart-breaking decoration clinging to its branches.

'It is because I mean it that I will not.' She reached for her robe, shrugged it over her shoulders. 'Come, sit beside me.'

No, the last time he was that close to a Christmas tree love had died. To sit again among evergreen branches, the ornaments which had been so special now staring at him, mocking the bond he had shared with his mother, would suffocate him.

He crossed his arms over his chest, staring down at his opponent in this battle of wills. He unsheathed his sharpest expression, pointing it at her as if to slay her point of view. To his surprise, he did not see answering combat in her eyes. Neither did he see surrender.

She had called him husband. The expression in her beautiful green eyes said she had not spoken the endearment idly. There was not a single weapon she might have drawn against him more powerful than that word.

'Isaiah…' she patted the quilt '…sit with me. Help me understand why you hate this tree.'

He did not know how she could understand a moment of it, having grown up all smiles and laughter as she had. But if speaking with her would eliminate her objections when he took the tree away, he would sit.

As long as the tree was gone by dawn, he would tell her whatever she wished to hear.

'What do you need to understand?'

He sat down, folding his legs beneath him, preparing to withstand the siege. So he told himself. If he was really doing that, he would not be sitting so close that he could smell whatever flowery scent she had bathed in. He would have put enough space between them that he could not feel the heat of her skin nipping—battering, rather—his defences.

'What is it that makes you act like someone you are not?'

He nearly gasped at the emotional impact of that question. He did it to prevent anyone from seeing inside him as she was so clearly doing right now.

Oddly, because it was Felicia searching him out, he was not fighting it as hard as he might have been. Feeling her probing his heart made him want to run away from her—but, oddly enough, towards her, too.

He would never confess it, but if someone—if Felicia—looked past the thorny barrier he had erected about himself and cared for him anyway, well, he might respond to that in a way he should not.

He might care back.

Dash it, he already cared for her. How could he deny it without being a liar?

She really was the most endearing person he had ever met. Sweet, caring and cheerful, but not without a dash of stubbornness—she was everything he was not.

One did not have to look deeply to note the staff were falling in love with her. The Christmas tree would be on the woodpile destined to be kindling for the Yule log if that were not the case.

'What makes you certain I am not exactly the person I look like?'

Because she clearly did not think so. No one looked at another with tenderness if they were shaking in their socks in fear of their crusty temperament.

He would know if she was shaking since she was not wearing anything on her feet and her slim, fascinating toes were curling then and relaxing in apparent contentment.

It could only be assumed she was more at ease with this conversation than he was.

It did not matter. Lady Scarsfeld could appear as tranquil as Eloise did while lying in a sunny window, but the freshly scented tree looming over him would still be gone before daylight.

'I have seen how you are with your sister. That is who you are, Isaiah. All the rest is bluster to hide it. What I would like to know is why you do it?'

'I would not expect you to understand. How could you having grown up as you have? From what you say, your family has always been a devoted one. Not everyone has had your advantage.'

And there was the truth, uttered with a bitter edge to his voice, an edge that she did not deserve to hear.

No doubt she would rise from the floor at the insult, rush to her chamber and give him time to dispose of the tree.

'Do you resent the way I grew up?'

Wait! Was that compassion lurking in the turn of her lips?

'I can understand it if you do. Life has not been fair to you.'

Surely she was not reaching for his hand to give it a brief squeeze.

'I'm sorry. I spoke poorly. I do not resent the way you

grew up. But I do envy it. I wish I could look at your tree, see it as a joyful thing and sing carols around it. I will admit, this is something you and Abigail ought to have.'

'Let's put that aside for a moment.' Because she fully meant to have this tree. She stated so, not with words, but by the expression in her eyes. 'How would you rather have your sister grow up? Do you want her memories of these years with you to be lacking joy? Or rather, remember them with joy? Do you want her to feel she grew up happy in spite of you? Or that she found happiness in her days because of you?'

'Abigail is happy!'

Of course she was. Had he not spent his life making sure she was? Had he not married in order to keep it that way?

'Shall we put it to a test?' She reached behind her and plucked an ornament from the tree. She held it to the lamplight, turning it this way and that to catch and reflect sparkles on the decorations he and his mother had pasted on it. 'I will help you take down the tree and remove it from the house.'

He suspected her words were a trap in which he was neatly ensnared.

Carefully, she placed the glass ball in his hand.

'We will know how happy Abigail is when she comes downstairs in the morning. Both of us will be waiting right here so we can judge whether she minds the tree being gone or not.'

Damn it! Of course she was going to mind.

'I say, toss that ornament into the fireplace. It would make as good a start as any.'

He ought to take her up on the challenge, for clearly that was what it was.

Tossing the ball from hand to hand, he stared at it.

'Here, I will do it.' She snatched the blue orb from him, lifting her arm.

Something twinkled in the depth of the glass. The sparkle reflected a memory of his mother's smile, of her kiss when she told him how proud she was of his creative work.

Before he could think better of it, he grabbed it out of Felicia's fingers. Quickly, before he could change his mind, he placed it back on the tree.

'Would you have done it?' he asked.

'I would not have. No more than you will destroy Abigail's Christmas tree knowing that, by doing so, you will break her heart.'

'There is too much that you do not understand.'

'You said so before and I asked you to tell me why I do not.'

Wiping his hands across his face, he sighed deeply within himself. Looking at her, trying to see behind her thoughts the way she so easily read his, he wondered if he could tell her what he had never told another person.

'For me, Felicia, love died the Christmas my mother left me. The last I saw of her she was standing in my bedroom doorway, looking at me as if she did not know who I was. I wonder if she was maybe looking through me as if she was already gone. She sneaked away in the night without a goodbye. I lay down under the Christmas tree, looking through my tears at these ornaments, remembering how we had made each one. All of them have a story. I cannot bear to look at them.' He closed his eyes, pressing the lids hard together to keep from seeing it all again. 'You look at this tree and see joy. I look at it and I am reminded that I will never love anyone again. I could not bear the loss.'

There, he had confessed it. The world had not collapsed around him. He felt fingers in his hair, gently stroking from temple to the curve of his ear.

'But you do love someone, Isaiah. You love Abigail. You would not be sitting here enduring the tree if you did not.'

Yes, he did—and he might lose her.

'You also love your mother.'

At those words he opened his eyes, staring hard at Felicia. While she was right about many things, she was not right about that.

'If I do hold an ounce of love for the woman, I do not wish to. She buried a little boy's heart with her own two hands. The last thing I want is to resurrect it.'

'Then why did you not shatter the ornament?'

'It would have been a mess for the servants to deal with in the morning.'

'That, yes. But why else?'

'Felicia, you have neatly pointed out my duty here. I love Abigail and, in order to make her happy, I must not destroy her tree. Now, if you have some magic to help me deal with having to keeping it, I would be happy to know what it is.'

What kind of smile was that?

She did have something!

He greatly feared what sorcery she had in mind.

Chapter Ten

'I have an idea, only. There is no magic to it.'

In fact, she had drawn on all the magic she could expect to in one lifetime simply getting him to leave Abigail's tree in place.

He shifted his position, inching slightly closer to her, inclining his head towards hers as if expecting some great and mysterious wisdom to spout from her lips.

'What?' he asked, his brows lowered and his expression half fearful of what she might say.

'It is a simple idea, Isaiah, and logical. We must find a way to replace your bitter feelings for this Christmas tree with happy ones.'

'Simple? Logical? Do you believe I can put away what my mother did?'

'No. And you should not. But perhaps balance the hurt with understanding?'

He sat up straight, gazing at her as if she were a madwoman. 'After what she did? I do not know what there is to understand. I am raising a child. I know what that commitment means. There is nothing that could make me choose to live apart from Abigail.'

'As my presence here attests to.' In spite of the fact that he had kissed her, she had freely entered into a marriage of convenience. She should not hope for more than that and yet she did. The truth was the truth and sitting next to her husband wearing nothing but her nightgown clearly pointed that out. If only he would touch her—but that was something to think of later. 'But just for a moment, let's stand in the place of your mother, see the world as she might have.'

'I would rather not.'

'Being a man you probably could not anyway. But follow her through my eyes, Isaiah.'

He did not look pleased to be doing so, but neither did he leap up and walk away in a huff.

'I am the happiest woman on the planet. I adore my husband and have just given him the most beautiful and amazing son. I am certain she thought it to be true so you may put your frown away. You know in your heart she did. Then, a short time later, I am the saddest woman on the planet. My husband, my best friend, has died. Oh, but I still have my baby. I will pour all my love into him.'

'She did do that. It was why what came later nearly killed me.'

'It nearly killed me, too. You see, I was a young woman suddenly all alone in the world. We had run out of money and I had no one to turn to. Society expected me to remarry. So I wed a man who seemed an ideal match. For both of us.'

'Seemed, but he was far from ideal in the end.'

'It was too late to do anything about it then. You will remember how he was heavy handed, cruel to me and to you. When, after a time, he decided you should grow up at Scarsfeld, it was an answer to my prayers. At least one of us would be safe from him. At first he allowed me to visit you?'

Isaiah nodded. 'Short visits which became fewer and fewer until she never came again.'

'It broke my heart, you have to know it did.' Standing in Lady Penfield's slippers was not an easy thing to do. Felicia felt tears pressing behind her eyes. 'But I was fairly beaten down by then. I closed my heart. I refused to feel anything.'

'I did see that deadness in her soul on that last Christmas Eve. Your imagination is more than accurate.'

Oddly so. Her emotions were as engaged in this recitation as her imagination was.

'After many years I did give him the child he wanted. But he died of…?'

'Of an apoplexy, the lawyer told me. It was the week before my sister was born.'

'Yes, it was before he knew the baby was a girl and not an heir. I was glad he never knew. I was so weak from giving birth, I knew I would not be the one to raise my pretty Abigail so I sent her to you. But do not fear that I was unhappy in that moment, Isaiah, because there was something that I learned, from you and from my baby girl. Children are the ones who make everything right. You cannot regret a past that has brought them into the world.'

For some reason tears were slipping down her cheeks. It felt almost as if Juliette had been there, a guide through her past.

'Isaiah, I feel that if your mother were here speaking to you, she would want you to understand that she always loved you.'

He was silent for a very long time, staring at the fireplace.

His forearms rested atop his bent knees while he curled his fingers into fists.

'I do not know about that,' he finally said, brushing a spot on his cheek. 'Those might have been her feelings, but we are only playing a game. But one thing you said did strike me, Felicia. It's to do with my sister. Had the past not been as it was, she would not be here. I think she is worth it all.'

'It is a start, then.'

He swung his head to look at her. 'I'm still going to need to make some very good memories if I am to gaze upon this thing without feeling sick.'

'It stands to reason.' It was up to her to supply a good memory to ease the bitter. She glanced about. 'Are there any games in here we could play? Chess, perhaps?'

'If you would rather go to bed, you may. The floor cannot have been a comfortable place to sleep.' Reaching across the short distance between them, he squeezed her hand, then smiled. 'I promise not to destroy your Christmas tree while you sleep.'

'Do you realise what you just did?' And left her heart all dizzy over it.

'I made a promise. Do not worry. I will keep it.'

'But you smiled when you gave it. You grinned and said "Christmas tree" at the same time.'

'An accident, clearly.' Then why was he still smiling?

'I think our tactic is working.'

'I do not know what memory we created to erase the old.'

'We simply spoke to each other, openly and truthfully the way friends do.'

Now, fully understanding his wounds and how he believed that love had died for him, she did not feel it was the time to tell him all of her heart, how a moment ago she had concluded she wanted more of his.

A time would come, she hoped, when she could convince him love had not died.

'Chess?' she asked.

'I'll get the board.' Isaiah stood up and walked out of the room.

When he returned he carried the chess game and half a dozen buns.

'I stopped in at the kitchen. At this hour Mrs Muldoon is asleep so these are not warm with doilies underneath. But I thought we needed sustenance for our endeavour, don't you agree?' He sat down beside her and set up the game.

She could not help but be encouraged since he might have more easily set the game on a table next to the window and not under the tree he detested.

He had beaten her twice, then she beat him once before she yawned.

'It is very late,' he pointed out. 'We should retire.'

He was correct. They ought to have done so some time ago, she thought while he gathered the game pieces and put them away. The problem was, they would now part company.

She truly did not want to.

He stood up, then reached his hand down for her. Naturally she took it, making sure to take a long time to come to her feet.

She need not have because he did not let go of her hand. Instead he lifted her fingers to his lips and kissed them.

'You said something earlier, Felicia—I need to make something clear about it.'

'What is it?'

He looked into her eyes, his expression unguarded. She wanted to throw herself into his arms and hug him. With his barrier down was he about to let her into his heart? Did she dare hope it? She must, because her heart was beating madly and it would not be doing so for no reason.

'It has to do with what you said—about being my wife. When I said I would do anything for Abigail, you replied that it was the reason you were here, or words to that effect. Do you recall it?'

'Yes, and it is why I'm here. The reason is no secret between us.'

'You also called me Husband.'

'You are that, are you not? And a rather good one since you have promised not to harm the Christmas tree.'

'I must have been half-insane when I vowed it. But vow it I did—Felicia, the bit about Abigail being the reason you are here? It was true in the beginning, but no longer. I will admit I proposed marriage to you only as a means of protecting my sister. What I could not see at the time was that luck was smiling upon me when you fell out of that tree. I am grateful, but that is not quite right since I have always been grateful—what I am is happy. Felicia, I am glad you are Lady Scarsfeld. Even if we are not successful in keeping Abigail with us, I am thankful you will still be here.'

All right, that was something close to what she wished to hear and it warmed her through.

'I'm glad, too.'

For him to say he was glad she was Lady Scarsfeld was wonderful, but not the same thing as him being glad she was his wife. Being a wife implied a certain intimacy, whereas Lady of the manor was simply a title.

'And we will be successful, Isaiah.'

'In everything, is what I mean. Home is where the heart is, so they say. I hope it is true for you. I want you to feel this is where you belong.'

'I am beginning to.'

'Perhaps you require a good memory as much as I do. In order to help the process along?'

He slid both of his arms around her back, slowly drawing her towards him.

'One can never have too many good memories,' she whispered close to his lips and closer, she thought, to his heart.

The game apparently forgotten, he dropped it. Playing pieces clattered on the wood floor.

Oh, my—she leaned into him, felt all soft and gooey. Completely melted by his kiss.

Whose good memory was this?

Hers? Indeed, it was. She felt so—so consumed she could not quite put the feeling to words. Of course, no words were required, only that she lean into her husband and let her senses soak in the essence of Isaiah.

His heart beat hard against hers. She was engulfed in muscle, hot breath and masculinity.

This memory was not hers alone. Oh, no, it was so much more than that.

It was their memory to be cherished together.

And what was more, it had happened in front of the Christmas tree.

Please let him be drinking in this moment without the bitter taste of the past to poison it.

Coming downstairs to breakfast the next morning, Isaiah wondered if last night had been a mistake. It did not feel like one. In fact, he had slept better than he had since receiving the letter from Lord Penfield. Even upon waking he did not feel the weight of fear pressing upon him as he often did.

Following his nose towards the breakfast room, he wondered if the contentment he felt in the moment would hold if he turned aside towards the parlour.

Looking at the tree might change everything, cast him back to his normal, ill-humoured self.

He would find that out later—at the moment, the scent of bacon and the sound of his sister's laughter drew him towards the breakfast room.

It hit him hard, realising that, had he acted on his own selfish motivation and destroyed the tree, Abigail would not be laughing.

It hit him harder, knowing that, if not for his bride's intervention, it would be weeping instead of laughter that he heard.

Rounding the corner and entering the room, he saw Felicia and Abigail together, their heads bent while giggling over something.

Isaiah had raised his sister all these years and never understood that she needed a close bond with a woman. All these years she had been lacking and he had never known it.

'Good morning, Isaiah.' Felicia glanced up at him, her smile twinkling and cheerful. 'I trust you slept well?'

All these years, he thought, while watching the curve of the smile meant just for him—all these years, how could he have failed to recognise his own need of a woman?

Not a carnal need, he did not mean that as much as he meant the close tie that came from bonded hearts.

Perhaps he had not known it because he had not known

her. Felicia was the only person who had ever cared enough to scale his wall.

What he could only wonder was, how did she feel about him now that she had?

He picked up a plate and filled it with food from the sideboard. Sitting down, he wondered if his wife was correct in her game of easing bad memories by gathering new ones. Just watching his sister and Felicia chatting, laughing, was making a good memory.

'How is your foot, Abigail?'

'Much improved. I slid down the banister this morning to avoid putting too much pressure on it.'

The first thing to come to his mind was to scold her. Sliding down the banister was a safety risk and forbidden.

Just in time he recalled what Felicia had told him about what he wished his sister to remember during her life with him.

A scolding was not the thing.

Felicia rose from the table all of a sudden. She hurried to the window.

'It is snowing!' She clapped her hands. 'We should go out and have a snowball fight.'

'Oh! Let's do!' Abigail started to rise and then winced.

'You are hurt and a big storm is coming. We shall remain safely indoors.'

It was a lucky thing he was here to add a voice of reason to the discussion. Left to their own choice, his women would dash outside in spite of the danger.

'But it is not big yet, which is all the more reason to go out now,' Abigail persisted. 'We ought to get fresh air and exercise while we are able to.'

'You are not able to,' he pointed out since she was ignoring the fact that it was painful for her to walk.

'I am if you carry me out and set me in a chair. I can easily form my weapons while I sit.'

'Are you forgetting what a target you will make?' In spite of his reservations he was beginning to imagine the possibilities. 'Sitting chairbound and unable to dodge out of the way of my assault?'

'Your sister and I will be a team!' Felicia rang for their coats. 'She will throw her weapons at you while I deflect the ones you throw at her!'

'Two against one?'

If this was going to happen, he had best be out there with them. For one thing, he would be the judge of when it was time to come in, but, more than that, he did not want to miss a second of it.

'It has been pointed out,' Felicia stated, her eyes alight with mischief, 'that you are stronger than you appear.'

Within a quarter of an hour, the three of them were bundled up and ready to go.

He carried Abigail. Even in layers of clothing she was light which served to remind him that, in spite of her rather large personality, she was but a child.

'Thank you for taking me out to play.' She hugged his neck. 'This will be the best snowball fight we have ever had.'

'Why do you think so?'

'Because Felicia is here. We will have great fun.'

'You and I have always had fun.'

'Yes, but now that we have her it will be better.'

Mr Phillips hurried past them, carrying a chair. He set it down a safe distance from the lake.

Carefully, Isaiah placed her in the chair. She tugged his sleeve when he would have gone off to form his weapons.

'I only meant to say I'm glad you married her. Scarsfeld has never been so happy a place as it is now.'

'I can only agree.'

It was happier. He had yet to decide if that condition comforted him or frightened him.

What would happen if he fully let go of his heart, trusted it completely to another person? It would be a great risk, yet had he not already given Felicia a part of his heart? So far nothing hurtful had come of it.

'Be ready for defeat, Brother!'

'Come, Felicia.' Isaiah plucked on her coat sleeve. 'We shall craft our weapons together.'

There were a few mounds of good snow close by, but he led her towards the furthest one.

Something was on his mind and he needed her opinion on it.

That was something in itself. All his life he had made his decisions, for good or for ill, on his own. It felt good to be able to count on another person's advice. Especially when it was given by his wife, whom he was coming to believe was a very wise lady.

'I need to know what you think of something, Felicia,' he said, reaching down to scoop up a handful of snow.

'As you might have guessed by now, I am accomplished at giving opinions.'

'This is advice more than that.'

'What is it, Isaiah?'

They bent and scooped while they talked, pounding snow into balls and stacking them.

'You know I never told Abigail why her aunt and uncle are coming. But, in fact, I did not tell her they are coming at all. Do you think I ought to? They will be here in two days so I cannot put it off for ever.'

Felicia smashed a snowball on his head with a great mischievous smile. In doing so she made their conversation appear to be competitive as would suit the game they were about to play.

'I think she has to know they are coming for a visit. Otherwise she will wonder why you did not tell her about it. But as for their reason for coming? We will pray she never discovers it.'

'Very well. I will tell her about it after I beat the two of you in this game.'

'Abigail!' Felicia called while carrying over their share of snowballs. 'Your brother thinks he is going to slay us in this battle.'

His sister's laugh was young, carefree. He could listen to it for ever. He only hoped nothing, or no one, would ever change that. He only hoped that the fact he was married and therefore a stable family man would be enough to discourage the Penfields from taking her away. That they would put her well-being over their desire to raise her in London.

Abigail pitched the first ball and hit him in the shoulder.

Felicia prepared for his retaliation by standing in front of her partner, shielding her by waving her arms and dancing about on her toes.

Oh, yes. This added twist to the game was going to be great fun.

Taking aim, he launched his shot, hitting Felicia in the

knee. Next Abigail got him in the hip. Then he landed a ball on Felicia's upraised fist where she was about to launch a blow at him.

Felicia and Abigail were laughing to the point of being breathless.

It startled him to hear his own laugh. Until this moment he had not been sure he still had one.

Apparently it startled his opponents, too, for all action stopped while they stared at him, jaws hanging agape.

Their mistake. It gave him an instant to snatch up a ball in each hand.

One of them, a purposefully soft one, hit Felicia square in the nose. While she swiped the snow from her face he delivered the other to Abigail's lap.

'I win!' he shouted, feeling exultant in victory. One defeating two was a great triumph.

'We surrender!' Abigail's sly grin belied her words.

Felicia strode forward, hands behind her back.

'Congratulations, Lord Scarsfeld,' she said, then shoved two snowballs in his face. 'Own your loss!'

Blinking through ice crystals, he grabbed for her and missed. She spun neatly away, dancing on her toes.

There would be payment for this treachery! He was vaguely aware of hearing his sister laughing while he lunged after his opponent.

Felicia was quick, he would give her that. Each time he reached for her she bounded adroitly beyond his grasp.

'Do you concede defeat, Isaiah?' she asked, breathless.

Ah, here was where his superior strength would gain him the win! 'Do you?'

'I am far too fleet of foot to be caught by the lumbering likes of you!'

And so he lunged, taking aim at her middle. The trouble was, the superior strength he had mentally boasted of also gave him the greater weight. It would be a hollow victory if he injured his wife to achieve it.

Mid-fall he flipped her so that she ended up on top of him, which made it falsely appear the victory was hers.

Winded, her breath puffing in his face, she asked, 'Which of us is the winner?'

'We should vote on it!' Abigail called.

'Yes—vote,' she muttered, her breath changing from exertion to something more breathy—more intimate.

'Ha! A guarantee of my loss. I do not agree to it.'

One of them needed to make a move to rise. It was not as if they were alone. Yet here they were, lying breast to breast in the snow, gazing at one another.

There was more going on here than met the eye. Yes, whichever of them got up first would be admitting defeat, but that was not all of it. Something was changing between them that his sister would not be aware of—at least he did not think she would be.

Something began to change in the weather, too. Snowflakes blew sideways instead of drifting gently down. Wind picked up, moaning through the tree tops and making winter-bare branches scratch together.

It was time to go inside. Not because of the change in the weather, but because of the change in him.

If it were not for the fact that Abigail was sitting only feet away, he would—

Ah, but she was there and peering at them with a strange little smile.

Also, the conservatory door opened.

No doubt Miss Shirls was going to demand they come

inside. He was going to have the devil of a time explaining this 'game' as it was.

But why should he be obliged to explain anything? Felicia was his wife.

'This is a good game. We ought to play it again,' he said, revelling in the heat of her breath on his face. It felt extra comforting since he was growing cold from taking the brunt of the snow.

'Oh, indeed. We need a rematch in order to know who the winner truly was.'

He was the winner. This was one more memory his wife had presented him. Another small step out of the dark place he'd chosen to keep his heart.

A throat cleared. Someone gasped.

A second later Mr Phillips announced, 'Lord and Lady Penfield, my lord.'

Here? Now!

'I suppose you ought to let me up now, Felicia.'

'Indeed.' She raised up, casting a glace over her shoulder at the Earl and the Countess. 'We are on the same team now.'

Even with the frowns being cast down from the terrace, Isaiah could not recall when anything had made him feel better.

Preceding everyone into the parlour, Mr Phillips's expression appeared pinched.

Of course it would, Felicia thought. The guests had arrived days ahead of schedule. The staff would not be prepared for them.

Miss Shirls, ever in charge, had acted swiftly and swept Abigail away the instant they stepped inside the house. She insisted the child must be changed into a dry gown. It was interesting how the governess all but shielded her from the guests' view. It was almost as if she knew they were not here to share holiday cheer.

If only Isaiah had informed Abigail they were coming. How on earth was he going to explain why he had not?

'Welcome to Scarsfeld. It is good to see you, Penfield.' Isaiah extended his hand in greeting to the rigid-looking man. To be fair he probably could not look any other way because of his nose. Sharp, as much beak as nose, it would slice the most earnest of smiles.

'Lady Penfield.' Isaiah turned his attention to the woman who looked like a fluffy round sparrow to her husband's hawk. 'I am delighted you came to visit.'

Of course Felicia knew he was not delighted. They surely knew it, too, because of what passed as Isaiah's smile.

While Mr Phillips helped Felicia off with her wet coat, the Penfields' gazes swung her way. They must be wondering who it was that Isaiah had been carousing with in the snow, right in front of Abigail's innocent eyes! They could not know it had been but a game.

'Allow me to introduce my wife, Lady Scarsfeld.'

Both of them had to look up at her while offering a greeting.

Casting a loving smile at Isaiah, Felicia was reminded how glad she was not to have to look down at him. All right, there was the inch, but it did not signify.

She took a steadying breath. Let this show begin, then. Although, given how her heart spun a dizzy jig when Isaiah smiled back at her, clearly it was not all for show.

'Welcome to Scarsfeld!' Felicia held out both of her hands to Lady Penfield, making sure her smile of welcome would make up for Isaiah's lack of one. 'How perfectly wonderful that you were able to make it. We feared the weather would prevent your visit.'

'As did we,' Lady Penfield answered. 'It is why we travelled early. I hope our untimely arrival will not inconvenience you.'

'Not at all. We are only happy you were able to come. Christmas spent with family is ever so much better than spent alone, do you not agree?'

Felicia wished Isaiah would stop trying to smile. Their guests were going to feel as unwelcome as they actually were.

'Oh, I do.' Lady Penfield's smile showed such relief that Felicia felt more kindly towards her. 'Given the reason we are here, I thought—well, you might not welcome us.'

'Oh, but you are family through Abigail. She would be grieved to think there were hostile feelings between us.'

'Scarsfeld,' Lord Penfield stated from where he had taken a position in front of the hearth, 'I did not hear that you had married.'

'It was a quiet affair.'

'And convenient, I suspect.'

'Oh, dear,' Lady Penfield muttered for Felicia's ears alone. 'My husband is not as beastly as he appears. Truly, we are overjoyed to hear your happy news.'

Isaiah opened his mouth, probably to return vocal fire. Felicia hurried over, insinuating herself under his arm. As she had expected, tension rippled through his chest.

'Delightfully convenient.' With a half-lidded gaze at Isaiah, she sighed. 'Once one is smitten it is foolhardy to postpone one's vows.'

'Only trouble can come of it, otherwise,' Lady Penfield agreed.

'I, for one, believe this marriage is a sham. Carried out in order to make my niece's life here appear favourable.'

'Do not be a dolt, Henry. It is rude of you to suggest such a thing. Look at the two of them and tell me you do not remember how it was to be young and in love.'

Oddly enough, the hawk blushed. Lord Penfield and Lord Scarsfeld had some things in common. Perhaps there was a chance for them to rise above the ill will sparking between them.

Peter would accuse her of looking at things through rose-coloured spectacles. Yet it was the Christmas season and unlikely things—wonderful things—might happen.

Right behind her the tree, still standing and all a-glitter, was proof of it.

'Her life here has always been favourable, my lord.' How brightly could one smile without freezing one's face? Felicia wanted to know. 'You shall see it for yourself soon. Abigail is a delight, which of course is a credit to her brother. I have rarely seen siblings so devoted to one another.'

That part was easy to say since it was the truth.

It was also not what their guests wanted to hear. It would be easier to remove Abigail from her home if they believed it was for her own good.

Felicia's job was to make them see the truth, to understand it was in Abigail's best interests for her to remain at home with her brother, which meant she needed to do what she could about softening her husband's image. This would involve appearing to be completely besotted with him, which was not so far from the truth.

'You must be weary from travel,' Felicia said. 'It looks as if you arrived in the nick of time. Just look at that snow out of the window! It is growing heavier by the moment.'

It truly was. Great sheets of white sailed past the windows. It was difficult to see ten feet beyond the glass.

'We saw it developing while we were still in Windermere,' Lord Penfield remarked. 'I must say, I was relieved to arrive at your door when we did.'

'The worsening weather all but pounced upon us. We were involved in a snowball fight and had neglected to notice how hard the snow was coming down. Isaiah...' she said, giving him her full attention. 'It was a lucky thing Abigail and I defeated you as quickly as we did.'

It was important to establish from the start that Scarsfeld was a fun place for a child to grow up and what was more fun than a battle with snowballs?

Isaiah arched his brows at her, his smile rare and, she felt, genuine. 'As I recall it, we agreed upon a rematch.'

'I hoped you had forgotten that part.' She patted his cheek as if it were the most natural thing to do, as if he were the most fun loving of souls.

He, in turn, kissed her cheek. It felt so lovely even though she knew it to be play acting. But he had kissed her cheek before, and her lips, had done it with only the two of them to know it. Dared she hope this was not play acting?

'We will have our rematch,' he stated.

In that moment, tea and sandwiches arrived. Felicia might have known Mrs Muldoon would have begun preparing when the coach was first spotted coming down the lane.

With a sweep of her hand that was sure to show off her beautiful wedding band, Felicia indicated that they should sit in front of the fireplace where flames leapt in friendly welcome.

It could not hurt that the scent of the Christmas tree added a heart-warming mood to the parlour.

With any luck the undercurrent of hostility between the men would ease in the homely setting.

At least Felicia sensed no mood of antagonism in Lady Penfield. With luck the woman might be made an ally rather than an opponent.

'A rematch we shall have, then,' Felicia announced, returning to the paused conversation. 'If our guests agree to participate, you will have aid this time, Isaiah. It will be you and Lord Penfield matched against me, Abigail,and Lady Penfield.'

'My word! That sounds like grand fun.' Lady Penfield clapped her hands. 'Oh, Henry, let's hope the weather clears.'

'Of course, my dear.' Lord Penfield's smile at his wife was affectionate. It was clear to see he doted upon her. 'I shall hope just that.'

What a blessing to discover the Earl had a softer side. All it needed was a bit of cultivation.

Perhaps there was hope that, in the end, the couple would act in Abigail's best interest and not their own.

Isaiah could finally breathe. With tea finished and the Penfields retired to their suite of rooms, he felt he could act himself—whoever that was. The past few hours had revealed a side of him he had thought lost.

Playtime in the snow with his sister and his wife had been genuine fun. How long had it been since he had allowed himself to give over to joy with anyone but Abigail? It was when life had been good with his mother.

Very clearly he had married sunshine personified. If only he could trust that storm clouds would not come racing in to snuff it out. The truth was, he had known her so briefly, how could he be aware of every facet to her character?

Just as true, even though their acquaintance had been

brief, she had given him no reason to doubt she was who she seemed to be. Day by day, even hour by hour, he was becoming ever more fond of her. Her smile and the happy sound of her laughter took up the greater part of his attention. He was eager to find her in order to discuss the conversation he'd just had with his sister, to discover what her opinion of their guests was.

He did not find her in the parlour guarding her precious Christmas tree, nor was she in the kitchen watching Mrs Muldoon buzz about.

Turning down the corridor that led to the library, he heard someone singing 'Away in a Manger.' He followed the pretty, if off-key, rendition down the hallway.

As soon as he opened the door, she looked up from the book lying open on her lap. As always, she greeted him with a sunny, welcoming smile. All of a sudden he barely minded the blizzard pounding the estate.

'Well?' she asked first thing. 'How did you explain this to Abigail?'

He sat down beside her on the couch. 'It didn't come to me until the last second. But I told her I did know about the visit and that I did not let on because it was meant to be a surprise—a Christmas gift.'

'And she believed you?'

'Yes, after Miss Shirls stepped in to confirm it was so.'

'I have a feeling Miss Shirls knows a good bit more about our situation than she lets on.'

He had to catch his breath. Felicia had called it 'our situation.' Spoken so easily, she had no idea what that meant to him. In the past, every problem he had encountered was one he faced alone. Just like that, his wife clicked another number on his heart safe into place. The amazing thing was, not only was she able to do it, but he did not fear the end result as much had he had only days ago.

'I never have been able to keep a secret from Miss Shirls. I wonder if the canny lady has some sixth sense.'

'Well, what do you think of the Penfields?' Felicia asked.

'I cannot say for certain, not yet.' He leaned his head on the back of the couch, closing his eyes. 'Matters are strained between us. Lord Penfield has made no secret of it.'

'Nor have you.'

He felt fingers brush the hair at his temple, the touch so brief and light it might have been a moth fluttering past.

'Here,' she said, tapping on the book. 'I have looked up the meaning of their names. Perhaps it will give us some insight to them.'

He opened his eyes to peer at her. 'You really do believe in names meaning something?'

'Sometimes meanings are spot on. But even when they are not, it is fun to study them.'

'All right, let's try out "Henry."'

She turned a few pages, trailing her slender finger down the list of names.

'Here it is. Henry…"ruler of the home."'

'He is the Earl, so clearly that. What kind of ruler is what I want to know?'

'We will need to learn it for ourselves. But I do get the sense he cares very much for his wife and would go to great ends to make her happy.'

Would the visitors have the same sense about Isaiah? That he cared for Felicia? It was important they did, yet was it not more important for Felicia to know it?

'What about Diana?' he asked. 'Let's look up her name.'

'I already did, before you came in.' Felicia thumbed to

the page where the name Diana was at the top of the list. 'It is very interesting. There are a few definitions. One of them is meaningful, but as a contrast. Diana means fertile.'

'Were she that, we would not now be facing this challenge.'

'I feel sad for what she must have gone through all these years, wanting a child and having one denied her month after month. It would break one's heart.'

Would it break hers? By continuing to dodge intimacy, would he doom Felicia to the same fate?

'Do you want a child, Felicia?' He had to know.

'We have discussed this.' She was not looking at him while she spoke, but rather at the names in the book. 'It is a decision for two people to make.'

'Indeed, we have.' And they would discuss it again, but in the moment his attention must be on keeping the child he had. 'So, Henry is the ruler of the home and his wife desperate for a child, be it her own, or mine. I agree the ruler would do whatever it takes to make his wife happy, even if it meant raising the daughter of his brother.'

All of a sudden he felt half-sick. Was Henry Penfield so different a man than his late brother? Would he claim Abigail as his own and then in the end resent her?

'We do not know that he and his brother are anything alike, Isaiah.'

'How did you know what I was wondering?'

'It only made sense you would be.'

Maybe, but she did have a way of seeing inside him whether he wished it or not. Somehow, he found the notion comforting and it was possible that he did wish it.

'But I think he and his brother are not alike. Certainly not in age. Henry Penfield must be much younger than Palmer.'

'Fifteen years, if I remember correctly. I met him once when I was five years old, but I do not recall much about it.'

'As far as I can tell, Lady Penfield is not a bit reserved with her husband. She speaks her mind without fear.'

Unlike his mother, who had been decidedly reserved in the presence of his stepfather. Even as a child he had known something was wrong with that.

'But I think I must speak to Lady Penfield.' Felicia closed the book and patted his hand. 'She needs to know that Abigail is not aware of the reason for their visit. I hope to be able to convince her not to reveal it until—well, there is no until, is there?'

Latching on to her positive attitude, he clung desperately to it, praying she was correct.

After an early dinner, Isaiah and Lord Penfield retired to the library, as men tended to do. Felicia could only wonder how stilted their conversation would be. They had not warmed towards each other during the meal.

'Come, Lady Penfield,' Felicia said. 'Shall we go into the parlour and enjoy the Christmas tree?'

Unlike Isaiah, Felicia was looking forward to spending time with her guest.

'That would be grand. I will soak up every bit of your beautiful tree.' She clapped her hands in clear delight as they turned into the parlour. 'I will admit to shedding a tear for not having put one up this year. No boughs of holly or winter berries either. But Henry and I were so eager to meet Abigail, we made the sacrifice.'

So far she and Isaiah had managed to put off that meeting with one excuse or another, but they could not do it much longer.

No doubt Abigail was as anxious to meet her aunt and uncle as they were to meet her.

'I understand your regret. Christmas really is the best time of year. Abigail and I went into the woods and cut this tree ourselves while Lord Scarsfeld was on a visit to Windermere. We had such fun with it. I am so happy to be able to share it with you, Lady Penfied.'

'It makes me warm all over just to look at it.' Lady Penfield touched a branch, then looked up, and up, with a smile. 'But, please, you must call me Diana. We are family, after all.'

'I would be delighted to! And you must call me Felicia.'

Good, here was the first step towards forging a friendship—but not one that was for the sake of the battle she and Isaiah were waging. No, indeed, because no matter where Abigail ended up living, it was important to form a genuine kinship with Diana Penfield.

Nothing would be worse for her little sister than to have to go and live with people she and Isaiah were at odds with. The poor child would have her heart ripped down the middle.

'Shall we sit and enjoy the fire?'

'That would be lovely. I do thank you for having dinner served early. Travelling makes Henry hungry. I have never been able to work out why. I wonder, do you have anything to sip while we relax?'

'I was hoping you would suggest it.'

Felicia poured them each a small glass of sherry. They sat in silence for a few moments, sipping while taking in the warmth of the fire, the beauty of the tree.

'I am so anxious to meet Abigail,' Lady Penfield said at last.

'I'm sure she is also anxious to meet you.'

'What is she like? I've wondered and wondered.'

Felicia could do nothing but tell the truth. It could not be long before Abigail came bounding in the room to make her acquaintance, or hobbling as the case was. Lady Penfield would see for herself who the child was whom she hoped to raise.

It would do little good to lie. More than that, it would do a great deal of damage. One could hardly cultivate a friendship born of deception.

'She is quite bright and very inquisitive to go with it. I enjoy her company greatly.'

'You are aware, I'm sure, that Henry and I wish to bring her home with us.'

Felicia could only nod. Discussing this caused a great lump to swell in her throat.

'May I tell you something of myself, Felicia? So perhaps you might understand.'

Again, she could do nothing but nod. She did not want to understand anything except that Abigail would grow up here at Scarsfeld.

'My husband and I have had some disappointments—I have suffered miscarriages. I get to a certain point early on when most ladies would become ill. But then, apparently the pregnancy does not take. Each time it happens my heart breaks a little more and I cry a little longer. After the last time, Henry suggested we bring Abigail to Penfield. I am no longer a young woman, after all, and my chances of conceiving are not—' She swallowed, blinking to hold back the moisture welling in her eyes.

'I'm sorry for your losses, Diana, truly I am.'

And yet, ought the lady's heart be healed at the cost of Abigail's happiness?

The battle for her sister had now become a muddled mess. At first it had seemed so reasonable to do whatever was needed to win the fight. Now that her heart ached for her 'adversary' it was all quite troubling.

If the time ever came when Felicia waited anxiously for her courses to stop, she would be devastated to have them begin again time after time.

Poor Diana. Felicia scarcely knew who to weep for now, Abigail, her brother, the Penfields—or even herself. In the short time she had lived here, she had come to love the child as much as she did the sisters she had been raised with.

'She is full of adventure,' Felicia said past the lump. 'And she has quite a bit to say on every subject you can imagine. Isaiah says she has been stating her opinions from the time she learned to speak.'

'I think she and I will get along famously. I must confess the idea of instructing her to become a lady of society is thrilling.'

This was the time to reveal to Diana what she must. It could not be put off any longer.

'There is something you must know. I hope I can trust you to—well, it must be told regardless.'

'You need not fear, I am good at keeping a confidence.'

'I did not mean to suggest otherwise, but you see, Abigail does not know why you have come. Isaiah told her it was for a Christmas visit only.'

'But surely she must be informed.' Diana's distress was evident. 'It cannot be wise to remain mum on the matter.'

'Perhaps it is not. But you must understand leaving Scarsfeld will not be what Abigail wants. She and her brother love each other deeply. Since the night she was delivered to Isaiah he has been devoted to her—and she to him, of course. Neither of them had the good fortune to be raised by their mother, but in the end Juliette Penfield did give them to each other.'

'But surely she will want a mother?'

'That is something she can never have—but she will have a sister to stand in a mother's place, or an aunt. If it is you at the end of it, I hope you will come to love her as much as I already do.'

'But of course I will! Never fear on that count.'

Even knowing Diana Penfield for such a short time, she suspected it would be the case.

'She is rather lovable.'

Felicia's next question would put what Diana said to the test. She only hoped Diana would be able to sway her husband's view on the matter.

'I must ask you something, Diana.' It was hard to speak past the cramp in her throat. 'Please do not tell Abigail of your intentions. Wait—get to know her first. If you feel she will not suit for your household, it will spare her grief.'

Diana drank the remaining sherry in her glass in one gulp. Felicia thought it a splendid idea and did the same.

'Yes.' Diana set her glass on the table next to the couch. The glass made a decided clink. 'You make a valid point. Also, it will make the transition easier for her if she knows us first.'

'So you will not tell her yet?'

'I am inclined not to, but there is Lord Penfield to be considered.'

'Do you want to know what I think, my friend?'

'Indeed, I do.'

'I think that Lord Penfield is inclined to think whatever you encourage him to think.'

Diana laughed softly.

'How wise a thing for one so recently wed to understand.'

'I did have the benefit of my mother's example to go by.'

Diana squeezed her hand, smiling. 'I cannot promise anything, but I will see what is to be done in regards to my husband's silence.'

'I meant it, you know, when I called you friend a moment ago. I only hope that, however this turns out, we will remain so.'

'Of course, we must—'

The pleasant exchange was interrupted by the arrival of the men.

It was clear to see by their matching scowls that they had come to no such accord.

Felicia stood, hurrying across the room towards her husband. While she went she gathered her weapons, her arsenal being a smile and a kiss on Isaiah's cheek.

Stiff as starch, he uttered a few words in admiration of the Christmas tree.

And so the skirmish between the Maxwells and the Penfields carried on.

Chapter Eleven

Lord Penfield was as bristly a fellow as Isaiah was. As custom dictated, after dinner he and Penfield spent a few moments in the library, but they were not particularly comfortable.

Such did not seem to be the case with the wives.

After he returned Felicia's brief kiss and then pretended to admire her Christmas tree, she sat back down on the couch beside Lady Penfield.

If he did not know better, he would have thought them great life-long friends.

Listening to them laugh, seeing them smile, he thought women must be very different creatures from men. He did not believe he was mistaken when he heard them already calling each other by their first names. It would be a long time before he and Lord Penfield did the same, if they ever managed it.

'I'll race you down!' Abigail's voice came from the upstairs landing.

'Oh, no, young lady, you will not—' All of a sudden Miss Shirls gasped. The snap of the nanny's starched petticoats rustled with her quick dash down the steps.

Isaiah spun away from his guests, dashed into the hall and caught his sister before she could fall off the end of the banister.

'How many times must I tell you not to do that?' he whispered in order to keep the Penfields from knowing he was overbearing.

He set Abigail on the floor.

'Our girl will do as she pleases, I fear, no matter how many times you caution her.' Miss Shirls bent to smooth a wrinkle from his sister's skirt.

'Are you able to walk?' he asked. 'Otherwise I will carry you.'

'Balance me only. I should like to meet my aunt and uncle while standing. And thank you for letting me stay up to meet them. I would not sleep a wink otherwise.'

It went against everything he thought was best, but he understood her wanting to walk in on her own.

Supporting her under her elbow, he led her into the parlour. It was a relief to see that she hobbled along much better than she had done this morning.

Evidently Miss Shirls did not want to be left out of the introductions. Most servants would remain in the hallway, but he heard her steps firmly walking behind him.

Lady Penfield stood when Abigail inched into the room. Lord Penfield was already standing, but went to the couch to take a place beside his wife.

Isaiah noticed him take her hand, holding it unseen within the folds of her skirt.

It was clear that this meeting meant very much to both

of them. As much as he wished to believe they were a self-ish pair, coveting what was not theirs, he could not help but wonder if they were also nervous.

This was the last thing he wanted to wonder because he did not wish to witness vulnerability and longing in the couple. All he wanted was for the two of them to leave Scarsfeld without Abigail and never come back.

'Good evening, dear girl!' Lady Penfield hurried forward, her hands clasped at her middle. Isaiah had the sense that she wanted to go down on her knees and embrace Abigail. 'What a pleasure it is to meet you at last.'

Balancing on his arm, his sister presented a small curtsy.

'Thank you, Aunt, it is a pleasure to meet you, too.'

'My lady,' Miss Shirls said with her own slight dip. 'Welcome to Scarsfeld.'

One thing that Isaiah and the nanny had in common was the inability to hide a displeased emotion. It might be why they got on so easily together.

But he got along with his wife, too, and she was always smiling. Even in this critical moment when one of the Penfields might blurt out their intention to steal his sister away from home, Felicia was nothing if not poised.

What he should do was strive to be more like her.

'Oh, my goodness!' Lady Penfield exclaimed, noticing the bandages wrapped around Abigail's ankle. 'You have been injured.'

His sister lifted her hem, turned her foot this way and that. 'It was all in the name of fun so it is not as horrid as it seems.'

'I'm sure it will not hamper your visit with your niece in any way, Lady Penfield,' he admitted.

Calling this a visit was not what it was. To his way of

thinking, it was more of an abduction. One of the Penfields was surely about to point it out at any second.

Lord Penfield stepped forward, lifted Abigail's chin and peered into her eyes.

'I assume, young lady that you know why my wife and I have come?'

Isaiah opened his mouth, having no idea what words were going to burst out, only that they would not be pleasant.

'Oh, Henry...' Lady Penfield neatly stepped between her husband and Abigail, breaking the contact of his hand on her chin. 'The whole household knows that we have come for a visit. To spend Christmas with our family and get to know them all.'

'I, for one, believe there is no better way to spend Christmas,' Felicia added, slipping her arm about the Countess's waist and giving her a hug.

There was more happening here than met the eye.

'But should the child not—' Lord Penfield looked perplexed.

That was something he and his opponent had in common: perplexity.

'Get to know us?' Lady Penfield arched a brow at her husband. 'And we get to know her? This will be the happiest Christmas we have spent in a very long time, do you not agree?'

He raised one brow back at her. 'Oh, yes, indeed. I have no doubt of it.'

'Yes, quite so. Being stranded at the estate because of the storm, we could not ask for a better chance to become acquainted,' the countess said.

Isaiah looked at Felicia, who was smiling brightly at Lady Penfield.

Hmm… Things were afoot that mere males had no idea of.

Thankfully, for the moment at least, it appeared that Abigail would not know how her future hung in the balance.

The next afternoon Abigail decided it would be grand fun for all of them to decorate the pine cones and twigs that Felicia had gathered.

Isaiah looked up from his place at the long table where they were seated.

Lord Penfield twisted a twig in his fingers, staring at it in bewilderment.

Glancing up at Isaiah, he shrugged. What was he to do with the thing? his expression asked. At least Isaiah and the Earl were allies in something.

Abigail rolled a spool of ribbon towards them. It was red and green plaid, edged in some fragile-looking white lace.

'Simply wrap the ribbon around however you like.' She held up the one she was working on. 'Like this.'

Penfield cut a length of ribbon and draped it over the top of the cone. It resembled a limp noodle.

'Really, dear, it is not so difficult. Just wrap the ribbon around and tie it in a bow.'

'Ever tie a bow, Scarsfeld?' he asked while fumbling with the ribbon.

'Only knots in rope.' He snipped a length of ribbon longer than the one Penfield had cut. It tangled in his fingers when he tried to copy what the ladies were doing. 'I'll just watch and see how you do it.'

There was an undercurrent of competition going on between them and, oddly, it felt—fun. It took him aback because he had not expected any sort of camaraderie with this man.

When he thought about it, he realised his animosity towards the Earl was not only to do with Abigail. Indeed, he had always harboured an uncomfortable feeling towards the fellow. He did not know this for certain, but it was likely that Lord Penfield had known his mother. While Isaiah had been weeping his seven-year-old eyes dry, was Penfield basking in Mama's love?

That was an unfair way to think. It would hardly be his fault if Isaiah's mother had showed Penfield favour as a young man.

'Between you and me,' Isaiah said softly in hopes that the women would not hear, 'your bow is sensible and to the point.'

'Perhaps, but by its very nature a bow goes against sensibility. It will secure nothing heavier than a feather, I fear.'

'That is not our concern. It is for us to simply get the ribbons on in a fluffy way.'

'Yours is sagging.'

All of a sudden Isaiah wanted to smile. He could not possibly, though. He would do well to remember the man was a foe and not a friend. To make him one would be a betrayal of his sister.

Yet, watching his wife laugh with Lady Penfield, he had to wonder. Clearly she had no problem with the divide between friend and foe.

Had she ever met anyone she considered a foe? It might account for her cheerful attitude towards life if that were the case.

Looking at her now, ruffling Abigail's hair, advising

Lady Penfield on which shade of red lace to use, he could only admit he was grateful she was this way.

What if life could always be lived how it was at this moment? With family gathered about a table and the only storm the one now beating the walls of the mansion.

What if—never mind. There was a storm inside this house as well as outside. In the end it, hearts would be ravaged, not bonded.

After tea, Felicia carried an armload of decorated pine cones into the hall. She set them on the floor while the men carried the rest into the parlour.

'This will be the most festive our house has ever been!' Abigail declared cheerfully, limping past and hugging a large spool of ribbon to her chest.

'Will it?' Lady Penfield asked, following behind with more ribbon.

Felicia did not miss the slight frown creasing her brow.

'Yes, but because you are here.'

Lady Penfield's frown dissolved into a smile. She tugged the bow in Abigail's hair. 'And we are so pleased to be, my dear.'

'Do you think our husbands have made a bit of peace with each other?' Felicia asked, feeling a bit shaken watching a bond begin to form between aunt and niece.

Lady Penfield tapped her chin, watching the men's efforts to hang a ribbon from a rafter. 'They could not help but feel each other's misery during the decorating. So perhaps, yes, they have—in as much as they can.'

'Let us hope. It does a family no good at all to be at odds with one another,' Felicia whispered out of Abigail's hearing.

Or to fear growing bonds.

'I like feeling that we are family,' Felicia whispered again even more softly. 'I must thank you for encouraging Lord Penfield to keep his silence. Whoever wins this tug of war over Abigail, we do not want her torn up over it.'

'Of course not. Love does not behave that way. I think that we can agree any decision which is made must be done with love.'

'I never expected to like you so quickly and so well, Diana.'

'And I never expected to be welcomed into your home so genuinely.'

Inside the parlour everything was a bustle with Abigail directing her brother and her uncle on where to hang the decorations.

Mr Phillips came in with a ladder and stayed to lend a hand with the hanging.

Eloise wandered in. Within a moment Lord Penfield began to sneeze so she was shooed from the room. Wasn't it interesting that a cat could actually look affronted?

It took a long while to finish. It was not until the time to dress for dinner that the last pine cone glittered from its spot on the mantelpiece.

Glancing about, Felicia had to catch her breath. She stood in a place of enchantment, of wonder which would thrill the most sober of hearts.

Everyone retired to their rooms, but Felicia lingered, a riot of leftover ribbon curling about her skirt.

What a beautiful afternoon it had been. One could nearly forget the heartache that was coming to sadden them all.

She no longer believed that the Penfields would be able

to take Abigail away from her home and not suffer remorse for it.

Closing her eyes, she let the scent of the Christmas tree fill her up. Lovely memories of the past with her family blended in her heart with the ones she was making today.

What would life be without Christmas? So much love was expressed at this time of year.

A flutter tickled her neck. Opening her eyes, she found a wide ribbon settling in place across her shoulders.

'You need a lesson in colour co-ordination, Isaiah. This blue plaid does not suit my gown.'

Wrapping the ends of the ribbon in his fists, he drew her towards him.

'What are you doing?'

'What do you think I am doing?'

Evidently he meant to kiss her. Her knees would not feel like mush and her heart would not be beating triple time if it were not true.

'My question is, why are you doing it? Everyone has gone upstairs so we need not put on a show.'

'Are you really who you seem to be, Felicia?' He tied the ribbon in a bow, of sorts, across her bosom.

'I imagine I am. You are the one who is a chameleon.'

'Are you sorry to have married such a crusty fellow?' he asked while fingering the loops of the bow and drawing her closer.

'Crusty?' Lightly, hesitantly, she touched his vest, felt his heart thumping hard under her fingertips. 'You are wounded, Isaiah. You are not crusty in here.'

'Abigail says I am.' Closer now, his breath warmed her cheeks.

'Well, she is only eight and must be excused for it.' Felicia held his gaze because for once his heart seemed open and so very vulnerable. She could all but hear his thoughts.

'I need to know—do you regret our marriage? If you had it to do over again, would you choose a love match instead of what I offer you?'

She touched his lips, thinking how wonderful it would be if he did kiss her. 'I am not convinced that I have not made a love match.'

'What are you saying, Felicia?' Even her fingers thrilled to the touch of his lips.

'I am saying you ought to give me this kiss so that I might learn the truth of the matter.'

'You undo me.' His voice was raspy and, she thought, expressed fear of what she just revealed.

Ah, but then his kiss fell upon her, possessive and capitulating all in one hot, breathless moment.

She knew the truth, as unlikely as that truth was. In spite of everything, she had made a love match.

When the kiss finally ended, she spun away, clutched the bow to her heart and dashed out of the parlour.

The very last thing she wanted was for him to respond to what she'd admitted.

He was not ready yet. She only prayed that one day he would be.

The truth of the matter was that he had kissed Felicia, yet again. He not could say he regretted doing it, but he could not say acting upon the impulse had not left him sleepless—yet again.

That must mean something, other than he would be tired in the morning.

But tonight's restlessness was different.

Words had been spoken which did not fit in with what he had first expected of this marriage. In the beginning he had been fool enough to imagine any woman would be satisfied with what he offered, a title and his beautiful estate.

His wife was not merely any woman. She was exceptional—she was relentless and he feared she would not be satisfied until she had all of him.

But did he fear it, really?

Sentiments had been shared which rocked his core, shook his heart. Was it possible that his shaking foundation might have as much to do with anticipation as dread?

He was the one to have brought up the subject of a love match. Her response was not at all what he had expected to hear.

No. In asking he sought an affirmation, a reassurance that she would be content even if she did not have one.

It nearly laid him out when she suggested that she might have found it.

And then she had fled, the ends of the ribbon that did not match her gown flapping like blue wings in her wake.

He had not thought before speaking, but only blurted out what was on his mind.

The shock of it was that it *was* on his mind. Why was it on his mind?

Had he, too, made a love match? If he had, did he dare to accept it?

If he did accept it, it would mean Felicia was well secured in his heart. It would mean losing her, for any reason, was something he could not endure.

To say he was troubled did not begin to describe the state he was in, which was why he was on his way to the library in the wee hours. He had never spent time wandering about his house late at night until Felicia came to him.

The library door was closed, but light seeped out from under it, casting a warm glow on the hallway floor.

He nearly turned away to seek another place to brood. He did not want to discuss matters of the heart—not yet. He needed time to think, to search his soul and discover what he really wanted from her.

Still, he would not flee his own library.

He opened the door, stepping boldly inside.

It was hard to know if he was relieved or disappointed that it was Penfield sitting in the chair in front of the fire and not Felicia.

One thing for sure, he would enjoy his wife's company more than he would his rival's.

Yet he did have it in his heart to speak to the man. There might not be a better opportunity.

'Good evening, Scarsfeld, or rather later than that, isn't it?'

'I've lost track. It might be early morning.'

'Perhaps you are losing sleep because of a woman, just as I am?'

'In fact, yes. Three of them.' Tonight his mother was on his mind along with Felicia and Abigail.

'You have my condolences.'

Settling in the other chair, Isaiah stretched his feet towards the flames.

'It is hard to imagine this storm could get any worse,' Isaiah muttered. Only he knew he had not referred to the weather, but to the storm whooshing about the walls of his own home.

'And here you are stuck with guests you must wish to be rid of.'

It was not they as much as what they threatened, he did have to admit that much truth. Lady Penfield was a good-hearted woman and he thought she would not love her husband unless he had a few redeeming virtues.

'I assume you had my sister's presumed best interests in mind when you decided she should come to live with you.'

'We can offer her many things in London.'

'It was my mother's wish that I raise Abigail. I have never regretted a moment of it.'

'My wife and I have many regrets.' Lord Penfield drummed his fingers on the arm of his chair. 'We desire a child, you will know that, I think. I fear it is the one thing I am unable to give her. Loving her so much, I would do anything to make her happy. Surely you understand what I feel?'

Lord Penfield gave him a look that clearly accused his presumed marriage of convenience as one lacking in affection.

'I would do anything to make my sister happy.' It was not the answer Penfield was seeking, but the only one he was going to get.

'I do not doubt that. You may rest assured that Lady Penfield and I will do no less for her.'

Penfield became quiet for a time, looking down his long nose at the flames snapping in the fireplace.

'There is something I can put your mind to rest about.' When he glanced over at Isaiah, he saw sincerity reflected in the man's expression. 'I am nothing like my brother was.'

No, he would not be. Palmer Penfield had wanted nothing to do with another man's child. Henry Penfield clearly wanted everything to do with his brother's child.

Arguing over who had rights to Abigail would be futile right now so Isaiah turned his mind to the other matter pressing upon him.

'Did you know my mother?'

Even under the beak Isaiah saw a genuine smile.

'Of course. Before I left for Oxford I lived at Penfield. What would you like to know?'

Why did she stop loving me? Did you replace me in her heart? Why did she never come back home?

'Was she happy?' He wondered that, too. Was she content after she left him behind?

'No one was happy living with my brother. Especially not your mother. She tried her best to please him, but he was a man who could not be pleased. Even if she had given him a dozen heirs, he would not have been satisfied. Do you want to know the truth, Isaiah? It will not be pleasant to hear.'

'I do not, but I think I must.'

'Your mother was under my brother's control—what she said, who she met—she did nothing without his approval and he approved of very little.'

'Did he forbid her to come and see me?'

'He did and I watched it break her. I imagine you will be wondering, did I take your place?'

He nodded because his throat closed so tightly he thought he might strangle.

'I tried to. I hoped it might help her, you understand. But I think I only reminded her of what she had lost in you. She could not speak of you, my brother did not allow it. He hoped she would forget you eventually. When I made my escape to college, she was deep in melancholy. I'm sorry. I wish I could have done something but—a mother's love—she needed you and no other.'

Isaiah sat silently, his resentment for his stepfather growing more bitter than ever.

'In the end there is Abigail,' Lord Penfield muttered. 'The former Earl did one thing right.'

Yes, there was Abigail. How ironic was it that the man who had taken the love of his mother from him had given it back in the form of his sister.

'You will think me uncharitable to say so, but I've often thought it was good that he died before he knew he had fathered a girl and not his heir.'

'Do you think he would have mistreated his own child?' The thought of anyone being unkind to his sister blurred his vision in a red haze.

'He mistreated his wife, so, yes, I do. Women were of no value to him.'

Isaiah curled his fists, digging his fingernails into his palms. All this time he had resented what his mother had done to him when all along she'd had no choice because of what had been done to her. She was the late Earl's victim as every bit as much as he had been.

The rub of it was, he had been so consumed with his own unhappiness that he had never considered that to be the case. He must have grunted or growled, because Penfield slid his glance sideways.

'I would have done something if I could have. Please do not think I would not. My brother kept me away much of the time in order to prevent it.'

'I believe you are telling me the truth.' Isaiah forced his hands to press flat on the chair arms. 'I will also be truthful with you, Penfield.'

'If you must.' The comment was softened by his smile.

'I did not want you to come here. I bore you hostile feelings—even as far as thinking of you as my foe. I confess, I no longer think that.'

'What man would not feel the same?' Lord Penfield asked.

'Not many I know of. But our wives—have you noticed how they became fast friends from the moment they met?'

'Indeed. They deal with the issue between us far better than we do.'

'I will strive to follow their example,' Isaiah promised. 'But you might know some people believe me to be less than cheerful.'

'Reputations do not necessarily reflect the truth. I would know this since I have struggled with people seeing my brother in me.'

'I do not see him,' Isaiah admitted because the truth was the truth.

And yet, it changed little. Abigail lay between them as solid as a wedge lodged in a log.

Chapter Twelve

In Felicia's opinion, Lord Penfield was the perfect choice to read from Charles Dickens's *A Christmas Carol*.

Somehow the shape of his nose alone added to the drama of the Christmas ghost story. Added to that the storm scratching at the windows, moaning and howling to get in... Well, a delicious shiver prickled up her back.

Back at Cliverton House, Christmas could not fully arrive until the book was finished, which always happened on Christmas Eve.

With three days until then, the timing was perfect.

Abigail sat on the floor in front of the hearth. It was odd to see her without Eloise contentedly purring in her lap, but Lord Penfield would never have made it through the story had she been. The poor man burst into sneezing fits whenever the cat was nearby.

Lord Penfield turned his chair so that everyone could see and hear him clearly.

"'Stave One: Marley's Ghost,'" he read, his brows shooting up and his voice going deep, as if the said ghost might suddenly drift into the parlour, his white robes aflutter or perhaps even followed by Scrooge, his chains rattling. '"Marley was dead to begin with. There was no doubt whatever about that."'

Felicia closed her eyes to better allow the author's words to come to life in her mind.

A few days ago she would not have thought the five of them could be gathered so happily. Indeed, even yesterday there had been an air of wariness between Isaiah and Lord Penfield. While there was still a sense of stress between them, she no longer feared they would go for each other's throats.

'"Old Marley was as dead as a doornail."' Lord Penfield nodded while he read. 'Mind, I don't mean to say that I know, of my own knowledge, what there is particularly dead about a doornail.'

Abigail began to giggle.

'Really, my dear.' Lady Penfield smiled brightly at her husband. 'No one reads this story as well as you do! Had you not been born to a title you might have been a great success on stage.'

'I would run to see your performances, Uncle!' Abigail's delight at having her aunt and uncle here to share Christmas was evident in her smile, in the happy sparkle in her eyes.

Of course, if she knew the true reason for their 'visit' she might feel quite differently. For all that Lord and Lady Penfield were not the despicable and selfish relatives both she and Isaiah had first believed them to be, they were still a threat to Abigail's well-being.

It made matters all the harder because they were well intentioned. Felicia truly felt great sorrow for their plight.

'At Penfield I read the story every year to the servants' children.'

'It is the best time,' Lady Penfield added. 'When the story is finished we give gifts to the children and everyone eats jam tarts.'

'What a grand time!' Abigail's grin with her missing tooth was one of the most endearing things Felicia had ever seen. She felt all warm inside just looking at it. 'Until this year it's been only me and Isaiah to give out Christmas treats.'

'I wonder if you would like to come back to London with us?' Lord Penfield asked.

It was as if a shroud soaked in icy water had been cast over the adults. Lord Penfield blinked at his wife's frown, realising he had spoken out of turn, and his large Adam's apple bobbed up and down.

'For a visit, I mean.'

'May we, Isaiah? I would love to visit London.'

Lord Penfield cleared his throat and pressed on with the story. '"Scrooge knew he was dead. Of course he did."'

Lady Penfield nodded once quite sharply.

With any luck Abigail had not noticed the sudden tension between the adults. No one in this room wished her to feel frightened for her future.

Felicia's joy in hearing the story was dimmed. She knew very well that Lord Penfield had not been suggesting a visit. What she wanted to do was weep but, of course, Abigail would wonder why she was.

So she sat, hands folded on her lap while presenting a smile her heart did not feel.

At last Lord Penfield said, '"...went straight to bed without undressing, and fell asleep upon the instant."' Then he closed the book.

Abigail hopped up. 'Perhaps Cook has left us tarts in the kitchen!'

One by one they trailed behind her. Felicia hoped there were tarts. Everyone could use a dash of sugar in the here and now.

Isaiah walked up the stairs beside Felicia, shoulders nearly touching while they made their way towards their chambers.

After the turn the evening had taken, he was beyond grateful to have her beside him.

'What do you think?' he asked. 'Are they going to tell her?'

'Lord Penfield nearly slipped up,' she said. He wished her sigh did not sound so resigned. A response more like a battle cry would have made him feel better. 'I thought Diana had managed to convince him to wait until after Christmas. I do not think he meant to say what he did. It's only that the evening was so pleasant... All of us gathered for the story like a proper, affectionate family. Honestly, Isaiah, I think he was simply speaking from his heart. I do think they care for her very much.'

Standing in the hallway between his suite of rooms and hers, he could not help himself and let out a resigned sigh. He shook his head, feeling confused and defeated.

'Do you think it is unfair of me to keep her from them, Felicia?' He looked at the rug while he spoke because he was cut up by what he was about to say. 'I wonder if she would be happier in London. They can give her social benefits that I cannot.'

He felt her fingers in his hair, gently stroking a trail from his temple to the curve of his ear, as she had a way of doing. The gesture was amazingly comforting.

No one had comforted him this way since he was a very small child. How had he managed all these years without Felicia?

'She is only eight years old. Perhaps ten years from now that will be a boon to her, but not yet. She belongs here with you.'

'But I only wonder if she ought to be able to choose.'

'If it came to that, she would choose you, never fear it.'

He turned his face, kissing her palm.

'May I come in?' he asked with a nod at her side of the hallway.

It had been a night for ghosts, it was time to put one of them to rest.

'I would enjoy your company. This is not a time for being alone,' she said while opening the door.

He followed her inside, prepared for the rush of pain that always came from entering this chamber.

The space was warm from the small fire snapping and popping in the hearth. Only one lamp was lit so everything was cheerfully aglow in amber light.

He stood still, glancing at dim corners while Felicia sat down at her dressing table and began to take the pins out of her hair.

For once, his mother did not come to him joyful and laughing, nor did she stare at him with vacant eyes. In fact, she did not come to him at all.

Pain did not rip his heart apart even though it was no longer as dead as Mr Dicken's doornail.

'It is no longer snowing, thank the good Lord.' She glanced back at him with a smile. 'I imagine you never thought to hear me say that.'

He walked across the room, holding her gaze as if it were a lifeline and he a sinking man.

But he was not sinking, except to his knees beside Felicia's chair.

'I think—well, there is something I wish to point out.' He caught a lock of red hair as it tumbled free of its pin, then twined it between his fingers. The thought coming to his mind was that her hair was a Christmas ribbon and she the gift he would unwrap.

'It will be less tangled after I brush it.' Her cheeks flashed a beguiling shade of pink.

She must know he was not speaking of untidy locks.

'Yes—and I will be less tangled once I—' Was he really going to say this out loud? Perhaps it would be wiser not to, but more than that, he would be a huge fool not to say it. 'It is my belief that there cannot be a love match when there is only one involved in it. A match requires two, don't you think?'

'There are unrequited loves in which—'

'Still, not a match.'

Before she could try to convince him of her point he kissed her. He gently tugged her hair with one hand while sliding her off the chair, his arm firmly around her waist.

He set her on the floor, his thighs braced on either side of her.

'Felicia,' he whispered across her cheek. 'I am the other side of your love match.'

What?

Felicia slid away, but not so very far that she could not slide back in a hurry.

Surely she must have misheard? Or, if she had not, perhaps he had declared it on a whim and would now take back those very precious words.

'I beg your pardon?' If he *did* mean what he said, her response was the least romantic in the history of declarations of love.

His smile was the best and brightest she had ever seen. It turned her into a puddle—not mud, but chocolate—rich, smooth and simmering.

'No, I beg yours.'

Well, then! She slid back to him.

He gathered her into the circle of his arms. Strong muscles hugged her so solidly and yet at the same time so tenderly that she felt as if nothing could ever go wrong again. Or if it did she need never face it alone.

'It is a wonder you did not run for home on our wedding day. I beg your pardon for doing it all so poorly... I truly regret I was so...'

He seemed to have trouble coming up with a suitable word.

'Overwhelmed?' she suggested. 'We were strangers committing our lives to each other. Both of us were rather staggered with what we were about to do. One thing about it, Isaiah, I do not regret that there was no music. Otherwise you would not have sung me down the stairs. I think I would follow your voice anywhere, it touches me so.'

'Everything about you touches me. From the very start you have gone straight to my heart. It only took me a while to trust it.'

'And no wonder. You suffered what no child ever should have done.'

Had they not married to try to prevent such a thing happening to Abigail?

Of course the silver linings of their situation were beginning to gleam. Was she not sitting on the floor with this man, nearly ready to make her way from here to the bed?

The great miracle of love was that it was sometimes born of pain. This was a profound thought that only just this moment had occurred to her.

'But love finds a way,' he whispered as if he had made the discovery in the same instant she did.

What were the odds that they would think the same thing at the same time? Very slim—unless the spirit of love explained it to them, both in the same thought.

No one could know that for certain, but it seemed a lovely and reasonable way to account for it.

'Felicia Merry Penneyjons, I love you. Will you marry me—continue to, I mean?'

'Isaiah Elphalet Maxwell, you know very well I will. And I will love you "in the city of gold, my dearest, dearest heart."' She did not sing that last for fear of ruining the moment.

'And I,' he murmured, his voice going low and husky—a sound which thrilled nerves she had never expected to be thrilled, 'will love you in that bed.'

He stood, giving her a hand up.

For the longest time they simply looked at each other, as if the moment was enchanted and they were loath to leave it.

But in Felicia's opinion, a moment even more magical awaited.

'I'll race you to it!'

When she made a dash for the bed she heard him laughing.

Nothing that happened under those covers would be more magical than that.

Isaiah Maxwell was a married man.

Not that he hadn't been one all along, but now he felt like one.

Isaiah Maxwell was also a happy man—a cheerful man.

If anyone could see him now sitting at his desk in the library, staring at the ledgers and grinning, they would not know who he was.

No more than he knew who he was. How could he have guessed that when Felicia spun the final number on the lock of his safe, light would come spilling out? That it would flash into every dark corner and send darkness packing?

He tapped his finger on the page, not really seeing what it said. It was a wonder that he saw anything but the love glowing in his wife's eyes when he had made love to her—until the early hours of dawn.

How many more hours until he could hunt her down, sneak away from company and fall upon the bed with her? Find joy in a place where there had been only pain.

Felicia had been quite right in her belief that good memories could vanquish bad ones. Until last night he had not been fully convinced.

Oh, but he was now. Sitting here waiting for the house to quiet down for the night—he was completely, irrevocably persuaded.

A movement in the doorway caught his eye.

'Would you like some company?' Leaning against the door frame, Felicia shot him a wink.

Excellent! He would not have to waste time finding her.

Posed as she was, he thought she looked like—there were too many wonderful things she looked like for him to pick one.

'You were already keeping me company.' He tapped his heart to show her where. 'What is everyone else up to?'

'Our guests have retired early.' She winked and he knew the gesture had something to do with romance. What he did not know was whose romance it was. Lord and Lady Penfield's? Or had they sensed the change in him and Felicia today and gone upstairs to give them a bit of privacy?

Which he intended to take full advantage of.

'Close the door behind you, Felicia.'

The smile she gave him while she leaned into it, fingers splayed against the wood, was one he would store in his memory for ever. Keep it as a treasure to look at whenever he wanted to.

All of a sudden Felicia lurched forward.

Miss Shirls burst into the library.

'Are we to make a trip to London? Abigail is all abuzz over it.'

'Where is my sister, Miss Shirls?'

'Tucked into her bed and reading a good-night story to her cat.'

'Abigail is mistaken. We are not going to London.' Dash it, he did not want to think of going anywhere but upstairs with his bride.

'That is good news. But she is quite certain of it and I, for one, think something is afoot. I have felt it in my bones since the moment Lord and Lady Penfield marched grandly in our front door.'

'You should tell her, Isaiah. Abigail is as dear to Miss Shirls as she is to us—her employment is—'

'They have come to take her away!' The governess slammed her hands on her hips. 'I know it without you having to speak the words.'

It was a lucky thing his sister was upstairs. The governess was not expressing her displeasure quietly.

'It is not for certain they will. But, yes, Miss Shirls, it was their intention to take her back to London with them.'

'They will not take her from me, I can tell you that! She has been my poppet since she was a few days old and that she will remain, even if I have to move to London with her. And believe me, Miss Eloise will not be going to London. Not with His Lordship sneezing his nose off whenever she is within sight.'

'Lord and Lady Penfield are not heartless,' Felicia said, 'They…'

Her voice faded, then she gasped.

Eloise pattered into the room—followed directly by Abigail.

'You promised!' Tears dripped down the child's pale face. Her bottom lip trembled. 'Isaiah, you promised I would not have to go anywhere I do not wish to.'

'Are you certain you do not wish to?' Clearly she did not, but the question needed asking. 'Your aunt and uncle can give you many advantages.'

'I will not go! No one can make me!' She dashed out of the room. 'Eloise and I will run away to live with the circus!' her voice sobbed from the hallway.

She must think he had betrayed her. What she said cut him to the quick. It felt as though he had done so even though he had fought to prevent this moment.

Still, he had kept her ignorant of what was going on. Yet he had been correct to do so. Anyone young enough to threaten to run off with the circus was too young to be told the truth.

Her tears cut his heart, filling him with guilt whether or not it was warranted. With her emotions undone, would she run outdoors in search of the circus? But, no, she was wise enough not to. When she had wandered off as a baby she had not understood what could happen.

'She does not mean it.' Felicia leaned her head on his shoulder, watching the cat rub her tail on the doorway going out.

'Children do say such things without meaning them,' Miss Shirls declared, then hurried after Abigail.

He thought the same. Her disappearance was not a problem he would need to deal with. Addressing her fear of being taken away was.

'We will work a way out of this,' Felicia whispered. 'Do not worry, Isaiah. Between us, we will.'

For all that it felt as though life had come crashing down upon him, it was not only him. His wife stood shoulder to shoulder with him.

Because she did, his heart went on beating. They would find a way out of the nightmare.

'I cannot find her!'

Felicia looked past Isaiah's shoulder at Miss Shirls standing in the hallway outside her bedchamber. A moment earlier her loud rap on the door had jarred them from a lovely moment. From bliss to dread in the space of a heartbeat.

'What do you mean?'

'Gone! I do not know where she is.'

'Where have you looked?' Isaiah grabbed his robe while he spoke.

'I came here straight away when she was not in bed where I left her.'

'What about Eloise?' Felicia asked, watching her husband stomp into his slippers. 'The cat will likely be where Abigail is.'

'I have not seen her, either.'

'Alert the household, even those who have retired for the evening. We will search the house.'

'What if she has gone out?'

Already in the hallway, he paused to say, 'She won't have. Even if she did not have a care for her own safety, she would for her cat.'

And then he was off on a run, shouting his sister's name.

Within seconds she heard other voices calling.

A dozen or more people would be searching inside, but someone needed to make absolutely certain she had not gone out.

Hurriedly, Felicia put her coat on over her nightgown. She stepped into her boots without a thought for stockings.

There was but one thing on her mind: finding her little sister.

Dashing out of the room, then down the steps, she hurried past the Penfields standing in the hall. Lady Penfield was crying while Lord Penfield patted her back.

'Check the cupboards!' she called.

It would help them to be doing something useful. Give an outlet for the fear. And perhaps Abigail was hiding in a cupboard.

Felicia rushed to the conservatory. It was where she, herself would hide if she needed to. There were shrubs and trees to duck behind. It was also a likely place to sneak outside.

'Abigail?' she called, softly. Perhaps if she sounded calm her sister would emerge from hiding.

Nothing. Not even a rustle of fabric gave answer.

Felicia hurried to the set of doors. They were closed, but something caught her eye on the stone floor. She bent to touch it, then recoiled from the icy drops of water.

Someone had opened the door and not so long ago.

Could Abigail have heard everyone calling for her and run outside, thinking she might be disciplined for causing such a stir?

It would be sensible to find Isaiah and show him what she had discovered. Two would be able to search outside better than only one.

As logical as that seemed, it would take too long. If Abigail *had* gone out, there was no time to be spared.

She stared hard out of the window, praying Abigail had not ventured beyond the terrace.

Even though it was not snowing, wind blew every which way. It disturbed the surface of the powdery snow, making it look something like fog, shifting this way one moment and that the next.

She stepped outside.

'Abigail!' Her shout was caught away as if it had never been.

Chapter Thirteen

Hearing a shout, Isaiah bolted up from looking under a bed in a seldom-used guest room.

'We've found her!'

The cry came from the floor below and he could not tell who it was who'd made the discovery.

He took the stairs down in three, sliding leaps.

People from all over the house came running to the hall.

His sister stood surrounded by her searchers, looking small and distraught.

'We found her in the pantry in the company of her cat,' Lord Penfield stated, looking troubled rather than relieved.

But he would be. The Earl must understand that she had hidden away because of him and his wife—or what they wished of her.

If anything could make them reconsider, surely it was this. Nothing Abigail said would be more convincing than what she had done.

Which was to scare the life out of them all. As much as he did not wish to address it, he must.

'Come with me, Abigail.'

Just because he needed to address her behaviour, he did not need to do it in front of everyone. He held his hand out to her and she took it.

Going into the parlour, he closed the door.

He sat in a chair. She climbed on to his lap and curled into a small, sad heap. She had grown a bit too big to be doing it, but she did fit and so he wrapped her up.

'I am sorry I did not tell you why the Penfields came. I hoped they would see how happy you were living here with me and give up the idea.'

'Well...' she smeared the tears on her cheek with the back of her hand '... I like them very much. But I love you and Felicia. They cannot force me, can they?'

'I imagine they could. Your uncle outranks me socially. If it went to court, he would probably win. It is not what you want to hear, I know. But I do not think it will come to it. You know by now they are decent people. Your uncle only wants to make your aunt happy and since she seems not to be able to have a child of their own—'

'They think I might be their child! But I am eight years old and halfway done with being one already.'

'Abigail, you must promise that no matter what happens, you will not hide from us again. The whole household was turned out of their beds to search for you.'

'I'm sorry, Isaiah. I ought to have thought first.'

'I'm only glad you knew not to go outside to find a travelling circus.'

'Even I know how dangerous it is out there.'

'Now you must apologise to everyone.'

'I suppose I do owe them that.'

He lifted her off his lap. She followed him back to the hall.

A few people frowned at her while she gave her regrets, but not many. Everyone just seemed relieved that she was safely found.

Isaiah looked around. Where was Felicia? Perhaps she was in the attic, still searching, but a stir had been created when his sister was found. She ought to be here.

'Where is Lady Scarsfeld?' he asked, cutting off Abigail's speech of contrition only halfway finished. 'Has anyone seen her?'

Heads shook as everyone glanced around as if puzzled to find she was not among them.

'The last I noticed she was going in the direction of the conservatory,' offered Mrs Muldoon. 'But that was some time ago.'

Rushing across the conservatory, Isaiah heard footsteps thumping behind him.

'Surely she would not have gone out!' Lord Penfield caught up to him, breathing heavily from the run.

'She would if she thought Abigail went that way.'

'But—'

'The door is not properly shut, Penfield. She has gone out.'

'Then we shall, too.'

The Earl nearly beat him on to the terrace.

'You look near the lake. I'll search the front road.'

Near the road where years before he had hunted for his mother on a night similar to this one, searched in vain until he was a broken child, both in heart and body.

This search would not be in vain. He would not return

to the house without his wife. Not even if he froze where he stood, he would not stop searching.

He would not huddle under the Christmas tree and weep as he had then. Forcefully, he shook the memory off. Back then, his mother had not been there to find.

Right now, Felicia was out there waiting for him to bring her home.

He did not think she was still looking for Abigail. If she were, he would see her, hear her voice.

Unless she was near the lake. But so far Lord Penfield had not called out to alert him she had been found.

High stepping in order to clear his feet of the deep snow, he plodded to the front of the house.

If Felicia had fallen, she would be covered by the icy powder blowing across the ground.

What if he had walked past her unknowing? Even though she could not have gone far, she might freeze before he found her.

He shouted…shouted again. The only answer was Felicia's name distantly echoed by Lord Penfield.

Wind buffeted him, scratching bare branches together, which gave them the effect of laughing at him, the same as they had done all those years ago.

Once again—this was now, not then. Felicia had not ridden off in a carriage, she was somewhere out here waiting, urgently needing him to find her.

Stare as he might, he could not see her. It could only mean the thing he dreaded.

She had fallen.

He had to fight the panic creeping into his brain, turning his stomach inside out and making him ineffective.

Branches! How many times had he warned his sister not to play under trees when the wind was blowing?

But there were hundreds of trees! If she had been hit by a limb, it would probably have happened near the road since that was where Felicia would have very probably been searching.

The crackle of splintering wood came to him, sharp in contrast to the moan of wind.

Spinning about, he spotted a limb crashing on the ground.

There were branches missing above the one that had fallen.

Knees pumping high, he raced for the spot where the limb lay half buried in snow.

There! The streak of red was nearly covered by drifting snow. Had he been scanning the area more quickly he would have missed it.

Within one long heartbeat he was kneeling beside Felicia. He lifted her out of the icy blanket.

A movement at the front door caught his eye.

'Mr Phillips!' he shouted. 'Over here!'

Lord Penfield must have heard, too, because Isaiah caught his shout of 'huzzah' from down by the lake.

The butler was beside him in only a few moments even with the snow dragging his steps.

'Praise the Good Lord you have found the mistress!' He helped Isaiah carry her. 'That is a nasty-looking gash on her head. Shall I go to the village and fetch the doctor?'

'You must not risk your safety, Mr Phillips. I will not forget that you offered. And no doubt she will come around before you get halfway there.'

Speaking those words, he only half believed them. Felicia looked very pale. She lay utterly still and limp.

'Any of us would go, my lord. All of us are so very fond of Lady Scarsfeld.'

* * *

Three hours later Felicia was still limp and pale. Isaiah sat beside the bed watching her breathe, looking for any sort of expression to cross her face. A smile, a frown—even a grimace would do.

She was no longer cold. He was grateful to the staff for quickly heating bricks and tucking them into her bed. Within a quarter of an hour her hand had warmed in his.

He stroked her cheek. His fingers were colder than her skin. No doubt his face was paler than hers was, too.

Once again he stared loss in its ugly face.

Felicia might wake up and smile at him, but she might not. He could only guess how much damage the blow to her head had caused.

'Felicia?' he whispered close to her ear. Nothing. No tug of a lip or twitch of an eye.

'Felicia!' This time he shouted. Still, there she lay, as still as the branch that struck her.

'My Felicia...' His voice cracked on her name this time.

Whatever came, he would never regret the cost of loving her. Never again would he shutter his heart as he had done as a child.

He lay his head on the mattress beside her shoulder wanting to weep, needing that release.

Not that he would indulge in it. Doing so would toss him back to the past, to that bitter night when he had been inconsolable.

The past few hours hit him hard, trying their best to drag him back to the nightmare.

No matter what happened, he was not going back to the boy he had been, nor to the bitter man who had grown from the boy's sorrow.

He was changed for ever.

Besides, Felicia was not gone. Here she was where he could touch her and talk to her.

Directly behind him a sob erupted.

Straightening up from the bed, he gazed into Abigail's red, tearful eyes.

'Would you like to wait with me for her to wake?' He patted the cushion of the chair beside his.

She shook her head, bit her bottom lip. 'This is all my fault. If I hadn't gone to hide, it would not have happened.'

'No, sweetheart, this is not your fault at all.' He reached for her, but she backed away.

'If I hadn't lied and said I was going to join the circus, she would not have gone outside looking for me.'

'You could not have known she would.'

'Yes, I could.' She sniffled hard, wiping her sleeve across her nose.

'You are blaming yourself needlessly.'

'But I almost did go outside… I opened the door, but it was so cold I thought better of it. She must have noticed melted snow on the floor.'

'Felicia will not blame you for what happened.'

'But I don't even like the circus!'

'If your sister can hear you, there is a good chance she is laughing.'

'I'm sure that is not true.'

'Sit here with me, Abigail. Talk to Felicia while we wait for her to wake up.'

Sitting with a thump, she crossed her arms over her middle.

'I am too ashamed to speak to her.'

'Have you ever known her to be angry or hold a grudge?'

'Well, no. But I haven't known her all that long.'

'But you know her well enough.'

Abigail shrugged, clasping her hands tightly together on her lap.

'I present myself as proof of her forgiving heart,' he pointed out.

'Yes, you were rather a curmudgeon and yet here she is.'

'Tell her what is in your heart.'

'I'm sorry, Sister,' she murmured, her voice quavering. 'I never would have done any of it if I'd known you were going to go looking for me outside. Everyone was upset by what I did and they didn't even leave the house. Well, Mr Phillips did. And so did Lord Penfield. Isn't it odd how, of everyone, they frowned at me the least? They were so happy to find you, in their joy they quite overlooked what I had done. I suppose they will remember soon enough, though.'

'I'm sure she knows you regret it.'

'When you awaken you may reprimand me as much as you like. I will stand and take what I deserve.'

'You will not get what you deserve, not from Felicia. Neither did I.'

In order to comfort his sister he was encouraging her to believe Felicia could hear everything being spoken. Could she really, though? He had no idea.

'You should sing to her, Isaiah.' She shot him a blurry-eyed glance. 'If she can really hear you, she will appreciate it.'

A song might make these unbearable moments of waiting better for everyone.

Yes! Much in the way a bad memory could be banished by a good one? A moment and a memory were not so different. One simply happened before the other.

His bride had healed him in this way, perhaps he could…

'I need your help!' He stood so suddenly his chair tipped.

Abigail caught it, then set it upright. 'You wouldn't if you rose more carefully.'

'You have a smart mouth, miss. Never lose it.' He ruffled her hair, relieved to see the beginnings of a smile on her face. 'We are going to move the Christmas tree up here.'

'Oh, that will be grand! But why?'

'You know how partial Felicia is to it.'

Isaiah took long, quick steps towards the door. Abigail had to run to keep pace.

'She is devoted to it…luckily for me.'

'What do you mean?'

'I think you know, but I can be as forgiving as my sister is.'

'I'm grateful to hear it, for whatever crime I have committed.' She could not know he had taken down her tree and Felicia had restored it. Could she?

'Do you expect her to revive for the joy over having the tree near her bed?'

'I hope it, only. But run and see who is available to help.'

He did not expect this to work, but he prayed most fervently that it would.

The darkness was comfortable. There was no cold, no pain, nothing at all unpleasant…just floating in a vast, soft nothing.

Oddly enough, there was also singing. It was all so very nice down here in the depths, listening to 'Jingle Bells,' 'What Child is This?' and 'O Come, O Come, Emmanuel.'

The last carol was the nicest. The singer's voice so full of emotion it nearly faltered over the words.

"'O come, O come, Emmanuel, to free your captive—'"

Oh, was that a sob? But why? It was so beautifully done. Surely the singer could have no regrets in his performance.

Even if he did, it was not her concern. All she needed to do was sink a bit deeper into darkness and concern for the singer's trouble slipped away.

Wasn't it strange that the darkness smelled like a Christmas tree? How very lovely.

"'On the first day of Christmas my true love sent to me...'"

Something jolted the dark. Her head began to ache. She tried to swim back down, but that something was drawing her, up and up.

"'A partridge in a pear tree...'"

That meant something to her! Whatever it was that jarred the peace beckoned her to float towards it. It seemed she ought to, but everything was so snug where she was.

The song went on. She heard 'five gold *r-i-i-ings*'!

Her body began to feel like—something. Not real, but no longer a vapour mingled in mist. No, she felt like a jellyfish being rolled upon the beach by a wave.

Five gold rings? Wait, she wore a ring on her finger. A wedding ring!

'Felicia!' Isaiah! That voice, so dear to her, sounded harsh with desperation. 'Come to me...follow my voice.'

It was easier where she was, in the nothingness. Yet she must try because she loved him.

Oh, but it was difficult, as if she were swimming in one of those dreams where one's movements were restrained by something unseen and threatening.

If she focused on his voice, calling to her...pleading with

her...it was easier. She would do anything to prevent him from grieving because of her.

And then, there he was. Darkness receded, giving way to the greater power of light. His face looked fuzzy at first, but second by second it came into focus.

'Welcome home,' he whispered, his voice somewhere between a sob and rejoicing. 'You had us worried.'

She tried to ease up to her elbows, but everything went dizzy and she lay back.

'Why are you weeping, Isaiah?'

Oh...no! Something had happened to her and as a result of it she had she failed to find Abigail!

What had happened? One moment she had been calling for her sister and the next she was here.

'Abigail?' Why did her voice sound so weak? Surely only a few moments had passed.

'Aside from feeling wretched with guilt, she is well.'

'She is safe, then?' Felicia would have sagged in relief had she been able. As it was, she was pressed heavily against the mattress by her own weight. 'Where is she?'

'In bed.'

'At this time of day?'

'It is two in the morning.'

'Surely not!'

'You were unconscious for a long time.' He bent to kiss her cheek, then slid his mouth to gently kiss her lips.

'I do not remember any of it. What happened?'

'When you went to search for Abigail you were hit by a falling branch.'

'How did you find me?' He could not have known she'd run outside.

'You left the door cracked open so Lord Penfield and I

went searching. But how I found you? I suspect it was by the grace of God.'

'Really?' She was beginning to think something along the same lines, but for a slightly different reason.

'I had no notion where to look. It was all blowing snow. Everything, even bushes, was invisible. Then a branch broke and I wondered if you might have been struck by one. I ran over and saw a strand of your hair peeking out of the snow.' She watched a shiver race over his shoulders. Reaching up, she wanted to smooth it away, but her hand fell back limp on the mattress.

It was hard to believe she had become this weak so quickly. That must be why it had been so difficult to come back, why the dark had been so deceptively peaceful.

What he must have been going through in those moments, probably recalling how he searched in vain for his mother, believing she had perished because he could not find her.

Knowing him as she did, she thought he would have been reliving that horror all over again, fearing he had lost another woman he loved.

She felt wretched that it had been her actions, no matter how well intentioned, which must have shot him to the nightmare of his past.

Horrible, wretched, yet perhaps, in the end, what had happened might be for his healing.

'I would like to sit.' She reached her arms up to him.

'Are you sure?'

'I've been lying far too long, have I not?'

He nodded, eased on to the bed, then positioned her so that she lay against his chest. His bent knees supported her on either side.

'This is so nice.' Carefully so that her head would not hurt, she shifted her gaze to the fireplace.

What? 'Isaiah, what have you done?'

'Brought the Christmas tree to you.'

'I don't believe it! Truly, you did this?'

'I had help with the moving, but the decorating? I did do that myself, took a long time at it, too.'

'I cannot even start to say how happy this makes me. I hope it was not too painful a thing to do.'

She felt the rise and fall of his breathing against her back. Oh, but she did cherish his strength and warmth. If only this moment could go on for ever.

But life was meant to be lived with all its joys and challenges. What a blessing it was that the two of them faced them together.

'It was, at first. But the strangest thing happened. Each time I hung one of them on a branch, memories came to me, good ones of me and my mother.' He nuzzled her neck gently, breathing in deeply where her pulse thrummed. 'I must confess something to you, Felicia.'

'Is it something delicious—perhaps even wicked?'

'Shocking more like it.'

'Truly?' She turned to look at him too quickly. Her vision went fuzzy, pain shot an arrow through her skull.

Isaiah lightly kissed her temple, erasing her wince.

'I confess it, I am glad you and Abigail brought home the Christmas tree. Don't let it get about, but I have grown very fond of the thing.'

'Now you are teasing me.'

'I would not. Not about a subject as serious as Christmas decor.'

'Decor? Pine cones and garlands are decor! A tree is

more than that—somehow it feels as though the magic of Christmas is alive in its branches.'

'I'm the last person who would have thought it, but once again, you are right.'

'About Christmas, at least. And there is one other thing.'

'Only one?'

'It has to do with what you said about finding me by the grace of God. I wonder if what happened didn't only have to do with finding me, but with making some sort of peace with your past.'

'I did wonder that. I struggled with it—the feeling that somehow time had slipped backwards. If I had not found you, would I have gone back to being who I used to be?'

'You mustn't do that. No matter what happens to us over the years, you must promise me you will not.'

'The thing is, I didn't. When I feared the worst it was loving you that kept me from it.'

And she could say the same of his love. 'Do you know, Isaiah, when I was unconscious, I heard you singing—at first I wanted to stay where I was, but then I heard your love coming through it and I remembered us.'

'As long as we do that, we can face all the arrows coming at us, don't you think?'

'I do. Even the well-intentioned ones flung by the Penfields.'

'Especially those,' he said, then snugged his arms tighter about her. She grasped his hand where it rested close to her heart. 'I imagine I should spread the word that you have returned to us.'

'I imagine so.'

He made no move to do it.

'Let me hold you a while longer,' he murmured into her ear. 'When you are ready I will get us some tea.'

'Some of our best times have involved tea.'

'Some of them, but lately...' his voice grew low and husky, tickling the hair near her ear '...our tea would grow cold before we gave it a thought.'

And so they sat in silence, feeling each other breathe, wrapped up in the relief of being together.

She must have started to doze because she was startled awake by a soft knock on the door.

Mrs Muldoon came inside carrying, of all things, a tea tray.

'Oh! My lady, you have returned to us. I knew it was the right thing to bring two cups.'

Isaiah's muscles shifted as if he would get up to take the tray.

'Ach, no! Stay where you are, my lord.'

Cook shuffled about, pulling over a small table and setting the tea and cups on it. There were also pastries which made Felicia feel half-queasy to look at.

'I shall spread the good news.' Even as late as it was and the lady ought to have been abed, she smiled brightly at them.

'There is no need to wake anyone.'

'Wake them?' Mrs Muldoon laughed quietly. 'Everyone is gathered in the parlour, waiting for news.'

'Surely not!' Felicia tried to exclaim, but only croaked.

'And where else would they be, my lady? But I will tell them and they will take to their beds soon enough.'

With that she bustled out of the chamber.

'Do you know,' she said. 'I feel that I am completely at home.'

'No matter where we are, wherever we go, this place right here...' He hugged her tighter to him, she thought, in order to make sure she knew where here was. 'You will always be at home.'

Chapter Fourteen

In the morning, the first person to come hesitantly into Felicia's chamber was Abigail.

Her face looked far too sombre. She was a child, one who ought to be smiling. She clutched Eloise tight to her chest. It was a wonder the cat did not struggle to get out of her arms.

There was nothing Felicia could do about her sadness if the reason for it had to do with what she had discovered about the Penfields wanting to take her with them.

If, on the other hand, it had to do with feeling guilty for Felicia venturing out in the storm in search of her, she could do quite a bit about that.

'Sit here beside me.'

Felicia patted her mattress. Abigail set the cat on Felicia's lap and then climbed up on the tall bed.

'Can you tell me why you look so sad?'

'I nearly killed you. If my brother had not found you when he did, I would be a murderer.'

'Silly little bird.' She ruffled Abigail's hair. 'You were the one clever enough to remain indoors, not me.'

'But you thought I was in danger, it was why you went out.'

'You must understand, it was my choice and I would do it again.'

'The need will not arise. I promise it will not.'

'I should have known you had sense enough not to. This was more my fault than yours. And in the end, no harm was done.'

'But there was! Tomorrow is Christmas and you are stuck in bed.'

'And the tree is stuck in my room.' She would need to get Isaiah to move it back downstairs so that everyone could enjoy it. Father Christmas could hardly deliver his gifts to Felicia's chamber, after all. 'Besides, I am perfectly well. It's only that your brother will not allow me to get out of bed yet.'

'Truly? You are feeling recovered?'

'Completely.' Nearly that, at any rate.

'I will be downstairs in the morning to see what Father Christmas has brought you.'

'If I have your forgiveness, nothing he brings will be as good as that.'

'I hold no ill feelings towards you, little Sister. I love you too much for that.'

'Isaiah told me you would not, since you didn't hold a grudge against him either and we both know he deserved it.'

'For any particular crime?'

'For taking down our Christmas tree and then making you put it back and sleep under it to keep him from doing it again.'

It only hurt Felicia's head a little to laugh, which was a relief. With Christmas so near she was ready for merriment. Troubling matters could be put away for a day. She had every intention of having a joyful time with those she cared for. Among whom were Lord and Lady Penfield.

They could only feel wretched over what happened. All they wanted was a family and, as far as Felicia could tell, they would be devoted parents.

But sometimes good intentions went awry. Her going out into the storm was a perfect example. Her thought had been to save, but had her husband not found her it would have brought heartache upon them all.

'Do you like Eloise?' Abigail asked, her expression brightening somewhat.

'Indeed I do, she is a wonderful cat.'

'Good, then. I will leave her here with you.' She placed Eloise in her lap, then petted her slowly from nose to tail. 'To keep you company for the afternoon. You can become great friends with her.'

With that, Abigail got off the bed and hurried towards the door.

Before closing it behind her, she turned to say, 'I'm very grateful to have a sister, no matter what else happens.'

'And I am grateful to have your company, Miss Eloise. I could be up and about were not someone so much stronger than I am forbidding it.'

It was Christmas morning!

Isaiah would have sprung from the bed had not Felicia been sleeping so peacefully beside him.

But it was Christmas and he had not felt the thrill of rising to greet it in far too many years.

He bounced on the mattress to judge how deeply Felicia was asleep.

One bleary-looking green eye blinked open.

He bent over her to peer into that one eye. 'It's morning!'

'Good morning.' She rolled over on her side, snuggling into the pillow.

'Good Christmas morning!' He bounced more forcefully this time. 'It's nearly daylight.'

This time she opened both eyes, a smile shining in them. 'Is it light already? How could you let me oversleep?'

She tried to bolt out of bed. He caught her balance before she toppled.

'Hand me my robe and slippers.' She wagged her finger impatiently at the chairs where they lay in a heap on the cushion. 'We must get down before Abigail does! I can't wait to watch her come down the stairs and see all that Father Christmas has brought. It was such a beautiful sight I could hardly sleep with all the excitement.'

He nearly laughed because she had given an excellent impression of a deep night's sleep.

Going down the steps, he could tell she was much stronger than she had been last night. For all that it was encouraging, he had no intention of letting go of her until they stepped into the parlour.

As it turned out, they were not the first to come down.

Lord Penfield and Lady Penfield stood beside the window, the merrily snapping Yule log casting a happy glow over everything. Judging by the grins on their faces, the Penfields were as excited as the Scarsfelds were.

It sounded nice in his mind. The Scarsfelds—Isaiah and Felicia Scarsfeld. Lord and Lady Scarsfeld.

He wondered what people would think if he held a party

here at Scarsfeld. It would be appropriate to properly introduce his wife—appropriate and a great joy.

His neighbours were no doubt wondering why he had wed so quickly. As soon as they met Felicia they would understand—applaud him, even, for his wise choice in a bride.

Yet he had had been very lucky, very blessed.

'I hope you don't mind us rising so early,' Lady Penfield said, her expression bright and sparkling. 'It is a thrill to be able to spend Christmas with a child. To share the excitement of Father Christmas's visit. I'll admit we were both restless with excitement all night long.'

Isaiah and his supposed foes had that in common. Of course, it was difficult to think of them in that light any longer. Not with all they had been through and with their shared affection for Abigail.

Apparently Mrs Muldoon was awake as well for the Penfields each held a cup of what smelled like hot chocolate.

'I think the sun will be shining today,' Lord Penfield commented. 'The sky is bright and starry.'

'Yes.' Lady Penfield sighed. 'As much as we have so truly enjoyed staying with you, if the weather permits we must be going home tomorrow.'

Abigail's footsteps on the stairs prevented him from asking if it was still their intention to take his sister with them.

Maybe he should continue to fight, but not this morning.

Peace on earth, good will towards men, was what the day was about. For the first time in what seemed for ever, he felt the sentiment fill him up.

Abigail bounded into the parlour, her injury seeming to be healed or forgotten.

'He came!'

'But of course he did.' Lady Penfield stood, clapped her

hands then took a place beside Abigail while she danced and spun in front of her pile of gifts. 'Father Christmas always comes.'

'I thought I might get a lump of coal.'

'You see…' Felicia walked slowly over towards the pair '…even Santa believes you did not misbehave.'

Then something happened that he would have believed impossible on the day he read Lord Penfield's letter.

Abigail wriggled into the space between her sister and her aunt, wrapping one arm around each of them. The ladies, in turn, hugged each other's shoulders.

Of all the gifts happily waiting under the tree, the one he was looking at would outshine them all.

Lord Penfield glanced at him, cleared his throat, but made no move to engage Isaiah in a hug.

As for the gifts wrapped under the tree, there were more of them than had been there when he and Felicia had gone up for the night. The Penfields must have come prepared to spread cheer.

Again, not at all what he had expected them to spread.

Abigail dipped out from the hug, snatched a present and waggled it at them.

'Now?'

'Now.' Isaiah nodded, feeling a grin reach all the way to his toes.

Gift opening began sedately enough, but soon dissolved into beautiful chaos.

To his surprise, Lady Penfield presented gifts to him and to Felicia.

Laughter, hugs, and good wishes were what this day was all about.

More than that, it was what family was all about.

This, what was happening in his parlour right now, was what he had been missing all his life. Yet when it had first arrived he had distrusted it, had judged his sister's family to be a threat.

Of course, he had not been the only one. In the beginning he and Lord Penfield had gone at each other as adversaries. Yet here they were, discovering that friendship was better than ill will. If only a decision did not stretch painfully between them, their joy in each other's company would be complete.

He hoped that when tomorrow came, the spirit of December the twenty-fifth would slip into December the twenty-sixth.

But tomorrow was coming. In the morning the Penfields would be going home and things would be strained.

'This is so beautiful, Abigail!' he heard Felicia exclaim. 'Thank you so much.'

'It is from Eloise. The feathers are not from birds that she caught.'

'That is a great relief.'

To his way of thinking, Felicia's laugh was the first of the carols they would sing.

This was a day of days and he would not allow himself to think beyond it.

Felicia had to admit that the morning after Christmas was strained. Although Abigail sat at the table with them, it was as if she was not there.

Who would expect anything different, given what she must be going through?

Worry etched lines on her husband's face. He picked up

a piece of toast, set it down, then tried to sip his tea. The wonder was that he did not choke on it.

Of all the people in this house, he alone fully understood what it was like to be ripped from home.

'It was such a lovely Christmas,' Felicia said because anything was better than this silence. 'What was your favourite gift, Abigail?'

'There were many wonderful gifts.' She looked at her plate while she spoke. 'Spending time with my aunt and uncle—that was my favourite.'

'It was,' Isaiah said, his fingers turning white gripping his spoon, 'a very great pleasure to have them visit.'

But there was one thing puzzling her. The Penfields were going home to London this morning. Were they taking this child with them or were they not?

They ought to have said, one way or another. Abigail was not the only one who would suffer the heartache of the coming decision. There were four adults in the house—two of them would end up heartbroken.

Eloise strode into the room, leaping from the floor to Abigail's lap. Abigail picked her up, rubbing her face against the cat's cheek. Then, with a great sigh, she set her pet on the floor. 'Shoo, go away!'

Shoo...go away? Felicia had never heard her sister say such a thing to her cat. Two days ago she had fed Eloise a quarter of a piece of ham, then cooed to her while carrying her from the dining room.

All of a sudden she stood up, chased after the cat. Pausing in the doorway, she looked back at them. 'I love you both very much.'

The pair she had mentioned stared silently at the kick of her petticoat as she fled into the hallway.

Isaiah placed his hand on the table, palm up, wordlessly asking for comfort.

At least this, their marriage and their love, came of this turmoil. It was the silver lining they must cling to.

So she did cling to his offered hand, to give support as much as to get it.

'Whatever happens this morning, I must say nothing that will add to my sister's pain. If I have to smile and pretend I am happy for her great opportunity to live in London, it is what I will do.'

'If you smile, she will know you do not mean it. Better that you look at the toes of your boots when you lie.'

'Or at you. I will look at you and you will pass the smile to Abigail.'

'Should we refuse to let them have her? We could take them to court.'

'It would be a long and painful thing to do. Whatever good will has grown between us and them would be destroyed. The lawyers would see to that.'

'But it might take a very long to be resolved. She would stay with us for that long,' she pointed out.

'I hear what you are saying, Felicia, and I think you do not mean it, not in your heart. Those are words meant for my comfort.' He squeezed her hand hard, but she did not tell him it hurt a bit. 'We will appear happy for her, no matter what occurs.'

'And we will travel to London as often as we are able,' she said.

'I used to hate London, but I suppose if my sister is there I will tolerate it.'

'London can be lovely, you know. You will see it for yourself when we visit my family.' She touched his frown, trying to smooth it away. 'And perhaps they do not intend to take her at all. Perhaps it is why they have not informed us of it.'

'Maybe you are right. As long as I have you, I can bear whatever happens.'

And so she gave him a kiss, hoping he understood it was the promise of a lifetime.

Three hours later, Mr Phillips entered Isaiah's office to inform him that the carriage had been brought round and the Penfields were in the hall, waiting to bid their farewells.

Dreading this moment, he had hidden from it by burying his attention in the ledgers. With the butler standing in the doorway he could hardly ignore it any longer.

'Do you know where my sister is, Mr Phillips?'

'I believe she is in her chamber with Miss Shirls.'

The Penfields were packed, ready to depart and waiting in the hall. Abigail was not with them.

Hope surged in his heart, pumping in his blood to his feet and back.

Had they intended to take her they would have said so and she would not be in her room! No, Abigail would be waiting with her aunt and uncle to go out to the coach.

'Where is my wife?' he asked on half a run across the office.

He could be wrong about this. But, no, he thought he was not!

'In the hall, my lord, saying farewell to your guests.'

By the time he burst into the hall his heart was beating hard, nearly slamming against his ribs.

Lady Penfield smiled when she saw him. She hurried across the carpet and took his hands in hers.

'Getting to know you has been a great joy,' she said and

he knew she meant it. The lady had never been anything but sincere.

The only luggage being carried to the coach was that which they had brought in with them when they arrived.

Lord Penfield stepped forward and extended his hand.

Isaiah did not take it, but instead wrapped the man in a brief hug, then pounded his back.

'I meant to tell you, something, Henry.' He cleared his throat to ease what he had to say. Oddly, he realised this was going to be easier than he would have expected. 'Thank you for trying to help my mother—for trying to be the son she left behind.'

'It would not have worked. You were her flesh and blood. That is much too strong a bond to try to replace. In truth, I'm not sure it is even possible.'

From the corner of his eye he saw Felicia and Lady Penfield hugging and probably shedding a tear or two.

Isaiah felt a lump in his throat to be saying goodbye to the Penfields, but weeping—well—he and Lord Penfield would leave that to be expressed by their wives.

'We will visit you in London,' he said. Funny how he truly wanted to. 'Now that Abigail has got to know her family—that we have got to know you—we will miss you.'

'Given the reason we came here, I would not have expected it.'

He slipped his arm over Lord Penfield's shoulder in a companionable way and lowered his voice. 'Do you know, I would never be a married man had you not come? You were right when you accused me of making a convenient marriage and disguising it as a love match. But it is not that now and I have you to thank for it.'

Lord Penfield laughed out loud, slamming his open palm

on Isaiah's back. 'I'm no fool, Isaiah. The fact is clear to see. I fully expect to see you carrying a babe in your arms when next we meet.'

How could he respond to that? He could not. Not when it was what the Penfields wanted with their whole hearts.

They might have had what they longed for in his sister, but had chosen not to break up the family she already had.

It would be his nightly prayer that the Penfields would have the family they wanted so desperately.

'Where is our niece?' Lady Penfield asked. 'We cannot leave without saying goodbye to her.'

'Here I am,' came Abigail's voice, sounding younger and more subdued than he had ever heard. 'You need not say goodbye, Aunt. I have decided to come and live with you.'

He must have gasped out loud, because she looked down at him, blinking furiously.

'I'm sorry, Isaiah!' While she stood ringing her hands, Miss Shirls came on to the landing, dressed for travel and carrying three valises, one in each hand and one tucked under her arm. 'It is a wonderful opportunity and—and I think, well, it is what I am called to do in order to make amends for nearly killing Felicia.'

Lady Penfield clasped her hand over her mouth, turning her startled gaze to her husband.

'A penance, do you mean, my dear?' Lord Penfield asked.

'Yes, but I have grown fond of you, Uncle, and my aunt, too. So I'm not quite throwing myself on the sacrificial fire.'

'But ought you to let your poor cat suffer?' Lady Penfield asked. 'She will miss you, you know.'

Abigail seemed to have nothing to say to that. But Isaiah knew that in her heart she was making a great sacrifice for what, in her very young heart, she considered her duty.

Felicia came to him, insinuating herself under his arm. Had his body begun to sag the same as his heart had?

Here was Lord Penfield and Lady Penfield's dream handed to them on a platter, so to speak. All that needed doing was for one of them to raise an arm in welcome and Abigail would come down the steps and go with them into the coach.

Even without that she did come down.

Going to Felicia first, she gazed up at her. 'I am grateful to have a sister. Eloise has asked if you will love her in my place.'

'Of course I will, but—'

Lord Penfield and Lady Penfield stared at each other in some silent communication that long-married couples were so adept at.

Next thing he knew, Abigail threw her small arms around him, hugging tightly.

She began to weep. She had made what she considered to be a brave decision, but she was only eight years old and could not hide the emotions that came along with her choice.

'I love you, Isaiah...' She wiped her nose on his sleeve. 'I will never...but you will come to visit...and—'

Lady Penfield touched Abigail's small, trembling shoulder, turning her away from him.

Cupping Abigail's face in her plump hands, hands that Isaiah noticed shook a bit, she bent and kissed her forehead.

'You really are the bravest girl, Abigail. I am proud to call you my niece. But you see, your uncle and I, well, we would be so grateful if you were to come and visit. But...'

Lady Penfield cast a look at her husband, her eyes blinking back tears.

'The thing is,' Lord Penfield continued when his wife

had difficulty finding the words, 'your aunt and I feel you are happy where you are.'

'I will learn to be happy with you.'

'But what your uncle and I were thinking is that it is not fair for one sweet girl to have two families to live with and be adored by them both, when there is a child out in the world who has no family to love them.'

'We hoped you would not mind,' Lord Penfield said, his voice going low and strained, 'sharing us with a less fortunate child.'

'You mean I needn't go—that is—it would be more a penance to stay here and make up for my wrongdoing?'

'Oh, indeed,' he answered. 'Giving another child a chance at a family would more than make up for that.'

Abigail hugged her uncle tight. 'I will miss you every day, Uncle Henry!'

'As I will miss you, child.'

Isaiah knew how deeply he meant those words because Lord Penfield looked steadily the ceiling while he spoke.

'Next Christmas you shall visit London!' Lady Penfield exclaimed. 'We shall have the best and brightest time. But come now, Henry, let us be on our way before we wear out our welcome.'

'You could never do that, my dear friend,' Felicia said, holding Lady Penfield by both hands and kissing her cheek.

Moments later the Penfields were gone.

The house seemed very quiet—too quiet.

Had there really been a time when he preferred it this way?

What a fool he had been, a wounded one, but a fool just the same. Now that Felicia had let his heart out of its dreary iron safe, he was never looking back at it.

In his mind, he picked it up and tossed it on to a fire so hot it melted, never to be made into anything ever again—except perhaps for a dozen keys to a dozen houses where a dozen happy families lived.

And for all that his wife and his sister stared mournfully at the closed front door, they were a happy family.

Joyful, blessed and in need of—

'As I recall it, the two of you owe me a rematch of our snowball fight. The sun is shining and I say you must pay up.'

'You might be sorry.' Felicia turned to him, the smile he loved playing happily on her lips.

'I'll run upstairs and get Eloise! She will not want to miss your defeat!'

Abigail dashed up the stairs laughing, twirling about on every other step and acting every bit the eight-year-old girl she was.

'Do you know what day this is, Felicia?' He held his arms wide and she stepped into them.

'December the twenty-sixth.' She snuggled into him with a wiggle.

'Yes, and yet it still feels like Christmas. Why is that, do you think?'

'I do not think, Isaiah. I know. The love that came down at Christmas was not for one day only. Even after the carols have been sung, the gifts opened and the feasts eaten, it carries on to fill us with the strength we need to face whatever comes the rest of the year.'

'Well then, I am armed with love and ready to face whatever it is.'

'For all the good it will do you in our snowball fight!'

Abigail cried while racing past them towards the conservatory, the cat dangling rag-like from the crook of her elbow.

'Just hold that love until tonight, Husband, we shall see what kind of strength you need.'

Felicia kissed him lightly, then tugged on his hand to urging him towards the battle.

London—December 20, 1890

It did not appear that it was going to snow while Felicia snipped branches. Given that the clouds dotting the sky were no more than wispy puffs, it was not likely to drizzle either. Yet she smiled while cutting greenery in the Penfield garden.

'If the weather was any more pleasant, I would outright weep for joy.' Lady Penfield cut a branch of spruce and set it in the basket looped over her arm.

'I will confess, my friend—or whatever relation we might be, I have not been quite able to pinpoint what it is called—that this is a lovely day.'

'It is great fun to see ladies walking and showing off their fine gowns,' Abigail pointed out while reaching for a clump of berries to snip.

'Oh, and the bonnets! Are they not the most delicious things you have ever seen?' Lady Penfield asked.

Clearly, Felicia's young sister was taken with London fashion, sighing and pointing to every pretty frill they spotted parading past the garden gate.

'You will be parading with them in only nine more years, my girl. I can hardly wait to present you to society.'

Nine years did not seem nearly long enough to Felicia. Time went by too quickly. She could scarcely believe she and Isaiah had just celebrated their first anniversary.

'Tell me, Felicia, how was your visit with your family?'

'Wonderful. For all that we spent a lovely week with them, we are glad to be spending Christmas with you.'

'We are so happy you came. Truly, we have missed you every day since we left Scarsfeld.'

'Eloise wandered about searching for you for a week,' Abigail said. 'I would have brought her, but Isaiah thought it better not to. I see he was right about it. I can hardly believe so many people live in one place.'

'It is not as lovely here as where you live, of course, but there are many things to do. When you are of age I shall enjoy showing you each and every one of them.'

'I think I will find a kind and handsome nobleman to wed among so many people.'

'You might, my dear, but you must be open to finding such a man anywhere.' She smiled at Felicia. 'Your family must be relieved to see with their own eyes how successful your marriage is. Some arrangements between strangers go all wrong.'

'But sometimes they go very, very right.'

'I would imagine your sister, Ginny, was relieved that you and Isaiah have made a success of things.'

'Greatly relieved. I have only just discovered she took to her room for a week, overcome with remorse that she did not step in to fulfil our mother's wish.' It had taken a very private talk with her sister to convince her that she was as happily married as she appeared to be.

'And your other sister is wed, I understand?'

'Yes, for six months now. Peter has yet to settle down.'

A step on the terrace drew their attention.

'My lady, the children are ready to be put down for their

naps.' The nursemaid crossed the garden, a child in each of her arms.

'Well, my darlings, come to Mother, then.' Lady Penfield's smile was all happiness as she set down her basket and reached for her daughters, one about a year old and the other about three.

They were thought to be sisters at the orphanage run by Lady Fencroft. The Countess had found them together on a poor, mean street in town, the older one holding the younger in her skinny little arms.

Knowing that Lord and Lady Penfield were looking for a child to adopt, she brought them straight away to Penfield, where they remained.

'There is not a day that I do not thank the good lady who brought them here. Few people care any longer that she was an American heiress who snatched up an eligible earl. No one can match her in good works for London's poor children.' Giving each small girl a kiss, she carried them back towards the house. 'I will see you at tea, Felicia,' she called over her shoulder.

'So will I.' Abigail snatched up her aunt's basket and hurried after her and the children.

Abigail loved babies. Indeed, she had not mentioned missing Eloise since she first set eyes upon the little girls this morning.

Felicia continued to cut greenery while listening to the sounds she had not heard in a long time. The music of life in London was vastly different than the less hectic music of life at Scarsfeld.

Truthfully, she enjoyed them both, but in the end she would be happy to return home where the creak of carriage wheels beyond the gate and the sound of a dozen voices all coming to her as one indiscernible murmur would be replaced with the peaceful sough of wind tickling treetops.

As if thinking of tickling had summoned it, a rush of air shivered her neck.

A very special rush of air, one that she knew intimately.

'I challenge you to a duel with holly branches since there is not a snowball to be had,' her husband whispered in her ear. 'With our little sister involved with babies, it will be a more even match. One against one.'

'Here is your weapon, sir.' She handed him a short, prickly-leaved branch, then chose a longer one for herself.'

She took a pose, waving her weapon under his nose. 'Be ready to meet your doom, my—'

He struck before she was ready, the sly fellow. He tossed her weapon into a bush and his after it.

'I suppose I must pay a forfeit.' She touched his lips with her fingertips. It had been a year and still she did not tire of touching them. 'I imagine it will be something wicked that I will regret very soon.'

'Later tonight you will pay, for now I will take a kiss.'

He did, a very long and lingering one.

'Here,' she said, picking up the shears which Lady Penfield had left behind. 'You may be useful between now and then. Now that you no longer dislike Christmas decorations, this will be fun.'

'I no longer dislike Christmas trees. Having ribbons and lace tangled up in my fingers is quite another matter.'

'For now we will snip and talk.'

He took the basket from her arm and slung it over his much stronger one.

The shears went click, click, click, nearly making a melody.

'If we time the cutting just so, I think we can play "Jingle Bells."'

'Only someone named Felicia Merry would think of such a thing.'

'Let us try, then we will explore your name meaning. We never did fully discover why it fits.'

While they clicked the blades in tune, Isaiah sang along. Somehow he made the piece sound very nice. She would have joined in the singing, but she thought she ought not to.

'God is salvation and has judged mercifully,' he quit singing to say. 'It is not a contradiction. It suits my life rather well.'

Felicia set down her shears, then traced the line of his jaw where he was in need of a shave. She never tired of touching him there, either. There was not an inch of the man she grew weary of touching.

He set down the basket and looked up an inch to hold her gaze.

'God did judge me mercifully and with a bit of humour. Did he not?'

'I think you will need to explain it to me.'

'Well...' He twirled a slipped lock of hair in his finger. There were areas of her body he never seemed to tire of touching as well, her hair being one of them. 'He found a crusty grump of a fellow and gave him a woman named Felicia Merry.'

'And he gave me a man with the most beautiful singing voice. A man I can never hope to sing to and have it come out anything but a screech.'

'No, my dear wife, you sing to me every single day. Your

heart sings me a carol which makes it Christmas every day and nothing is more beautiful to my ears.'

'Oh, well…then. Shall I carry on with our song?'

'Yes, let us make Christmas a lifelong affair.'

Then he kissed her—and it was.

* * * * *

THE VISCOUNT'S
CHRISTMAS PROPOSAL

Author Note

Thank you so much for reading *The Viscount's Christmas Proposal*. At this time of year life can keep us extra busy and I appreciate that you have chosen to spend a bit of your valuable time with Anna Liese and Peter.

This is a Christmas reunion story that, this year, is more fitting than ever. I hope the holiday finds you spending joyful time with friends and family.

You might remember Peter Penneyjons from *The Viscount's Yuletide Bride* and *To Wed a Wallflower*. Now the time has come for Peter to wed, but he really would rather not. Not if such a union involves giving his heart. Naturally that all comes into question when he reunites with his childhood friend Anna Liese, who will settle for nothing less than a true love match.

Peter wants a marriage of convenience. Anna Liese wants one of love. I hope you enjoy seeing how they bring it all together.

Wishing you every blessing of the season.

Dedicated to Jeremy Iaccino,
my awesome and much-loved son-in-law.

Prologue

January 1873—Woodlore Glen, England

He was dying and he was only twelve years old.

Peter Penneyjons heard footsteps tapping across the floor. They paused at his bedside. Whoever was standing over him gave a great, sad sigh and pronounced, 'Poor lad. It is better this way with his family all gone in the night.'

Mother gone? And Father?

Someone was fibbing. Because they would not go away without him—not go anywhere with him lying abed and sick to death. They would wait for him to heal and then all go to London together just as they'd planned.

'If you please, speak your negative thoughts outside this room. He might hear you.'

'Not in his condition. He has only the slightest grip on life as it is. You may count on him not hearing anything.'

'Doctor Fillmore, you may wait in the hallway. I will summon you if you are needed.'

But he could hear! Voices seemed like scratches in his ears. He had to strain to listen. What he could not do was open his eyes or his mouth to tell them that he could.

More than anything, he was confused. If his family had gone to visit his uncle in London, why was his uncle here holding his hand?

He would have returned Uncle Robert's squeeze, but he could not flex his fingers. All he could do was feel too hot and too cold in turns—and thirsty. He was so thirsty.

'You must prepare yourself, Lord Cliverton, the boy is very ill and with his family dead—'

'I am his family and I am here.'

What did the doctor say? He thought he heard but—no… he could not have heard that!

'I feel duty bound to remind that you should not be in this room. This strain of influenza is more deadly than usual. It will do no one any good for you to perish along with the child.'

'The child will not perish, nor will I. I cannot say the same of you if you do not quit your blathering and leave this chamber.'

A door closed. Uncle Robert lifted Peter's hand, pressing it to his cheek which felt prickly, as if he had not shaved in some time.

An odd thought drifted through his mind—he would never grow old enough to have a beard. He felt sad about it, although in a rather detached way.

'If you can hear me, Peter, I promise I will not leave you. You will recover and I will bring you to Cliverton where you will never be alone.'

There was no reason for his uncle to say this unless his parents really were dead.

Peter wished he could not hear. He wished he could not feel the beat of his heart or the rush of blood in his veins.

Mother and Father were gone for ever. It hurt too much to think—to feel. As if the fever were not awful enough, this revelation made him fear he would vomit and choke.

It did not matter if he did because being dead with his parents would be better than alive without them. If he died, they could be together again.

But what would become of baby Deborah? His sister was only two years old and she would need him to live and take care of her.

But had the doctor not said that his family had perished? Could he have meant Deborah along with them? His uncle had not said he was bringing Deborah to Cliverton.

With his sister gone there would be no reason for Peter to stay alive. All he needed to do was stop breathing and they would all be together for eternity.

Very well. He would simply stop—

'Peter!'

At Uncle Robert's bark, his lungs jerked, filled with air.

'You will not die, do you understand me?' Peter felt his shoulders being squeezed, firmly yet with utter tenderness. A tremor shook his uncle's strong fingers. 'Your Aunt Grace has forbidden me to come home without you.'

He did love his aunt. She would weep if he died and he did not wish to make her weep. Nor did he wish to make his three younger cousins sad. If he died, who would be their prince when they played castle and dragon?

Was it possible for a boy who only had 'a slight grip on life' to hold on tight and survive? The yes or no of it might not be up to him—or to Uncle Robert.

The click of his bedroom door opening sounded distant—

everything did, even Uncle Robert's voice telling whoever had entered to come no closer.

'Please, Lord Cliverton, may I sing to Peter?'

Anna Liese! If only he could sit up and warn his friend to run from the wicked disease slithering about his room. His sweet neighbour was only ten years old, which was even younger to die than twelve was.

'The doctor says he cannot hear, my dear. You should not risk being here.'

'But we do not know for sure.' Her voice caught on a soft sob. 'Perhaps, sir, it might be a comfort to Peter—and to me.'

It would be. He had always thought his friend had the voice of an angel, there was not much he liked better than hearing her sing.

Still, if he could tell her to leave, he would.

Since he was unable open his mouth or summon his voice, he would cherish the sound of her voice, imagine she was singing him goodbye of an evening while they stood on the stone bridge over the stream which separated her grand manor from his family's humbler cottage.

Of all the songs, he liked the evening one best. Hopefully, she would sing that one.

Mostly he joined in, but since he was no good at tunes, they ended up aching with laughter while they sang. It was all the funnier because on its own the song was sentimental, but they changed the lyrics to silly ones which was great fun. On days when they were weary of climbing trees or the weather kept them indoors, making up silly song lyrics was what they liked doing best.

'By yon bonnie banks and by yon bonnie braes, Where the sun shines bright on Loch Lomond, Where me and my

true love will never meet again, On the bonnie, bonnie banks of Loch Lomond.'

This was the right tune, but also different! She had never used the actual words to the song before—especially the 'true love' words. 'Where me and my true friend will always meet again' is what they sang, because they were only children with long lives ahead of them—and they were too young to be 'true loves'.

Trapped within his useless body, he was crying great loud sobs because he understood what she was doing. She was saying goodbye, perhaps singing of what might have been had he grown to be a man.

She sang a bit about the high road and the low road, but then she stopped. Her soft weeping crushed his heart. Uncle Robert whispered something to her, but Peter could not make out what it was.

Then Anna Liese began again, the sound pure and angelic. No one would know how desperately he wept inside since he could make no sound and the fever burned up his tears.

''Twas there that we parted, in yon shady glen, On the steep, steep side of Ben Lomond, Where in soft purple hue, the hieland hills we view, and the moon coming out of the gloaming...'

'I'm sorry, Lord Cliverton.' Anna Liese's voice caught on a sob. 'I cannot go on.'

Peter knew why. There was a bench on the hilltop overlooking their village. He and his sweet friend often sat on it, gazing down at folks hurrying about their business. They giggled over how good it was to be children, free to spend their days racing each other over meadows and wading in the stream which gurgled happily between their homes.

He heard the bedroom door click in closing.

It hurt to know it, but they would never share such moments again—never again stand on the stone bridge while bidding each other goodnight with a song.

How was it possible to sob so awfully on the inside without tears leaking from his eyes?

Because he was dying of a fever and was as dried out as an old bone.

'Take your rest, Peter, my boy.' Uncle Robert picked up his useless hand, held it between both of his. 'Rest and heal.'

He would, in one way or another. Either he would awake in heaven and be healed, or he would rise from this bed and be healed.

Until either of those things happened, he would hold on to his uncle's hand and keep Anna Liese's song in his heart.

'The wee birdies sing and the wildflowers spring,' he imagined the rest of the words. In his imagination they were as clear as if he and Anna Liese were standing on the bridge with the sun slipping behind the trees. 'And in sunshine the waters are sleeping. But the broken heart kens, nae second spring again, Though the woeful may cease from their grieving.'

Grieving felt very wicked. He would not put his aunt and uncle through more of it if he could prevent it.

No, he would live if he could.

Feeling his uncle stroke back the hair from his hot, dry forehead, Peter decided he would not stop breathing again. At least, not on purpose.

He would try to heal and perhaps one day he would meet his friend again.

Chapter One

~~~~~~~~~~~~~~~~~~

December 1891—Cliverton

It was too quiet in the garden, but not as quiet as in the manor house.

Quiet was not something Peter Penneyjons was accustomed to. Who would have guessed how much he would miss the hum of feminine activity that used to buzz about the premises at all hours, both indoors and out?

Standing alone among the hedges, watching the last golden leaf of the autumn garden drifting down from a sycamore, he found himself listening for the rustle of skirts.

He ought to be used to silence by now since the last of his cousins to marry had left home months ago.

Ginny, the youngest of his cousins, had surprised everyone by overcoming her shyness and reuniting with a childhood friend. She had wed him quite hastily in Gretna Green. Had Peter been there at the time, he would have tried to dissuade her. Just because her husband had been her perfect match as a child did not mean he would be as a man. Time would tell, he imagined. For now they did seem did seem devoted to one another.

Felicia had been no wiser. Before Ginny got married, his middle cousin, had wed a surly stranger. Peter knew he was surly because he had met the man when he'd delivered Felicia to him in a marriage arranged by their late mothers. Frankly, he was surprised and relieved to know his cousin was blissfully happy.

Of his cousins, Cornelia was the only one to make a match involving a properly long engagement, observing her vows with appropriate pomp and circumstance.

Becoming guardian to his former playmates had not been easy. When he had made the transition from carefree young heir to Viscount Cliverton, the shift in his relationship with them was the most difficult of all the changes he had been required to make.

It was one thing to act their prince and slay their dragons in play and quite another to enforce rules the girls were to live by.

Or try to enforce them, at any rate. Until he had taken on their care, he had never fully understood how lively a trio they were. No doubt it was because he had been lively right along with them.

In the end he had done his duty by them and seen them safely married—not that it was really any of his doing. One and all they had been set on their marriages. His opinion on any of it made not a whit of difference.

But married they were and here he stood, listening for echoes.

Loneliness was not an emotion he cared for. After his parents and baby sister had died, he had lived with the weight of a crushed spirit. Were it not for the love showered upon him by his aunt, uncle and cousins, he was not sure he would have managed to dig himself out from under it.

A bird chirruped overhead but received no answering twitter. Did the poor creature feel as companionless as he did?

Were it not for the company of his friends in the Anerley Bicycle Club, he would be bereft of any sort of interesting company.

As a gentleman of society he attended the obligatory social engagements, but they were dull affairs compared to pedaling about with other bicycling enthusiasts.

Indeed, only last evening he had attended a soirée and been speaking to a young lady on the fascinating subject of the 'safety bicycle', but the woman had looked uninterested. By the time he had mentioned the invention of pneumatic tyres, she was glancing about for a more interesting companion to speak to.

Perhaps he ought to invite Aunt Adelia to visit. His late aunt's sister was a vibrant lady who scattered good cheer as naturally as trees scattered autumn leaves.

With her quick mind and keen sense of adventure, Aunt Adelia would probably enjoy talk of the growing bicycle craze. It was his firm opinion that within a few years everyone would be pedaling merrily about.

But of course, he could not impose on his aunt to visit again. She had spent a week here last month, planning the ball to be held at Cliverton during the week before Christmas.

It was said that 'time is a healer' and he supposed it must be so. Here at Cliverton, he had learned to put the past away, to be happy and love without fear of loss.

No. If he were to be truthful, he did fear loss. It would be more correct to say that he had learned to go about his day-to-day life in spite of the fear.

Losing his mother at such a young age had crippled his heart until Aunt Grace stepped in to fill it. But then, he had lost her, too.

The passing years did help with grief, but not with the fear of experiencing it again.

Glancing about the familiar garden, seeing long shadows of evening creep across the stones, he felt as at home as if he had been born here.

While he might not have been born within these walls, he had been born for them.

After his uncle produced three girls it was understood that Peter would become Cliverton. Sadly, he had not expected to fill the role when he was twenty.

A carriage accident, an uncontrolled skid on ice had left the family bereft of both his uncle and his aunt.

He thanked the good Lord daily for Aunt Adelia. She, in large part, had pulled them through the tragedy. It was that dear lady who had helped him deal with the responsibility suddenly pressed upon his shoulders.

Evening shadows crept longer, grew darker and chased the lingering light from the garden.

He had always enjoyed this time of day—but at this moment he felt rather alone.

There were staff aplenty, but still, they were not family.

The rustle of dry shrubbery caught his attention. A kitten dashed out of a bush to bat Peter's trouser leg. He picked it up.

'What do you think, little chap?' There were always cats in the garden, not tame exactly, but not wild either. 'What this place needs is a family. I imagine you would enjoy having children to romp with.'

Yes, children to dash about the house—to play dragon and princess. For that to happen Cliverton needed a viscountess, which meant it was time to fulfil his obligations and wed an acceptable lady.

Which was the reason he was hosting the Christmas ball.

Setting the kitten down, he smiled, watching while it scampered after leaves blowing on the path.

He was not certain he wished to wed as his cousins had, for love and nothing less. An acceptable match would suit him better. He would be quite content with it, in fact.

The thought of losing another woman he loved was too much to bear. First his mother and then his aunt. There was only so much grief a soul could bear. He was not convinced that love was worth the price.

In a sense he had lost his cousins, too, albeit not to sadness and he would see them again soon. Until then house was far too quiet.

Sitting down on a garden bench, he watched the full moon rise above the treetops and thought about society's eligible ladies, both the debutantes and those in their second and third Seasons. There were a few who would suit nicely. Happily, none of them made him view marriage as anything but the fulfilment of duty.

A duty he had neglected for too long. It was beyond time he got married.

While he watched the moon creep slowly higher into the sky, a voice came to him from the other side of the garden wall. Faint at first, the sound grew louder as the woman passed by. She had a clear, lovely voice, but it was her song more than her voice which touched him unexpectedly.

It is not as if he had not heard 'Loch Lomond' performed over the years—but he had not heard it in the quiet of early evening. Not heard it sung with the same light, sweet quality that his long-ago friend had possessed.

The singer beyond the wall was not a child, but still she brought to mind Anna Liese. How long had it been since he had thought of his young friend?

So long that he could not remember it. There had been a time when spending all day with her was all he had thought of.

Eighteen years had passed since he had last heard her voice. Eighteen years spent making a new life at Cliverton—a good and happy life.

Looking back at the past, to the blissful times he had spent with Anna Liese—with his parents and sister—was not something he often did because in the end, happy thoughts turned to grieving ones.

He had even heard whispers that Anna Liese had fallen ill with the flu. Of course, no one had spoken to him of it for fear he would never come out of the sorrow consuming him. One more loss would have been more than he could have borne. It was better not to know.

But, for a time, his childhood had been idyllic.

His father had disliked London and society. He had often made a point of saying how glad he was to be a younger son to the Viscount and not the one burdened with the title. The family had lived in a sweet cottage beside a stream. It was larger than most cottages. In fact, what they had called home had long ago been an inn.

Papa had always said he had the best brother there could be because, knowing how Papa was uncomfortable in London, he had purchased the large cottage which, at the time, was a part of the Barlow estate. Uncle had also settled a large sum of money on Papa so they had never wanted for anything.

While they lived simply, Papa had been wealthy—although Peter had not been aware of it. Those had been the best of times, and they had ended in the blink of an eye.

Over the years he had not allowed himself to look back. If he did, his good memories might be tainted with shadows of tragedy. Even though he had later discovered his friend had survived, he refused his uncle's offer to take him to visit. The past hurt too much to be revisited, so he had put the cottage, Anna Liese and their lost friendship, behind him.

Ah, but this evening the woman's song shot him back to Woodlore Glen, to the bridge where he used to say goodnight to sweet and pretty Anna Liese.

What had become of her?

Being the daughter of a baron, she would naturally have married long ago. It was highly likely that she was mother to several children every bit as lovely as he recalled her being.

Full dark was now settled over the garden. Inhaling a breath of fresh evening air, he watched stars begin to take their ancient places in the sky while he thought of his first home.

It was not easy with so much time and shadowed memory between then and now. He had only vague memories of the place. After offering to take him back that one time, Uncle Robert had not pressed the matter again. No doubt it would have been as painful a visit for Uncle Robert as it would have been for Peter.

Over the years his uncle had rented the house to various tenants. After becoming Viscount and in charge of the property, Peter continued to do so through a property manager. For all that he had avoided visiting the place, he had no wish to sell his first home.

Perhaps the time had come to pay a visit. The house had now been vacant for a more than a year. In all the hustle and bustle of weddings, he had given the place little thought, but now that he had, he realised it was irresponsible to let it go unoccupied any longer. With his cousins settled he now had time to devote his attention to the cottage—personally—without the buffer of a property manager. There would be plenty of time to visit, see to its care, and still get back in time for the ball.

'There you are, my lord!' Mrs Boyle, his housekeeper, exclaimed. 'Why are you sitting in the dark while dinner is growing cold in the dining room?'

Growing cold in the dining room where he would sit at the long table with only a footman keeping him silent company.

He could not imagine why the housekeeper seemed surprised to find him here since it was where she found him most evenings. Well, perhaps he could imagine after all. She had clucked about him like a mother hen since the day he first came to Cliverton. Now that he was the only Penneyjons in residence she was even more devoted to his care and keeping.

'Mrs Boyle,' he said as he kept pace behind her rustling skirts—was it silly to find the swish of fabric comforting? It was what came of being raised with girls, he supposed. 'I will be taking a trip to Woodlore Glen next week.'

Mrs Boyle stopped, spun about to stare at him, surprise arching her brows nearly to her hairline.

'It has been many years—are you certain, my lord?'

'Quite.' Perhaps he was certain—but perhaps not.

'When shall I inform the staff to be ready to travel?'

'I won't need staff. It is only a cottage, after all.' He would much prefer to spend a day or two alone. He could not say if the home was even fit to live in having been neglected all these months. More than that, though, he had ghosts to visit and he would prefer to greet them on his own.

'You will need me, sir! I would rather not see you starve.'

'I can manage my meals in the village for a time. I'll send for you and some of the others after I have seen the condition of the house.'

'Very well,' she answered with a sniff. 'Between now and then I shall be sure cook puts a few pounds on you—just to tide you over.'

'Thank you, Mrs Boyle. I do appreciate it.'

Following Mrs Boyle, her lantern swinging golden beams across the stone path, he decided he was excited to go to Woodlore Glen. Before he turned his attention fully to the duty of finding a bride, he would attend to his first home.

Duty was duty and he would not shirk it, but a visit to the past was in order.

Chapter Two

⁓⁓⁓⁓⁓

Anna Liese stood at the drawing room window watching her pet goose, Fannie, waddle across the stone bridge, her tail feathers flicking while she squawked at a bristle-backed cat.

She refused to shiver over the tingle creeping up her neck and smoothed her hands over the chill prickling her forearms.

The uneasy sensation had nothing to do with the goose or the cat. Nor did it have to do with the temperature in the drawing room. No, indeed, a bright fire snapped cheerily in the hearth and spread warmth to every extravagantly decorated corner.

More than likely the unwelcome sensation had to do with her stepmother. The crawly feeling was familiar enough that she knew better than to ignore it.

Over the years Anna Liese had developed something of a sixth sense—an intuition—when the Baroness was hatching a scheme. A scheme directed against her.

Without moving her head, Anna Liese shifted her gaze towards her stepsister. Mildred was frowning at her mother, her bottom lip curled in an unattractive pout.

Mildred swung her disgruntled expression at Anna Liese, then grunted in an unbecoming way.

What, she wondered, was Stepmama up to this time?

There was little doubt she was concocting some trickery which might land Anna Liese in a compromising situation with a man—someone she would thereby be forced to wed. Her stepmother did not care how it happened or what unscrupulous person she became saddled with, only that Anna Liese was no longer a stumbling block to Mildred's prospects.

Ever since Anna Liese had come of age and gentlemen began to show her favour, Stepmama had made it her goal to get her out of Mildred's way.

Would the woman never tire of it? If gentlemen callers were not attracted to Mildred, it was not because of Anna Liese, it was because Mildred was not the most congenial of ladies.

Which was understandable, in her opinion. How else could Mildred have turned out given that, for all the sixteen years they had lived together, Stepmama had compared her to Anna Liese and found her own child lacking?

It was hard not to feel some pity for Mildred. How would anyone have an ounce of respect for themselves growing up and hearing things such as, 'Mildred, do you see Anna Liese having a second helping of tart?' or, 'Watch and learn how your stepsister smiles at a gentlemen, otherwise you have no chance at surpassing her.'

Then there was the worst comment, which Anna Liese had overheard shortly after her father had married Lady

Hooper. 'You shall try harder to be pleasant to your step-father, Mildred. The Baron must see you as his favourite daughter. Anna Liese is prettier than you are which means you must be more charming than she is.'

It was a horrid thing to say to Mildred. To this day, she recalled her younger stepsister's sobs as she ran out of library.

The saddest part was, that, in the beginning she and Mildred had begun a sisterly relationship. Had it not been for Stepmama putting them at odds, perhaps they still would have been friends.

And yet Anna Liese did have some pity—almost—for Stepmama.

What kind of joy could there be in a life consumed with seeing one's daughter wed to a title? As far as a life goal went, what happiness could it really bring her in the end?

And honestly, at twenty-six years old, Mildred was not the most sought-after lady in society. It was unlikely that Stepmama would ever see her dream satisfied.

Besides the issues with Mildred's age and disposition, there was the difficulty of residing in Woodlore Glen. It was a quaint and lovely village, but, being a few hours from London, they were isolated from society. It was a rare day when a gentleman paid a call.

Sadly, there was truly little which Anna Liese and her stepsister had in common.

But there was one thing.

They were pawns of the Baroness's ambition. The woman would do anything to get what she wanted which was to see both girls married.

While most mothers wished for the same, they also had a care for whom their daughters wed. Stepmama did not.

It was not their happiness she sought, but only that Anna

Liese be out of Mildred's way, and that Mildred should have a title. And that said title would be above the rank of Baroness.

While love and romance meant nothing to Stepmama, it meant everything to Anna Liese. If she decided to spend her life with a man it would be because she adored him— because if she did not marry him, life would be colourless. If her life was to be colourless, she might just as well remain here in the home she loved.

Honestly, she had made up her mind long ago that without love there was no point in marriage. Memories of her parents' marriage was her guiding light. She would settle for nothing less than the love she recalled shining from her father's eyes for her mother.

'Anna Liese, my dear.' There it was—further proof that Stepmama was scheming. She never used an endearment towards Anna Liese unless she was up to something. 'I fear I have left my shawl in the carriage and my old bones are feeling chilled. Do be a dear and fetch it from the stable.'

Where, Anna Liese suspected, she would find some brash overzealous gentleman hiding. She would not find Stepmama's cloak. The woman had come in earlier wearing it.

How much had Stepmama offered him? Quite a lot, she imagined. Lady Barlow was an extravagant spender. Her late father's fortune had to be nearly gone. Mildred would need to wed a wealthy peer in order to see them through.

She wondered why her stepmother continued to see her as such a threat to Mildred. There had been a time when Anna Liese was sought after. While a suitor might still see her as a better choice than Mildred, she had no interest in a marriage—would refuse one outright if it were not based upon love.

With each passing year, spinsterhood seemed the likely outcome for both her and Mildred, yet Stepmama did not stop her attempts to compromise Anna Liese into matrimony. And it mattered little who the man was, as long as he was not titled and someone who might offer for Mildred.

As it had been when she was younger, her choice was love or spinsterhood. Since she loved Maplewood, she did not mind so much. Surely in time, watching couples walk arm in arm, laughing and clearly in love, would not make her heart ache. Indeed, she had only cried into her pillow over it twice this year.

If she was going to cry into her pillow, she did not want it to be because she had a husband who considered her an obligation fulfilled—one who did not really see her at all.

Stepmama was looking far too congenial, her smile bright and friendly. Anna Liese knew she must be on guard. On one occasion after such a smile, she had found her evening stroll interrupted by a stranger stepping out from behind a tree. He had tried to embrace her, which had not worked out best for him. Another time the third son of a baronet had attempted to secrete her away and keep her in a shed. He, too, had lamented that action.

The most daring, and most recent, of Stepmama's schemes had involved a gentleman who had looked for all the world like a pirate. His narrow chin had sported a black pointed beard and his small eyes had glittered as he peered over the windowsill of her bedroom. Truly he had been the most menacing of the gentlemen that Stepmama had sent her way.

She had managed to blacken both of his eyes before he had gained entry to her room. The cad had not seemed nearly so threatening as he scrambled back down the heavy trellis, sobbing like an injured child.

Anna Liese might be small of stature, but years spent hiking the woods and walking beside the stream had made her strong.

If they lived in London, her stepmother's schemes would be easier to accomplish. All she would need to do would be to get Anna Liese alone with a man at a ball, in the garden or an alcove.

But then, no. There were titled gentleman at balls whom Mildred might steal away with into a garden or an alcove. More often it was scoundrels of lower social status who Anna Liese had to fend off.

'I would be happy to do it, Stepmama, but I would not wish to offend Thorpe.' Whom she suspected would be hiding behind a haystack waiting to witness her fall from respectability. 'He does dote upon you and might be hurt if you do not ask him to see to it.'

'The footman is under the weather.'

'Very well, then,' she answered, making sure she sounded as unsuspecting as a newborn lamb. 'Would you like to walk with me, Mildred? It is not quite dark and the air is crisp and lovely.'

'I would enjoy a walk.'

Would she? That was not the answer Anna Liese expected. Mildred disliked venturing out of doors especially with evening settling in. Her willingness to do so now must mean she knew of the scheme and wished, for some undreamed-of reason, to quash it.

Perhaps Anna Liese's surprise 'suitor' was Woodlore Glen's banker, or someone acting on his behalf. Mildred did her best to disguise her interest in the man, but, sadly for her, she was not adept at hiding her emotions.

It would be a great coup for her stepmother to force Anna Liese to wed Mr Grant. In doing so she would have Anna Liese out of the way while at the same time ensuring the man's false admiration would go no further.

And false it was, most sincerely false. Mr Grant had an expression in his eyes that was easy enough to see if one looked behind his deceitfully handsome face. That expression was greed, for both money and social status. While Mr Grant would like to elevate that status by wedding the daughter of a baron, Stepmama would never allow Mildred to bear a title lower than viscountess.

Yes, it made sense that it was the banker awaiting her since Anna Liese was also the daughter of a baron. Mr Grant might be quite willing to settle for Anna Liese.

Poor Mildred. It was no wonder she had grown to be bitter and petty, having been little more to her mother than a means to achieve her own ambitious ends.

'It is too cold for you to venture out. You will remain here with me.'

'I shall wear a coat, Mother.'

Oh, good for Mildred for speaking up for herself! It was a rare thing when she did.

Stepmama's mouth thinned, the tip of her nose beginning to pulse the same red colour as a beetroot when sliced open.

Anna Liese and Mildred both knew it would be risky to push the woman further.

'Hurry along, Anna Liese, before he—' In her rising ire, the Baroness nearly blurted out the secret which they all knew anyway. 'Before I catch a chill.'

'It might take me a while to find it, Stepmama. You should sit close the hearth.'

Where she might swelter.

Perhaps it was not charitable to wish the woman to roast, but neither was it charitable to try to trap one's own family.

Slowly, Anna Liese strolled out of the drawing room, then mounted the steps to her bedroom.

'I'll need my coat, Martha,' she said to her maid who was drawing the curtains closed against the night.

'Surely you are not going out, miss. It is time to dress for dinner.'

'I will not be needing you until morning. You may enjoy the rest of the night off.'

'You are hiding away from that old besom again! If you will forgive me saying such a thing about your—your relative. Although I hate to call her such. I remember how it used to be when your mother was alive. Oh, your father adored her so—and you. Then that woman came and Maplewood Manor has not been the same since, believe you me.'

Nor would it ever be. Until the deadly influenza robbed them of Mama, life had been so lovely—a bit of paradise fallen to earth.

Anna Liese, too, remembered how it used to be.

'You will be in your secure place? Wherever it might be.' Martha settled Anna Liese's cloak about her shoulders, then buttoned it under her chin. 'You always come home in the morning so I suppose you must be safe enough.'

'You need not worry. I'll be close by and far safer there than here.'

Ever since the 'pirate' in the window she had been extremely cautious.

'Sit by the fire for a moment, my dear, and I will bring you a basket of food.'

Moments later Martha returned, setting the basket on Anna Liese's lap. The scent of warm bread wafted from under the napkin.

'You are too kind, Martha. I thank you.'

'It is not my place to say so, miss, but I do have an opinion on all of this.'

Having cared for Anna Liese all her life, Martha rarely withheld that opinion.

The bread smelled delicious and she was hungry. She broke off a piece of crust and nibbled it.

'It just seems to me you would save yourself some trouble by marrying one of the better gentlemen the Baroness sets in your path. You could move away from here. Surely there is one among them who can offer more than what you have now.'

'It is the banker this time.'

'Oh, my. Well, not Mr Grant. But perhaps the next gentleman.'

'I have no wish to leave my home.'

Martha shook her head, several wisps of grey hair shimmering in the brown. 'I fear it has not been the home we knew for a good long time now.'

'It is where I—where we all—knew love. At least here I have my memories of that time.'

It was where she had been crushed with grief. But it was also where the memories of love wrapped her up, then healed her. Grief was strong, but love was stronger.

'You might learn to love a husband. Many women do.'

Annaliese looped the basket handle over her arm, then stood up.

'And many do not. I will be in love with my husband first and he with me. Otherwise, I shall remain here just as I am.'

'But are you happy, my girl?'

Well, no. She could not claim she was, but at least she was not happy in the home where, for a time in her life, she had been.

Ordinarily, Anna Liese enjoyed moonlight. But not to-night when it shone so brightly on the bridge that anyone looking out a window might see her crossing.

Although such a thing was unlikely. If her stepmother did happen to look out of a window it would be on the east side of the house where she could spot Anna Liese walking 'un-awares' to the stable. No doubt she was even now wringing her hands in anticipation of her scheme working this time.

Quickening her pace, she wondered how long the banker and his witness would wait.

They would become good and cold while they did.

Since the scoundrels lay in wait by their own choice, she did not feel an ounce of pity for them.

With the temperature dropping as quickly as a stone in a wishing well, she shrugged deeper into her cloak and hurried along the path towards her sanctuary—the abandoned Penneyjons cottage. She had spent many happy hours there as a child and still felt the welcome within those walls.

Naturally, she did not enter by the front door, but by a window in back. Luckily for her, the previous tenants had failed to properly shut up the cottage when they left. She used this back window as her secret entrance.

As always, it screeched when she shoved it open, then again after she climbed over the sill and closed it behind her. Securing the latch then testing it, she sighed. The night was shut out along with the mischief lurking in it.

Taking a deep, grateful breath, she removed her cloak and lay it across the back of a chair. She had always loved this cottage, but never more than she had over this last year when its vacant rooms had been at her disposal. Crouching beside the hearth, she put in enough wood to start a cosy little fire.

There now, this was lovely. It was unlikely that anyone from the manor would notice a tiny smoke swirl coming from the chimney. Until morning, time was her own. There would be no one to demand she fetch a shawl or comb their hair before bed. If Mildred misplaced a bed slipper, she would have to find it on her own. Or as often happened, if Stepmama required a cup of midnight tea, she could fetch it from the kitchen herself.

The reason she was treated as more of servant than a daughter was clear. Her stepmother must believe that if living at Maplewood was difficult, Anna Liese would be willing to marry anyone just to be free.

Stepmama was quite wrong in that. Unless her one true love came striding through the doorway, she would reside at Maplewood longer than they would. The home was hers, legally given to her by her father. Nothing Stepmama did could force her away.

She opened the dresser drawer where she kept a few things and withdrew a jar of salve. Sitting upon the bed, she smothered her chapped hands with it.

Perhaps next she would read, or sing.

Or sleep. Ever since the incident with the 'pirate', his beady little eyes peeking at her over the sill of her bedroom window, a peaceful night's sleep was rare and found only when she escaped within the cosy walls of this room.

Peter's room.

Taking off her shoes, she lay down on her side, plumping the pillow under her cheek. From time to time, she dreamed of her old friend. She had loved him. Quite adored him as only a girl with her first crush could. Although, she would have told anyone that what she felt for her neighbour was more than a passing infatuation. He had been her only friend and she, his. During those wonderful days, they had spent every day together doing what children do.

Those had been the best days of her life. She and Peter had raced each other across meadows, waded in the stream and climbed the hill which overlooked Woodlore Glen. They had spent hours watching busy villagers go about their business. Sometimes, back when life was still safe and innocent, they had crept away into the night to sit on the hilltop bench, trying to identify the constellations moving across the sky.

Precious days and treasured nights that came to an end when death had slithered through the streets of Woodlore Glen.

The last she had seen Peter was in this room. He'd lain in his bed, closer to death than life with only his uncle to hold him back from it—and perhaps she had in some way as well with her song.

She had not known for sure if he had heard her singing. Halfway through, she had fled home, her heart caught in intolerable grief. She could not lose her friend, she simply could not.

But of course, she had lost him. Not to death, as she had her mother, but to his uncle who had taken him away to live in London.

'Peter,' she whispered. 'I still miss you still and our friendship. Whatever became of you?'

She had thought of writing to him, back then—but life had been in such upheaval with Mama dying and Papa remarrying. And she had not known what to say to him. How many times had she set her pen to the paper, only to stare at it, then push it away, her eyes too damp with tears to see what she was writing?

Sitting up, she decided she was hungry and not yet ready to sleep. Opening the basket of food, she asked God's blessing upon Martha for thinking to send it.

Nibbling a square of cheese, she tried to remember what Peter looked like. For some reason it was easier to recall how she felt about him than what he looked like. Eighteen years could create quite a blur.

'Let's see…' She closed her eyes, chewing a bite of bread while attempting to conjure his image out of time and space. 'You had freckles on your nose—oh, and your hair! It was something between red and blond, I think. You had the best smile and the worst singing voice—I remember that quite well. And you did know how to make me laugh.'

Indeed, she had never had a better friend—or another friend, truth to tell. While he had lived here, they had had too much fun together to want to include any of the village children. Afterwards, Stepmama had not liked other children visiting the manor.

There was a brief time when Mildred might have become a friend, but then, after Papa remarried, love had not been the reigning banner at Maplewood.

This cottage, though—it seemed that everyone who lived here over the years had been happy within its walls. How many times had she gazed across the bridge in envy?

She had learned from its example. If she ever married, she would live in a joyful home which took its spirit from a couple in love with each other. Nothing less would do. Her longing for true love was not some fairy-tale idea of romance and happily ever after. Not the fluffy sort that every little girl fantasised about.

No, it was bone-deep love she craved. The kind which saw people through trials and lasted over years. Love which rejoiced in good times and grew stronger even when hair turned grey and wrinkles etched smiles.

True, abiding love.

Setting aside the basket, she lay down again, closed her eyes and drifted towards sleep. In the instant balanced between reality and dream, she saw a funny, freckled face laughing at her.

Chapter Three

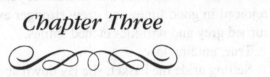

The train arrived in the village of Woodlore Glen behind schedule.

All in all, Peter did not mind disembarking near midnight. The village was peaceful in these wee hours.

He instructed the porter to have his luggage delivered to Myrtle Stone Cottage—to home—in the morning. There was no point in dragging anyone from their beds at this hour to do it.

He also refused the ticket-master's offer to give him a ride home. The man had already worked late, waiting for the train to arrive.

The walk from the village to the cottage was just over a hill, no more than half an hour's walk. He welcomed the exercise, even though the chilly air forced him to draw his coat collar up and his hat low.

Memories popped out at him from every street corner of the village, events long forgotten drew fuzzy pictures in his mind.

He stopped in front of the village's bakery, surprised to find Victoria's Sweet Shop was still in business. The establishment was closed at this hour, but that did not prevent him from seeing himself and Anna Liese as children.

Yes! Just there they rushed out of the shop grinning, each of them gripping a bag of gingerbread squares.

He could nearly feel the children they had been brush past his trouser legs in their haste to rush to the top of the hill where they would sit on a bench and gobble them down before an adult could tell them not to.

Was the bench still there? He could not imagine it would be, but why not walk to the cottage that way and find out? Going over the hill would take more effort than walking the easier but longer path around, but would be worth it.

Coming to the crest, he found there was a bench. Not the same bench, but one remarkably like it.

Since no one was expecting him, why not sit here for a moment? The sky was bright, twinkly and worthy of admiration.

Since he was sitting here, why not imagine he was holding that bag of gingerbread, laughing through a mouth full of crumbs with his long-ago friend?

It would be easier to do if he recalled exactly what she looked like. So much time had passed, he could not expect he would, but he did remember thinking she resembled a princess. Smaller than other girls her age, she was delicate looking. But strong, he recalled that clearly. And her hair…it was blonde and it sparkled in sunshine and in moonlight. She liked running, singing and twirling while her skirt flared around her.

Perhaps he would pay a call at Maplewood tomorrow. It

might be that whoever resided there now would know what had become of Anna Liese.

He sat a few moments longer and then a few more. Were his toes not beginning to ache from the cold, damp ground, he might have carried on sitting.

While he was indeed enjoying the night and the memories, there was more to him spending time on the bench than that.

If he were to be honest with himself—and what was the point of not being so?—he was afraid of seeing his old home.

He was bound to be overwhelmed with emotions, good and bad. It had not been for no reason that he and his uncle had never paid a visit over the years.

This was where his family had laughed and loved—it was where they had died.

None of which would change by him continuing to sit here. What had happened had happened. Could not be changed. What could be changed was what would happen from here on.

Rather than leasing the abandoned cottage to new tenants he intended to make his former home a place where his family could gather. Only Cornelia still lived in London and it would be good to have a quiet retreat for his cousins and their families to spend time together. Beginning this Christmas after the ball, he hoped.

Such a happy outcome would not occur unless he faced the place, assigning good and bad emotions—which were bound to pummel him—to the past as was reasonable.

Rising, he walked down the back side of the hill which would bring him to the rear door of the cottage.

He would think about Anna Liese, draw her memory out

of cobwebs if he could. Recalling his time with his childhood friend would give him the smile he needed to face
the rest.

Coming closer, he decided he would not sleep in the master bedroom tonight, rather he would take his old room. Perhaps he would find peace in it, the same as he had when he
was a child. Until that awful day when—

Never mind. It would be better not to dwell on that, but
allot it a place in the past as he had resolved to do. He would
think of the time before when life had been as wonderful
as a boy could wish for.

But—wait! What was that?

He almost stumbled over his boot toes, squinting hard
through the darkness at the cottage. Pale light leaked from
around a curtain in a window. If he recalled correctly, it was
his childhood bedroom. An intruder, a vagrant it seemed,
had taken up residence. Well, that is what came of neglecting his property for nearly a year.

He drew the key to the back door out of his pocket, glancing about for some sort of weapon in case the intruder resisted being evicted.

Ah, just there to the right of the door was a stick. Something of one at least—it was more of a thick twig. He curled
his fingers around it. Having never chased off an intruder,
he could not imagine what to expect. But he could scarcely
let whoever it was remain.

Entering the dark kitchen, he caught not a scent, but the
memory of one. Gingerbread. He'd forgotten how often his
mother used to bake it. He nearly called out 'Mama'.

Noiselessly, he took off his boots, setting them beside
the door. It would be important to get the upper hand on
the vagrant, not allow him time to become the aggressor.

Tiptoeing down the hallway, he twirled the flimsy stick in his fingers. Perhaps the man would leave willingly and he would not have to poke him with it and be humiliated when it snapped. He paused outside the door, trying to determine if the interloper was sleeping.

No snoring, but he did hear light breathing, soft and regular. The doorknob clicked sharply when he turned it. He might as well have fired a warning shot! His breath caught and held in his lungs as he quickly shoved the door open.

What the blazes? Not a man, but a woman!

Or an angel.

Dim light from the fireplace softly illuminated her face. Dammit, if the lady did not look more ethereal than flesh and bone.

All at once her eyes snapped open. 'Pirate!' she screeched, springing from the bed. She fired a pillow at him. The twig snapped in half.

'Pirate!' Anna Liese screeched.

'Miss?' The man looked as stunned as she felt.

How had he discovered her? And how had he got in?

Of course, he'd broken in! What else would a coldblooded predator do?

'Fiend! Get back!' Her fingers trembled. Her heart trembled more. Who was this? It wasn't the banker!

He obeyed—but took only one step. She wondered briefly if he was as surprised to see her as she was to see him.

But that could not be since the only people who would come looking for her were the one, or two, who had been waiting to trap her in the stable.

'You wicked, vile cad!' She had not a second to spare for cloak or shoes. She opened the window and escaped into the night, casting glances over her shoulder all the way across the bridge.

Oh, but those stones were cold!

At least it did not appear that he was chasing her. Gradually her heart slowed enough that she felt confident it would remain within her ribs. But where was she to go now? The manor house would be locked for the night and she did not dare knock to be let in. Oh, dash it! Her wonderful hideaway was now lost to her. The hired villain was bound to report where he had found her.

The stable was really her only choice to flee. It was risky. What if one of the men remained? And she did believe there were two of them, one to do the deed and one to witness.

But she must find shelter. Given a choice between freezing to death or fighting, she would face fisticuffs. Years ago, Peter had taught her a thing or two about it—but all she recalled was to ball up her fist and aim for a nose.

The stable door was ajar. She slipped inside without sliding it closed behind her. The less noise she made, the better. Towards the back of the stable was a tall heap of straw. Shivering, she burrowed inside it, clearing a small hole to peep out of.

With the door left open it was exceedingly cold inside. She could only hope the chickens and their only horse were not shivering the way she was. Still, all in all, things were not as bad as they could be. She was hidden. If not in her lovely, secret room, she was at least grateful not to be cowering among reeds growing near the stream.

Nor, apparently, was Fannie cowering among them. Not one to cower anyway, she must have been roused by the pirate fellow. Even from here Anna Liese could hear the goose honking an alarm.

Oh, drat! The squawking was coming closer. Her pursuer, probably realising she had no place to go but to the stable, was returning. Through her peephole she saw the door slide open. The miscreant strode inside, the loyal goose attached to his trouser leg.

'Miss?' he called while swatting at the bird and missing. 'Are you in here?'

By the heavens, she was not likely to answer that!

'Do not think you must remain here and freeze.'

What was that he was holding? Her cloak!

This man was not as ugly as the pirate who had peered over her chamber sill, but he was more cunning, attempting to lure her with the promise of warmth.

'You may return to the cottage. We will discuss this in the morning.'

Discuss it? Was the man mad? She would punch him in the nose before she discussed how he might compromise her.

'Very well, have it your way.'

How congenial of the rogue. But if she truly had her way, she would kick him in the rump. Although Fannie was doing a rather splendid job of accosting that area of his anatomy as it was. There would be an extra treat at breakfast for the good goose.

The man stood for a moment, frowning. His gaze passed over the haystack. As rogues went, this one was rather amiable looking. In other circumstances she might consider him handsome. And he had not wrung Fannie's neck as he might have. Still, she supposed his air of congeniality made him even more dangerous.

He shrugged, then draped her cloak over a barrel.

She watched it cover the oak, wishing it covered her. It was not as if she could venture out to retrieve it. Mr Handsome Pirate would no doubt pick that instant to pounce upon her, whereupon she would be hauled before a minister and wed within a week.

No, thank you very much.

She would freeze in the haystack before she would spend her life with anyone who did not share at least a few qualities in common with her first true love. Suddenly, she missed Peter Penneyjons more than she had in a long time.

One dull-sounding thud hit the floor, followed by another. Having dropped her shoes, the handsome, wicked man pivoted sharply, then left the stable, sliding the door closed behind him.

The woman had not returned to the cottage overnight and he felt sorry for it. She must have been awfully frightened of him, coming upon her in the dead of night as he had.

Returning to his room last night, he discovered that she must have been staying there for some time. There was a brush and comb in the bureau drawer, a small mirror—and a blue ribbon twined about the bedpost.

In her flight the woman had left behind a basket with half a loaf of bread in it along with a wedge of nibbled cheese. Also, she had run away without her cloak and shoes. He dearly hoped that she'd had the sense to pick them up off the stable floor after he left. The haystack she had been hiding in could only provide scant warmth.

There was nothing he could do about it now, except wonder about her. Who was she? Why had she felt it necessary to seek shelter in his cottage?

He had not slept last night, but rather spent the hours wandering the rooms and revisiting his ghosts. To his surprise he found the good ones more comforting than the bad ones grievous. Glancing about, feeling memories fall into place, he had smiled more than he wept, although he had done both.

In all, the cottage was in fair condition. It needed cobwebs swept off ceilings and walls. Fresh paint, perhaps cheery new wallpaper and new curtains. Certainly, a good airing out and vigorous scrubbing. Every corner of the cottage needed attention, except for his boyhood bedroom. That space was clean, well kept.

It smelled good, too. Even though the lady was not here, a fresh, delicate scent lingered—lavender, wasn't it? It was unlikely he would see her again, so he tried to put her out of his mind.

Today brought a bright new morning with much to look forward to. First, he would walk to the village and have breakfast, over which he would come up with a strategy to renovate the cottage and get it done before Christmas. It needed to be done quickly in order for the family to gather and celebrate.

After breakfast he would pay a call on the manor across the bridge. The current resident of Maplewood might know what had become of Anna Liese. He had no hope that she lived there still. Certainly, she would be married and be mistress of her own home. His childhood friend had been on his mind a great deal since arriving at Woodlore Glen.

And, despite his best efforts for her not to be, so had the angel from last night. While he had every right to be resentful of her intrusion, he was not. No, what he felt was guilty for having turned her out, although, that had not been his intention. She had fled before he could reassure her and he felt sorry for it. Frightening women was not something he normally did.

No doubt, in her eyes, he was the interloper.

As interlopers went, she was lovely—he could hardly deny what he had seen. A sleeping beauty, her bosom rising and falling in peaceful slumber, her fair hair splayed across the pillow. And when her eyes snapped open, he had discovered them to be an exquisite shade of blue. Even in the dim light cast by the hearth he could see how pretty they were.

More than her beauty, which was quite stunning, he had been taken with her voice. What she had shouted at him had been odd. Pirate?

Then by the time she had called him 'cad', his heart had taken the oddest tumble. There was something about the quality of her voice that had caught his heart. Made him want to smile and weep all at once. He had never had that disconcerting reaction to a stranger before.

Perhaps it had to do with the fact that she seemed so vulnerable. Until recently, he had been guardian to his cousins so that might have something to do with it. Relinquishing his role as protector might take some time to accomplish.

Anna Liese stood in the hallway outside the dining room, trying to decide if eating breakfast was worth joining her stepmother and stepsister at the table. She was hungry, but was she hungry enough to face Stepmama's ire?

No doubt she was steaming because Anna Liese had not gone to the stable as instructed to do and once again her stepdaughter had not fallen into a scheme to get her married off and out of Mildred's way.

The only sound coming from the dining room was the irregular click of utensils on china. Then, 'You ought to have done more with your hair this morning, Mildred. What if we have a gentleman caller?'

'A gentleman caller?' There was a clack, as if a fork had been intentionally dropped on a plate. 'That is quite unlikely, Mother.'

'But you must be prepared, in the event.'

'When was the last time such a miracle happened? Two months, three? But it was not a gentleman who called last, was it? As I recall it was the banker trying to sell a loan and you sent him away before I could have one word with him.'

'My, my... Your mouth is impertinent this morning, Mildred. Do remember that you are not meant to be the wife a common banker. Both your father and your stepfather were barons. I will not settle you upon anyone less than a viscount.'

'I shall dry on the vine waiting, then.'

'No doubt you will if you fail to take care of your appearance. As I said, your hair needs attention.' Suddenly Anna Liese heard a quick, sharp slap. 'Are you certain you wish to eat a fourth slice of bacon?'

'You need not strike my hand.' Mildred sniffed. 'Besides, Martha dislikes my hair. She never puts it in the pretty curls she does Anna Liese's.'

'And do you know where your dear sister is?' The word 'dear' was clearly uttered with a sneer.

'I imagine you would know better than I do. Did she not return from fetching your shawl last night?'

The shawl which was never in the stable to begin with? The one which had been a ruse to get her out there and was probably hanging neatly in her wardrobe?

Yes, she had returned, but only after shivering in the

haystack for two hours. It had taken that long for her to be certain the man was good and gone. Half-frozen, she had climbed the sturdy trellis to her second-storey window. Once inside she collapsed in a heap on the rug in front of her hearth, more grateful for warmth than she could ever recall being.

Bless Martha for having the forethought to keep the fire going. Not only in case she returned, but because anyone looking for her would assume she was within and search no further.

But, by the heavens, what was she to do now that her sweet hiding place at the cottage had been revealed?

'Would that she had not returned. Mark my words, Mildred, gentleman callers will not give you a second glance, not if they see Anna Liese first.'

Anna Liese flinched as if she were the one to have been cut by Stepmama's words. With comments like that it was no wonder she and Mildred did not get on. One could only wonder what might have been had Stepmama had a different attitude towards her only child.

'Honestly, did you think I would allow you to dally with a banker?'

A sniff. Silence. And then, 'I would not lower myself to the likes of him. As you say, I will have a viscount.'

How belittled must Mildred feel.

It was no wonder her stepsister had a misguided attraction to the banker. The society climber often smiled at her in a less than wholesome way. Being desperate for attention, her stepsister mistook it for admiration.

While Anna Liese did not often agree with Stepmama, she did in this instance. The banker, preening peacock that he was, would make an awful husband to any woman.

Anna Liese hoped Mildred did manage to wed well. It was the only way she would be free of her mother's hurtful comments. On occasion Anna Liese dreamed of being free of them, too. She wondered if she ought to run away and, despite her position in society as a baron's daughter, seek employment.

But, no, she would not—could not.

Her heart was as much a part of this home as the walls and gardens were. It was where she had grown up, been a part of a loving family for a time. She was not about to lose the home her father had given her, where at every turn she still saw his smile and heard Mama's laugh.

If she went away, she feared the Baroness would find a way to steal Maplewood. As long as she remained in residence, it was not as likely to happen.

'Put the toast down. It will go straight to your waist.'

'My sister eats toast and look at her waist.'

Mildred's sister wished she had a slice of toast with jam and a cup of hot chocolate to go with it. But she did not wish it badly enough to join their company.

Instead, she decided to go to the kitchen and see what was to be found. Last night she had promised Fannie a treat. Given what a beautiful December morning it was, going outdoors in the crisp air would be a delight.

She was a dozen steps down the hallway when she heard a knock at the front door. Being the closest to the door it would make sense for her to answer it, but Stepmama had forbidden her from doing so, insisting it was the job for the butler and not a lady.

Rubbish and more rubbish. Stepmama never considered any of the other chores she assigned her to do to be beneath a 'lady'.

The knock came again. Hurried footsteps hastened from the back of the house. The elderly butler who had served the family ever since Mama and Papa wed rushed into the hall, winded.

If Stepmama did not spend so frivolously on things of no real value, they might be able to afford to give him his retirement and hire someone younger.

The knock sounded a third time. Who could it be possibly be?

She slid behind a curtain. This was not the first time she had made use of this rather perfect hidey-hole which made her privy to what was said in the drawing room. Even better, there was a rip in the curtain just the size for a curious eyeball to peer through.

A man's voice ushered from the hall. She could not make out his words, but he spoke like a gentleman. Given the rarity of such a visit, Anna Liese could imagine the stir going on in the dining room. She did not need to see Stepmama's face in order to know her eyes would be glittering, her mouth set in a thin, calculating smile. By the time she greeted her guest in the drawing room a mask of charm and congeniality would be settled over her features.

Poor man. Whoever the butler was leading to the drawing room had no idea what was coming down upon him, that while he waited to be introduced, a wedding was being planned. Perhaps the man was not titled and would be safe from them.

'If you will wait here in the drawing room, sir, I will announce you.'

The visitor walked past the rip in the curtain. No! It could not be! But it was! Bold as day, the less than dastardly-looking pirate strode past her hiding place. This was an outrage! How dared he look so—so—pleasant?

Anna Liese clamped her hand over her mouth to keep from gasping aloud. She backed up against the wall with a hard thud which made him stop and glance about. Oh, how brazen he was, acting the part of a welcome guest and not a knave come to collect his ill-gained due. Not that Stepmama was likely to hand it over since he had failed to malign Anna Liese's virtue.

Standing utterly still, she listened to footsteps approaching the drawing room from the dining room.

'Lift your chin and for pity's sake smile like—' she heard Stepmama say when she and Mildred passed by.

Stepmother's greeting carried out of the drawing room. Could she gush any harder over the man?

But wait. Why would she do that? Surely once she recognised who he was, she would chastise him rather than welcome him. The fact alone that he was not the gentlemen visitor she had hoped for ought to turn her stepmother's mood sour.

It was imperative for Anna Liese to listen to what they were saying in case they concocted another plan to waylay her, especially as she no longer had a secure hiding place to flee to.

'I hope I have not called at an inopportune time,' the man said.

Truly? She nearly snorted aloud. He excelled in doing so, she would point out if she dared speak up.

'Not at all, sir. Guests are always welcome at Maplewood.'

Sir? All right, she did have to confess the stranger had looked handsomely dressed when he passed by her peephole. But it did seem strange that Stepmama did not seem to recognise him.

Perhaps she had made her negotiations with the footman only and that is why she was acting so politely towards him. Once he stated why he had come, the fur would fly. She could not help but smile at the thought of him getting his due—or a small portion of it—at least.

'I arrived in Woodlore Glen late last night.'

Indeed he had! No one knew it better than Anna Liese did. Why, the worm did not sound at all ashamed of it.

'Since we are to be neighbours for a time, I thought I would come by and make your acquaintance.'

What? Neighbours!

'Are you the new tenant of Myrtle Stone Cottage, then?' Stepmama asked.

'No, I own the cottage. I grew up there for a time.'

Oh, what a bald lie. She did not recall anyone but Peter growing up there, not boys, at least.

This man was up to something. If she were not in hiding, she would charge into the drawing room and accuse him of—whatever it was he was about.

'What a delight!' Anna Liese could all but see Stepmama rubbing her hands together in anticipation. 'I am Baroness Barlow and this is my lovely daughter, Mildred Hooper.'

Anna Liese's hands grew damp with the sinking feeling in her stomach that something shocking was about to be revealed. Nothing about this conversation made sense.

She knew who the true owner of the cottage was. Only last night she had slept in his childhood bed.

'I am Viscount Cliverton and I am quite pleased to meet you both.'

Her stomach took a dive straight to her toes, which

knocked her off balance. Why could the earth not open and swallow her? Her one true love—of a sort—had come home at last. Of a sort indeed. This man was not her Peter! Not the boy she'd held fast in her heart over the years. Viscount Cliverton did not have freckles on his nose or a mop of windblown hair. He certainly was not gangly. And his voice was deep!

For some reason he had never aged in her mind. How could he have imagined him older, when he might have grown to be tall or short, slim or muscular? Some people's hair darkened as they aged. Had she aged him in her mind, she would not have come up with the handsome man on the other side of the curtain.

Mildred was surely casting cow eyes at him while Anna Liese hid behind the drapery!

Oh, drat and curse it! Yes, curse it that she was wearing a serviceable gown and not one fit for a happy reunion involving an embrace and happy tears.

For most of her life she'd dreamed of being reunited with Peter. Somehow, she had never imagined it would be as a trespasser in his house! Who could ever imagine such a thing? What would he think of her once he made the discovery?

Nothing could be worse. How long did he intend to stay in Woodlore Glen? She pressed her fingers to her flaming cheeks, blinking back the moisture gathering in her eyes. It was out of the question to be reunited with him now.

Peter Penneyjons had known her as a cherished daughter, a beloved friend. Not as a squatter in his home! Clearly, she must avoid him. No matter what, she was determined to remain a memory to him.

Unless…

Perhaps he did not remember her? That possibility left her feeling rather ill at heart. But truly, it had been such a long time since his uncle took him to live in London. Eighteen years was an awfully long time. It was possible he did not remember her. His life in London would have been full elegant people and grand events.

Thinking reasonably about it, it was likely that he did not recall his childhood friend from the quiet countryside. Which broke her heart, made her want to let loose of her tears and sob into the curtain.

'May I ask you something, Lady Barlow?'

'Of course, my lord!' There was a rustle of fabric, as if perhaps Mildred had been thrust forward. 'But perhaps you would like to take a walk with Mildred. I'm sure she will have the answers to anything you would like to know.'

'It's one question only. I am looking for someone. I wonder, do you know what became of the Baron's daughter?'

'Why, she has grown to be a well-tempered and beautiful woman, as you can see.'

'Indeed, yes. I can see that. However, it is Anna Liese I am enquiring about.'

She pressed her palms against her chest to keep her wild heartbeat from giving her presence away—it did seem that loud to her own ears.

This development was wonderful and horrible all at once. How on earth was she to hide away when she wanted to speak with him more than she wanted her next breath?

'Oh. I see. My stepdaughter is away from home.' Stepmama might have found a career onstage, her voice sounding as warm as sunshine on a summer morning as it did.

'We were close as children and I was hoping to see her again.'

'Why, naturally. But, if I might say so, old friendships are rarely as wonderful as we remember them. People do change. But Mildred would be delighted to reacquaint you with the village. What could be lovelier than a new friendship, I always say.'

Wouldn't sugar melt in Stepmama's mouth? It was acting such as this which had captured her father years ago. The last thing Anna Liese intended was for Peter to fall prey to it, although, she was not sure how to prevent it since she was going to avoid encountering him.

With goodbye greetings exchanged, she peeked at Peter who, accompanied by the butler, walked towards the front door. Seconds later she heard Stepmama and Mildred chattering excitedly as they went back to the dining room.

Dashing from behind the curtain, she ran for the drawing room window. Now that she knew the man to be Peter, she needed to see more of him than the slice she'd had through the drapery.

Of course, she had seen him last night, but only briefly and she had believed him to be a scoundrel and a knave. A very well-knit-together knave. Even in her fear she had recognised his handsome bearing.

Hopefully, he would not turn to look back. If he did, he might spot her watching him through the glass with great admiration. Not that he would recognise her as the girl he had gambolled about the estate with, any more than she recognised him.

Suddenly he halted, taking off his hat and scratching the top of his head. The gesture went straight to her heart. This man was very much her Peter, after all. Oh, dear. He spun about, caught her staring at him. In the instant it took for her to stumble out of view, she noticed his brows draw together in confusion.

She pressed her chest to settle her heart. That frown was remarkably familiar and completely endearing. It did not matter how long it had been since she had seen it on his boyish face, it seemed as if it had only been yesterday. What a horrid and wonderful turn the day had taken. She could not decide whether to rejoice or lament.

Cry. She would do exactly that when she got the chance. Happy tears and sad ones came from the same eyes, after all.

Chapter Four

Peter walked beside the stream listening to the rush and gurgle of water, to the chirrup of birds seeking a meal before sunset. Given the afternoon he had spent, he needed this soothing peace.

What he had intended was to spend the day in the cottage, taking note of what needed to be done and making lists. He instead found himself in the company of the Maplewood Manor ladies.

All the live-long afternoon.

No matter how many times he courteously suggested they part company for the day, he found himself more deeply sucked into their company.

There had been lunch in the village, then a stroll about the grounds of Maplewood, which were as beautiful as he recalled them being.

For a time, he thought himself free of the ladies' company. He had been whistling while crossing the stone bridge leading to his cottage when Mildred scurried after him, insisting he remain for tea.

Since he had no ready excuse not to and the lady did seem exceptionally needy of company, he agreed.

Unfortunately, tea dragged on interminably.

One would think he was Prince Charming the way the women seemed rapt on each word he uttered. Of course, he was not fool enough to think it was he they were so enamoured of, but that a viscount had come to call.

This sort of attention, the kind that bordered on unhealthy adoration, was something he was not used to. In London he associated with people of equal or better rank. Among his peers no one was impressed overmuch with his status.

Being isolated in the country, he imagined the ladies did not have much opportunity to entertain. He supposed it was understandable they would enjoy company. It was also understandable how relieved he was to be free of it for the moment.

But only for the moment. He had been invited for dinner and once again could find no polite way to turn the invitation down. Besides, he might see the lady he had spotted in the drawing room window at Maplewood.

No doubt the pretty woman was a servant in the employ of Lady Barlow. Which did nothing to explain why she had been sleeping in his cottage.

The day might not have been such a loss had he been able to get an answer to his first question of the day: What had become of Anna Liese?

Each time he turned the conversation towards his old friend, Lady Barlow redirected it towards her own daughter. He still knew nothing more of Anna Liese than that she was not at home. After all this time he doubted he would even recognise the child she had been in the woman she would have become, if he happened upon her.

Free for the moment to be with his thoughts and not having to supply clever conversation, he let his mind relax, wander where it would.

While Anna Liese was greatly on his mind, so was the servant he had chased from his childhood bedroom. Why had she been there?

Rather than spending the day with the ladies, he ought to have been trying to find her. Clearly, she was in some sort of dire circumstance otherwise she would not have broken into his house. Hopefully, she would not seek refuge in the stable again. A haystack was no place for a woman to sleep.

Perhaps on his way home from dinner, he would search there for her just on the chance she had returned.

There must be something he could do to aid the lady. In a sense, he owed her a safe place to sleep. It seemed his bedroom had been her sanctuary for some time until he burst in upon her.

It was hard to forget the way she had looked at that moment—so beautiful and peaceful. How she had seemed part-angel and, at the same time, quite a desirable woman.

Over the course of the day he'd found himself smiling at the picture she'd made. Which he wished he had not done because he suspected Mildred construed the expression on his face as having to do with her. He did not wish her to misunderstand. He was not here to find a wife, but to restore the cottage.

Once he returned to London, he would hold his Christmas ball, face that next step in his life and seek a bride. For now, he had but two desires regarding women: first, to discover what had become of little Anna Liese and, second, to find the angel woman.

A bird settled upon a low-hanging branch, fluttering its feathers. Peter stood still, closed his eyes and listened while it sang the day into evening. He had nearly forgotten how much he enjoyed simply standing quietly and listening to birdsong. There were birds in his London garden, but here in the country they were easier to hear.

But wait—what was that? Not a bird but a woman singing, her voice far lovelier than a twitter. From here he could not identify what it was she was singing, but it was beautiful beyond words. There was a quality to the woman's voice that shook him.

It was hard to know if he felt like weeping or humming along.

Peter Penneyjons was coming for dinner which meant Anna Liese was not. Just where she would be at eight o'clock, she could not imagine. While it would not be possible to avoid him for ever, she simply was not ready yet. Nor would she be ready by dinnertime.

Maybe she would remain here, sitting on the stream bank watching Fannie paddle about in the water. What an awful prospect that was. This was December, not July, and the tips of her toes had only now warmed from last night's misadventure.

Neither did she wish to be inside where the temptation to leap upon Peter and enfold him in a great, teary hug of reunion would be difficult to resist. Better to avoid the temptation for the time being. Wherever she spent the evening, it would not be in the Viscount's company.

Some things were too humiliating to be borne. To be revealed as his intruder would be mortifying beyond the pale. Why, she did not know what his reaction to discovering her intrusion would be. He would be within his rights to hand her over to the village constable. Young Peter would never do such an unkind thing, but he was no longer young Peter. London and society might have changed him so she had no idea what he might do.

And would it not be a dream come true for Stepmama to get her out of the manor, shamed and incarcerated?

Well, shamed at least. Being incarcerated might reflect badly on the family.

Afternoon sunshine faded, giving place to early twilight. Fannie waddled out of the water, shook her tail, then settled into the tall grass for the night.

Not ready to go back to the manor house, Anna Liese decided she might as well sit for a bit and sing.

Singing always calmed her soul.

Did Peter know that she had sung to him the last time she saw him? Perhaps not. The doctor hadn't thought so but, thankfully, Peter's uncle had allowed it.

How awful it had been, believing he was dying and singing a bit of peace to him. She remembered the song well, although she had not found the heart to sing it since. Sitting with her knees drawn up to her chest, she now felt it rising in her lungs.

Peter was home. The sun was setting and the urge to sing their goodnight song overwhelmed her. Closing her eyes, she let it out.

'By yon bonnie banks and by yon bonnie braes, Where the sun shines bright on Loch Lomond...' Words springing

from her lips were born of her heart rather than her lungs. *'Twas there that we parted, in yon shady glen...'*

She did not realise she was crying until salty tears dripped into the corners of her mouth. Words and melody welled from her soul, the past becoming as present as the cool, damp ground beneath her. She had not been able to finish the song that wicked awful day, but now...

'O ye'll take the high road and I'll take the low road and I'll be to dinner before you, where me and my true friend will always meet again, On the bonnie, bonnie banks of Loch Lomond.'

She sniffed, wiping her eyes with her sleeve. Her true friend was here and yet a thousand miles away. It was unlikely they would meet again since she intended to avoid him.

'Is it really you?' A man's voice yanked her completely into the present time. 'Anna Liese?'

Gasping, she opened her eyes and leapt to her feet. Oh, no! No, no, no! She spun about, set her feet to flee and would have had she not glanced over her shoulder.

Peter, her Peter, stood mere feet away, a hesitant smile on his face. It was as if a veil was lifted from her eyes, from her memory. Knowing now who he was, she could only wonder that she had not recognised him from the first.

'It is you!' he said, his grin breaking wide.

'No, it isn't.' She backed away. This was not a fib. She was not the child he knew any more than he was the boy she knew. What they were...were strangers.

'Who else would sing our lyrics?' He stepped closer. She did not run as she ought to have. 'But why are you crying? Are you not happy to see me?'

'All right, I confess it. I am she. And why would I not be

crying? Last I saw you I thought you were dying and now here you are.'

For a moment he simply stared at her, silent and his grin gone flat. But then—

Then he opened his arms. It was as if time and distance vanished and he expected her to run into them, exchanging hugs as they used to do. But there had been time and distance. He was a man and she was a woman.

'Why didn't you write to me, Peter?' she said, uttering the first protest to come to her aid. She could not simply go back to the way they had been as children. Neither of them was that carefree person any more. 'Would no one bring you to visit?'

He shrugged one shoulder, tilted his head to the side. His smile slipped and a frown creased his brow.

'I imagine I meant to. As soon as I recovered.'

'And yet you did not.' Perhaps it was not right to feel offended that he had not thought of her over the years. But she had thought of him so often, wondered about him, prayed he was well and happy.

'Life dealt me a wicked turn, Anna Liese.'

As it had done to her, but that had not kept her from thinking of him.

'If I'd looked back, I think I never would have moved forward again. It took a while before I even wanted to live. Longer than that to be able to smile. I was afraid of coming back here, even for you.'

'My mother died, too. Did you know that?'

'Your father sent word of her passing and I'm deeply sorry for it. I remember how loving she was. So much loss, Anna Liese. It is a wonder we made it through. Won't you forgive me for not writing or visiting?'

She must, of course, since she never had been able to write to him either, although she had tried.

'Yes.' She had never truly held it against him, anyway. The only reason she brought it up now was because she needed to distance her emotions from this man who was, by now, a stranger.

Except for the way he shrugged his shoulder and tilted his head. That gesture was quite familiar. So was the curve of his smile and the brackets that lifted each corner of his mouth. Oh, have mercy, but a hint of playful mischief shone out of his eyes now, the same as it had in years past. Perhaps he was not such a stranger.

Regardless, he was bound to recognise her any second now as the one who had been trespassing in his cottage. Light in the bedroom had been dim, but not completely dark. If she did not wish to face her crime, she must hurry away.

'It is growing late and I must go home. But it was pleasant to see you again, Peter.'

As goodbyes went this one was formal, meant to let him know—well, she was not sure what, but...

Giving him a nod, she turned.

'One of the things I remember best about you is your singing. I forgot a lot over the years, but not that.'

Oh, well, for some reason hearing him say so made her go soft inside. Shot her back to who they used to be. The Anna Liese and Peter who roamed green hills and splashed in the stream without a thought of their world ever changing.

To the children who loved each other in complete innocence.

'I'd hoped you did, but—well—goodnight.'

She would have made it safely away but then he opened

his arms once again, nodded, asking for the hug they had always shared before going to their own homes in the evening.

Well, then, what could it hurt? A quick embrace to complete the circle of their friendship. To put a period to the years that had passed rather than a question mark.

Stepping forward, she raised herself up on her toes to give his neck a quick hug, same as she had done a thousand times. But unlike the thousand times, Peter did not laugh and instantly let go of her. His embrace drew her to his chest, which was no longer all ribs and gangly adolescent angles, but well muscled, manly and—oh, my word.

Oh, my word, indeed! Grown-up Peter made her aware of herself as a woman and not a flat-chested child. Her heart racing madly in confusion, she pressed her palms on his chest, pushing back out of his arms.

This man might be called Peter Penneyjons, but that was all he had in common with the boy she had known. All right, there was the grin, but it was hardly enough to erase years of being apart.

If, like they had done as children, they stole away in the night to sit on the hilltop bench, it would not be to point out constellations. She had better not let her mind wander to the bench because she was growing rather warm…flushed.

Spinning away from him, she was too aware that it was not a boy's scent lingering in her senses while she crossed the bridge and ran for home.

Peter stood in front of the bedroom mirror, tugging his necktie into place. It was not as easy a task as his valet made it appear to be, but then nothing was as easy as anticipated, he decided while shooting his mirror image a grimace.

In the beginning this visit had seemed simple enough.

Come to Woodlore Glen, repair the family cottage and deal with the ghosts of his past. Then, while he was about it, enquire about Anna Liese.

That was all he had wanted: knowledge. To discover what had become of her and then put her away with the rest of his ghosts.

It ought to have been a simple thing.

But, no, as startling as it had been to find a woman in his bed last night, it had been even more of a shock when he realised his angelic-looking intruder to be Anna Liese.

More shocking, he had hugged her.

The scent of her hair lingered in his mind. He could not forget her quick intake of breath when she had pushed herself out of his arms. Even now he could scarcely believe he had done such an impulsive thing. What had prompted him to do it?

Enchantment brought on by December twilight and her song, no doubt. Hearing her voice had nearly brought him to his knees, his heart quivering in his chest. Even so, the last thing he had intended to do was hug her, certainly not to linger over it as he had. In his defence he had been astonished to discover his playmate had turned into a woman more appealing than he could have imagined—far more enchanting than any woman he had ever held in his arms.

Anna Liese had intriguing curves and smelled like lavender. Coming back from the stable last night he had stood over his bed, the fragrance drifting up from the pillow. In case he had any doubt as to who his intruder had been, the scent put the question to rest.

Another thing he had not anticipated was her reaction to seeing him. He had thought she was not best pleased by the surprise. Perhaps she really had been harbouring ill feelings towards him all these years because he had not written.

While dressing for the coming dinner at Maplewood, he had many questions and not many answers. The only answer he did have was that he knew where Anna Liese was. Not what had become of her, only where she was.

His childhood friend presented a mystery. Why had she been sleeping in his bedroom when she resided in the manor across the bridge? While it made no sense, he intended to make sense of it soon.

For the moment he would struggle with this cravat, grateful to know she was, if perhaps not doing well, at least whole and sound. And he would think of her voice—her song—which was even more beautiful than he recalled. All of her was more beautiful than he recalled.

'Why, there you are, Anna Lise!' She had only stepped on the bottom stair when Stepmama's voice brought her up short. 'Where have you been? Your sister and I have been beside ourselves with worry.'

'I cannot imagine what dire thing could happen to me here at Maplewood, can you? We must have missed each other in passing, that's all.' She started up the steps, but paused, looking down. 'I trust you had a pleasant day in spite of the worry, Stepmama?'

A pleasant day trying to trap Peter. She'd heard the servants whispering about it. They had spent much of the day together and he was coming to dinner tonight.

'It was mostly uneventful, as our days tend to be. But, my dear, something has come up and I fear I must ask for your help.'

The staff was all abuzz about Viscount Cliverton coming for dinner tonight. It was unlikely that she wished for Anna Liese's help in keeping him entertained.

'It seems there is a fox prowling about the stable and the hens are nervous about it. Would you mind spending a few hours with them tonight? If they do not calm down, I fear it will be days before we have eggs again.'

'Is there not a lad you might send to do it?'

There was certainly no fox. Even if there were one, the door would be shut against the animal.

'Oh, but you have such a way with animals. The hens will settle at once when they know you are with them.'

Another scheme! Anna Liese was becoming weary of them. The only fox close by was the one speaking to her. In any case, it would suit Anna Liese very well to be absent for the evening. If Peter had not yet recognised her as the woman sleeping in his bedroom, he soon would. It would be beyond humiliating for it to be revealed in front of Mildred and Stepmama. It simply would not do.

Hurrying up the stairs, she entered her bedroom and closed the door, leaning against it with a relieved sigh. After the events of last night, she was content to remain here, snuggle into the chair beside the hearth and read a book. She would become so engrossed in the story that she would forget altogether that Peter was downstairs, that he was likely to be under assault from Mildred and Stepmama.

Poor man, but there was nothing she could do about it unless she was willing to join them for dinner, which she was not. Even if there was not the issue of her being exposed, she would not go down.

Life with those women would be miserable if she intruded. Stepmama clearly did not want her there. Anna Liese's mere presence at dinner would cause the Baroness to redouble her efforts to trap Anna Liese into marrying the next cad who wandered by the gate, or perhaps the banker.

Yet, despite the wisdom of remaining here, she could not help but imagine how nice it would be to spend the evening with her old friend. She did want to know about him—about how his life had been since they parted.

Hmm, what would she wear if she did join them for dinner? It could not hurt at all to wonder. She did not have many gowns, not compared to the number Mildred had, but the few she did have were quite pretty.

Walking across the bedroom to the wardrobe, she drew open the doors. What on earth...? Her pretty gowns were gone! All that hung inside were the serviceable dresses she wore every day.

How clever of Stepmama to have them removed in order to ensure she remained in her room. She would have realised that Anna Liese would recognise the story of the marauding fox to be a ruse and so taken this step to ensure she would not come down.

She need not have gone to the effort of making it up. Anna Liese plonked down in her chair which was positioned to give her a view of the fireplace and the window. This was where she would spend the evening. It was where she would remain until she spotted Peter crossing the bridge going home to his cottage.

Apparently, he would be walking back in the rain. Big fat drops began to hit the window. They rolled down, making the glass look as if it were weeping. Which is not what she would be doing sitting here. It did not matter that Peter was downstairs being entertained by Mildred.

He really was no more than a childhood friend. It was none of her business whom he found attractive—although she could not imagine he would be attracted to Mildred. Then again, she did not know him well enough to judge the kind of woman he was drawn to.

The bedroom door opened. Martha bustled inside, carrying Anna Liese's favourite gown over her arm.

'I thought Miss Mildred would never be satisfied with her hair. But here now, there is just enough time to arrange yours before dinner.'

'You needn't bother, Martha. I'm not going down tonight.'

'There is not time to play at refusing. Our young man is already here—and look, I retrieved your gown from the laundry. Miss Mollie, bless her soul, set it aside in case you might need it.'

Playing, indeed. She was not playing at anything. She was not going downstairs. She simply was not.

Chapter Five

'Will your stepdaughter be joining us for dinner?' Peter asked, glancing at the empty chair at the far end of the long dining table. It was oddly placed since the chairs they sat in were close together at the opposite end.

His hostess appeared to suck in a breath, then release it in a slow, barely concealed hiss. In an instant, her expression transformed, the corners of her mouth perking up in a smile. Even her cheeks blushed a congenial pink shade.

'I do hope so, but I fear she will not even though she has returned.'

'Is she ill?' Anna Liese had not seemed to be a few hours ago, but the question bore asking.

'Healthy as can be—however, she is a bit of a shrinking violet. Mercy knows I have tried to draw her out of it. As old as she is, she still rejects the suitors I introduce to her. Perhaps she simply distrusts men. Some ladies do.'

'You cannot blame her, I suppose,' Mildred said, her fork halfway to her mouth. 'Poor Anna Liese withdrew into herself after dear Papa married my mother. It must have been a sad thing to discover her own father preferred my company to hers. I tried to tell her it was not so. Still, discovering such a thing is bound to influence a young girl.'

He could not imagine this was true. Anna Liese and her father had shared a close and loving bond. The man he remembered had always been devoted to his child. But years had passed, people did change, so perhaps it was true.

It hurt to think that his sweet friend had grown to be a recluse. If she had, it might go some way to explaining why she had been sleeping in his deserted cottage. Perhaps she was avoiding visitors.

Mildred chewed her food, her expression elated. It was odd, but she gave the impression of savouring the bite as if it might be her last. The woman was not terribly attractive, with narrow eyes set in a round, cheeky face. She was saved from being homely by a pretty smile, though.

How sincere was that smile? he wondered. He had no way of knowing whether she would give Peter Penneyjons the same coy attention she gave Viscount Cliverton. Both Mildred and her mother were attempting to win him over, of that he had no doubt. He did not judge them for it, naturally. It was a lady's role in society to marry as high as she might.

He had a role as well when it came to marriage, which made him no different than Mildred and her mother were. But since he had no intention of considering marriage until after his business here was completed, the Baroness and her daughter were wasting their efforts.

'I fear we will simply have to carry on without Anna Liese,' Lady Barlow said cheerily.

'Good evening, everyone.'

Pivoting in his chair at the sound of the voice, Peter saw

the most beautiful woman imaginable standing in the doorway. Truly, she had to be. Dressed in a gown that looked like pink froth floating about her shoulders and feet, with a white rose tucked into her hair at her temple, she was ethereal.

Earlier, when he'd come upon her by the stream, she had stolen his breath. In this instant she did it again, only this time he was certain he would not get it back.

'Good evening, Anna Liese.' He stood to greet her.

The footman pulled out the chair at the far end of the table as if it was where she was to sit. Did Peter imagine the brief, but smug glance the fellow shot the Baroness? And her even briefer nod?

'If you please, bring the chair to this end of the table,' Peter instructed.

'Yes, my lord,' the footman answered, then carried the chair and set it down next to Mildred.

'How lovely that you could attend dinner, Anna Liese.' Lady Barlow maintained her smile and her happy blush—however, the welcome was oddly absent from her eyes.

'Lovely, as always,' Mildred muttered, casting a sidelong frown at her stepsister.

'Please accept my apologies for being late.' Anna Liese melted his heart with her smile before she turned her attention to Lady Barlow.

'It was reported that there was a fox disturbing the hens. It turned out not to be true.' Anna Liese cast the Baroness an odd, speculative glance. 'Whoever reported the warning was mistaken. But rest assured, the hens are content and we will have eggs for breakfast.'

As much as he would like to devote his attention solely to Anna Liese it would not be appropriate, so he turned the conversation to one of his favourite subjects: bicycle racing. Surely speaking of his visit to George Singer and Son's establishment, where the newest in bicycles were made and distributed, would distract everyone from Anna Liese's late arrival. Her family was clearly annoyed with her and he supposed her tardiness was the reason why.

While he told them about the Anerley Bicycle Club, he kept part of his attention on the sisters. Watching them, he found it difficult to imagine that Baron Barlow had shown a preference for Mildred over Anna Liese. It simply did not fit with the man he remembered.

Apparently bored with talk of bicycles, Mildred said, 'Your hair looks especially pretty tonight, Sister. Martha must have spent a good deal of time seeing it so nicely styled. And a rose to go with it.'

'Your hair looks lovely, too, Mildred.' Looking at Anna Liese's smile, Peter was certain she meant it.

'Oh, yes. Martha did not spend nearly the time on mine as she did on yours. But of course, she would not need to. Isn't that right, Mother?'

'Oh, my dear. You have the loveliest hair of anyone in Woodlore Glen. It has been remarked upon over and over again.'

Love was blind, people liked to say. It must be especially true when it came to one's daughter.

Anyone with eyes could see that Anna Liese's hair looked like sunshine even with only lamplight to illuminate it. Not that there was anything wrong with Mildred's hair, but since she had brought it to the fore of conversation, he could not help but notice the difference.

The meal passed in pleasant conversation. At least he thought so, but that might have to do with how pleasant he felt inside himself. Being in Anna Liese's company again after all these years made him want to grin. It was going to be a delight over the next few weeks getting to know her again.

'Would you care to join us for breakfast, Lord Cliverton?' Lady Barlow asked with a bright smile—and a wink? Yes, that is exactly what it had been, a wink. 'Apparently we will have eggs.'

'As lovely as that would be, I fear I have burdened your staff far too much already.'

'I'm certain they do not find their jobs to be a burden,' Mildred stated.

'Nevertheless, I will take breakfast in the village.'

Now that it was time to return to the cottage, he found he did not wish to. Not because he would be drenched before he dashed halfway across the bridge, but because he did not wish to lose Anna Liese's company.

Looking at her, watching her smile and hearing her voice, he was beginning to remember how life had been for him as a carefree child…how innocent and happy he had been in the time before death altered their lives.

'Anna Liese,' he said when Mildred and her mother seemed to be involved in a discussion about the rain. 'We have much to catch up on. Would it be appropriate for me to ask you to join me for breakfast at the inn in the village?'

For all that being alone with her was not quite acceptable, it did feel the most natural thing in the world. Feeling the other ladies' attention shift to him, he added, 'All of you ladies, I mean.'

'What a grand idea!' Lady Barlow declared, clapping her thin fingers. 'We shall be happy to join you.'

He was not certain Anna Liese thought so. She smiled at him, but he read hesitation in her eyes.

'I would like that,' she said.

'Good, then.' He stood to take his leave, greatly regretting that he had been required to extend his invitation to them all. At some point he would find time to be alone with his friend. There was so much to talk about without the other ladies to divide his attention.

'I was all but forced to go downstairs to dinner, Fannie.' Swimming, the goose kept pace with Anna Liese while she walked on the stream's bank. 'After Martha went to the trouble of going out in the rain and picking a rose to put in my hair, it would have appeared ungrateful had I not. Not to mention what a waste of a lovely flower it would have been. What a wonder it was to find one this late in the year.'

Fannie dipped her head underwater, came up with a waterweed, then gobbled it down. She shook the water off her beak, giving a loud, strident honk.

'It was picked from an old bush Mama planted so you see what sort of a situation I was in.'

Fannie waddled out of the stream, honking again. Anna Liese stooped down, swiping water from the bird's feathers with a flick of her fingers.

Those were excuses, not reasons. She wanted to go down and so she had. There was no point in pretending there was any reason for it but that she wanted to see Peter again. So down she had gone to dinner, feeling something of a princess thanks to Martha's effort.

She had been all but chilled by the frigid reception she got from Stepmama, although the woman had done her best to hide it from her exalted guest. It was hard to think of Peter as exalted, but she imagined many people did.

Standing, she walked on, the goose waddling beside her. 'Honestly, I was not all that sorry for sending Stepmama into a mood. But, why am I explaining this to a goose when I ought to be explaining it to Peter? It is time I owned up to sleeping in his bed. If I do, perhaps we will find a way to strike up our friendship again. That would be…' She stopped walking, gazing at blue sky broken by a single white cloud drifting west. What a pretty backdrop to imagine ways a renewed friendship would be wonderful…ways it would be different.

Leaving the goose at the water's edge, Anna Liese proceeded to cross the stone bridge spanning the water between Maplewood and Peter's cottage.

If she did try to rekindle a friendship, she must accept that it would not be the same as it had been years ago. She was not who she had been and neither was he. Oh, indeed he was not. All night long she had been restless, comparing the differences between the boy and the man.

Pausing to stand on a point exactly halfway across the bridge, she listened to the wind playfully whistling through bare branches. A single yellow leaf blew off and tumbled across the surface of the water where it was caught, then floated away.

Standing where she was, she knew she must make a decision: keep her distance from Peter as best she could or continue across the bridge and knock on his front door. She did not know if renewing their friendship was for the best or not. Things might not be the same between them as they had been. And if they were not, the memory of what had been between them could be tainted.

Nonetheless, she needed to know. The affection they shared might remain and, given time, it might become even better. The seeds of a lifelong friendship had been planted when they were children. Had they never been separated, what would their lives be like now?

Taking a long, slow breath, she shook her head. The past could not be changed and the future had yet to happen. All she had was this moment and what was she going to do in it? Over the years she had crossed this bridge hundreds of times—why was it so difficult this time?

She could tell herself that it was because she was about to become hugely embarrassed when she admitted it was she who had trespassed in his house. While true, it was not the reason she remained standing on the halfway point of the bridge.

Was she willing to risk the memories of the past for what might be in the future? That was what her hesitation came down to. Could she replace her laughing, freckle-faced friend with a stranger who made her feel fluttery when he smiled?

If she chose to knock on that door, things would never be the same. But perhaps they would not be anyway. The fact alone that Peter had come home changed things. Nothing could go back to how it had been. Well then, off she went over the bridge, relieved to have the decision made. What she had set in motion could not be gone back from now.

She raised her hand to rap on the door, but it swung open before her knuckles touched wood.

'You cannot imagine how relieved I am to see you, Anna Liese.'

'You are?'

Even after years of separation her smile felt familiar. It was as if a forgotten flicker of sunshine radiated from his heart.

'How wonderful,' she said.

Indeed, it was wonderful and he was awfully glad to see her.

It had been a disappointment when she had not joined them for breakfast in dining room of the village inn. The meal had become an ordeal with Mildred consuming his attention.

Whenever someone approached to make his acquaintance, she put herself to the fore, giving the impression that she was his close friend and anyone who came between was intruding. It had been beyond troublesome since he did wish to make the acquaintance of people in Woodlore Glen.

'I missed you at breakfast.' He swept his arm in a gesture, indicating she should come inside.

He wondered if she would be offended by the invitation given that they would be unchaperoned in the house. But neither of them was a blushing youth. Besides, since they had spent so much time together as children, to his mind this was not unfitting. Also, with the village over a mile away, strangers did not wander this way so no one would know.

'My cook is still in London so I cannot offer refreshment.' This said, she now knew they would be alone and could gracefully decline if she wished to.

With a nod, she stepped inside.

'Stepmama decided my time this morning would be better spent taking inventory of the pantry, or I would have come.' Her smile brightened the hall far better than the vase of green foliage he had placed on a table beside the front door.

Filling vases was not something he normally did, but his mother had always placed a display of seasonal colour in the hall. Just seeing it gave him the strangest feeling. Longing for her was all he could think it was. He had never got over missing his mother.

'What a lovely way to honour your mother,' Anna Liese said, pausing to touch a sprig of red berries.

His heart took a leap. It was as if in touching the berries, she touched his heart.

'I can scarcely believe you remember.'

'Berries and holly in the winter, daffodils in the spring, roses in the summer, leaves in the autumn. How could I forget?'

'Filling the vase was my way of telling her I remember.'

Seeming at ease, Anna Liese walked ahead of him into the drawing room. It made sense that she would be comfortable in the cottage. Since she had been staying here, she was probably more familiar with it than he was.

'I have always loved this room, Peter.' She sat down on the sofa, spreading her cheerful-looking yellow skirt while glancing about with a smile.

Good, then.

He sat beside her, relieved that her casual attitude set the stage for their renewed friendship to develop naturally and not be stifled by societal rules. Rules such as having a chaperon in attendance at all times. As children, they had tended to ignore rules in favour of fun. Deep in his gut he felt they were still those children, that something remained of who they had been.

'Anna Liese, I must ask you something.' For some reason, she glanced away from him, staring at the rug as if the vined pattern were suddenly mesmerising. 'It has to do with why you were not at breakfast. One would think taking inventory of the pantry would be a job for the cook, not the daughter of the house.'

He could not imagine why, but his question restored her smile.

'You have no idea how offended Mrs Graham would have been had I tried. We passed the time speaking about her grandchildren. Did you know they are the brightest and most handsome children ever born?'

She laughed. The sound soothed the stress of the morning. Even as a small girl she had a way of settling him. How often had he been anxious about something, only to have the very look she was giving him now make the day better?

'I missed you, Anna Liese.' Until this moment he had not understood how deeply he had. Years had gone by without him thinking about her, and now? Now he regretted the years they missed. He ought to have asked his aunt and uncle if she might visit Cliverton.

'Would it have caused a great problem for you to ignore your stepmother and come to breakfast?'

He caught her hand, in a simple, friendly squeeze, but then had to release it. The touch of her warm, smooth fingers cupped in his palms was not all that simple. Indeed, the kick to his heart left him confused.

'It would, of course. My stepmother can become quite cross when her will is thwarted. I imagine Stepmama has rather grand plans for you and Mildred, so be forewarned.' She twirled a strand of hair around one, slim finger. He could not help but stare. It resembled silk around a maypole. How lovely that she did not wear it bound in some frivolous hairstyle. 'It wasn't because of her that I did not come, though. It was because of me. I chose not to join you.'

That statement was a dagger to the heart. He placed his hand flat on his chest in an exaggerated gesture of deflecting pain. Which he did truly feel.

'Oh, but I wanted to. Do not think I was not miserable all morning, imagining what you were suffering in the company of my family.'

'I must admit to being confused.'

'After I have made my confession and offered an apology, it will be clear.'

'I'm sure you have no need to—'

'Peter.' She touched his arm, looking him steadily in the eye. His heart kicked against his ribs.

Suddenly she blinked, sucking in a breath, as if touching him had been—well, he could not guess what she thought of the touch. To him it had felt comforting and exciting at the same time. And still confusing.

He might have also sucked in a sharp but discreet breath.

'Surely you recognise me as being the intruder in your bedroom?'

'I didn't at first, only later. How was I to know it was you? But why did you run away?'

'Because I did not recognise you, either. I thought you were—' Her voice faltered. Her cheeks flared bright pink.

'A pirate?'

'Something of the such.'

'We are a bit inland to be troubled by the likes of them.' She waved her hand as if to dismiss that last odd bit.

'In the event, thank you for bringing my shoes and my cloak.'

'Why were you hiding in the haystack, Anna Liese? If you were afraid of me, why not simply go home?'

'I did go home eventually, once I was certain you were not coming back.'

'Surely you did not think I meant you harm?'

'Not harm in the usual sense of the word. Had I known

who you were, it would have made a difference. I must say, my friend, you have changed a bit over the years.'

'So have you. Had I recognised you, I would have made sure you did not mistake me for a pirate.'

'Neither of us look a bit like we did then.'

For what seemed a long time, they stared silently at each other, no doubt each taking a moment to observe the differences brought by the years.

He admitted he liked the differences he was seeing. While she had grown to be an exquisitely beautiful woman, what did she think of him? He could not help but wonder. Outwardly they had changed—but inside? Pray there was enough of the friendship they used to share to begin again.

Now that he remembered how it had been between them—how she had been as dear to him as his own family—he wanted that again. It would be good to have a friend in Woodlore Glen, a place where he knew no one. There was the Baroness and her daughter, but—

'I don't mind that you were using my house,' he said. 'But I would like to know why you felt a need to.'

For as flattering as it would be to think she had been in his bedroom because she missed him, he doubted that was the case.

'Sometimes a lady has private reasons.' She glanced away when she said it, which made him wonder if she intended to reveal them.

Private was private—he would respect that and not press the matter. Her reasons were her own. Perhaps in time she would confide in him.

'Now that I have confessed my sin, you understand why I could not join you for breakfast. I simply could not face you until there was only truth between us.'

'Think no more of it.' He would because he was intensely curious about her rather vague, private reasons. 'With that out of the way, I could use your help with something.'

Now that he thought about it, she might be a great help to him if she wished to be. Her eyebrows arched in what he hoped was interest. Her eyes flashed brighter blue and her smile—it was exactly the smile he remembered from when they used to find mischief to get into. Young Anna Liese had always enjoyed a bit of fun. It made him happy to know she had not lost that quality.

Although it was not mischief he had in mind, but work. She might not consider helping him renovate the cottage to be of interest.

'I want to revive this place.' He took in the drawing room with a sweep of his hand. 'The whole cottage needs renovating. I could use your advice.'

'Please say you are not renovating it in order to sell it, Peter. If you are, I must say no, I would rather not.'

'Why?'

She shrugged, looking thoughtful. 'I suppose it would feel as if you were selling a part of my past—giving it to strangers.'

'The tenants who lived here in the past were strangers.'

Even though the last thing he wanted was to sell the cottage, he did want to know what she was thinking.

'Only until I made their acquaintance. Over the years I felt that as long as you owned the property, you might return one day. And look, here you are.'

Now he felt like a cad. All this time, she been hoping for him to return, while he had assigned Woodlore Glen a place in the back of his mind. The idea that she had been thinking of him over the years—perhaps trying to keep his memory vivid by living in his house—made him feel something of a worm.

'I have no intention of selling. My past is here, too.' He stood up and walked to the wall. He tapped a finger on the image of a faded flower in the wallpaper. This was only one place the house looked dingy and sad, if a wall could look sad. 'What I plan is to bring my family here for holidays.'

'What a lovely idea.' Once again, the vine on the rug captured her attention. 'I did not hear that you had married. Have you children, too?'

'Not that sort of family. I realise I am late fulfilling my obligation to the marriage market, but I have been occupied with seeing my cousins settled first. Do you recall them? Cornelia, Felicia and Ginny?'

'They visited from time to time. I do remember them, of course. I enjoyed it when they came.'

'Now that I think about it, I remember wishing they would go home so that you and I might resume our romping.'

Anna Liese laughed, which made him feel odd—in a dizzy but pleasant way.

'I recall how I disliked it when you went to visit London. Romping on one's own is not nearly as much fun.'

'What I intend will not be as fun as a romp, but I hope you will help me turn the cottage into a holiday home, a getaway from London.'

'As much as I would enjoy helping you, I do have a concern.'

'I promise I will not occupy all of your time.'

'What I mean is that it must appear as if you are not occupying any of my time. If Stepmama and Mildred discover we spend time together, I cannot tell you the misery that will follow.'

'Because we will be unchaperoned… I do understand. The last thing I wish is to cause you trouble.'

'Chaperoned? Truly, I am not all that concerned about it. I am hardly a blushing, susceptible debutante. It is not me I am concerned about, Peter. It is you. They will make your life unbearable if they know. Believe me, they must never know we are meeting.'

'That adds some adventure to the prospect,' he noted, following her out of the drawing room. 'Clandestine meetings and secret plans.'

He opened the front door, feeling years younger. More carefree than he had been since—well, he could not remember when, but before his uncle died and left him as the new Viscount.

'Are you still an early riser, Peter?'

Knowing she remembered that about him made him warm and fuzzy. Many were the mornings he used to get to the bridge first, watching the sun crest the hilltops while waiting for Anna Liese to emerge from the manor.

'I still do my best work early in the morning.'

'It could work. My stepmother and Mildred sleep late so we will have time.'

He watched her walking away through a last drizzle of late autumn leaves. She had grown graceful over the years. He was certain in the old days that her hips had not swayed in such a manner.

All at once she turned, waved and grinned. For half a second he felt thrown back in time to the boy he had been, but in the next second, he realised her grin was not at all the same. Her lips were rounder, pinker and quite desirable.

Looking back was all very well, but, all things considered, the present was going to be more interesting.

Chapter Six

For as much as Anna Liese would prefer keeping out of the way of her relatives, at some point she would need to go inside the house. The wind was rising, sweeping in a mass of dark, stormy clouds.

Coming in the back door, then through the kitchen, she heard feminine voices issuing from the library. She could not determine what they were saying since the voices seemed to be trying to speak over one another.

Curious, she paused in front of the library door. Bolts of fabric in every imaginable hue and texture were strewn across sofas, chairs and half of the floor.

Anna Liese watched while Woodlore Glen's modiste, Mrs Creamer, held a bolt of fabric underneath Mildred's round chin.

'That colour makes you look ill,' Stepmama announced, dashing the other ladies' comments of approval.

Mildred frowned. Alice, Mrs Creamer's assistant,

dropped the bolt on the floor with a thud while the modiste bit her lip.

Anna Liese did not envy the two women having to do business with Stepmama.

'What we need is a hue to bring a blush to Mildred's bosom. Chartreuse, I think.'

Stepmama never did have an eye for colour, nor was she able to discern the difference between what was becoming and what was ostentatious.

'If I may point out, my lady,' Mrs Creamer put in, 'the bosom should be hidden enough so that one does not know it is blushing. By raising the bodice, one raises the mystery of what is behind the bodice. If there is a blush, it is more properly displayed in the cheeks. Fabric colour can help with that. It can also enhance the eyes which are on display no matter the cut of the gown. Hold up the ivory, Alice.'

'I have chosen chartreuse, and chartreuse I shall have.' Next thing, Stepmama was going to stamp her foot and pout.

'As you wish, naturally, but I assure you that some skin tones call for bright shades and some for subtle.'

'Are you suggesting that Mildred is not attractive in both? Surely you must agree that wearing such a pale shade as ivory will cause my daughter to fade into the wallpaper. Our gentleman will not fail to notice her in the bright one.'

Oh, dear, poor Mildred would be seen, just not in the way the Baroness intended. Clearly it was what the dressmaker wished to point out, but did not dare. Speaking one's mind to Stepmama was rarely worth the ill temper sure to follow so the woman usually got her way.

Taking pity on them, Anna Liese entered the library, stepping carefully over rejected bolts of fabric. Hopefully, a new presence would change the mood in the room.

'Good afternoon,' she said, giving each woman a smile. 'New gowns? Are we having a grand event, Stepmama?'

'A small event, to welcome Viscount Cliverton to Woodlore Glen.'

'How thoughtful.' How calculating. 'When will it be?'

'Soon. Our Viscount returns to London before Christmas.'

'And I have not had a new gown since, oh, I cannot recall when,' Mildred said, casting a frown at Anna Liese as if, somehow, her presence interfered with it.

'Three weeks ago,' Anna Liese supplied helpfully.

'Yes!' Alice exclaimed. 'It was a lovely thing. Rose with ivory stripes. I remember because I spent until the wee hours sewing the hem.'

'It's an adequate gown,' Mildred admitted, pushing the another bolt away from her face. 'But now that we will be frequently entertaining Lord Cliverton, I will require something more elegant.'

Frequently? Peter was here only for a short time. Did they mean to commandeer every moment of it?

'Something chartreuse,' Stepmama persisted.

Anna Liese wondered if she had failed to notice the grimace which shot between Mrs Creamer and Alice.

The women had vast experience at dressing ladies and, in Anna Liese's opinion, they were wise to advise a colour other than bright, glaring green.

'I've a solution, perhaps. Stepmama, you are right about the colour being beautiful and that Mildred will shine wearing it. However, taken all at once it is intense.' Anna Liese stooped to snatch up a bolt of fabric near her foot. 'What if we use this lovely cream lace for the body of the gown and accent it with a chartreuse border and sash?'

She swirled a swathe of lace in the lamplight to show off its sheen.

'That way Lord Cliverton will remark on how pretty Mildred is rather than how pretty the gown is,' she said, noticing a flash of hope cross Mildred's expression.

'Hmm…yes, then. I suppose that might do. Just be sure that you add chartreuse to the bodice. The pink of Mildred's maidenly blush will look outstanding with green.'

Oh, dear, poor Mildred and her blushing maidenly bosom. For all that she and her stepsister were not close—not even allies most of the time—she did feel sorry for her.

'And what colour gown shall we make for you, Anna Liese?' Mrs Creamer declared. 'It has been ever so long since we have designed one for you and you have the prettiest figure—I quite enjoy sewing your gowns.'

Glancing about with a smile, the dressmaker clearly did not notice Stepmama's scowl.

'Here we are!' Alice picked up a bolt of blue satin the shade of the sky on a summer afternoon. She draped it across Anna Liese's shoulder.

'Why, it does look stunning with your hair,' the designer pointed out.

'That one is for Mildred.' Even if Stepmama had dismissed the fabric a moment ago, it was not to go to her stepsister.

'I look pitiful in blue, Mother—you know I do.'

'If you insist on having a new gown, Anna Liese, you may have the grey silk on that bolt in the corner.'

While the rest of them turned their attention to the creation of yet one more gown, Anna Liese quietly left the library. She was only steps down the hallway when Alice came after her.

'It is not a horrible shade of grey,' she whispered. 'And once I adorn it with what is left of the blue, you will hardly notice the grey at all.'

Anna Liese suspected Peter would not know the difference between a new gown and an old one, let alone which colour combinations worked. He was not the sort to entertain fashion as uppermost in his mind.

Since it was uppermost in Alice's mind, Anna Liese said, 'Thank you, Alice. I have no doubt it will be the most beautiful gown I own and a great credit to your skill.'

'It is my pleasure, Miss Barlow. I will make sure you are the loveliest lady at the Christmas ball.'

'Christmas ball? Are we to host a ball? I thought it was a welcome dinner.'

Alice must have realised she had revealed something she ought not to have because she blushed.

'Your stepmother discovered that Lord Cliverton is holding a Christmas ball in London. She is ordering gowns in anticipation of being invited. I fear I have said too much.'

'The Baroness will not hear it from me.'

With a nod, which seemed quite relieved, Alice returned to her duties in the library.

Anna Liese dashed upstairs to her bedroom where she intended to remain for the rest of the afternoon and evening. A Christmas ball in London? Peter should not have let that be known. He would not have a moment's peace until he added both Stepmama and Mildred to the guest list. As for Anna Liese? She was content not to attend a grand ball. She imagined London would be interesting, but Woodlore Glen was where she preferred to be.

Spending a rainy evening in her room, going over this idea and that for the cottage, seemed delightful to her. She was anxious to jot them down and picture the result in her mind. Also, to imagine Peter's smile when she offered her suggestions. A smile which was different from the one she recalled from their childhood years. While she had always been delighted in his boyish grin, she was now delighted and fascinated.

A flash of white light blazed beyond Anna Liese's eyelids. Lightning brought her from deep sleep to awareness.

Awareness of someone touching her hair!

Feeling the slight tug, hearing the bare whisper of the strands shifting between someone's fingers, she kept her eyes closed, feigning sleep. If this was an intruder bent on impugning her virtue, he smelled intensely of rosewater.

Mildred's preferred scent.

Thunder rolled over the roof, barely covering the sound of a metallic click. Snip, snip, snip, she heard inches away from her ear.

Lurching out of bed, she saw her stepsister's face illuminated in another flare of lightning. Mildred's jaw fell open, her narrow eyes blinking as if she were confused to be standing in Anna Liese's chamber.

Anna Liese snatched the scissors from her hand. 'Were you going to cut my hair?'

'I suppose...' she stammered, an odd, startled look on her face. 'Yes, I did mean to. But...then you woke up.'

'Truly, Mildred?' Handing back the scissors, then gathering her hair into a hank, she extended it, calling her sister's bluff—hopefully calling her bluff. 'Here it is if you want it so badly.'

Mildred looked at the scissors, then glanced at the offering. 'What do you want it for?'

She let out a long sigh which sputtered her lips. 'I don't want it. But I don't want you to have it either.'

Mildred sat down hard on the bed, setting the scissors beside her on the mattress. Anna Liese sat down next to her.

'I realise we are not close, Mildred—but this? Did Stepmama tell you to do it?'

Mildred shook her head, silently denying it. 'Had I gone through with it, she would have had a raging fit. How would she explain such a scandal?'

'Do you think we might find some common ground? Trying to keep from being bullied by your mother, I mean?'

'It is true, Mama is a bully. But if she did not bully you, I would be hidden in your pretty shadow. If she did not bully me, I would probably remain there. So, I will do what I can to marry to her wishes, in part to be away from her. What a wonder that the Viscount seems to have fallen neatly into my lap.' Mildred tapped her cheek in thought. 'But I wonder why you do not do the same—not with Lord Cliverton—but what is so awful about Mr Grant? The banker would have you.'

'I have no wish to marry him, but I thought you might.'

'Would it matter if I did? The man is smitten with me, of course, but he has no social position. Surely you see that our neighbour is a far better choice.'

'What about love?'

'What about it? Love can fade, but being Viscountess, that will last.'

This was by far the longest and most heartfelt conversation they'd had since they were small. Not friendly, but they were speaking of their feelings honestly.

Mildred started to stand, but Anna Liese caught her hand.

'Your mother is right, you know. You do have very pretty hair.'

'Mouse brown. It wants to go every which way regardless of how it is styled.' Mildred snorted. 'It is your hair everyone comments on. Light and sparkly as sunshine—it is enough to make one ill to be compared to you.'

Sadly, what she said was true. Thoughtless comparisons had been made over the years.

'Tell me something, Mildred. Do you think Isabella Haverton is beautiful?'

'Everyone says so. Yes, I think she is.'

'And yet she has no suitors. But look at Olivia Green—she is modest in beauty and yet has half a dozen men seeking her hand.'

'Please, do not preach to me that "beauty is only skin deep". Men are rather aware of beautiful skin.'

'It is true, some are shallow that way. What I was pointing out is that Olivia smiles and Isabella does not. Everyone responds to a smile.'

Mildred stood, grabbed the scissors and gripped them in her fist. 'I may not have your winning smile, but you, my dear sister, are every bit the spinster that I am.'

Evidently Mildred missed her point, or ignored it.

'You do have a winning smile! You simply need to use it.'

'Simply? Really, Anna Liese, what do I have to smile about with you sucking up all the attention?'

With that, Mildred stamped towards the bedroom door. Yanking it open, she stood for a moment. Thunder rolled over the roof and rain beat down hard. Her stepsister gave her a look, one which Anna Liese had never seen before.

'I apologise for nearly cutting your hair.' That said, she clicked the door closed behind her.

Stunned, Anna Liese sat on the bed blinking, her jaw in danger of an unladylike drop. While she could not pretend there was anything resembling friendship between them, they had spoken from their hearts. And this was the first time Mildred had ever apologised to her—or perhaps to anyone.

Although last night's rain continued to fall, Peter stood on the bridge, sheltering under a large black umbrella. He supposed it would have been more sensible to wait for Anna Liese inside, but for some reason he wanted to do it here, on the spot they used to meet as children, and at the time they used to meet.

Somewhere beyond these storm clouds the sun was rising. While he and Anna Liese had not assigned a precise time to meet, he hoped she would remember their schedule of old and come dancing out of the manor as she used to do.

Ah, just there! The door opened. Out she came, not dancing and twirling as in the past, but huddled under an umbrella and carrying a basket. Bless her if she had thought to bring breakfast. Once the rain stopped, he would need go to the village and buy a few things, then hope he could work out how to combine them into some sort of edible state.

Perhaps he would send a telegram, asking his cook to come and bring one or two of the maids. The cottage was large, having been an inn before his father purchased it, but not nearly big enough to summon more than those few. He was not sure that even those few could be spared with all the bustle of getting ready for the ball.

For all that he would like to have his cook here, he did not mind it being only him and Anna Liese this morning, especially if she was going to feed him.

Breathless from the dash over, she handed him the basket. 'Good morning, Peter! I am bursting with ideas for your cottage. I can hardly wait to tell you of them.'

'Over breakfast.' Judging by the aroma lifting from the cloth over the basket, he was in for a treat. 'We can eat and talk if you don't mind.'

Her cheeks being nipped with cold looked pink and fresh. Excitement made her eyes bluer than he had ever seen them. 'I don't mind, but let's get out of the rain.' She was laughing when she said so. Some people complained about foul weather. As he recalled, young Anna Liese had never been a complainer. He was glad to find she still was not.

As anxious as he was to get a start on restoring the cottage, he was more anxious to get reacquainted with his neighbour.

By the time they reached the front door, Anna Liese's face was dotted with raindrops. She blinked dampness off her eyelashes. Suddenly breakfast was not as urgent as it had been. If he could, he would simply stand in the hall and watch her sparkle in the glow of the lamp he had left burning against the dimness of the morning.

Ah, but it was not to be because she folded her umbrella, then wiped her hand across her face.

'There is a fire in the drawing room hearth. Shall we have breakfast in there?'

She nodded, so he hurried to the drawing room, dragged over a small table and placed it in front of the fireplace. Then he carried over a couple of chairs.

He could not recall a time when the drawing room had looked cosier. The vision he had had of his old home was of it being homely and warm. This was just how he remembered it. Beginning with Christmas, this would be a happy spot for the family to gather, play games and laugh.

He was anxious to discover what Anna Liese's thoughts on it were. He hoped her taste did not run to the formal. Cliverton was formal in its common areas. He did not wish the same for the cottage since it was not meant to entertain the public.

Coming back to the hall, he slipped her coat from her shoulders, hanging it on a rack to drip and dry.

Anna Liese walked into the drawing room ahead of him which gave him a moment to simply look at her, watch how she moved with such grace and confidence.

As a child she had been confident, but her grace had been more of a gangly sort. Perfect for a child, but now she was—

'This is lovely, Peter, so warm and inviting. It's this area which has been on my mind all night.' She withdrew a sheet of paper from a pocket of her skirt. 'I have made notes on my thoughts.'

She'd made notes? Part of the reason he had asked for her help—a great part—was because he wanted an excuse to spend time with her, to get to know her again.

'Are you certain you do not feel awkward being here without a chaperon? Society would frown on this meeting.'

'Society is in London. The only ones who will care about it here are asleep and will not know.'

'If you are certain.'

'I would not be here if I were not. Let us speak no more about it.'

That would suit him since he was finding it difficult to recognise that their relationship should change from what it had been.

Sitting across from her, he could not help watching her

hands while she unwrapped their breakfast from the napkins, such slim, graceful hands, lyrical in their movement. He nearly chuckled aloud at himself. He was not usually as poetic as to make up mental odes to long, lovely fingers, or to anything else. What he must keep in mind was that her reason for being here was practical, to be a helpful neighbour.

Nothing more.

If he forgot that, began to wonder about the way her lips had grown fuller and her slim little figure was no longer so slim, he ran the risk of feeling things he refused to feel. Risk a sort of grief he refused to feel again.

While it could not be denied that Anna Liese had grown to be an exquisitely beautiful woman, she was and would continue to be his neighbour, his pretty and ever-helpful neighbour.

'I appreciate your help. And breakfast. It was kind of you to think of bringing it.'

She smiled while spreading jam on toast. 'That is to Mrs Graham's credit. She rose in the wee hours to prepare it—all I did was put it into this basket.'

'Wasn't Mrs Graham here when we were children? As I recall, she used to pack us bags of biscuits for our daily romps.'

'She was. A few of the staff you knew are still here.'

'It was good back then, wasn't it?' He thought about it for a moment, during which he forgot about the clotted cream piled on his spoon. 'Your family and mine got along so well. We were lucky, I think. Not everyone is as blessed as we were with our families.'

'It is because we had parents who loved one another. It

makes all the difference in a child's life. I have lived it both ways, Peter, so I know of what I speak.'

Recalling the clotted cream ready to plop from his spoon, he spread it on a scone.

'I'm sorry that your father did not find joy in his second marriage. I think, perhaps, you did not find joy in it either.'

'Papa married because he was lonely and Stepmama gave every appearance of being the answer to his sadness. He did not recognise that she only married him because he was titled.'

'It's not uncommon to wed for social position.' He would be doing it soon, after all. 'Such a thing does not exclude a satisfactory marriage.'

Indeed not. He reaffirmed his stance that it was better to wed for satisfaction rather than to invest one's heart in a wife who could be ripped from him in death.

'That is all well and good if one wishes to settle for satisfactory. But, Peter, you and I have seen what a happy marriage is. We have experienced the affection when a family is founded upon it.'

'One does not always have a choice.' Or might wish to choose a safer way.

'Of course one does and I have made it. I refuse to marry for any reason but love.'

'I cannot imagine that there have not been dozens of men in love with you over the years, Anna Liese.'

'Not as many as you might think—besides, there was never one whom I was in love with.'

'You've never been in love?'

She blinked, then glanced away.

'Perhaps once.' She shooed her fingers as if she did not wish to discuss a former swain. 'What about you? Have you been in love? I would think dozens of ladies would be infatuated with you.'

'With my title only. As I said, I haven't pursued marriage because I felt it best to see my cousins wed first.'

'I hope you did not force them into anything. A woman ought to be able to choose her course.'

'As if I could force them into anything. Of them only Cornelia wed at a proper pace. Felicity rushed headlong into a marriage arranged for her when she was a child. You will be happy to know I did not force her into it, but rather advised caution. She and her husband are in love. Then Ginny! Do you happen to recall how shy she was?'

'She did cling to your mother's skirts rather than play with us.'

'She eloped with her childhood sweetheart, a fellow she had not seen in years. I missed the wedding.'

She tapped her lovely, slender finger on the table for a moment, then said, 'I am happy for them all. Perhaps you will be as lucky one day and find a wonderful stranger to love.'

He would guard against it. Better to find an acceptable stranger to admire—to respect. For all that his cousins had married for love, he most fervently prayed they did not live to regret the risk to their hearts.

'More than likely it will be a proper marriage to a proper lady. As Viscount, I do not see myself indulging in a grand passion in my search for a wife.'

Rain beat on the windows while they ate in silence. Clearly their expectations for marital bliss were not the same. If his cousins were here in the room, they would tell him, *Peter, you must not close off your heart to love.* That was exactly what they would say. He nearly glanced about to see if they were here.

'If you wish to fill this home with the joy it used to have, you will need happy children which come from a happy marriage.'

'I didn't say I would not have a happy marriage, only that it was not likely to begin with a mad passion.' For a second, he looked at her lips where she licked a smear of jam from her finger, wondering if he should say what was truly on his mind. Since she was comfortable enough to do so, he said, 'I hope you do not live a lonely life because you refuse to settle for anything less than a mad passion.'

'I hope for exactly that, Peter.' And then she grinned at him. 'Now, how many people do you anticipate gathering in this room? With the way your cousins are so happily wed, I expect there will be plenty of children. It seems to me you will need more sofas.'

Sharing a modest breakfast in front of the drawing room fireplace with Peter had been better than a feast. They had shared more than mere food. To simply sit with him in quiet conversation, to discuss ideas for the redecoration of his cottage, was simply bliss.

Beginning the day knowing that tomorrow they would go the village to hire a painter, and visit the carpenter to make some furniture, made the day bright.

Even the weather seemed to be reacting to her mood. Walking over the bridge, she watched rainclouds scatter, revealing bright blue patches of sky. Still, it was chilly and the breeze stiff.

Hurrying in the front door, she came face to face with Stepmama, who was scowling at her.

'And where have you been, miss?'

'Visiting my friend.'

Stepmama's face flushed and the tip of her nose pulsed the bright red shade it took when she was angry.

'You must under no circumstances visit Lord Cliverton!'

'The Viscount? I was spending time with my goose.' It was partly the truth. Fannie had been there waiting for her when she stepped out of the cottage. 'We took a short walk together. It was brisk and lovely.'

'I'm sure it was, although I do not understand how one can form a friendship with something which is not even human.'

'We should get a dog, Stepmama. A pup will teach you how it is entirely possible.'

The Baroness snorted. 'Absolutely not. I have no wish to make friends with the fleas and ticks which come with a dog.'

Mildred had wanted a dog desperately when she was a child, but had been refused repeatedly.

'I require your help with something, my dear.' Oh, no. What was the woman up to now? 'You have such lovely penmanship and I need you to write out the invitations to our modest dinner to honour Lord Cliverton. Come to the library.'

She sat down at the secretary, quickly jotting down the details of the invitations as Stepmama recited them. Then she made note of the names to go on the invitations.

To her surprise, it really was a smallish gathering with only about twenty people invited. How interesting to note that there were no young ladies among the guests. When she thought about it further, she realised it was not surprising after all. Stepmama would not want any young lady to compete for Peter's attention except Mildred.

'The guest list seems unbalanced, Stepmama.' It was

bound to be embarrassingly apparent why. 'Perhaps you should add Lord Hampton and his family.'

'Lord Hampton has two eligible daughters, both of them quite lovely.'

She heard the quiet rustle of fabric coming from the hallway. Glancing up, Anna Liese spotted the hem of her stepsister's gown barely visible where it peeped out from behind the frame.

'But you have no need to worry. They are not as pretty as Mildred is,' she said because her stepsister had to be feeling cut by her mother's words. 'Their presence will only serve to show her off.'

She would like to point out that in the event Stepmama managed to secure invitations to Peter's Christmas ball, there would be many lovely ladies in attendance and every one of them with matrimony on her mind.

Not that she could point such a thing out, since she was not supposed to know about the ball. Peter had not even mentioned it to her. Perhaps the reason he had not was because Woodlore Glen seemed a thousand miles away from London and his mind was not on the matters of Cliverton.

But for all that London seemed so distant, in truth it was an easy train ride which took less than half a day. The distance she was thinking of had more to do with the way life was lived. The peace of Woodlore Glen must be vastly different than the bustle of a London street. Although she could not say for certain, having never been to London.

'I'm looking forward to our little gathering,' Anna Liese said even though she assumed, when the time came, she would not be in attendance. Her stepmother would find a way to make sure she was not. 'What a nice way for the Viscount to become acquainted with our neighbours.'

Having said that, she knew that between now and then she would need to be wary. Just because Mr Grant had not succeeded in trapping her the other night did not mean he would stop trying. Although he was as handsome as the day was long, she did not believe him to be patient, let alone honest. He was a shifty-eyed fellow of low moral character, in her opinion.

Now that she had lost her hiding place, she must be more cautious than ever.

'Have them ready by morning.' Stepmama started to go out of the library, but stopped just outside the doorway. Apparently Mildred was no longer standing in the hallway. 'I would have Mildred help you, but we are dining at the inn tonight with Lord Cliverton.'

'How lovely. Please give Peter my regards.'

'Really, Anna Liese! You must not call him Peter, Lord Cliverton is the appropriate address.'

'But we have known each other since we were quite small,' she answered without looking up. 'He will think it odd if I call him that.'

'Nevertheless, you will address him by his title.'

When they met in the morning, she was going to call him Peter and it would feel the most natural thing in the world.

'You are correct, of course,' she answered.

It was unlikely that Stepmama was pacified by her apparent acquiescence. Indeed, no more than Anna Liese was fooled into believing that when her stepmother used the words 'my dear' it was a term of endearment.

The woman was cunning and, no doubt about it, Annaliese's freedom from matrimony depended upon which, of the two of them, was more cunning.

Chapter Seven

A gust of wind whistled past the window of the village tea-room, making the table beside it seem snug. Peter was grateful that the place opened so early for tea and light breakfast.

He and Anna Liese would be finished before the laya-beds at Maplewood roused themselves. The last thing he wished was to cause Anna Liese trouble for helping him.

'Christmas is coming,' Peter remarked. 'One can nearly smell it in the air.'

'Only three more weeks.' Anna Liese's smile made him feel as cheerful as the morning sunshine streaming through the lace curtain. 'Soon the shops will be putting holly and berries in the windows. Do you remember that?'

He did! It came back to him how cheerful everything had felt at this time of year. There had always been the anticipation of a visit from Father Christmas which made everything sparkle.

'Holly and mistletoe?' Joy and carols. 'I do remember now. I kissed your hand under the mistletoe once.'

'I remember it, too! Our parents were looking on, laughing at how sweet we were.'

'Sweet? I felt mischievous.'

'For us back then, mischief was sweet.'

The waitress carried a tray to their table, setting down two cups of hot chocolate along with a vase of holly and berries.

'It's as if you summoned Christmas cheer, Anna Liese.'

She tapped a red berry nestled in the greenery with the tip of one finger. 'Abracadabra.'

Her quiet laugh sounded like Christmas bells. There he went being poetic again, which was not like him in the least. Next thing, he was going to pluck that sprig of holly and place it in the buttonhole of his coat.

He had not anticipated feeling particularly festive this year. Not with the obligation of finding a viscountess pressing upon him. Especially not with his cousins off and married, leaving Cliverton absent of family. Yet here he sat, feeling light-hearted. It could only have to do with the woman sitting across from him.

'May I tell you something, Anna Liese?' He did not wait for her answer. 'I've missed our friendship more than I ever realised.'

He caught her hand, giving it a friendly squeeze. His heart rolled over at the feel of her hand squeezing back. He should not touch her. It never turned out to feel as casual as he meant it to be. If she had not been blushing when she lifted her cup of chocolate, he might have been able to breathe.

'To lost friendship being rekindled,' she said, lifting her mug in salute.

He picked up his cup in answering salute, took a sip of

warm, rich sweetness, unable to deny that it was how she made him feel. Warm and sweet.

'Who could have imagined that choosing wallpaper and paint would be amusing?' he said, steering the conversation to the practical.

'We shall see about that. We might yet come to blows over whether the drawing room wallpaper should be green or yellow.'

'Blue.' Because that would remind him of her eyes. He suspected blue was becoming his favourite colour.

'Blue might be—'

A movement caught his eye. A gentleman pedalled industriously past the window on a bicycle.

'Come, Anna Liese!' He stood up, reached across the table and snatched her hand.

'Sit down, Peter. I see the waitress coming with our food.'

'I'll ask her to pack it up in a basket.'

'But—'

'Look!' He pointed across the street at the village shop. 'It is opening up.'

'As it usually does this time of morning.'

'But do you see what is in the window? Come, we are going cycling.'

Half an hour later, Anna Liese was the proud owner of a bicycle which she had no idea what to do with.

'You expect me to sit on this?' Not likely. 'I'll tip over.'

'Trust me, I won't let you fall.'

That remained to be seen, but at least they were on the little-travelled path which meandered around the outside of the village so if she did fall no one was likely to witness it. Still, she would rather remain upright.

'Ha! Like the time I was carrying a basket of eggs and you said you would not let me fall off the skinny plank crossing the stream? You said "trust me" then, too.'

'Did I?' He looked puzzled while he seemed to be searching for the memory. He shrugged, apparently not recalling the mess the basket of broken eggs had made. 'This time you can trust me. Watch this.'

With a great grin he mounted his new bicycle, then rode about in front of her, manoeuvring expertly in large circles, then small ones, cutting a figure-of-eight shape, and how proud of himself he seemed while riding backwards.

'It's easy.' He grinned.

Responding to his enthusiasm was easy, but getting on that risky, wheeled vehicle, that did not appear easy.

'For you. You're a member of a bicycle club and are clearly accomplished at dashing about. I am more confident of getting from here to there on my feet.'

He set his bike against a tree.

'Here, I'm going to help you.'

He held the bike steady. She could hardly refuse to try it even though she was certain to fail.

'No need to look so frightened. This is not one of those old-fashioned vehicles. It has pneumatic tyres. They are filled with air. It's a Rover bicycle with a chain drive.'

'I'm sure that is impressive, and I am grateful for the gift, but, Peter—' Suddenly the bike rolled.

She screeched, then grabbed his arms where they firmly steadied the contraption. It was on her tongue to demand he let her off, but then that would mean she would no longer feel his arms braced about her. They felt too strong and reliable to be let go of. Oh, but they were more than that. The strength made her feel excited as much as—no, more than—safe. She wanted nothing more than to lean into them and sigh.

'I won't let go until you have the hang of it.'

For all that she feared it, she thought perhaps she would not rush to learn the skill.

Being so close, she felt his breath near her cheek, heard air rushing in and out of his lungs as he trotted alongside her. She took a deep, discreet sniff. Beside her was a man, one who was not a thing like the boy she remembered. She knew the boy quite well, but who was this man he had grown into?

In truth, he was a stranger, one who at the moment held her life in his hands and was laughing over the fact. After years of waiting and watching for his return, she could scarce believe it had happened, that he actually here. Perhaps this was a dream and when she fell off the bicycle she would wake up, startled and alone.

'Are you beginning to feel your balance?'

Quite the opposite. What she felt was off balance. A woman would need to be made of marble to not react to the heat pulsing from his body.

Balance, indeed!

'I'm not meant for this,' she gasped in the instant he let go.

'You've got it!' he shouted while chasing after her.

She imagined he was waving his arms madly and whooping, but she did not dare to turn her head and look. Being on a downhill slope, she could not stop even had she wanted to, which she quite desperately, did.

But then—

Suddenly, amazingly, she did feel her balance. Oh, what a grand sensation! It was as if she were flying. She had never moved so fast in her life. She was like a bird winging joyfully along.

Until something jerked. Oh, no! The safety bike with its air-filled tyres hit a stone. The handlebars wobbled madly. The next she knew she was sitting on top of a pile of leaves and twigs, her arms and legs every which way, her skirt tangled about her knees and her petticoat exposed.

Peter was bent over at the waist, hands on his knees while laughing his noble head off.

'You did splendidly, Anna Liese.'

'I am lying in a bramble patch, in case you have not noticed.' In truth, it was not a bramble patch, merely a shrub. However, something sharp was poking her rump.

Rather than helping her up, Peter sat down next to her. 'I can't tell you how many times I've ended up just like this.'

'You could not have! Otherwise, you would not choose to get on that thing again.'

'Tell me the truth, Anna Liese. You felt liberated, like you were flying.'

She turned her face away, silent because he was correct and she did not wish for him to know he was.

His fingers touched her chin, turned it so that she could do nothing but look into his eyes.

'Admit it, my friend. You had fun.'

What she would admit was that she was happy he had not lost his playful nature over the years.

'Many things are fun which do not involve breaking one's neck in a fall.'

'Hmm, broken, is it?'

Boldly, he reached under her tangle of hair, touching the back of her neck, making slow, gentle circles with his fingers.

'It does not feel broken to me.'

Emotions crowded her throat, making it swell to the point she felt she might weep. Peter, her Peter, not a lofty viscount, sat beside her in the shrub, teasing her, laughing at her. Life, as it used to be before their parents died and her father remarried, clicked neatly into place. Nothing was different than it had been back then. The realisation brought her close to tears.

And yet, everything was different.

He was a man, she was a woman. Years ago, young Anna Liese would have flopped back on the ground, giggling and laughing at the sky.

Right this moment, she wondered what she would do if she did flop back. Would she grab Peter's shirt front, drag him down, so that she gazed into his eyes instead of the sky? She might.

His fingers stilled, then moved around to her throat, his thumb rested on the spot where her pulse raced. If, in the weeks to come, they happened to pause under a sprig of mistletoe, she feared she would not settle for a mischievous kiss to her hand.

'Are you nervous, Anna Liese? You really must get back on the bicycle. It is the golden rule of cycling.'

The actual golden rule was of a 'do unto others' nature.

What she would have him 'do unto her' right now was kiss her. It was bold, but true, none the less. Did it now follow that she ought to kiss him?

She leaned forward, into the press of his fingers on her neck. Would he be stunned? Or would he—?

Oh, he would. Heat from his mouth skimmed hers. She could almost feel his lips, although they hovered just beyond a kiss.

'My dear Miss Barlow,' said a snide, unwelcome voice. 'I trust you are not being assaulted by this gentleman?'

Of all the wicked timing. The fellow must have come upon them while on his way to open the bank.

'If I were being assaulted, you would be aware of it, Mr Grant. I would not be sitting here involved in a pleasant conversation. I would screech and defend myself against any unsavoury and any unwise person to attempt such a thing.'

'Conversation, was it?'

Peter stood, helped her to her feet.

'This gentleman is my dear friend. He is teaching me to ride a bicycle.'

'An odd way to do it if you ask me.' Mr Grant's dark skinny brow inched up in his forehead. 'You must realise that many people consider bicycling an unladylike pursuit. Perhaps you need a proper friend who will not lead you to behave in questionable behaviour.' How anyone could put such a sneer on the word 'friend' was beyond her. 'One who will instruct you in respectable behaviour. Come now, I shall escort you home.'

He reached for her. Peter clamped his hand around the banker's wrist.

Hmm, what appeared to be a handshake hid a warning. At least Anna Liese suspected it did.

'You seem to admire respectable behaviour, sir, and yet you have failed to introduce yourself.' Peter sounded every bit the Viscount and not at all the boy she remembered. 'Allow me to introduce myself. I am Viscount Cliverton. And you are?'

A change came over Hyrum Grant's face. A mask of civility fell deceitfully into place.

Peter's answering smile was equally pleasant. No doubt

he had been trained in false civility when he came to his title.

'Lord Cliverton! What a pleasure it is to make your acquaintance. I have been anxious to ever since I heard of your arrival. I do hope you will consider my bank for your financial needs.'

With a curt nod, Peter dismissed Hyrum Grant, took her hand and helped her to stand.

'I am certain you will find my establishment on a par with the best in London.'

'Come, Anna Liese, let us resume your lessons.'

They were silent while walking the path away from the village. There was one thing on her mind and it was not the banker or bicycling.

It was Peter and the kiss he had nearly given her, or she had given him. She was not sure whose idea it had been, but was certain that had they not been interrupted they would both have been quite involved in it. At that point it would not have mattered whose idea it was.

Was he thinking of what might have been? She could not tell, and the silence was stretching uncomfortably.

'If I were you, I would not trust that man with a penny of my money, Peter,' she said because someone must say something.

'It is you I do not trust him with.'

He nodded at her bike, indicating she should mount.

She sighed. It truly had been great fun before she had spilled into the bushes and Hyrum Grant had made his intrusive appearance to ruin it all.

The bike began to move slowly along, she pushed her feet on the pedals, but not so quickly as to outpace Peter gripping the back of her seat.

'I would have a care about that man, Anna Liese. I have a bad feeling about him.'

'He is not one you would wish to encounter alone at night.'

'Did you think I was him that first night when I burst in upon you?'

'Him, or someone like him.'

'I'm sorry. I had no idea who you were that night or why you were there. If I had, I would have made sure you stayed.'

'Peter! Really, you could not have. Woodlore Glen might not be London, but it would have been a great scandal if it came to light that we spent the night alone in the same house. It is one thing to travel about without a chaperon, but that would be something else! Your reputation would be tarnished.' She cast him a sidelong smile. 'You may let me go now.'

He held on a moment longer. She thought he wished to say more on the subject. She did not.

Then he let go. Off she went, peddling down the path, Hyrum Grant forgotten, near-kiss remembered and her happy mood restored.

In order to return to the cottage by a ridable path, they were forced to pedal past Maplewood. Hopefully, no one was peering out a window. Still, it was early and they were likely to be safe.

Crossing the bridge, the stones were uneven and she nearly toppled. She did not, though, and felt emboldened by her newfound skill. Upon rising this morning, she would never have imagined she would learn such a thing.

'Thank you so much for this, Peter. I cannot recall when I have had more fun. Do you mind if keep my bicycle at the cottage?'

'Naturally not, but is there some reason you cannot take it with you?

'It is for the best that Stepmama does not know.'

'Why? What would happen if she did know?'

She would rather not reveal how her stepmother treated her. Becoming submissive in order to avoid a temper tantrum was not much of a character quality. Along with it she had become an interesting mix of clever and wary. What she was not was who she used to be. Before she had come to dread her stepmother's bad moods, she had been brave. Brave enough to face down grief and come out smiling.

In her heart she felt this man was the Peter she remembered, her best friend and companion and that his opinion of her would not change if he knew. But he was also Viscount Cliverton and she knew nothing of him in that role. He had been gone from her life far longer than he had been in it, after all.

In dealing with Hyrum Grant, Peter's rank had been clearly on display. At that moment she had wondered if she knew him at all. Who was this man she did not completely know? Surely there were things about him she did not know just the same as there were things he did not know about her.

But then, just as quickly, the years fell away again, the Peter and Anna Liese of old as fast friends as they had ever been.

'She might feel that Mildred has been slighted and fall into a mood. If that happens, we will all be miserable.'

Should she let him know how badly Stepmama meant to have him for Mildred? That behind the friendly smiles and invitations it was all trickery? Or reveal that if Stepmama knew they were spending time together she would redouble her efforts to get Anna Liese out of the way?

She had hinted at what they wanted, warned him to be wary, but he could not know who those women were at heart. What they would stoop to in order to get what they wanted.

'There is more to it than you are telling me.' Peter leaned his bicycle against a tree trunk, then took hers, putting it next to his. 'How can I help?'

How good it would be to lean into his arms, to unburden her heart by revealing to him how her life at Maplewood really was. She knew that her young friend would not judge her, but a viscount? How could she know for certain what his opinion would be?

Her secrets were humiliating. Any woman with a backbone would stand up to Stepmama, not run and hide the way she had been doing ever since she was thirteen years old.

'When my stepmother gets into one of her moods, no one can help.' She shrugged. 'But if you wish to wed my stepsister that would cure her of it.'

She found she was holding her breath, wondering what his reaction to that would be.

'While I will have to marry someone soon, I do not—'

Discussing his potential marriage made her feel rather sick at heart. Now that she was looking back, she recalled how she believed it would be the two of them getting married and living happily ever after. She had been as certain of it as sunrise, as the coming of Father Christmas and of ending each day in song.

Those carefree days had been so innocent. She would never have dreamed then that life could rip the joy out of one's heart.

'I will see you in the morning, my friend. We will make a decision on the wallpaper.'

With that she dashed across the bridge. It really was for the best that he did not know to what villainy Stepmama would sink. He did not need to know how desperately the Baroness wished to be rid of her.

It would be humiliating if he knew that she, the Baron's true daughter, was treated so disrespectfully and in her own home. A home which she intended to keep no matter what.

The girl he had known would never stand for such effrontery. Of course, the girl he had known had been adored by her family. For all that she wondered if he was the boy he had been, she thought he might not find her to be the girl she had been.

Halfway home, she nearly stopped to weep. She had thought herself clever by outwitting Stepmama. What she ought to have been doing was standing her ground and Maplewood was her ground! All at once, she missed the Anna Liese of old. That girl had disappeared so gradually she had failed to notice the change.

If only she could always feel as free as she had a short time ago, whizzing along the path on her gleaming new bicycle. She had not felt so carefree since she was a small girl, basking in Mama and Papa's love.

It was decided. Blue wallpaper for the drawing room.

He and Anna Liese had bicycled to the village tearoom, had breakfast while arguing between yellow and blue decor, then had gone to the village shop and placed the order for what they needed.

Peter supposed it was time to send a wire asking for his cook and one of the housemaids to come to Woodlore Glen.

If his cook was in residence, he would have no reason to have breakfast in the village with Anna Liese each morning. This was a routine he had grown fond of.

He could honestly say he enjoyed her company as much now as he had when he was a child. Clearly, she kept secrets. Something was going on beyond her stepmother's ill temper, but unless she wished to speak of it there was little he could do to help her.

This afternoon he would concentrate on what he could do: make a trip to the village and hire a crew to clean the cottage. Before he could move ahead with new paint and wallpaper, everything needed a good scrubbing. He wished Anna Liese would join him, although she never did at this time of day. He could not help but wonder what she did in the afternoon.

Plucking his coat from the hall tree, he shrugged into it. The days were getting colder and the nights frigid. Opening the front door, he found himself looking into Mildred's face. Her blank expression bloomed suddenly into a smile. With a lift of her elbow, she brought his attention to the basket draped over her arm.

'Good afternoon, Lord Cliverton.' Quite boldly she took a step forward as if she would enter his house uninvited.

He blocked her way, which she might interpret as being rude, but he did not intend to be alone with her inside his cottage. He would hope to have a bit more choice in a marriage partner than being forced by scandal. Indeed, he had a couple of weeks until he needed to direct his attention to marriage and he intended to enjoy them. Enjoy them in the company of Anna Liese, not her stepsister, insofar as he could avoid it.

'Good afternoon, Mildred.'

'Oh, it is sunny and lovely, my lord.'

Sunny, yes, but it was more cold than lovely. He hoped to make it to the village and back before it turned bitter.

'I just stopped by to see if you would care to share a pie with me. We have had so little time to get to know one another without being interrupted by this and that. The manor is a beehive now with all the preparation going on for your welcome dinner.'

He was rather stuck with sharing the pie, he supposed. Although he was not going to allow her to put one foot across his threshold.

'Shall we take a walk along the stream?' he asked, offering a polite smile while inwardly grimacing.

'How lovely, perhaps we shall find a nice quiet place to sit.'

It would need to be got out of the way quickly since it was the worst weather for sitting outside.

They had not walked far before Mildred spotted a place near the bank which was more secluded than he would have liked. Since she sat down, he did not know what else to do but sit beside her. Unfortunately, this spot gave a clear view of the cottage's back porch where the bicycles were stored. Since she seemed to be engrossed by the contents of the basket, she might not wonder why there were two of them.

He found he did not need to worry about keeping up his side of the conversation since she flitted from subject to subject with him only needing to nod occasionally while huddling in his coat.

Apparently having run out of topics, she sat in silence, shivering.

'Silly me,' she murmured while sidling closer to him. 'Rushing outdoors and forgetting to bring a coat.'

Silly or calculated, he had to wonder.

'I will escort you home.'

He began to rise, but she lunged for him. He leaned out of the way. Unable to stop her momentum, she landed face first on the grass. Rolling onto her back, she covered her eyes with her forearm, then reached her other hand towards him to be helped up.

The last thing he was going to do was touch this woman, if only she had not started to whimper. What was he to do now? He was nearly certain she intended to entrap him, but he could hardly walk away and leave her like this.

Staring at her, he was surprised when someone tapped his elbow. Jerking his gaze sideways, he sighed with relief. Anna Liese. Thank goodness!

She pressed one finger to her lips, indicating for him to remain silent. He nodded. Anna Liese grasped her stepsister's hand and began to draw her up.

'Oh, my lord, you must not touch me,' she wailed, eyes pinched closed. 'I will be compromised for certain.'

'Do not fear, Mildred. Your virtue remains,' Anna Liese declared, shooting Peter a wink. Her playful expression made him want to laugh, though he thought it was best to refrain.

Mildred gasped and yanked her hand out of Anna Liese's. Scrambling up, she glowered at her 'rescuer'. Snapping her skirts into place, she settled her gaze upon him.

'Well, I must say it is a lucky thing she came along— from wherever it was she came from—who can say what might have happened. We must be more cautious in the future, my lord.' With a sniff, she snatched up the basket and hurried away.

'I cannot say how grateful I am that you happened along.'

'The truth is, I didn't happen along. I saw Mildred coming over and predicted you would be in peril. Good friend that I am, I followed.'

'You are a good friend, the best I ever had.'

All at once, he had the strongest urge to kiss her, this time really do it, not hover close to her mouth in delightful hesitation. Her smile, the humour shining in her eyes and the way the breeze caught her hair and blew it softly across her mouth...

His racing heart was engaged in battle with his mind which was urging him, quite strongly, not to act on the delicious impulse. He should not, not if he wished to avoid the risk of ruining the friendship growing between them. Their bond was renewing, but it was still fragile. He did not wish to make a great blunder.

Yesterday he had acted rashly in nearly kissing her. All things considered it was a lucky thing that that Preston chap had interrupted. Anna Liese was important to him. He did not want to lose her again.

It had nearly done for him years ago. So much loss—his fear of losing her again so great that he had refused to come and visit. He had shut her out without realising it, built a wall against future loss. Now here it was, tumbling down all about him.

What kind of cad would he be to kiss Anna Liese, knowing he would soon be proposing to someone else, whoever that someone might be?

A whisper tiptoed through his mind so quickly he nearly missed it. *Why not marry Anna Liese?* it suggested. They did get along well and had since they were children. Perhaps it would not be a love match, but he had not expected one— not wanted one. Not at the risk of exposing his heart to pain.

The question was, what did she expect of marriage? Love? A grand passion? Is that what she was waiting for and so had yet to wed?

He had never considered such a thing for himself. Having never experienced anything more than affection for the women he had been attracted to, he did not believe he was destined for grand passion. Was afraid of it, even.

As he looked at Anna Liese, feeling a distinct softening of his heart, it was getting harder to remember that it was better to wed a stranger whose affection did not matter greatly.

'Let this be a warning, Peter. You must be wary. I have reason to know that my stepmother and stepsister will do whatever they feel they need to in order to win you.'

'How do you know it?' he asked, even though after what had just occurred, he had a good idea.

Were they doing something to Anna Liese was the question on his mind? Perhaps the Baroness's moods were not at the heart of what troubled his friend.

He took her hand, cupped it in both of his. Far from the kiss he wanted, the feel of her soft warm fingers went straight to his heart.

'Good afternoon, Peter,' she whispered softly, backing away from him. 'I will see you tomorrow.'

He watched her go home over the bridge. Was his presence here putting her in some sort of danger? If so, he would discover what it was. The last thing he was going to allow was for her to suffer for being his friend.

Chapter Eight

Three days had passed without a visit from Anna Liese.

Peering out of the window this morning, he hoped today would not make day four. While he understood it was unreasonable to expect to take up her time every morning, breakfast without her was lonely. Beginning the day seeing her smile, hearing her laugh, set a positive mood for the rest of it.

Without Anna Liese the past few days had dragged by.

The cleaning team had been here and the cottage smelled as fresh as it looked. The past few days had also served to remind him how much he disliked living alone. Home was meant to be filled with bustle and noise. One could only revisit ghosts of the past for so long before one longed for actual company.

The company of one friend, in particular.

With Christmas getting closer—was it really little more than a fortnight away?—he longed for company more than ever. Yesterday the village had looked festive with fir boughs and garlands made of shiny red beads decking every window. And there had been carollers singing on a street corner. Anna Liese would have loved listening to them.

With the weather cold and uncomfortable, he had listened to only one song before he hurried home. Had his friend been singing, he would have lingered for an hour despite the chill settling in.

At least once his staff of two arrived, it would be more acceptable for Anna Liese to visit him here, indoors where it was warm. She had yet to see the cottage freshly scrubbed. Given that she had been involved in the renovation from the beginning, he thought she would be pleased to see it shine.

He ought not to spend too long staring across the bridge at the mansion's front door. What he needed to do was send another telegram home. Also, he had got word that the paint and wallpaper he had ordered were ready to be picked up from the village shop.

Surely Anna Liese would not wish to be left out of see-ing their plan for the cottage come to fruition. But where was she? It was unlike her to miss their mornings together. By the looks of the weather, it would soon be raining so he ought to be on his way.

As he stepped outside, it occurred to him that she might be ill and that was the reason he had not seen her. He ought to pay a visit and find out.

Then again, after what she'd had to say about the ladies' aspirations, he hesitated. It would do Anna Liese no good to have them believe he was singling her out for attention, which is what he would be doing because, when it came down to it, Anna Liese's needs were foremost in his mind.

Ah, just then the door opened and she stepped outside. Crossing the bridge, she looked as healthy as a sunray. He was certain she was singing but could not determine what the tune was. She stopped when the goose waddled towards her, then bent to pet it.

After she crossed the bridge, she turned aside, walked down a path, then out of his view. When she reappeared, she was clutching a bunch of greenery to her heart. She walked the path to his front door with the goose waddling behind, honking off-time to the tune she hummed.

He felt like humming along, too. If a goose could do it, why couldn't he? He met her halfway down the walk.

'Good morning,' he said. 'I've missed you.'

'I've missed you, too. But it is all hands needed at the manor getting ready for your welcome dinner. Even Mildred swept a floor.'

'I do not know whether to be flattered or embarrassed.'

'You will need to decide that on your own. But I will say, I've never seen Mildred near a broom.'

Peter closed the door on the goose.

Anna Liese placed holly in the vase, arranged the branches to her liking, then plucked a red and green plaid ribbon out of her pocket. She tied it in a festive-looking bow around the vase.

'My mother used to do that,' he said.

'I remember. She always made things pretty.'

It hit him then, rather like a hug to his soul, how grateful he was that he was not the only person to have memories of his past, of the people he'd loved and lost. This reminder of his mother was a small one, but so incredibly poignant it made his heart swell and his throat along with it. It would be a wonder if he was not reduced to unmanly tears.

How many other things did Anna Liese remember from their childhood? All he wanted was to sit and talk, rediscover buried memories—look at them again and walk among them in his mind—along with his oldest friend. They could pick one as if it were a ripe peach, savour it and then pluck another.

'I'm on my way to the village to pick up the paint and wallpaper we ordered. Would you like to come along? We can have breakfast first. I've missed starting my day with you.'

'As much as I would like to, I don't dare be gone that long. I am needed at home to pull everything together for your visit.'

'I'm looking forward to it, to being able to spend an evening with you for a change.'

'It will be grand, for certain. I hope you are not expecting a casual affair. My stepmother is taking advantage of the chance to entertain a genuine viscount. It might be the most elegant affair ever to be held in Woodlore Glen.'

'As long as you are present it will be delightful.'

'What a sweet thing to say. Have a nice day, Peter.' She turned for the door.

'You only came to bring the holly?'

'That and the ribbon for the vase, and to say good morning.'

'May I see you again later today?'

If not, it was going to be another long, rather dreary day.

'I will not have a free second until it is quite late.'

'Meet me at ten on the bridge. Is it too late for you? We shall sit upon the bench on the hill and look at stars the way we used to.'

'By the looks of the sky, all we shall see are clouds.'

'Very well, bring your umbrella in case it rains.'

He opened the door for her to go outside. The goose,

having settled on the porch, stood up. It gazed up at Anna Liese. Even though it was a bird, Peter could tell the creature adored her. If only he could be the one waddling after her swaying skirt. Young Anna Liese's skirt had bounced rather than swayed. He found he could not look away.

Arriving at her front door, she turned about and caught him staring. Laughing, she went inside. It was only eight in the morning. He feared it would feel like for ever until ten o'clock tonight came.

It was nearly the perfect time to meet with Peter. With the household bedding down for the night, no one would notice her going outside.

Except that it was raining—not a downpour, but still a steady drip which might keep Peter from coming out even though he was the one who had told her to bring an umbrella. A spot of wet weather was certainly not going to keep her from venturing out.

Anna Liese tiptoed to the kitchen, prepared a jug of hot tea, then gathered a pair of pottery mugs. Even though the tea was likely to be cooled by the time they drank it, it seemed sensible to bring it along. Even now she felt the lingering touch of Peter's hand from the other day. It would be wise to keep her hands occupied with holding the tea.

Peter had seemed anxious to spend time with her. But was he as eager as she was? All she thought of lately was being with him. Over the years she'd sat upon the bench on the hill, watching stars and listening to night sounds, but it had never been as lovely as when she used to sit there with Peter.

She shrugged on the heavy cloak she kept near the kitchen door, snatched her umbrella from the stand and then went outside. Her heart took a happy little hop to see him waiting on the bridge.

He placed his hand under her arm, then they hurried to the top of the hill. Neither of them spoke until after Peter had spread a dry canvas over the bench and they sat down. With their umbrellas forming an arched canopy, they had a rather snug and cosy shelter.

She poured tea, then handed him a mug. Having cooled a bit, the vaporous twirls of steam weakly curled up into the night, then drifted away.

'Isn't this like old times?' she asked.

'We would have been forbidden to come out in the rain when we were children.'

'So true. We were not forbidden much back then, but had our parents known we sneaked out at night to sit up here, we would have been.'

'I miss those days.'

She took a short sip of tea, nodding agreement while gazing down at the village. Streetlamps were still lit, causing raindrops streaking through the light to resemble tumbling diamonds.

This moment held all the magic that a starry night would—perhaps more, even. This night held a sort of enchantment which had been absent years ago. As children gazing at the stars, the focus had been upwards towards the heavens.

At this moment, her focus was on the man sitting beside her. She had a strong urge to lean in close, to feel his warmth and imagine what it would be like if he put his strong arm around her shoulders and drew her closer.

'The funny thing is, here we are running about together as if we were those children still and I cannot bring myself to feel improper about it. What do you think?' He arched a brow, giving her a sweet, crooked smile. 'I'm not wrong about this, am I?'

'To me it does not matter and we do breakfast in town openly. If we were to be caught out here, alone in the night? That would matter.' Each of them took a long, thoughtful sip of warm tea. 'But I, for one, do not intend to tell.'

'You can count on my silence, Miss Barlow.'

His funny, oh, so Peter-ish grin made her laugh, which gained her a laugh in return. Looking at each other, they became caught up in a fit of merriment which somehow morphed into side-splitting humour. It made no difference that nothing was all that funny—it simply felt good to laugh.

'We used to do this all the time.' He sighed softly, as if in his mind's eye he was looking at who they were once upon a time. 'Share a memory you have of us from before.'

There were so many they crowded her mind all at once.

'Well, there was the time we were sitting here one night and you felt something fall on your head from the branch above us. You jumped about, yelping and screeching. It turned out to be a kitten, a very small one, in fact.'

'Ollie! I remember Ollie. You took the little chap home with you. Whatever became of him?'

'He grew to be a sassy fellow and industrious at keeping rodents out of the stable.'

It had been a long while since she had thought of her cat. What a nice thing it was to sit here and remember, the steady *plink-plop* of water off the umbrellas notwithstanding.

'What do you remember, Peter?'

'I remember going into my mother's kitchen one after-noon—it was a few days before Christmas and raining then, too. You were there with her, standing on a stool and putting candy eyes on the gingerbread men you were making. I really wanted to eat one.'

'You did, too. Your mother was about to forbid it, but you dashed forward and snatched one up so quickly that you had it half gobbled before she got the words out.'

'I grabbed two of them, as I recall, and they were delicious.'

Back and forth they went, sharing stories, sighing over some and laughing over others. And some, the sad ones coming at the end of their time together, avoiding all together.

'I wish we could sit here for ever, sharing memories,' he said. 'But the wind is rising. We ought to go back.' He stood. With his umbrella clutched in one hand, he extended a hand to help her rise.

Coming up, she placed her hand in his. She had never felt anything like it before—so large and strong—so intriguingly male. She could not look away from his face. His eyes held an interesting expression. One which a young boy would not have.

She wondered if perhaps he meant to kiss her, but then he did not.

'Have you invited my stepsister to your ball yet?' she asked while they walked down the hill. 'If you haven't, she and my stepmother will be fishing earnestly for an invitation.'

'I shall be delighted to invite them, as long as you agree to attend along with them.'

She would like that, more than anything. But at the same time—London and its bustling streets? Ladies and gentlemen of society wherever one looked? She was not sure.

Even though, as a baron's daughter, she had been born to society, she was a country mouse.

'I really do not think—'

'Do not refuse me, please. I fear I cannot face the occasion without you.'

'Well, perhaps a ball would be interesting. But surely you are used to attending them.'

'As true as that is, I have never attended one in which I am actively searching for a bride. And the worst of it is, word will have got around that I am.'

'If that is the goal of your ball, so much the better. But you make it seem as if you do not wish to marry.'

'What I wish is irrelevant. It must be done, after all. It is the ball itself which will be a trial. The affair might look Christmassy—good will and peace on earth—but the truth is, in between the carols we will be merrily singing, battles between the ladies will be waged.'

'I'm not sure what I can do about it by attending.'

'Not much, I'll admit. I dread to think it, but imagine a ballroom packed with young ladies and their mothers, every one of them as ambitious as the Baroness and Mildred. Having you present, my friend, will keep me sane through the ordeal.'

Perhaps, but at the same time it would break her heart. Did he believe she could watch him searching out a bride when she herself had once wanted to be that bride? It had been her childhood expectation. She had even imagined her wedding gown being made of rose petals and dew drops. Now that she was a woman with a mature outlook... What? She still wanted rose petals and dew drops!

She had been fantasising about his return for years. And why was that? So that she could say, *Oh, how lovely to see you again and did we not have a fine time as children?* She would be fooling herself to believe it. The reason she had turned down suitors, hidden away from them even, was not only that Stepmama was forcing them upon her. No! It was because none of those men had been her Peter.

Every man she met had been judged by the friendship the two of them had shared. Every time they had been found wanting. She had not been aware of doing it, yet she had, which only went to point out how deeply he had always been a part of her. Of how loving him over the years had formed who she was then as well as who she was now.

She could not possibly attend his ball only to witness him pick someone else, no matter how badly he needed her to be there. Suddenly, the tea which had been so sweet a moment ago turned sour in her belly.

'Now that I have admitted to you that I have no genuine wish to marry, it is your turn to tell me why you have not chosen a husband. There must have been dozens of men infatuated with you over the years.'

'There is a vast difference between being infatuated and being in love, Peter.' Surely he knew that. 'We grew up as children of love matches and were lucky in that. But after that I grew up a home where there was no love match. Since I understand the difference, I will settle for nothing less than my true love match.'

'It is not the same for me. I will wed properly, as society expects me to. I have put it off too long as it is.'

What nonsense! She stopped walking, clutched his arm and looked him hard in the eye.

'Peter Penneyjons, do you truly believe that society will suffer if Viscount Cliverton waits until he finds a woman who will make him happy in marriage? One who makes his heart sing?'

'The ladies awaiting my title might suffer. They have been waiting anxiously for me to do my duty.'

'You make it sound as if you are a commodity and not a man.'

'That is not so far from the truth, Anna Liese.' He stepped closer. Their umbrella brims clicked. 'You confuse me.'

He confused her, too. 'How do I confuse you?'

'You...' He touched her cheek with his rain-slicked fingers. 'Well, you—you are—'

'Waiting for true love...' Was he going to kiss her this time? Would she allow it, knowing that love was not important to him?

Inch by slow inch, he dipped his head. She wanted this kiss more than she had ever wanted anything. She feared it even more. A kiss would make her fall in love with him in a vastly different way than the way she always had been.

Until this moment she had loved her young, childhood friend. In a blink, a touch, he would change everything. If his lips touched hers, it would all be different. The boy would be replaced by the man for ever.

What was she to do? How was she to resist what she wanted most? But, no! This was not what she wanted most. When she did kiss him, she wanted her love returned. She wanted him to look at her with love in his eyes. There was something in his eyes, something simmering and compelling. Whatever it was, it was not love.

She ought to step back, to run for home, not take a risk. She would if her feet were not rooted to the wet ground, her legs not leaden and useless. If her heart were not balanced on the head of a pin, unsure of which way it would leap.

His lips dipped slowly towards hers. She felt the heat of his breath, breathed in the scent of his skin. This was her dream come true and it was her nightmare. She turned her face so that his kiss connected with her cheek.

'I beg your pardon.' He set her at arm's length, breathing hard. 'I regret taking advantage of you.'

Not as much as she regretted not allowing it. She took a quick step away. Hopefully quickly enough that he did not taste the one tear that had escaped and run down her cheek.

What she needed to do was to make light of what had happened. If she did not, how could they go on? And she did want to go on. The thought of not spending time with him was horrid.

'Do not take it to heart, Peter. You did not take advantage.' It shattered her, wondering if he really would not take it to heart. 'We have been playing about at this kissing business. I suggest we put it behind us and carry on as the friends we have always been.'

She could scarcely believe her voice did not quaver while she lied.

'Thank you for not taking my indiscretion to heart. I do not deserve a friend like you, Anna Liese.'

If he assumed she had not taken it to heart, he didn't know her at all. What had just happened—or not happened, more to the point—was for the best.

'Goodnight, Peter. I will see you in the morning. We shall discuss what furniture to purchase for the cottage.' She sounded so ordinary, so every day. He would never guess how she wept inside.

Had they kissed, her world would have changed. His would not have, although she thought he was not unaffected by what had happened. Knowing him as she did—and she did know him—he had felt a moment of confusion where past and present collided.

The same had happened for her.

Unlike Peter, she was not confused about what it meant. She wanted to marry him now the same way she had when she was a child. Only, not at the cost of giving up true love.

Chapter Nine

The next morning, Peter bicycled back from the village with a box precariously balanced on the handlebar. The scents of breakfast wafted out and made his stomach growl.

Even though it was no longer raining, it was as cold as the dickens out here. What a relief it would be to get inside the cottage where he had built a fire in the hearth before peddling off to town.

Not certain what time Anna Liese would arrive, he wanted it to be warm when she stepped inside. It had taken him an hour or more last night to stop shivering after being out in the rain for so long.

If, in truth, it had been the weather causing his shivers. Facing facts, he had to admit to being nervous. He had done the unthinkable last night and came within a breath of kissing his childhood friend—again.

She would be within her rights to be incensed—to not wish to be alone in his company again. No one would blame her for it. Although she did say they should think no more about it and put the incident behind them.

In the moment he was finding it nearly impossible to do. Even though their lips had not met, their breath had mingled. He had breathed in and caught the scent of her desire.

What a surprise it had been when she turned her cheek to him. What he could not get out of his mind was her tear. He had seen it slip down her cheek, then tasted it when she turned away from the kiss.

He could hardly blame her if she did not come to the cottage this morning as they had planned. If she did, he would treat her with the respect she deserved, behave as the gentleman she expected him to be—treat her as the lady she clearly was.

Last night it had been pointed out quite clearly that his Anna Liese was now a woman. It was not as if he hadn't noticed it before—how could he not? But the difference now was that he felt it.

Ah, but what must she think of him? It was troubling to him that she might believe he kissed every woman he happened to be alone with. Far from it! He was exceptionally careful not to be caught in a compromise.

Stashing his bicycle on the back porch, he walked around to the front door, carrying the box of food. He stopped for a moment to sniff the air which was crisp and redolent of evergreen trees.

He glanced towards Maplewood Manor, hoping to see Anna Liese coming out. She was not, but someone was. Mildred stared at him. From this distance he could not see her expression, but she waved her hand vigorously. He waved back, feeling her eyes on him even after he closed the door.

'Do not come over, please do not.' he mumbled.

But what was that? Singing—a voice so pure, so ethereal it felt like breath whooshing around and through him. The shiver that had taken him last night raced over his skin again—but pleasantly warm. Oddly, the scents of pine and cedar, which he had only a moment ago been admiring, filled the cottage.

Following the sound of Anna Liese's voice, he entered the drawing room. What on earth?

She turned to him with a wink and a smile which warmed him more thoroughly than the fireplace she stood in front of. 'Do you like it?'

'You have "decked my halls with boughs of holly"!'

Swathes of greenery draped the windows on either side of the fireplace. Pinecones and holly made an artistic arrangement on the mantelpiece.

'Fa-la-la-la-la,' she answered, giving a quiet laugh.

'It is beautiful.'

More than that, it indicated she did not hate him for last night. That they remained friends despite what he had done.

'But is it not too early to decorate for Christmas?'

'Not when one will be leaving to choose a bride before then,' she said brightly and handed him a garland of pinecones dotted with gold beads. 'If we do not decorate now, you will not be able to enjoy how festive the cottage can be at this time of year.'

She pointed to the newel post and indicated he was to twine the garland around the bannister.

'I will be coming back before Christmas. And I will bring my cousins and their families.'

'These will be dried out by then.' She tapped her finger on her chin. 'You mustn't worry, though, I will refresh them while you are gone.'

Clearly, this was her way of saying she would not be attending his ball. If she did not wish to come to London, he could hardly press the matter.

For instance, he would not point out that she would meet many fine gentlemen in the city. Perhaps one of them would be the man with whom she would make her true love match. If he tried to utter those words, he feared he might choke on them. Which was absurd. Didn't he want her to find what would make her happy—or rather, who would?

Since she apparently wished him well on his marriage quest, she merited no less from him.

'I've brought breakfast,' he said. 'Over which I will apologise profusely for last night.'

While he dragged the small table in front of the fireplace and withdrew the contents of the box, he thought who among his acquaintances he would introduce her to if he had the chance. One after another, faces appeared in his mind and he rejected them.

Watching while Anna Liese sat down across from him, then fluffed her skirts until they were arranged to her satisfaction, he decided his sweet friend was too good for the lot of them.

'Thank you for breakfast, Peter. I am hungry. But please do not apologise for anything. Let us move past it and go on.'

Apparently in her mind the issue of kissing had been put aside.

'Very well. I'm hungry, too.'

She did look as though she had put the incident behind her. While he had been restless into the wee hours, she looked as fresh and cheerful as the bright bow she had fastened to the garland.

'Maplewood is sparkling in your honour, Peter. The house has not been so well adorned for Christmas in years.'

'I am looking forward to it, Anna Liese.'

'The affair is the talk of the village, you know. Woodlore Glen does not typically have such a grand visitor.'

'I am not grand and you well know it.'

'Oh, please, surely you have noticed how people fall all over themselves to do your bidding.'

One could not fail to since their attentions were pronounced. Here in Woodlore Glen he stood out from the average villager even though he never dressed in his London finery.

The only person to treat him as a genuine human being was the woman sitting across from him. To her he was simply Peter Penneyjons, her friend—the boy who had grown up across the stream from her. One could hardly romp through green fields, catch tadpoles in the stream and afterwards put said friend on a lofty pedestal. She knew his secrets and he knew hers.

'I'm glad you do not treat me that way.'

'We are too old of friends to observe society's nonsense.'

Indeed, she would not be sitting across from him having breakfast if that were the case.

'Anna Liese, I hope you know how much I value our friendship.'

'As do I, Peter.'

'The reason I say so is because—it is only that I hope that, once I am married, what is between us will not change.'

A delicate blush rushed up her neck and pulsed in her cheeks. Perhaps it was only the fire reflecting off her skin that made it appear that way.

'I'm certain—'

Whatever she was about to say was cut off by a loud rap on the front door.

'Mildred,' he muttered. 'She saw me come in.'

'She is up and about early today because the modiste is delivering her gowns.' She stood up when the pounding became more urgent. 'I will leave through the back door.'

'I hate for you to go so soon.' He had the strongest urge to restrain her with a kiss. Apparently, he was not doing a grand job of putting the thought behind him. 'We have yet to discuss what furniture I need to purchase.'

'Later. Perhaps once the dinner party is past.'

'Lord Cliverton!' Mildred's voice sounded strident, even though muffled by the heavy wood door.'

'Goodbye, Peter.' To his surprise she went up on her toes and gave his cheek a quick, friendly kiss. 'I will see you in a couple of days.' With that she rushed out of the room, through the kitchen and out the back door.

He went to the front door, wondering if one slightly plump lady could actually batter it down.

'Good morning, Miss Hooper,' he said, opening the door and glancing at her knuckles in the hope that she had not rubbed them raw.

'Good morning, my lord,' she said, peering past his shoulder as if she were looking for someone, then shifting her gaze to his face. 'Is there something wrong with your cheek?'

He jerked his hand way from the spot Anna Liese had kissed. Apparently, he had been caressing it without being aware.

'No. Just a—' He shrugged, stalling while trying to think of something. 'I hurried to answer the door so quickly I collided with a—door frame.'

She frowned, no doubt trying to picture such an unlikely occurrence.

'Do not worry, my lord, it does not appear that it will
leave a mark.' She lifted a napkin which had something
wrapped inside. 'I saw you coming back from the village
and thought, since your own cook has not yet arrived, you
would like a bit to eat. It is apple cake and I promise it is
delicious.'

'How thoughtful of you to come out in the cold and bring
it. Thank you for your trouble.' He nodded, starting to close
the door, but she placed her palm on the wood. 'I shall enjoy
every bite.'

'I did not realise how cold it was until I was halfway
across the bridge. Perhaps I might come inside? There is
enough cake for us to share.'

For a moment he could not help feeling some pity for
her. Even though she and Anna Liese had grown up in the
same household, they were quite different people. Despite
everything Anna Liese had been through, she was a lovely,
caring person. Mildred, by comparison, had grown up to
be disagreeable.

The reason for the difference might be what Anna Liese
had pointed out last night. Being a child of parents who
loved one had a great deal to do with one's outlook on life.
Mildred could not help that she had not been so blessed.

Looking at her rather desperate expression, he determined to treat her with kindness. Not that he would allow
himself to be trapped by her, but he would be polite, have
compassion for the past she had been formed by.

'I'm sorry, but I was just going out again. I have business
in the village. Perhaps you would care to accompany me?'

If she were as cold as she claimed to be, she would refuse, but the offer was sure to show his appreciation of her bringing him apple cake.

'How delightful! I would enjoy a few moments out from under Mama's thumb. It is not enough that she orders the servants about, she is doing it to me as well.'

The question in Peter's mind was how hard was the Baroness making Anna Liese work, the true daughter of Maplewood.

It did not set well that she was doing so in the cause of honouring him. He would rather not be honoured if that were the case.

'Wait one moment, Mildred. I will bring a second coat for you.'

He recognised his mistake when her face bloomed in undisguised pleasure. What a great blunder to call her Mildred instead of Miss Hooper. Please let her not consider them a step shy of becoming betrothed.

Having retrieved the coats, he set off at a brisk pace across the bridge. Clearly this was not the pace she preferred because she dragged her feet in a leisurely stroll. She slipped her hand into the crook of his elbow, no matter that he had not offered his arm.

A short distance along the path, she began to speak in a tone so low that he had to incline his head towards her in order to hear. He imagined they presented an image he did not wish to portray. Anyone who did not know better would think they were enamoured of one another and indulging in romantic conversation. He could only pray there was no one about to make such an assumption.

'Oh, look,' Mildred said. 'There is my stepsister standing over there near the stream, holding that goose of hers. She looks rather pathetic, don't you think? As pretty as she is, you would expect her to have wed by now. I think perhaps she is afraid of men. But do not worry, my lord, I have no fear of you.'

She might have no fear of him, but he certainly did of her. He was also worried that Anna Liese might misunderstand what she was seeing.

Mildred lifted her arm and waved energetically while leaning closer to him than was acceptable. Clearly, her intention was to make sure that Anna Liese did misunderstand what she saw.

Rather than returning her stepsister's greeting with an answering wave and her customary smile, Anna Liese offered a curt nod, then hugged her pet closer to her heart.

'It is rather sad, don't you think? Having a goose as your closest friend? It is not even a sweet goose. I cannot tell you how many times it has attacked the ruffles on my skirts. Perhaps I should speak with my mother about getting Anna Liese a dog instead.'

The goose had attacked him, too, but only in the cause of protecting Anna Liese.

Which was more than he was doing in the moment. He ought to be defending her against Mildred's spiteful comments and would be if his companion would give him a chance to speak. The woman chattered on as if this were a monologue and not a conversation.

Whatever business he came up with in town, it would be short. He would probably need the whole of the afternoon to recover from a few hours spent in Miss Hopper's company.

Exclamations of delight issuing from the library gave away the fact that the gowns had been delivered and none too early, given that the dinner party was tomorrow.

Anna Liese felt no great rush to see her own dress since Stepmama would have given special instruction for it to be drab. Just the same she did enjoy gowns, seeing the bright colours and pretty fabrics, even if they were not meant for her.

Standing in the hallway where she had a view of the library, she watched Mildred pose on the dais which was always kept at the ready for the frequent fittings her stepmother and stepsister indulged in.

Mildred's gown did have a nice swirl to the fabric and might have been lovely were it not for the abundance of bright green flounces and ruffles.

Although the modiste had done her best, Stepmama had insisted on getting what she wanted no matter how ugly the result was. No doubt Mrs Creamer cringed, imagining people would judge her work by her customer's taste, but business was business and the Baroness must be satisfied.

Which, given her stepmother's gushing exclamations, she was.

Spotting her, Mrs Creamer excused herself and hurried towards where she still stood watching from the hallway.

'Your gown is to your stepmother's specifications, my dear, and I am sorry for it. But there is another gown. I have given the box to your maid. She has taken it to your room. The Baroness knows nothing of this one.'

'I cannot imagine how I will pay you for it. The Baroness handles the finances.'

'No need to worry, my dear, the cost of your gown has been absorbed by the others. It is an easy thing to hide when there are so many of them.'

'I am grateful, Mrs Creamer. Although I'm sure the gown you made at the Baroness's request is lovely.'

'Oh, it is, indeed, for an afternoon at home. And not a thread of chartreuse in it.' She laughed quietly, careful not to be overheard. 'Come, let us go in and do our best to gush and pretend Mildred looks like a princess.'

Her stepsister had changed gowns and the one she now wore was pretty, being pale yellow and a nice cut for her figure.

She did not want to wonder, yet one could hardly help what one wondered about. But—would Peter think Mildred attractive when he saw her wearing it?

Earlier this morning, she had been stunned to see him strolling with her stepsister. His head bent down to hers, they had appeared companionable. She had thought Peter would have sent Mildred away rather quickly. Could it be possible that he was developing fond feelings for her? Had she tricked him into seeing her as a person she wasn't?

Perhaps not. But the day would come when she would see him walking with a woman. Peter would be bringing his future wife to Woodlore Glen. The only way she would avoid witnessing his possible marital bliss would be to accept the attention of a man she did not love, to marry him and move away from her home.

No—that was unthinkable. The best she could do was deal with the pain of seeing him with a woman who was not her. Better that than dealing with the anguish of giving up Maplewood where she relived happy memories of her past wherever she looked.

Moving away from home would not even help greatly since she could not move away from her mind. Just because she did not see Peter and another woman with her eyes did not mean she wouldn't imagine it.

Seeing her step into the library, Alice plucked a gown off the back of a chair and carried it to her.

It was a well-made dress, the stitches straight and even. The fabric was sturdy, durable and a shade of grey that ensured to make her blend into the background.

'I shall try it on in my room,' she said, lifting it from Alice's arms.

'Please let me know if it is suitable, miss,' Alice answered, giving her a discreet wink.

'I cannot say how grateful I am.' She glanced at Mildred before she exited the library, only to see her dressed in the bright green gown again. 'You are sure to catch any gentleman's eye, Mildred.' It was the truth, only not in the way her stepsister dreamed of.

'Do you think so, Anna Liese? Really?' The question seemed sincere, the look in her stepsister's eyes hopeful.

'You look lovely.' Despite the gown.

She hurried up the stairs and burst into her room to see Martha holding up the most exquisite gown Anna Liese had ever seen. The fabric was a pure sky blue and shimmered as if caught in a ray of sunshine. She had not seen this material among the ones the modiste had brought for the fittings.

The gown was so pretty, looking at it made her feel breathless. A princess could wear it and be utterly admired. The bodice was ruffled and tucked in such a way that it would appear to float about her bosom and shoulders. Attached to the sheer fabric were small silk butterflies and lace rosettes. It was hard to imagine how the cost of this gown had been absorbed by the others.

'Oh, my dear!' Martha exclaimed. 'You will appear an angel tomorrow night.'

'I do not dare wear it.'

If only she were bold enough to march boldly into Step-mama's presence without fear of something 'happening' to her beautiful gown.

'I suppose you are right—but put it on so we may appreciate Mrs Creamer's vision.'

It would be thoughtless not to do so. The ladies had gone to a great deal of trouble on her behalf.

Martha helped her into the gown.

Holding the skirt in her hands, she twirled in front of the mirror. It felt like a dream, as if she were whirling about in blue mist.

'You are a vision, my dear girl. Some day you will wear this gown and bring every gentleman in the ballroom to his knees.'

'It is nice to imagine such a thing. But I doubt I will be attending any balls.'

'Lord Cliverton is hosting a ball. Surely you will be going?'

'Help me out of the gown, if you please.' She maintained her smile with difficulty because she would rather not have Martha see what was in her heart. She certainly would not be attending a ball in which the man she loved would be picking a bride. A heart could only take so much misery.

She blinked, then blinked again. She did love Peter Penneyjons, loved him more each time she saw him. Funny how the understanding of it had not hit her as a grand revelation. Probably because love for Peter had always been a part of her, a bright and never-forgotten part of her soul.

She was not sure how it had happened, or exactly when, but the little girl's love for a friend had become a woman's love for a man. A man who did not return her feelings, not in the way she needed him to.

'We must hide it away. I do not want to know what would happen if my stepmother discovered it.'

'I shall keep it in my quarters above stairs. It will be safe enough since neither she nor Mildred visit the servants' quarters.'

'Thank you, Martha.'

'Now, let me see what you will be wearing tomorrow night.' She picked the grey gown from the back of the chair where Anna Liese had dropped it and grimaced. 'You might as well not attend for all that you will be noticed wearing that.'

Peter would notice her regardless of what she wore. She was certain he would. Even though he was a viscount, he was not one to be swayed by fluff and frills.

Doubtless her stepmother's message in presenting her with such a gown was that she was not welcome at the event. An event to be held in her own home to welcome her very dear—friend.

No matter what Stepmama's feelings on the matter, Anna Liese was attending. And she would not blend into the wall. She did have other gowns, after all.

She must simply make sure no one sent them to be laundered.

Chapter Ten

The event so anticipated by everyone from Stepmama to the scullery maids, from the village lamplighter to Alice, was at hand.

Descending the grand staircase, Anna Liese paused half-way down, glancing about with pride at what the staff's and her own hard work had accomplished.

Maplewood sparkled as it had not since her parents were alive.

Garlands of red and green were draped over windows and doorways in the drawing room. Through the wide door-way of the grand drawing room she admired pine and holly wreaths hung on the mantelpiece and in windows announcing that Christmas was around the corner.

The sounds of the string quartet, along with the muffled conversation of guests who had already arrived, wafted out of the drawing room door. She closed her eyes, simply listening to the lovely strain of the instruments playing 'Good

King Wenceslas'. One could nearly feel the excitement of the season dancing on the air.

Coming down the rest of the steps, she glanced about for Peter. She was beyond anxious to share this with him. They had spent so many happy hours at Maplewood when they were young. Just imagining his smile made her want to skip instead of walk. No matter what scheme Stepmama might have in mind to drive her away, she would not fall prey to it.

Apparently he was not here yet so she greeted the neighbours with one eye on the doorway.

She was not the only one to have an eye on the hall. Everyone was anxious to meet the Viscount in their village. Stepmama and Mildred stood in the hall near the front door, heads together in conversation. It would be best to know what they were saying. Forewarned was forearmed she had come to learn.

Anna Liese walked towards them, but then hung back from the doorway. She was not yet ready to have her stepmother see her wearing not the drab grey gown, but one of her old gowns which was a lovely shade of dusty rose. It was a pretty, festive dress of lace more appropriate for the Viscount's welcome.

'You ought to have seen how he admired me, Mother.'

'Perhaps he was simply being polite. You should not have shown up at his front door as you did. He might have taken you for over-eager. You must appear uninterested. It is a trick to get them to want what they believe to be forbidden.'

As if he would succumb to such trickery.

'He called me Mildred. That has got to mean something.'

By mistake, perhaps—Anna Liese hoped so at any rate.

'It well may. However, you must still charm him. Smile,

laugh quietly and, whatever you do, make sure not to eat too much.'

'What if I get hungry?'

'After you are wed you may butter your bread as thick as you like. Until then you will pick at your food like a bird.'

'I can be as charming and hungry as can be, but if Anna Liese comes downstairs Lord Cliverton will see no one else.'

Truly? Is this what Mildred believed? How interesting.

'If she does come down, she will not stay.'

'I fail to see how you can prevent it. Especially if the guest of honour wishes for her to stay.'

'Put away that pouty expression. You may trust that I have taken steps to ensure she will not be here.'

'What steps?'

'Never you mind. Your job is to be pleasant to the Viscount.'

'But I wonder if—'

'Hush now, we have guests.'

Whatever the scheme, Anna Liese would not fall prey to it. She would do nothing which would take her away from Peter's welcome dinner. Mildred would simply have to shine enough to attract Peter's attention. Anna Liese had no intention of getting out of the way in order to make it easier for her. If Peter held tender feelings for Mildred, Anna Liese's presence would make no difference.

It was time to make her presence known. She swept inside, making a grand sweep of her lacy skirt. She would be happy to wear the sturdy grey gown—tomorrow.

'Everything looks fit for a viscount, Stepmama. Lord Cliverton will be delighted by all you have done to welcome him.'

Not that her stepmother had lent a hand, only ordered

people about. But in the end, Maplewood was as festive as she had ever seen it. Or heard it. The Christmas carols wafting softly through the rooms—it was enchanting.

Some of the enchantment had to do with knowing Peter would be here soon, knowing she would have the evening to spend with him.

'Why, Anna Liese, what a lovely gown.'

'But do you not have a new one?' Mildred asked, casting her frown over the delicate pink lace. 'Do you not think it disrespectful to wear something old?'

'I cannot imagine he would think so. We are childhood friends and such things between us are trivial.'

So she said, but Anna Liese did want Peter to see her dressed in lace and looking pretty.

Footsteps thumped across the floor.

The three of them turned to see the footman, Thorpe, striding towards them.

'This was delivered by messenger for you, Miss Anna Liese.' He placed the tightly folded note in her hand.

'Who is it from?' Stepmama asked.

'I cannot say, my lady.' Turning about, he left them as quickly as he had come.

'Well, my dear, I imagine you would like some privacy to read this mysterious missive. Come along, Mildred. We shall wait for the Viscount with the others.'

Mysterious was a mild word for the folded paper in her hand. And why wasn't Stepmama more curious about what it was? Anna Liese might have expected her to be reading it over her shoulder. Something felt wrong, but she would not know if it was or not until she looked at it.

The only person she could think of who would send her anything was Peter. Why would he not just wait and speak with her when he came? Unless something was wrong. That sent a shiver along her neck.

She glanced out the window, hoping to see him crossing the bridge. He was not and the lamps were still burning in his front windows.

What on earth?

She opened it and read, 'Anna Liese, I am suddenly feeling unwell. I fear I will not be able to attend. Please give the Baroness and Mildred my regrets.'

It was odd that he not had the note delivered to his hostess. It might be a scheme to somehow make her lose interest in the party and go to her room. She had overheard Stepmama say she had some sort of plan.

On the other hand, Peter was not here and the drawing room lamps in the cottage were burning. If only she knew what Peter's handwriting looked like. Since they had never corresponded, she did not.

There was nothing for it but to cross the bridge and find out for herself. Opening the front door, she went out, leaving the lovely strains of 'Silent Night' behind her.

Just before she got to the bridge, she heard a voice calling after her.

'Miss! Your cloak!' It was Thorpe hurrying towards her with it slung over his arm.

Well, that was odd. How could he know she would be going out, let alone retrieve it so quickly and come after her?

He could not.

She started to run for the cottage, to shout for Peter, but Thorpe tossed the cloak over her head, trussed her up in it, then slung her over his shoulder and carried her away from the manor house.

She wriggled and squirmed, cursed even, to no avail.

At one point she was bound by a rope, then put in the back of a wagon and carted off by someone else. Kidnapped. Nothing but fear for Peter's safety could have made her act without caution.

But whoever had done this was not going to find her a compliant captive—and she had a good idea who was going to discover she was not. Trussed up as she was in the moment, she really did not wish to be in Hyrum Grant's shoes once she no longer was!

Entering Maplewood, Peter felt propelled back in time. Something, an echo of times past, enfolded him in a sense of well-being.

Perhaps it had to do with the melodies played by the string quartet. Music had always been a part of the Maplewood he remembered. Anna Liese was not the only one of her family to be musical. Her father had had a beautiful singing voice. And her mother—yes, he remembered now that she had played the violin. His family and Anna Liese's had spent many evenings together just this way. It was somewhat similar, but back then he had not been a viscount and the gathering intimate rather than grand.

But something of the feeling of how it had been in those days lingered. He could scarcely wait to find out if Anna Liese felt it too.

'Lord Cliverton!' The Baroness bustled forward, her hands extended in welcome. 'It is an honour to have you grace our humble home.'

Humble was not how he would describe Maplewood. In his mind it was large, yet at the same time warm and inviting.

He thought the appeal had to do with Anna Liese. This

was her home and, even though the Baroness and Mildred lived here, it was Anna Liese's presence giving it a sense of home. He understood how much she loved Maplewood. This was the place where she nourished memories of her past, kept them fresh and alive.

Now that he was in Woodlore Glen and had his own memories returning, he knew he ought to have been more like Anna Liese over the years. Rather than avoiding pain by forgetting, he ought to have sought solace in remembering.

He glanced about. Where was Anna Liese?

Mildred hustled towards him, looking flashy in a wealth of green. Bright, shocking green. He was not one to notice fashion even though he had grown up with women wanting his opinion on it, but this gown was—it was one to be noticed was the kindest way to think of it.

'How nice it is to see you again, my lord.' It was apparent that Mildred wished to reach for his arm and escort him to another room but withheld the impulse. 'I told dear Mother what a lovely walk we had yesterday.'

'I do feel the motherly need to scold you for taking my daughter off without a chaperon, Lord Cliverton. But I shall overlook it this one time. Young people will be young people, will they not? It is easy to get carried away when hearts are calling to one another.'

Young people? They were hardly all that young.

And hearts calling? This was far from the case.

The Baroness placed her hand in the crook of his arm and led him towards the large drawing room. The home had two as he recalled. A large one for entertaining and a smaller one for family. 'Come along, I will introduce you to the other guests.'

Mildred started to place her fingers on his arm then received a sharp glance from her mother.

'We are a small group tonight, my lord,' the Baroness declared. 'I prefer an intimate gathering where we can get to know one another more easily.'

'I prefer it, too.' He greatly looked forward to being able to spend time with Anna Liese in the same place they had as children. How many more memories would come back to him? he wondered.

Coming into the drawing room, Peter nodded to several guests who were seated about the room in comfortable-looking chairs, conversing and looking at ease. It was clear these people had known one another for a long time, if not all their lives.

Newcomer to Woodlore Glen that he was, he was anxious to know them as well as they knew each other. He intended to make this his home away from the city after all. It would be good to be on neighbourly terms with the people here.

The Baroness promenaded him in a circle about the room, introducing him.

In front of the fireplace there were three unoccupied chairs. Baroness Barlow indicated that he should sit on the one in the middle.

The ladies sat down on each side of him.

Where was the chair for Anna Liese? It only seemed right that she should be in this apparent place of honour with the rest of her family.

'Thank you for this fine welcome, Baroness. I do appreciate having the chance to get to know my neighbours.'

'Oh, but we are so humble here in Woodlore Glen. Please, you must tell us all about London,' she said.

'Oh, yes, please do!' Mildred clapped her hands. 'I would

love to hear about the grand balls. I have been to so few of them. Here in the countryside they are rare.'

'Have you never been to London, Mildred?' he asked, making polite conversation while glancing at the doorway whenever someone entered the drawing room.

Where was Anna Liese? Given all she had done in preparation of the event, he found it odd that she would be late.

'On the rare occasion and then only for a short stay.'

'But now that we have a friend who resides in the city, we shall make an effort to go there more often,' the Baroness said.

'Oh, yes, Mother!' Mildred spoke to her mother but stared at him while she spoke. 'I would love to see a grand ball. Even if we did not attend, I would be content to watch from the kerb while lords and ladies came and went.'

That was the last thing Mildred would be content with, in his opinion. Anna Liese had warned him that they would be casting about for an invitation to his ball. He would rather wait until she arrived and then offer it to all three of them at once. She had clearly said she did not wish to come. Still, he would give the offer one more go.

But where was she?

He was beginning to feel uneasy about her absence. Something about it felt wrong. Conversation stalled while Mildred stared at him, blinking and smiling. Better to get it over with, then. He would formally invite Anna Liese when he saw her, which he hoped would be soon.

'As it happens, I am hosting a ball. It is to be just a few days before Christmas. I understand this hardly gives you time to plan, but if you can manage, I would be delighted for you to attend.'

'Oh, my.' The Baroness frowned, as if she had not been

trying to extract this from him all along. 'It is rather late notice, with everything to be done in order to be made ready. I suppose I will need to give you my answer once I give the matter more thought.'

An hour passed by before dinner was announced and still there was no sign of Anna Liese.

He stood up to go to the dining room and was immediately latched on to. Each of his arms became possessed by Lady Barlow and Mildred. They led the way to the dining room with the other guests coming behind.

'Will Anna Liese be joining us for dinner?' Given how jealous these two were of her, he ought to have referred to her as Miss Barlow, but doing so would have felt unnatural in the extreme.

'I rather think not, my lord.' The Baroness sniffed as if there was something unpleasant in the air. 'She received a rather odd note earlier and I have not seen her since.'

'Perhaps it was bad news and she retired to her room,' Mildred suggested.

'How long ago did this note arrive?' Something was not right. He felt the wrongness down to his bones.

'Oh, well, let me see.' The Baroness tapped her chin. 'More than three hours ago.'

'Has anyone been up to check upon her?'

'I asked Thorpe to send an enquiry to her maid, but I have not heard.' She glanced about. Waved over the footman. 'Thorpe, is Miss Barlow in her chamber, do you know?'

'I cannot say, my lady. I took her cloak to her when she went outside without it. I did not see her return, but she must have done.'

'Well, I'm certain she has. Thank you, Thorpe.'

'I find it odd that Miss Barlow would work so hard and look forward to this evening so much to spend it in her room.'

'One never knows what my stepdaughter will do. She does tend to disappear without word on occasion. Ah, here comes the meal,' declared the Baroness, apparently satisfied that her stepdaughter was safe.

On this occasion? It was not likely.

'Should someone not check to see if she is ill?' Mildred asked.

'We saw her only a few hours ago and she looked quite well,' the Baroness answered.

Peter had not seen her and so could not be sure she was well. Until he was, he would not be able to stomach the meal.

'Thorpe,' he said. The man had not gone about his business, but lingered by the table. 'Will you send for Miss Barlow's maid? I would like a word.'

Moments later the maid arrived, but she did not enter the dining room, but rather stood by the door looking concerned.

'If you will excuse me?' He stood.

'Surely you are not leaving,' the Baroness gasped. 'I'm certain that even if Anna Liese is not in her room, she is well enough. She dislikes society, that is all.'

'She does not dislike my society.'

'Perhaps someone else might speak with Martha?' Mildred suggested. 'It is not your place to—'

He did not know what else she said because he was striding towards the hallway where Anna Liese's maid waited for him.

'No, my lord, she is not in her chamber. I have not seen

her since she went down. Thorpe came to collect her cloak quite some time ago.'

'Do you find it odd that she wished to go out?'

'Most odd, but Thorpe said she had received some sort of note.'

What the note had to do with anything he could not imagine. The fact was that Anna Liese had gone out in the dark and the cold and she had not returned.

Hurrying into the hall, he instructed the servant in attendance to bring his hat and coat. Shrugging into his coat, he asked the man if he had seen Anna Liese go out or return.

In the hour he had been in attendance he had not seen anything.

Standing on Maplewood's front porch, Peter took off his hat and scratched his head. Which direction would she have gone? And what, if anything, did the note have to do with it?

He walked the path towards the bridge in case she had been coming to see him. Perhaps there would be some clue to where she had gone.

Suddenly the wind picked up, blowing dry leaves across the path. But wait—not only leaves! A few feet away from where he stood, a scrap of paper blew towards the stream.

He rushed for it and caught it up a step before it tumbled into the water.

He went cold, reading it. It was supposed to be from him. Not only had he not written it, he was not sick! Or he had not been until he read the thing.

Shoving it in his pocket, he cursed. Someone had lured Anna Liese away by trickery. He meant to find her and discover why.

* * *

Anna Liese glanced about her cell, which happened to be the back room of the bank.

'I've finally got myself the Barlow lady. It has not been easy, I can tell you,' Hyrum Grant said, smiling as if he were quite proud of the nasty accomplishment.

'If you believe it will be any easier now that you have me, you are greatly mistaken.'

'I'm glad it is you and not the other one. Mildred—I cannot imagine being wed to her. I imagine your fine Viscount is enjoying her company.'

That was no doubt what Stepmama had in mind in instigating this outrage.

She was going to fight energetically to make sure she did not get away with it.

'You are wasting your time if you think to be wed to me.'

'I hardly think you are in a position to refuse me.'

Her strength pitted against his, this was true. She, however, would use a different weapon. For all that the man was stronger than she was, he was not very clever.

'I will procure a special licence in the morning,' he said with an arrogant smirk. 'Do not worry, my dear, you will be a respectably married woman in a day or two.'

'A special licence in Woodlore Glen? I cannot imagine where you will find one.'

'I do have many connections.' He grinned, showing off his straight, white teeth. 'But once I am your husband, I will gain many more influential contacts.'

'There are not all that many connections in our small village which you have not already made. I doubt if I will be much help to you in that.'

Anna Liese glanced about the back room. The curtains

were drawn against the night. As far as she could tell there was no easy way out. Even if she screamed no one would hear her. The village shops were closed and, even if they were not, the back door of the bank faced the little-used rear road.

The very road on which Peter taught her to ride a bicycle, where she had fallen off and landed in the bush and he had nearly kissed her. But the tender moment had been interrupted by this man—the one who expected she would meekly go along with his demands.

Well, they would see who was whose captive.

'If you think I will be married in anything but a proper gown, you are greatly mistaken. I am the daughter of Baron Barlow. It will bring shame upon you if I wed in rags.'

'You are not wearing rags. Besides, you have other things to worry about than fancy gowns.'

'What might those be? Gowns are of utmost importance to a woman of my position.'

Behind the curtains, she saw the shadow of bars on the windows.

'After we are wed, we will discuss what you will wear.'

'Can I be honest with you, Hyrum?'

'No, I would rather—'

'Being married to me might not be worth the supposed influence to be had.'

'It's not only that. Your stepmother has offered me a good sum of money to get you off her hands.'

'Surely you do not think she has enough to make this worthwhile.'

'I need a wife anyway. Why not get paid for it? It makes life simpler, two birds with one stone and all that.'

Upon their last meeting, Hyrum had indicated that he expected obedience in a woman.

Very well, let the battle begin.

'If you believe that being married to a woman who is forced into it will be simple, you are mistaken.'

What a nasty, arrogant smile he had. She wished to punch it so intensely that she had to sit on her hands. If she did end up doing so, it would be strategic and not an impulse.

'I think you will do.'

'Tell me then, what is it you require of a marriage, Mr Grant? Because I am certain you will not get it from me.'

'I'll need food on my table and my clothing washed. My house kept clean. I do not care much for children, though.'

'We shall have a large staff to see to those things. I will care for the children myself. All six of them,' she added when he stared at silently at her. 'Do you wish to know what I require of marriage?'

'Not that it matters, but I assume you are going to tell me.'

'I require a true love match. Will you be able to give me that?'

'Believe it or not, I have long admired you.'

She did not believe it, not for a moment. It was money and prestige he admired.

In that moment she wished for Peter's presence more than her next breath. If he were here, he would give this man his due. She would fear nothing if Peter was here.

For all that she pretended not to be, she was quite frightened. She was this man's captive and as much as she told herself she was capable of handling it, she really was at his mercy. Perhaps if she imagined Peter's arms tight and snug about her she would find the courage she needed to get through this unscathed.

'I do not believe it.'

'It doesn't not matter to me whether you do or not. The outcome will be the same. You will be my wife.'

'I'm hungry. Since I am your captive you must feed me.'

'Very well, Princess. Perhaps you should relax and get used to your new home while I am gone.'

'There are bars on the windows, Hyrum. I will never feel at home as long as they remain.'

There was little chance of him removing them, but it did bear pointing out. What she would be doing while he was gone was trying to work out a way out of here. If there was a way to be found. Banks were known for being secure.

'Feel free to explore, my dearest.' Oh, but that sneer made her want to strike him. 'Just keep in mind you will be wasting your effort looking for a way out. This door locks from the inside and the outside. And, as you say, there are bars on the windows.'

'Do you have bars on the windows of your home? If you do, I will insist on removing them. They will scare off our many guests. You do enjoy entertaining? I shall invite a dozen callers every day.'

She knew he did not enjoy the company of a great number of people—it was a well-known thing about him. It was odd since he wanted status, which by nature involved the society of others.

What else did he dislike?

'And we will have cats.' Many people were allergic, she could only hope he was one of them. 'Only two to begin with, but I do hate separating kittens from their mothers so the house will soon be overrun with the sweet creatures, although I imagine we will have to deal with fleas.'

With an ounce of luck, he was beginning to believe she

was a shrew and no amount of money would be worth living with her.

Grumbling, he opened the door and let in a whoosh of cold air.

'Do not forget to bring dessert, Hyrum. I adore sweets.'

And Peter—she adored his strength and his honest nature. He was everything that Hyrum Grant was not. Even if the banker did manage to ruin her reputation, she would not marry him.

He slammed the door going out. The lock clicked sharply into place. She really was stuck in here. What was she to do now?

Escape seemed impossible, which meant she must carry on with the weapons she had: her tongue and her superior wit. So far, her captor did not seem prone to violence. But she had no idea how far she might push the man until he was. Still, she had no choice in the matter. It was vital she give the impression that life married to her would not be worthwhile.

Seeing a desk, she crossed the room and opened a drawer. Perhaps it held something that might be used as a weapon. It would need to be small or he would see it. Drat, all it contained were pencils and other clerkish items. Scooping up the pencils she dribbled them on the floor. With any luck Hyrum Grant would slip, whereupon she would snatch his key and make her escape.

'Look at this,' she said to no one.

She withdrew a bottle of ink and opened the stopper. Since she did not wish to damage her gown, which had already taken abuse during the drama of getting her here, she did not dribble it on the floor. Instead, she poured it on the seat of the desk chair. A lovely black splotch bloomed on the navy-blue cushion.

'I would not want to marry me, especially after all these papers get scattered across the floor. They will be too crushed to read, I imagine, once I begin to pace about. He might begin to wonder what damage I will do to his home and regret this decision.'

Think, she told herself. *Think*. What in here might be used for a weapon?

Going to the window, she inspected the bars, yanking them one by one. Bars only went to point out yet another flaw in Hyrum's character. His judgement was off. Why on earth did he think he needed bars in Woodlore Glen? He was the least scrupulous of the souls living in the village. Was he barring windows against himself? She went from window to window, trying and failing to get out.

'Ouch!' A splinter pierced her finger, but she had no time to tend to it. She could not imagine where her captor was going to get dinner, but it might not take him long to do it.

And then something snapped. When she glanced at her hand a small bar was curled in her fist. It was only ten inches long, but it was a great deal more useful than a pencil.

Running across the bridge to get his bicycle, Peter could not recall ever being so worried. Or so angry! He swore his heart crept up his throat and the panicked beating was choking him.

Thorpe had been the person to give Anna Liese the note so Peter had sought him out. The man hadn't stood up to Peter's inquisition and admitted that he had delivered Anna Liese to the banker. Thorpe swore he did not know where Grant was taking her.

He'd let the footman go without punching him the way he had wanted to. The man already had a bruise swelling under his eye and he could only hope that Anna Liese had given it to him.

Whatever Grant had in mind for Anna Liese, it would not be to her benefit. He did not know that Grant would resort to violence against her, but neither did he know he would not. What Peter did know was that he, himself, would not hesitate to resort to violence if need be.

Although he had never had occasion to pummel anyone before, he knew he could. His hands clenching on the cold metal handlebars told him it would not be a difficult thing to use his fists in defence of his friend.

For all that he was running on pure emotion, he needed to act with logic and work out where the banker would have taken her. Somewhere secure where she would not be heard and where she could not get out. The bank would fit all those requirements. And Grant had the only keys to the place.

As fast as he was flying along the path, he risked going down. Uneven stones and pebbles hitting his front wheel made the bike wobble.

What did not wobble was his resolve to free Anna Liese.

To Anna Liese's surprise, the dinner Hyrum came back with smelled delicious.

'What is that, Hyrum? Did you find it in a rubbish heap? It smells rotten.'

He plunked the dinner tray on the desk, casting her a sneer.

'What has happened here?'

'It was an accident.' She glanced at the floor and shrugged. 'It looks like—what have you done?'

'Sit down here in the chair,' she said pleasantly. 'You might as well eat the food even though it is not up to my standards. Once we are wed you will need to do better.'

'Do not test me, Anna Liese.'

Oh, but he did sit down! He must be wondering why she, his captive, was grinning so broadly. She felt rather good about having the bar tucked into the pocket of her skirt. Now she only needed to discover a way to use it.

'Test you? I am not doing that. It has simply become apparent to me that I am trapped and will soon be your wife.' She nudged the tray towards him, smiling as prettily as she knew how while he scowled at the mess she had made of his shiny floor.

That was funny, really. If Peter were here, he would laugh. He would also rescue her. But he was not here and so she would wrap the thought of him around her as a buffer against fear.

'As a dutiful wife, and I believe such a lady is one you require, I merely meant to help.'

'Help?' he grumbled.

She nodded.

Still seeming to be unaware that he was sitting in ink, Hyrum began shoving food into his mouth.

She thought he cursed behind a mouthful of bread while he shook his finger at the floor.

'Well, I did get rather bored while you were gone. You should know that I require entertainment in order to keep myself in bounds—rather like a puppy, or so I have been told. You will need to make your own judgement about that in time. Well, I found the correspondence in the drawer, all these letters needing to be answered. When I picked them

up, I slipped and they all flew out of my hand and then...
well, you see for yourself what happened.'

'If you dislike tonight's dinner, you will detest our wedding feast. I am partial to goose and you have one, I believe.'
He slanted an evil, narrow-eyed glance at her.

Was he now about to burst into a fit of violence? What a
lucky thing there would be no wedding feast. Although, so
far, her portrayal of a being shrew did not seem to bother
him. Perhaps once he noticed the ink on his trousers...

Oh! But wait. Just there—a shadow moved across the
curtain from the outside. Her heart went still, then pounded
so madly in her ears she thought her captor could not fail
to hear it. Apparently, he did not, noisily chewing on some
sort of meat.

She recognised that beloved shadow, although it seemed
impossible that Peter could have found her. She knew the
way his shoulders moved when he walked and the way his
head tilted when he was thinking hard about a matter. She
was certain it was him—who else's presence would she
react to right through the walls of this building?

He had come to rescue her. Although in order to be able
to do so he would need to get inside. But this being a bank,
there was really no way to do it. The door would need to be
opened from the inside for Peter to rush inside and free her.

'I hate to bother you, Hyrum. And I would not mention it
if the matter was not urgent. But you did not supply a chamber pot. You ought to have done so because I—'

'I am beginning to think I do not admire you all that
much after all.'

He stood up. He would not admire her in the least once
he noticed the seat of his expensive-looking trousers.

'It does not matter a great deal if you admire me or not

because did you not say it was only the money which mattered? But the fact remains, I do require a way to relieve my needs.'

'Can you not wait until after I finish eating?' he asked with a regretful glance back at the half-eaten meal.

She shrugged, shifted her weight from one foot to the other and bounced up and down for effect.

'Are you willing to risk it? The floor is a mess as it is—my dear. I shall begin calling you that in order to be used to the endearment when we recite our eternal vows.'

He yanked the key from his pocket and marched towards the door. She followed close behind, curling her fingers around the hidden ten inches of bar.

She only prayed that Peter would be on the other side of the door when Hyrum opened it.

'I think that our wedding night would be more interesting if you continued to admire me, my dear,' she said, watching while he turned the key. Now was the time to keep his mind fully distracted. 'Would you like to know a secret, Hyrum? I do not know a thing about what goes on in the marriage bed except that it is better when the couple are—well, naked. I have heard that some sweating occurs, but that sounds odd to me. I will need your instruction on what to do, so—'

He glanced back at her, arching one brow while slanting her an unattractive smile.

The door crashed open.

There stood Peter, looking magnificently heroic. He balled his fist, ready to deliver a blow to Hyrum's razor-straight nose. Oh, dear, the cad began to close the door, which would land the blow on solid wood.

Whipping the bar from her skirt pocket, she smacked

the banker smartly on top of his head. The surprise gave Peter the opportunity to punch Hyrum's pointy chin. And then his stomach.

Ducking past the men, she ran a short distance and then glanced over her shoulder. She stopped and spun about, stunned to see Peter gripping Hyrum's collar and lifting him off the ground. My word, she had no idea he had grown to be so strong. If her heart had not already been galloping, it would now be, but for an entirely different reason.

Peter was shouting something in the banker's face, to which Hyrum was nodding vigorously. Once Peter set him back on the ground, the scoundrel scurried into the bank.

Watching Peter stride towards her, rolling his bicycle with him, she slipped ever deeper in love. She had never been rescued before and it made her feel—cherished.

Even after what she had just endured a sense of comfort wrapped her up. This sense of well-being had been lacking in her life ever since her father died. All she wanted was to stand still, right here on the path, and capture the sensation.

'He will not be bothering you again.'

'It appeared that you gave him a vigorous warning. I only hope he remembers it.'

'Don't worry, Anna Liese, he'll remember.'

'What did you say to him?'

'I reminded him of who I was—and who he was.' He grinned, his eyes sparkling and stern all at once. How did he manage such a glance? 'I made him understand that you were under the protection of a viscount. That if he bothered you again, I know people who could ruin him financially.'

She had heard of knees going weak and now knew it to be true. Her heart and brain felt mushy, too.

'You are my hero, Peter.'

What would she not give to kiss him and demonstrate her affection, her deep and growing affection? More than that, her love.

He drew her cloak from across the handlebars of the bike. 'I found it on the path further back,' he said, laying it across her shoulders and buttoning it under her chin. His large warm fingers lingered over the task for a moment.

She dug her fingers into her skirt. Peter was not in love with her. She would not kiss him again unless it would be answered with the same passion with which she offered it.

He shook his head, let his hands fall away from her. 'Do you wish to stay at the cottage tonight? I will take a room at the inn if you do.'

'I need to return to Maplewood. Would you mind taking me back?'

'It isn't that I mind, but after what your stepmother did— and I know she was behind this—are you certain you want to?'

'I must.' It was really the last thing she wanted to do, but she needed to let her stepmother know she had failed once again to be rid of her.

And how wonderful would it be to walk back into the party on the arm of her hero? To see Stepmama's face when she realised she had done nothing to keep her away from him.

'If you are certain, then,' he said.

'I do not wish for her to think she has intimidated me. Stepmama must be made to understand she must stop this manipulation.'

She was firmer in her determination to marry in a true love match than she had ever been. How could she not be when her true love was walking beside her, making her feel as if she were melting into her muddy party shoes?

It hit her that, unless Peter felt the same way about her, she might never have her love match. It was unlikely that she could transfer her feelings to someone else as if she were changing shoes.

'Let's go then,' he said with the grin she had always adored.

Even after what she had been through over the past few hours, going back to dinner with her skirt muddy, with her hair mussed and tumbled down her back, felt delightfully like mischief. It was almost as if she and Peter were children again, merrily bedevilling their parents.

'I'll just put the bike away.' Peter said. 'I imagine your stepmother will be glad to see you safe and hale.'

'She will be horrified.'

And for some reason a situation which ought to have been awful made them both laugh.

Stepmama was going to more horrified than Peter knew because in the instant she spotted her with the Viscount, she would read how very deeply Anna Liese loved him.

By the time Peter escorted Anna Liese into the grand drawing room, dinner was over, and people had gathered for drinks and conversation.

Conversation which ended abruptly when he strode inside, with a dishevelled Anna Liese on his arm.

'Baroness Barlow,' he announced, enjoying the stretch of a grin cutting his face. What had happened was not humorous in the least. Anna Liese's future had been threatened. But this! Watching the Baroness turn the shade of a bleached sheet on washday was satisfying. 'You will be relieved to know the note Anna Liese received was nothing of concern.'

'Indeed, it is a relief.' The drink the Baroness held sloshed in the flute and came close to spilling. 'I hate to think she might have received bad news.'

'It seemed at first that it might have been the case,' Anna Liese said, letting go of his arm and taking a step away from him. 'For some reason, Hyrum Grant was under the impression that the Viscount had fallen ill.'

'Hyrum Grant? I wonder why he would think that?' Mildred asked.

'As do I, how very odd.' The Baroness set her drink aside, no doubt fearing her scheme against Anna Liese was about to be exposed in front of her guests. 'I cannot imagine why he would think such a thing.'

'Or why he would send a note to Anna Liese?' Peter looked hard at Lady Barlow while he spoke. 'It is peculiar. I wonder how Mr Grant, being in the village, would come by any knowledge regarding my health, or be concerned about it.'

Mildred shook her head, taking in Anna Liese's appearance with a frown. 'What happened to you?'

'As anyone would, when I got the note, I walked over to the cottage to see for myself.'

'But I was already here and you know how concerned I was when Anna Liese was absent from our gathering. Well, I discovered from Thorpe that she was with the banker, discussing the meaning of his note.'

'And did you discover it?' The Baroness seemed to be holding her breath, staring hard at her stepdaughter while waiting for him to answer.

Anna Liese was the one to answer.

'I did not, even though he insisted I accompany him to the village to discuss it. But then Peter came along and—' she gazed up at him, her eyes warm and shining '—and insisted forcefully to know the reason for it.'

'But what was it?' Mildred asked looking puzzled so he thought that she, at least, had nothing to do with it.

'Mr Grant thought he heard someone say so, but try as he might, he cannot recall who. If he remembers, he promises to let me know.'

He did not wish to reveal the truth and make this uncomfortable for Anna Liese, especially with people looking curiously on.

'But, Stepmama,' Anna Liese said, 'you will be glad to know that he has promised not to cause us further trouble—with his notes.'

'He made me a particular vow about it.' Peter let his frown settle on the Baroness, letting it rest upon her until she slid her gaze away and stared at the flute on the table beside her.

Good, he believed she understood.

'But that does not explain what happened to your hair, Anna Liese,' Mildred half whispered, half hissed.

'It is nothing that cannot be repaired.' Lady Barlow shot her daughter a glance, clearly ordering her to carry the question no further.

Glancing at Anna Liese, he saw she was sucking on the tip of her finger.

'What happened?' he asked. He had not noticed her favouring her finger until now.

The Baroness stood up, looking a shade paler than she had.

'I clearly instructed him not to—that is, what I mean is

that I will instruct Thorpe not to deliver notes without coming to me first. Were you injured, Anna Liese?'

'A splinter, that's all.'

Beckoning to Martha, who was standing near the doorway looking concerned at what was happening, Anna Liese's stepmother waved her over.

'Come, take your mistress upstairs and see to her finger.'

'Do not bother.' Peter nodded to Martha. 'I shall see to it.'

With that, he led his frazzled-looking friend out of the drawing room. They had done what needed doing in letting the Baroness know her scheme had failed. The sooner they were out of her company the better. As welcome dinners went, this one was memorable.

The last thing he heard going out was Mildred's whine of complaint.

'My stepmother will be in a mood now,' Anna Liese said while sitting on a stool in a quiet corner of the kitchen.

'That is for her to deal with. She needed to know she had not got the better of you.'

Easy for him to say, but she would be the one left to deal with the aftermath. Ah, well, it was not as if she had not done so before. Trying to avoid her stepmother's moods was not easy even at the best of times.

A few of the staff bustled about, placing pastries and drinks on trays to be carried out to the guests.

One of the scullery maids cast Anna Liese a puzzled glance while she scrubbed a pot.

'Please carry on, Lucy.' The last thing she wanted was for the girl to have to work later than necessary in order to give them privacy.

Martha hurried across the kitchen, then placed a clean

towel, a bowl of steaming water and a pair of tweezers on the small table next to the window where she and Peter sat. Wind blew against the diamond-shaped panes, making one of them rattle.

Martha returned with a small lamp and set it on the table. 'Be gentle with her, my lord.' Martha gave them a smile, a wink, and then hurried away.

Peter picked up the tweezers, turned them this way and that so they glittered in the light, then he set them down. He held his palm open for her to place her hand in.

'Don't be worried.' He held her finger to the light, examining it, then dipped a corner of the towel in the warm water, wrapped it around her finger and gently pressed.

'Does it hurt?'

'It is tender, but I will do.'

'I'll make quick work of it.'

'You have done this before, when we were children.'

Then his hand had been slender and boyish. Not like now—now it was large, masculine and the fingers brushed with coarse hair. She hoped he did not make terribly quick of work of removing the splinter.

'I haven't removed one since then. Let us hope I have not lost the skill.'

'I remember once you pulled one out of my thumb with your teeth. Still, I shall try my best to be brave.'

He looked into her eyes for a long silent time while he pressed the warm cloth to her hand. The only sound was the loose pane of glass shivering the wind.

'You are the bravest person I know, but I have to ask. Anna Liese, you were with Grant for a long time before I got there—did he... What I am trying to ask is if he hurt you?'

'I do not imagine you had time to notice the condition of the bank while you were punching him in the jaw.'

'I've a vague impression of papers scattered on the floor as if there had been a fight.'

'He did not harm me, Peter, only scared me. But in the end, I think I scared him more.'

'How could you possibly?'

'I let him get a glimpse of what it would be like to be married to me. I can't think he would enjoy being trapped for ever with a nagging shrew.'

'You are clever, my sweet friend,' he said while picking up the tweezers. 'Perhaps you did not need me pedaling to your rescue.'

'I did, you know I did. He was bound to become angry after what I did to his paperwork, not to mention his trousers.'

'You came in contact with his trousers?'

His touch on her finger remained gentle, but his eyes sharpened in a way she had never seen.

'Not directly. I poured ink on his chair and encouraged him to sit on it.'

He grinned, but said, 'That was too risky. You should have been more cautious.'

'It would have been worse to cower and I did need to know how far he might be pushed.'

'Luckily, no harm came of it.' He lifted the tweezers to the light, showing her the splinter nipped in the small tongs. 'But there is still your stepmother.'

'She was chastised tonight, but honestly, Peter, the only thing that will make her stop will be for me to marry, or for Mildred to.'

'I cannot help but think marrying would be better than

being under constant worry. If you did wed, you could make a choice about your husband rather than having one foisted upon you.'

That not the case. She was kept away from any man worth consideration. And, more importantly, the only man she would choose had just let go of her hand. The man she would choose had an eye on a society wedding in which he would not be required to involve his heart. Such a choice made no sense whatsoever since he had the kindest and most giving heart of anyone she knew.

'I am exhausted, Peter. Go back to your guests if you wish, but I'm going up to bed.' She leaned across the small table, kissed his cheek and let her lips linger a bit longer than friendliness required. 'Thank you for capturing the splinter—and for saving me from having to marry Hyrum Grant.'

I love you, her heart declared while her lips said, 'Goodnight, Peter.'

She stood up, recognising by his frown that he did not wish to go back to the gathering in his honour.

'In case you have forgotten, the kitchen door is that way.' She pointed to a hallway which led to the butler's pantry and then outside.

'Ah, yes, it comes back to me now. So much is coming back—goodnight, Anna Liese.'

He strode down the hallway, but stopped halfway and turned about. He went back through the kitchen again.

'I suppose I must go back,' he mumbled in passing. Then stopping, he said, 'Will you come bicycling with me tomorrow? I believe we could use some fresh air to cleanse this evening from our minds.'

'Meet me on the bridge in the morning.'

He nodded and continued on his way towards the grand drawing room.

She smiled after him because she did not wish to cleanse everything from her mind. Parts of the evening had been harrowing. Had Peter not come to her rescue, she might be facing wedded misery with Hyrum.

But he had rescued her and she would never forget how brave and handsome he had been while doing it. Not every woman had a hero. Many had husbands, yes, but she had her knight in shining armour. No matter what happened in her lonely future, Peter Penneyjons would shine in her heart.

Chapter Eleven

The evening finally ended, Peter opened his front door and then decided he was still too restless to sleep.

Closing the door again, he turned and walked along the back path and then up the hill. At the crest, he sat down on the bench. How many times had he and Anna Liese sat on the bench, watching the folks of Woodlore Glen going about their lives?

Down below, the village was shut up for the night. Only a few lamps shone out of the windows below. It all looked so peaceful—so idyllic.

He might have been content with the image of perfection had it not been for one thing. The back door of the bank, although distant, was in his line of vision. Illuminated in the lamplight of one window, he thought he spotted a figure going past the barred glass. Grant was probably sweeping up the mess of papers Anna Liese had left on the floor. Peter could only guess he was hopping mad about it.

While it had been clever, tricking him into sitting in ink,

the situation spurring Anna Liese to take action had not been humorous.

A while ago, they had made light of the encounter simply because it was easier to do than to openly confront the danger she had truly been in. Which did not mean he was unaware of the evil that had nearly happened.

Had the man got away with what he had intended to, Anna Liese's future would have been a grim one. She had told Peter what she wanted of a marriage. For her it would be a love match or nothing. What the banker would have forced upon her would have been the opposite.

Wind blew briskly from behind, pushing his hair in his face and obscuring his vision. He gathered it in a clump on top of his head and held it there.

Overhead, gusts whipped through bare branches, sounding like a chorus of moans, as if it were singing a song of ill will—of impending doom. Feeling this maudlin was unlike him, but staring at Anna Liese's precarious future made him ill at ease.

For as long as he remained in Woodlore Glen, he would be able to watch over her. But who would do it when he returned to London? She had no man to stand up for her. Her maid, Martha, would do what she could, he thought, but she was a mature lady. What could she do other than report trouble to the Baroness who was the cause of the trouble to begin with?

Because of the wind, the sky was clear, the stars cold and sparkling. He gazed at them for a long time, hoping some solution to this problem would come to him. Short of going down the hill and strangling the man, he did not know what it might be. Since it was not in him to do murder, here he sat, as confused and troubled as he had ever been in his life.

If Aunt Adelia were here she would know what to do. The woman was as clever a lady as he had ever known. He could not recall a social drama she had not been able to sort out. This was not precisely a social drama, but if he pretended to be Aunt Adelia for a moment, thought the way she might think, an answer might come to him. Drawing upon her image, he imagined her sitting beside him, smiling while she tapped her finger on her chin in thought.

'Peter Penneyjons, you do know what to do,' her pretend image told him. Odd how her imagined voice sounded so real. He had to blink to bring her image in and out of focus to be certain she had not inexplicably appeared on the bench.

'No, Aunt, I do not,' he spoke aloud since he was alone on the hilltop.

'It is as simple as keeping her with you, my boy,' his imaginary advisor said in that vivacious way she had about her.

'There is nothing simple about that,' he grumbled. 'I live in London and she lives here.'

'I find marriage to my liking, Peter.'

What? This was his imagination he was conversing with—how could it possibly take such an unexpected turn? Just because Aunt Adelia had found her late-in-life marriage to her liking did not mean that he would find the same in his.

'Goodnight, Aunt Adelia. I will see you at the Christmas ball.'

What he needed was advice from her lips, not what he thought she might say.

A huff of wind bussed his cheek. Odd what one's mind could conjure. He imagined this gust was warmer than the others and that it had been a parting kiss from his aunt—who was not here.

He stood up, stretched and thought he might be able to sleep after all. Because present in the flesh or not, he thought his aunt had given him the answer to his problem. An answer he rather liked the idea of. Coming down the hill, he felt hopeful about it.

Once inside the cottage, he got into bed, looking forward to the morning and being with Anna Liese.

Surely she would agree that what he had decided to do was brilliant and a benefit to them both. With a great yawn, he crossed his hands over his chest and smiled.

Coming outside, Anna Liese decided it was not ideal weather for touring about on bicycles. Dark clouds skimmed the hilltops all about Woodlore Glen. She would not be surprised to see snowflakes at some point today. What a stroke of luck that the wind had stopped blowing.

Peter waited for her on the bridge, flanked by bicycles.

He looked fine and manly bundled against the weather. Watching his welcoming grin, she sighed inside at the way the way the brackets at the corners of his mouth deepened. The sight of him chased away some of the chill.

Not all of it, though—her nose and lips still felt icy. A kiss would warm them. A kiss which was not going to happen. She would have to be content imagining the heat that would simmer inside her—suffuse her from head to toe.

'Brrr...' Peter said, stamping his feet as if to warm them. 'May I suggest we ride no further than the village?'

'Please do say we will go no further. Sitting in front of the fireplace at the village tearoom would be wiser than freezing our toes off.' Sitting astride the bicycle and tucking in her skirt, she glanced up. The clouds looked darker than they had seconds ago. 'Do you think it will snow?'

'I wouldn't mind if it did. We don't see a great deal of it in London.'

'We don't see it much here either, especially this early in the year.'

By the time they parked their bicycles behind the restaurant and hurried inside, Anna Liese was convinced a blizzard was coming.

It was warm and festive inside with holly and berries on the tables and swathes of cedar and pine over the windows.

They had a choice of tables since they were the only customers. Ordinarily at this time of morning there were other visitors, but apparently they had hesitated to come out in the weather.

'I do not remember it ever being so cold,' she said, taking a seat at a table in front of the fireplace. Warmth washing over her from the flames gave her a delightful shiver. The sensation was so delightful that she wondered if the shiver did not have to do with heat from without, but heat from within.

What, she had to wonder, would Peter think if she admitted her feelings for him? How they had grown from those of a child to those of a woman. She would not dare to admit it because she had no reason to believe he felt the same way. She would rather not offer her heart up to be broken. Better to wait and hope.

Which was easier said than accomplished since she had spent the whole of the night imagining how wonderful it would be to be married to him. Each day they would awake with declarations of love and then end the day declaring it without words.

Hmm, her odd shiver probably was not caused by the fire. It skittered over her skin in a pleasant heat which mere hearth flames could not account for.

'I don't either. Since I have not been here at this time of year in so long, I don't remember the weather. What I do remember is how much fun we always had no matter the temperature.' He cleared his throat, seeming oddly ill at ease. 'You do remember what fun we used to have, Anna Liese?'

The serving girl came out of the kitchen carrying two cups of hot chocolate. She set them on the table, smiling. They had not yet ordered drinks, but the girl must assume anyone who was out and about this morning would welcome them.

'I do not need to go back so far to remember, Peter. It has only been a few moments since we had fun.' She took a sip of chocolate, sighing at the sweet warmth sliding down her throat. 'I find bicycling to be greatly entertaining. Thank you so much for teaching me.'

'You should come riding with me in London. Hyde Park is an interesting place to pedal about.'

'Hyde Park? That is for society nobs—oh, but you are one of them. Sometimes I forget it.'

'You are also one of them, my friend.'

'Sometimes I forget that, too.' On the social scale she felt closer to humble than noble.

The waitress returned to take their order for breakfast, then hurried away.

'Anna Liese, after I left you last night, was everything well? I hope the Baroness did not take her frustrations out on you.'

'I retired without seeing her and was out this morning

before she rose. I imagine I will need to deal with it later this afternoon.'

'I invited them to London, to attend the ball. I can only hope their attention will be diverted and they will leave you alone.'

Had he wanted to invite them? She could not imagine he did. But in the end, what did two more title-hunters matter? The occasion of the ball was for him to choose among the ladies, was it not? Certainly, he knew enough of Mildred not to pick her.

She imagined a few of the women attending his ball would suit his requirements of a convenient marriage—one which would not be marked with morning kisses and nightly declarations of love. Poor Peter. She did want better for him—although to be honest she did not want him to find it with someone who was not her.

For all that she felt left out at not being invited to his ball, she was relieved for it even more. It was difficult to imagine anything worse than watching him seek a bride—or having him ask her opinion on which of them might suit.

'I meant to invite you last night at dinner, but then you were not there to be invited. Afterwards, a social invitation seemed frivolous.' He reached across the table, curled his big, warm fingers around hers. 'Won't you attend? We will have a good time. I would like to show you what London has to offer. Just think of it, we can ramble about as if we were children again.'

It was crushing to know that was how he viewed her, as the child she had been. Had their relationship not progressed from that? In her heart she thought it had. Was it possible it had only been her heart to have progressed?

My word, but they had nearly kissed twice!

Maybe she ought to go the ball and wear the new gown which was secreted away in Martha's quarters. The flirtatious bodice would put the issue to rest, once and for all. She took a second to imagine what his reaction to her womanly figure would be. Better to let go of that image. A snapping fire in the hearth was quite enough heat.

But, no, she would not be attending his spouse-hunting ball.

'I fear you must find your bride without my help, Peter.' She wriggled her hand out of his. 'You are the only one who can make such a choice.'

'I have always believed my requirements in a bride are simple.' He frowned for a second, then blinked and resumed his smile. Something was shifting about in his mind, but she could not imagine what. 'I shall be content as long as she is companionable and of good character.'

'Peter Penneyjons! That is a cavalier attitude. You should care very much. You speak of your future as if the lady will make little difference in it, as if one was interchangeable with another. I am certain whoever she turns out to be will resent it.'

'I'm sorry, it did sound callous. I only meant that this is how it is for men of my station. I am expected to pick a bride for her position in society—for her large dowry. Every lady seeking my attention understands it.'

'As noble as you may be, Peter, you ought to know better having arranged love matches for your cousins.'

'I hadn't a hand in any of that. One and all, they chose for themselves.'

This was not a subject she wished to discuss. Let him choose where he would.

A bell jingled over the front door. A tall, dark-haired

young man rushed inside. He glanced about while brushing the shoulders of his coat.

His smile settled on the young waitress who was standing on a chair affixing a sprig of mistletoe to a beam.

'It has begun to snow, Catherine!' he exclaimed, grinning at them as well as her. 'We might have a white Christmas if it lasts.'

'I'm working, Glenn.' The girl shot him a grin over her shoulder. The handsome young man hurried over to help her down. 'You must come back later.'

Catherine's smile lingered on Glenn, her affection for him evident.

'Please say you will come sledding!'

'Off with you, now.' Catherine shooed her fingers at him. 'The snow has not yet covered the ground.'

Glenn did not seem to care. He took her hand and tugged her towards the front door. With the way his blue eyes were twinkling, Anna Liese could not imagine how Catherine resisted the invitation.

What Anna Liese saw in the young man's eyes made her heart yearn for what she was not likely to have in her own life. So far, she had seen no sign of anything like that in Peter's eyes.

In the face of the young man's affection for Catherine, Anna Liese was reminded that in Peter's eyes, she was only a friend—a dear friend—but not a true love.

'Later, then—I'll be back for you when the snow is deeper.' Not seeming to care that there were customers in the restaurant, Glenn kissed Catherine on her lips, quickly, joyfully.

Catherine swatted his arm, gave him a false frown. 'The mistletoe is over there.'

He pulled her under the inviting sprig, then kissed her again.

'I beg your pardon,' the girl said, pressing her fingers to the blush in her cheeks. 'Glenn asked me to be his wife last night and he has not settled from the excitement of it yet.'

With that, she spun about and half skipped to the kitchen. Clearly, Catherine's heart had not settled either. What a joyful thing it must be, to feel so flushed with love, with such hope for the future.

Peter was saying something to her, but she'd quite lost track of what it was. Witnessing the love the young couple shared for one another made her reaffirm her commitment not to marry until a man looked at her the way Glenn looked at Catherine.

Returning her attention to Peter, she found him blinking at her, his smile indulgent and—and friendly. Clearly, thoughts of mistletoe were not on his mind.

'I'm sorry, Peter, what were you saying?'

'I don't blame you for not hearing me. With the snow coming down harder, it is exciting.'

'We shall have great fun,' she answered, grateful that she did not need to make up a reason for her lack of attention. 'Build a snowman or go sledding?'

'I'm for a snowball fight—have we ever had one? I can't recall. But first I would like to discuss what you did not hear me saying.'

'Of course. By the time we have finished discussing it the snow will be deep enough for play.'

Peter cleared his throat, that odd sense of nervousness she had noticed a moment ago returned.

'Is something wrong?'

He nodded, pursed his lips. 'I am worried about you. I

need to know you will be safe when I return to London. Just because Hyrum Grant is not likely to be a threat, someone else might be.'

'You needn't be worried. I have been dealing with this sort of thing for years. You may return to London. Find your bride, Peter. I will get along as I always have.'

Except that she would not get along as she always had. In the past she not been in love. While it was true that she had always loved Peter, that love had been for a child—from a child. Now that she loved the man, nothing would ever be the same.

'Truly? Have you ever been kidnapped before?'

'I will admit, I did let down my guard, but it was only because I thought you were ill.'

'I will not allow that to happen to you again. I have come up with a solution to your problem.'

Had he? She could not imagine how since he did not know what her problem was: that she was in love with him and he was not in love her.

The reason he was unaware of it was because she had not told him. Perhaps she ought to. Right now, sitting here with no one to distract them, she should confess, 'I love you Peter'. In her heart she knew she must. If she did not, the regret would follow her for ever.

Very well, then—

He reached across the table, caught her hand again, held on and squeezed her fingers. 'What if you married me?' he said.

The confession died in her mouth—in her heart.

'Do not refuse me right off. If you think about it, it makes sense.'

Sense! As words of love went—sense was not one. Sense

was the last thing a woman—this woman—wanted to hear when being proposed to.

'Have you lost your mind, Peter Penneyjons?'

'Not at all. If we wed, the Baroness will not be able to force you to marry someone you do not wish to.'

'I do not wish to marry you!'

She did, of course. But not unless he loved her, which he clearly did not.

'We already know we get along well.'

'Getting along and being in love are not the same thing.' Her stomach roiled. If she did not lose her hot chocolate, it would only be by an effort of extraordinary self-control.

'Ever since last night I've been thinking about this.' Given that he was grinning, he was clearly not aware of cleaving her heart in half. 'To go into a marriage already knowing I like my bride will be a great relief. We both benefit from the arrangement.'

'A relief? Because you already like me?' She stood up, clenching her fists so he would not see them trembling.

'You know I do—you are and always have been my dearest friend. Many marriages begin with less.'

'The one I want—' she concentrated on breathing, in and out, slow and steady '—requires much more.'

Peter stood up, reaching for her hand with a pleading glance. 'Anna Liese, you must know how deeply I care for you.'

'I will never accept a sensible proposal from anyone, even you.'

She spun away. Out of the corner of her eye, she noticed Catherine frowning, shaking her head. As young as the waitress was, she knew more than Lord Cliverton did!

'I understand this proposal is not the romantic one you

wished for. I suppose I should have used prettier words, recited a romantic poem perhaps. But before you dismiss it out of hand, consider how it will benefit both of us. And is marriage not meant to be a beneficial arrangement for both parties?'

Marching to the door, she snatched her coat from the rack and jerkily put it on. If she did not escape this instant, he was going to discover how deeply he had wounded her.

Beneficial arrangement? Hang beneficial—stamp on it and curse it! Romance be hanged as well. He knew what she wanted of a marriage and yet he... Had the man no heart?

How shallow he made her emotions seem. What little value he placed upon them. Did he not understand that mere romance, hearts, flowers and vain poetry, came and went as if borne on a fickle breeze? It was bone-deep, lifelong devotion she craved. If she could not have that, she would have nothing at all.

And now she knew beyond a doubt he did not feel that sort of love for her. In his eyes, she was still a girl, fit only for laughter and adventuring. Worse—for a marriage of convenience.

'Good day, Lord Cliverton,' she snapped.

It had been on the tip of her tongue to say goodbye, farewell for ever, but despite what he had done she could not manage it. Tomorrow, or the next day, she would tell him goodbye. She would wish him success in finding a bride he would grow to like.

After she regained control over her emotions, she would wish him well in a life that was lacking the very thing that counted most in the world. The very thing she now knew for certain she would not have. Love to endure the storms of life, to withstand hardship and rejoice in blessings, was now unobtainable because, apparently, he was not capable of such devotion.

She had completely misjudged the man young Peter had grown to be.

Closing the door behind her, she went outside. Striding past her bicycle, she forsook the convenience of a quick trip home. She no longer wanted his gift. Huffing, she walked briskly through a hail of snowflakes.

The salt being rubbed in her soul wound was that Peter was correct. If she wed him, she would be beyond her stepmother's reach for ever. She could not help but see his point. Also, looking at the situation as Peter must be doing, he would be saved from the effort of finding a suitable bride. One whom he need not commit his heart to. It was all so logical.

'Anna Liese, wait!'

Wait for what? For Lord Cliverton to be struck by Cupid's arrow?

She glanced over her shoulder, saw him pushing both bicycles through a swirling gust. She walked faster, but not fast enough.

'Give my offer more thought before you dismiss it!'

'I already have!' she called over her shoulder.

Luckily, no one was about witness this sorry business.

'I will come for your answer tomorrow!'

At which time she would carry through with her intention of wishing him an adequate future without love.

Without her.

Chapter Twelve

That had not gone the way he had imagined it would.

All the way home he had walked several yards behind Anna Liese, trying to understand why she was so angry.

While it was true that she'd told him she wanted a true love match, it was also true that her safety was at risk—her future.

For as long as Mildred remained unmarried, Anna Liese ran the risk of being bound to a man who would treat her badly. There were worse men out there than Grant. Gentlemen who called themselves such, but were cads under it all.

He watched while she crossed the bridge, marched the path towards her front door, then went inside.

If she continued to refuse him, there was still one thing he could do to protect her—although the thing hardly bore thinking about.

Leaving the bicycles at the back door, he went inside, trying to forget the solution to protect Anna Liese which had just popped into his mind. Although once imagined, it was difficult to put aside because, for as awful as it was, it did make sense.

Kneeling to bring the fire in the drawing room hearth to full flame, he hated that wedding Mildred might be the only way to keep Anna Liese safe.

Anna Liese was correct when she told him the Baroness would not cease her efforts until one of them wed. Since Anna Liese refused his logical offer, what else could he do? The idea of marrying Mildred was so distasteful it left a bitter residue in his mind.

When it came down to it, perhaps he could not do it. For all that he did not require a love match the way Anna Liese did, he did require a lady more congenial than Mildred was.

Perhaps if he teased Anna Liese with this second idea, she would not wish him to sacrifice himself for her. Despite her rejection of his proposal, he knew she did care about him. Their friendship was a rare and beautiful thing. It was impossible to believe she no longer felt it.

Still squatting, he poked the flames with an iron, trying to understand why she had seemed so hurt. What had he said that was so objectionable? He had assumed their bond was deep. Even after all the years that had passed, they had easily picked up where they left off.

The moment they'd been reunited, the way they had been in the old days had slipped into place as easily as if the years had not happened. Even though they were no longer children and she had grown to be a beautiful woman, they were still who they had been or so he assumed until moments ago.

He stood up, glancing about the drawing room. Thanks to Anna Liese's help it was ready for the family to come for a visit. It had been such a pleasure working with her over the weeks. He felt she thought so, too. Surely, she must see what a pleasant life they would share if she married him.

'Curse it,' he whispered, even though no one would hear his frustration.

Wedding Anna Liese was not without risk—he had not thoroughly considered this before proposing. The fact was, he did love her. He always had. To lose his great friend to death would be more than he could bear, even without sharing the grand passion she wanted of him.

He didn't, did he? He had never allowed himself to feel that sort of emotion for fear of the crippling loss. He was not certain he could live through such grief again.

But right now, he did fear losing his friend. No matter what the thing he felt for her was called, he did not wish to lose it. Which, it seemed he was about to do. He must seek Anna Liese out. He needed to convince her of the wisdom of becoming Lady Cliverton before he returned to London the day after tomorrow.

Everything about this was right. They got along. She would fit in well with his family. Most importantly, she would be safe with him. Whatever it took to make her happy in their marriage, he was prepared to do it.

Suddenly he was struck by two thoughts at once. First, he wondered if marrying a woman only because she was appropriate was enough for him. It must be because he had always believed it to be so. He had seen that kind of marriage more often than marriages where love came first. That is, if one did not count one's own family.

And second, quite to his surprise, the thought of Anna Liese being married to her 'true love match' made him feel—queasy.

He strode to the window and watched the snow drift past

in whirls. An emotion he had never felt in his life snaked around his gut, flicking a barb at his heart. He thought he might be jealous—of a man who did not exist. The person, her true love, was an idea. Curse the dream lover.

How was he to compete with an idea?

Since it looked as if going out tonight would be impossible given the weather, he would have to wait until morning and then go see what was to be done about vanquishing Anna Liese's dream lover.

Upon rising, Anna Liese knew what she must do and do it without delay. Say goodbye to Peter. He was scheduled to go back to London tomorrow, but she would bid him farewell today.

Putting it off for another day would be too difficult. As it was her nerves felt like jangling bells. She was not sure how she would manage to part from him, but waiting another day to do it would only draw the tension out. She would simply—no, not simply—but none the less get it over with.

Putting on her warmest cloak, she walked to the stable. It was not that she was procrastinating, she merely needed to check on Fannie, make sure the goose had come in from the storm.

This afternoon would be soon enough to speak with Peter, to accept a future without him in it. Glancing at the cottage on the way to the stable, she wanted to cry. It was not entirely true that he would not be a part of her life. He would bring his adequate wife to visit—and his children who were bound be adorable.

It was hard to fathom how she would manage to be a friendly neighbour, to welcome them all as if she were not desperate to be that woman and the mother of those children.

Entering the stable, she found the stove lit and the space warm. Their occasional stableman must have come from the village to check on the animals.

'Fannie!' she called. She heard straw shuffling. Seconds later the goose waddled out of a stall, giving her a honk in greeting.

'There you are!' Anna Liese stooped down to pet the bird. 'You don't have a mate and you get along fine. You shall be my inspiration.'

Fannie ruffled her feathers, turned about and sauntered back to where she had been nesting.

It was too cold to go back out so soon and she did not wish to return to the manor. Stepmama and Mildred had risen early, buzzing about and preparing for travel. Twice already, Mildred had asked if Anna Liese knew whether Peter would be paying a call before leaving for London. It should not be annoying to hear her stepsister call Peter by his name, but it was. Mildred's obsession with their neighbour was wearing on Anna Liese's nerves.

'I'll need to get used to hearing it,' she explained while Fannie's white tail disappeared around a stall door. 'Very soon some woman will be calling him that. No doubt blinking great doe eyes at him, too.'

It did not have to be that way. She could prevent it by marrying him herself. She could accept his proposal, such as it was and perhaps in time she could make him see her as a woman. Perhaps he might come to love her...eventually. Perhaps...but perhaps not. So far, he hadn't fallen in love with her, even after they nearly shared two very perfect kisses. Perfect in her opinion, but clearly not his. But what if she had actually indulged in one of those almost kisses? Would it have made a difference?

Hoping for love to follow marriage was too great a risk. She did not think she could bear looking into his eyes, feeling so deeply for him and not seeing that love reflected back at her. To see him gaze at her in deep friendship would break her heart bit by bit as the days passed.

But wouldn't that be better than never being able to gaze into his eyes at all? Better than witnessing some other lucky woman gazing into them—wondering if he had fallen in love with her and then all the while be wondering if she, herself, had made a mistake? Would she wonder if the knife stabbing her heart might not be there if she had given him time to fall in love with her?

It was a bit much to think about. There was only one thing she knew of to soothe her stress and that was to sing. Someone had wisely placed a barrel in front of the stove. She sat upon it, let the warmth wrap around her, then began to sing 'The Holly and the Ivy'.

The gentle rise and fall of the tune filled her, took her away to a scene in her head—of a manger with a newborn baby boy lying in it. There were things of greater importance than her love for Peter Penneyjons.

Christmas was nearly upon them, bringing a time for joy and singing, for rejoicing no matter what one's circumstances happened to be.

Lost in her song, she did not hear the stable door creak open, but evidently it had.

'Anna Liese?' Peter's whisper drew her back to this stable and this time.

She did not turn at first because she was not ready to face him. However, she would need to if she were to carry through with bidding him farewell. Pivoting slowly on the barrel, she donned her emotional armour, pasting a smile into place.

'Hello, Peter.'

'I know you too well to believe that is a genuine smile and that you are not still angry with me.'

'You might be right about the smile, but if you believe I am angry, you do not know me as well as you think you do.'

'As well as I know anyone.' He shrugged, then held his hands out as if in supplication. 'And I care for you as much as I do anyone.'

She remained sitting, not trusting her balance overmuch. The man made her dizzy with the desire to show him how mistaken he was about what made for a good marriage. Certainly, he must be aware of the draw between them. It was impossible the attraction she felt was not returned. He was being amazingly stubborn in facing it.

Even with half a stable separating them, she felt the heat of wanting him pulsing under her skin. It was beyond belief that he could be causing her to simmer this way without being aware of it. She was no expert in male–female matters, but she did understand there was some force drawing them towards each other and it was not platonic.

If she had the boldness of a bird, she would give him a kiss to prove it. She would melt all over him and not release his lips until he admitted his passion for her. Unless he did not admit it, but pushed her away instead. She had never been so sure, and at the same time unsure, of anything in her life.

'Since you are here—' she folded her hands primly on her lap, which was far from what she was imaging doing with them '—I will bid you goodbye now and save either of us from having to venture out in the cold later.'

'How very thoughtful of you, Anna Liese.' His attitude seemed to turn as prickly as the one she was faking. 'But you need not be so quick to bid me goodbye. I will be back for Christmas with my family.'

'I am aware. Will you bring your fiancée as well? I shall be delighted to meet her—whoever she turns out to be.'

The oddest look of displeasure crossed his features. She could not recall seeing one like it before.

'I am still hoping she will be you.' He took two steps towards her, then stopped. Leaning his hip against a stall door, he crossed his arms over his chest.

The pose made him look manly, so virile and appealing she had to clench her fingers together. Harder to do, she shut tender yearnings for him away, pretended she was as unfeeling for him as he seemed to be for her.

'Tell me you will reconsider my proposal, Anna Liese.' His gaze softened to the one she was familiar with. 'If you marry me, I promise to be a decent husband to you. I will do whatever is needed to make sure you are happy. I will sacrifice anything to ensure you remain safe.'

'I do not require martyrdom of a husband.'

'You know that is not what I meant. Only that I will not see you shackled to some charlatan. No matter what you think of me for proposing a convenient marriage, I am bound to be a better choice than some man your stepmother has bribed to wed you.'

She was far too insulted to admit he was correct. She would be far better off with Peter.

'I am better off unwed if such are my choices.'

'At some point you will be forced into it. Please, Anna Liese—do not sacrifice your happiness for no reason. Marry me.'

What nonsense! In his opinion waiting for love was 'no reason'? He expected her to give that up in order to gain safe haven? Although, what was the point of waiting for something that was not going to happen? Still—

'No, Peter. Once again, I will not marry you.' She meant the rejection to sound forceful. Sadly, her voice emerged soft...whispery.

'Make me understand, my friend, because I do not. Am I so repulsive that you prefer a scoundrel?'

All right, then! He needed to understand. Words did not seem adequate to illustrate it, so...

Rising from the barrel, she took a fortifying breath, clasped her hands in front of her to keep them from trembling. Rushing for him before she lost courage, she grasped one of his hands, boldly placing it at her waist. His brows shot up. His handsome jaw dropped.

Undaunted, she took his other hand, curled her fingers through his, then tucked their joined hands behind her back. Lifting up on her toes, she leaned against his chest so that he could not miss the fact that she was no longer the child he remembered, or that her heart raced madly. She kissed his chin, nipping the prickly skin of a missed shave.

He turned his head so that her quick, hot breath mixed with his. He jerked her closer by their joined hands. She was not certain he meant to but, still, he had done it.

Emboldened, she turned her mouth a scant inch closer. She kissed his lips. She felt it when he cast away hesitation. The weight of his body shifted away from the stall while he drew her ever closer and up so that her toes almost lifted off the floor. Kissing her, he stroked the back of her hair, tangled his fingers in the strands.

Drowning in his presence, in his scent, in his heat, she knew she was correct to refuse sacrificing this part of marriage. But would she? This moment was intensely passionate—would he give in to it fully if she wed him?

His fingers felt bold, unhesitating, sweeping the hair away from her neck. When he kissed the tender flesh under her ear, she gripped her hand into the front of his shirt in order to keep grounded.

While she did not actually float off the stable floor, she was drifting away to a place where dreams came true and love was for ever.

Finally, with a gasp and great sense of loss, she pushed away. She was panting so hard she feared she would not be able to speak. But she must speak if only to keep herself from launching back into his arms.

'That, Peter Penneyjons, is what I will not sacrifice.'

He reached for her, clearly wanting to kiss her again. But any man could kiss a woman and leave her wanting. It was for her to leave him wanting—finally understanding.

'If you marry me—'

She backed several steps away. Watched while his hand clenched, dropped to his side.

'If I marry you, I will be safe. I realise that—but still, I cannot do it.'

Silently, he stared at her, looked as if he would speak and then did not.

'Very well, Anna Liese. I accept that you will not marry me. But do not think I will not do what I must to keep you safe.'

He spun about and strode towards the stable door.

She followed him because—what did he mean by that? She plucked on his sleeve.

He spun around, looking rather like a condemned man. The way he gazed down at her, his lips drawn tight and his eyes shadowed in misery, it was as if she were the one to condemn him.

Oh, no! This rift between them was his doing. She was the innocent party and quite correct to hold out for what she wanted in life.

'I do not understand how you—'

He opened the door. Cold air rushed inside, whirling loose straw into circles on the stone floor.

'But you do, Anna Liese. You said it yourself.'

She shook her head because she could not imagine what he was getting at.

'You said, and were correct about it, that the only way the Baroness will leave you alone is when either you or Mildred marry.'

She had said that and it was true. 'Neither of us are marrying, so I do not understand your point.'

'You are not willing to marry me.' He looked past her shoulder, silent for several seconds. 'I think Mildred will be. I will ask her to be my wife at the ball.'

'You cannot marry—'

'I will do it, Anna Liese.'

And the next she knew she was staring at the wood grain on the stable door. Struck dumb, her thoughts scattered to—to somewhere where they tried to make sense of this, but utterly failed.

There was only a dusting of snow at Cliverton, but what there was, Peter heard crunching under his boots while he came up the front steps of the town house.

He wished he could have remained in Woodlore Glenn a bit longer. He found that the place now felt like his home of old. His old memories were happy ones and he anticipated making new ones there with his family.

Had it not been for the ball which there was no longer a reason for, he would have.

Because invitations had been sent and accepted, he had to carry through with the gala. Ladies would have purchased expensive gowns and whatever went with them in anticipation of being selected as his Viscountess. The ball had not been announced as a bride hunt, but everyone knew it to be one.

It is how these things worked.

He wondered if his family had arrived already. The ball would be worthwhile if only to see them. Especially Aunt Adelia. What he needed more than anything was to speak with her—to get her approval on what he was about to do. As a member of society, she knew what was expected of a man in his position and would set his apprehension to rest.

And he did have a great deal of apprehension.

What would his family think of Mildred? She would become a member of the family and it was important that they like her. Or, at the least, tolerate her.

Tolerate—the word bounced around his brain as if it could not find a suitable place to lodge. Once he wed, that was how it would be—he would begin his day by finding a way to tolerate his wife.

If only Anna Liese had not refused him.

Looking at his future, at the woman he would spend the rest of his days with, he wondered if Anna Liese was correct in waiting for a love match. Living with a person one was in love with could only be a better choice.

The truth was, he did love Anna Liese! But just now, he was confused about what form that love took. After she had kissed him in the stable, he had little doubt of how she felt about him. That kiss had left him shaken to the core...it illuminated dark shadows in his heart.

Ever since going back to Woodlore Glen and renewing their friendship, he had been happier than he had been in a long time. Being with Anna Liese, rediscovering his past, faded memories clicked neatly into place.

Until he had asked for her hand in marriage, life had been complete. Had he been a wiser man he would have asked for her heart rather than her hand. No, not that. What was needed was for him to offer his heart.

He really did need to speak with his aunt. His heart was a three-ring circus with ideas and emotions spinning all at once. Holding Anna Liese in his arms had done something to him. He had been aware of a shift on that rainy night on the hilltop.

But after she had pronounced the near kiss something to be got out of the way, he had backed away from its importance, assuming he had misjudged her feelings.

Perhaps she had not been truthful that night. Would it have made a difference if she had been? Would he have looked at her as a lover and not a friend? There was no way of knowing. He could not blame himself for not responding to a heart that was not offered.

But yesterday's kiss had been different. Not only had she offered her heart in it, but he had responded in a way he had not expected to. The wall he had erected against deep intimacy crashed down on his boots. Which changed nothing about the position he now found himself in.

Anna Liese had stirred him, body and soul. Given time, he believed he would be able to offer her the true love match she needed. That it would be worth the price he might have to pay. But there was no time. She wanted assurance of it before she committed to being wed. What he wanted, needed, was assurance that she would be safe while he was away from Woodlore Glen.

He shivered. How long had he been standing on the porch lost in his thoughts? Long enough apparently for the butler to notice, because the door opened while he reached for the knob. Coming inside, he handed off his coat.

'Welcome home, sir, it is good to have you back.'

'Thank you, Conner. It is good to be back.'

But was it? The house seemed larger than it ever had—quieter.

Perhaps once his family arrived it would feel more welcoming. For a time, at least. The day would soon come when they would return to their own homes and here he would be, once again alone. Until he married and his Viscountess came to live at Cliverton, the house would be like this.

In the beginning, when he thought ahead to his marriage, he hadn't believed knowing the lady beforehand to be greatly important. He needed a viscountess and the lady would have been trained her whole life to become one. The way of courtship was traditional and uncomplicated—satisfactory.

Now he could not help but look ahead and wonder if having Mildred living under his roof would be worse than living alone. It was not as if he would go out of his way to be in her company. More likely he would retreat to his study and she to shopping and social engagements.

Glancing about his tastefully decorated walls, an image of Anna Liese came to his mind. He saw her rushing down the grand staircase, her arms spread to welcome him home, her smile happy and her fair hair streaking behind her.

Since yesterday, his mind pictured her everywhere. How could it not after she, his dearest friend, demonstrated in a poignant way what she would be sacrificing in order to marry him. It was as if he could still smell lavender in her hair, feel the heat of her breath on his mouth and the provocative nip of her teeth scraping his chin.

Yes, something had happened to him in that moment. He did not mean he had a sudden realisation of falling in love with Anna Liese, but more a whispered suggestion that he always had been. Never before had the idea of marrying for anything but obligation troubled him. Duty was duty, he had always accepted that, been relieved that his heart would not be involved in the affair.

Now, he must accept that he had been changed by Anna Liese. Not only by the kiss, but by every moment he had spent in her company. But when she illustrated a slice of paradise and then once again refused his proposal, she left him unsure of everything he had ever believed about courtship and marriage.

It was not right to be dwelling on Anna Liese's lips. Certainly not on the shapely swell of her hip under his hand when he had pressed her close to his—

He was a cad! How could he have lost all sense of propriety while kissing her? Of course, nothing about that encounter had been proper. It had been Anna Liese's way of pointing out where he was lacking.

Feminine laughter from the back of the house caught his attention. Praise the Good Lord. His cousins were home!

Chapter Thirteen

Anna Liese stood at the drawing room window, gazing across the bridge at the cottage.

Peter was gone. When he returned, he would no longer be her Peter.

She had always thought of him as hers. Even though he had rejected her attempt to demonstrate how she felt, she could not let go of feeling possessive of him. Aside from her parents, he was the best part of her childhood. This was not something that could be taken away from her.

What she must learn to accept was that when she next saw him, he would be Mildred's Peter. More than that, he would be Stepmama's Peter, her conquest.

It was going to be extremely odd to live with having the man she loved as a brother-in-law, of sorts. Odd and intolerable.

At least they would be living in London most of the time and she would not often have to witness them together as man and wife. Still, regardless of where they lived, she was going to be miserable.

In the unlikely event that Peter and Mildred were happy together, Anna Liese would feel envious. If they were not happy and Peter was miserable, she would feel responsible for it since she might have prevented it by marrying him.

Mildred fluttered nervously about, ordering everyone who crossed her path to be sure her packing was in order, that her prettiest gowns were put in her trunks.

Anna Liese was glad to see that the butler cast her a wrinkled frown and ignored her order when she instructed him to run upstairs and fetch three of her hats so that she could try them on, each one in the light of the downstairs mirror. The last thing he needed was extra work.

Mildred could not know that it didn't matter what she wore. Lovely or frumpy, she would be Peter's 'chosen one'.

Anna Liese jumped, startled from her thoughts by Mildred's voice suddenly close to her ear.

'What are you staring at? Its only snow and more snow.'

'Nothing, just… I like snow.'

'What a pity you are not attending Peter's ball.' Her sister shot her a smirky little grin. 'But without a proper ball gown, how can you? There is a higher standard for fashion in London than here in the country, you understand.'

Unknown to Mildred, she had the loveliest gown in creation stashed in Martha's chamber. It was sure to be the envy of any woman hoping to win Peter's proposal. If only she had been wearing it in the stable yesterday, perhaps then Peter would have viewed her as a woman and not his dearest childhood friend. Had she known she was going to—well, to do what she had—she would have done it in the gown.

With great flair she would have twirled about in a froth of gossamer blue, lifted her chin while catching his eye, made certain he noticed the swell of her bosom. Then he would have recognised who she was at the heart of her. A woman and not a girl.

But that was not how things worked out. Now Peter was set on making the biggest mistake of his life. And he was going to do it for her sake.

'Tell me true, Sister.' Mildred's softened tone startled her, especially after the peevish comment she had just made. Her voice sounded vulnerable, but at the same time hopeful. 'Do you think there is the slightest chance Lord Cliverton will choose me instead of a pretty debutante?'

'It is not for me to say.'

Although she could put her stepsister's worries to rest if she wished to. But she did not wish to. The thought of Peter giving Mildred the kisses and nuzzles that Anna Liese dreamed of having made her nauseous. She also remained silent in the hope that Peter would come to his senses and not go through with this insane plan.

Staring at the bridge, she allowed herself to fantasise that absence, if only for a day, had made his heart grow fonder. She could see him now in her mind's eye, galloping over the stones on a bold white horse, his formal black ball jacket flapping behind him. He had left the ball behind, dismissed his guests and his potential brides from his mind.

Especially the one standing beside her.

But back to the fantasy—her hero swept her up into his strong arms and carried her off to...to his cottage across the bridge where he declared his undying, true and ever-faithful love.

'I think that without you present, he might see me.'

She could not tell her stepsister that Peter would see only her, even if Anna Liese twirled into the ballroom wearing her princess-worthy gown.

He did not love her the way she needed to be loved and, clearly, nothing she did could change it.

'I realise that Peter will not love me at first, but I do not mind,' Mildred murmured. 'He might come to and even if he does not, I will have finally made Mother happy.'

Her voice forsaking her, Anna Liese nodded jerkily.

'You might look happier about it, Anna Liese, since with me married, you will not need to fear being trapped by Mr Grant or someone like him.'

Oddly, Mildred's voice softened on the banker's name.

'Did you truly like Mr Grant?'

'He was fond of me, I believe.'

'I do not wish to take away from that, but you are well rid of him. His handsomeness is a trick to hide his true nature. I have reason to know he is not a good person. You may be sure that Lord Cliverton will be a better husband.'

'For all that I hope he will choose me, I cannot be sure he will, not with all the others who are younger and prettier.'

'Just smile,' she advised, feeling her heart shred at the words of advice. 'You are pretty when you smile.'

'Ah! There you are, Mildred!' Stepmama's voice interrupted one of the few genuine conversations they had ever had. 'There is no time to waste in idle chatter. The carriage will be ready to travel within the hour.'

This had been far from idle chatter. While Anna Liese did not like hearing her stepsister speak of Peter and her hopes to become his Viscountess, she had at least been speaking from her heart.

'Thorpe!' Stepmama called to the only servant passing by in the moment. 'Have you made certain all of the gowns have been put in the carriage?'

'I will enquire, my lady.'

'Your sister's very future depends upon those gowns,' Stepmama muttered.

It did not. The only reason Mildred had a future with Peter was that Anna Liese had handed it to her. With each passing moment she felt a bit more guilty over what Peter was doing. The man was willing to sacrifice his future so that Anna Liese might have hers. Which was ironic since, without Peter, she had no happy future.

What she had was a great headache. She rubbed her fingers over her brow, not to ease the pain but to hide tears.

'Have a safe journey,' she muttered, then turned and dashed upstairs.

Halfway up she heard Stepmama's harsh laugh. 'I believe we need not fear she will follow.'

No, they need not fear that.

'My dear boy, what are you doing out here in the dark?'

Peter was standing in the garden, wondering about Anna Liese. What was she doing in the moment? What would she be doing next year or the year after that? Would she find her true love match?

'Aunt Adelia!' Finally, he would have a moment alone with her. 'I have been wanting to speak with you about something.'

'Oh, well, that is delightful. However, do you mind if we go back inside? It looks as if the weather will turn again. But what a lovely white Christmas we will have. London will look like a greeting card.'

Taking her arm, he led her to the drawing room where the yule log crackled with heat.

Glancing about his drawing room with its garlands, ribbons and the grand Christmas tree, he realised it, too, looked as welcoming as a greeting card.

'Apparently everyone has gone to bed early,' he said.

'Are you surprised?' She grinned at him with the twinkle he loved. 'If my husband were here at Cliverton, I would be abed, too.'

His aunt had a charming way about her. No other person he knew could be so sweetly scandalous.

Thinking of his cousins and their husbands, involved in whatever they were probably involved in, made him blush. He felt heat rising from his neck and creeping to his hairline. There were some things better not considered when it came to one's own family.

'Will he join us later, in Woodlore Glen?'

'He has promised to complete his business in time.' She sat down on the sofa, patting the space beside her. 'Tell me, my dear, is there a lady who has struck your fancy? Will you make an announcement at the ball tomorrow night?'

'I suppose I will.' He wished he felt some joy in saying so. 'It is past time that I married, isn't it?'

'You seem less than keen about it. Most young men look at least somewhat eager at the prospect of a wife and family.'

'That is what I was hoping to speak with you about.' He shrugged, not bothering to hide his lack of enthusiasm at the prospect of wedded bliss, since that was far from what awaited him. Hiding anything from Aunt Adelia was impossible anyway. 'What I want to know is, how important in a marriage is it to begin with a love match? I have always assumed that it is not something people of our station can hope for.'

'It is what many believe. But I will tell you what this old woman has learned. My first marriage was an arranged one.

Lord Monroe and I barely knew each other, let alone were in love. I thought the arrangement to be adequate because, as you pointed out, those of our position often do not hope for anything else. It was a short but adequate marriage. A few years into my widowhood, I met Lord Helm. We were great friends for a long time. But one day—it was at Violet Townsend's country party, the one where Ginny eloped—I looked at him in a way I never had before. I do not know why. Perhaps romance was in the air, but once seeing him in a romantic light, I could not see him in any other.'

He would never forget what a startling surprise it had been one morning at breakfast to receive a telegram informing him that not only had Ginny been married at Gretna Green, but so had Aunt Adelia.

'But you were content in your first marriage?'

'I thought I was, Peter, but it was only because I did not understand what it was like to be in love.' She tapped her chin in thought while she looked past his eyes and straight into his heart. 'This lady you suppose you have found, is she someone you love or hope to love?'

Love Mildred? He did not, nor did he hope to. His only question, really, was what was he willing to sacrifice for Anna Liese? Apparently, it was everything.

'I have a reason to ask for this lady's hand, Aunt, but it is not love.'

She shook her head, frowning. 'I doubt you have compromised anyone.'

'No, hardly that.'

Quite the contrary—he hoped to prevent someone being compromised.

'You only have this one life,' she said, seeming uncommonly sombre. 'If you want my advice, wait to wed. No matter that society deems it necessary, wait until you find a lady who will be your best friend in life, a companion you will be joyful with.'

Nothing she said could have shot more at the heart of his trouble.

'My true love match?'

'Precisely. Trust me, dear, it will be worth the wait.'

'May I confide something, Aunt?'

'I adore confessions, although I imagine yours will not be terribly scandalous.'

'I did propose marriage to my best friend and she turned me down.'

'But why would she? You will make a wonderful husband.'

'She is set on a love match and I told her I could not give her that.'

'And so you will now take a bride who will accept you without it? You will end up an unhappy man, Peter Penneyjons. Do you not hope to have the marriages your cousins have?'

'This woman, the one I intend to wed, is not one I would pick unless I had to.'

'Unless you have compromised her, you do not have to.'

'You are familiar with the Cinderella story?' At her nod and sigh, he continued. 'Well, my friend is something of a Cinderella. Her stepmother has often tried to force her into marriage to clear the way for her own daughter to have her pick of gentlemen. Since Anna Liese has turned down my proposal, I will offer for the stepsister so that Baroness Barlow will be appeased and leave Anna Liese alone.'

Why did his aunt's eyes sparkle as if she were about

to indulge in a fit of laughter? He had just admitted how wretched he was.

'Do you propose to be the lady's—Anna Liese's—fairy godmother, Peter?'

'I see no other way to ensure her safety. I hope that some day she will find her true love match.'

She patted his cheek indulgently, smiling and shaking her head. 'So, you are willing to sacrifice your happiness for that of your friend?'

He shrugged, nodding. It was exactly what he was doing.

'"Greater love has no man than this,"' she quoted with a wink. 'You are in love, Peter. I suggest you propose to Cinderella again and this time be honest about how you feel.'

Aunt Adelia kissed his cheek, then stood up. 'I'm for bed. Tomorrow is a busy day.'

He stared at the orange glow of the yule log for a long time after she left, thinking about what she said.

Could it be true, in the way she meant it? He did love her and always had. When she had kissed him the other night, he had wanted the moment to last for ever. For ever...as in a true love match and not the natural reaction of a man for a woman? Even if that were the case, what was he to do about it? He had proposed marriage and she had turned him down.

Not once, but twice.

But had she turned him down? Or had she turned down the sort of marriage he had proposed? In the end it didn't matter greatly. Turned down meant there would be no marriage between them.

It also meant there would be one between him and Mildred.

If Anna Liese had not overheard what she had while Stepmama and Mildred waited for the coach to be brought around, she might have slept the previous night. She might be able to pick up her fork and eat a bite of the breakfast set before her. Having heard, she could not sleep or eat—certainly she could not ignore the treacherous words.

They had been discussing a detailed plan to trap Peter, to make it appear that he had compromised Mildred. While Peter did mean to marry her, it would be horrid to have it happen the way they intended.

Why, they were even discussing what type of lace would make up Mildred's wedding gown as, laughing, sniggering, they stepped aboard the coach!

No man was more honourable than Peter. It would be beyond unjust to be accused of something so dishonourable. Had they not been pulling away from the front door, she would have given them a severe piece of her mind. A tongue lashing was what they deserved.

What Peter deserved was a woman who loved him. Which, Anna Liese did! Perhaps it did not matter as much as she had always believed that he did not love her in the way she wished to be loved.

'Miss Anna Liese.'

Oh, dear, how long had Martha been standing there watching her push food about her plate?

'Is there something wrong with your breakfast?'

'I'm sure it is delicious, but, Martha—' Martha was more than her maid. She was the closest thing she had to a mother and so… '—I need your opinion on something. Please be honest with me.'

'But, of course.'

Anna Liese indicated that she should sit at the table with her. With Stepmama absent, there was no one to be offended by it.

'What do you think—is it more important to love or to be loved?'

'That is a rather large question, my dear. I suppose it depends upon who we are speaking of. But in general, we cannot control what others feel for us. It is for us to love because we are in control of that.' Martha nodded at the neglected plate of food. 'If you wish to know the rest of my thoughts, you will eat what is before you. Once you have heard what I have to say, you might need your energy.'

How curious. She began to nibble, but it was delicious so it did not take her long to finish.

'Please, Martha, carry on with your thoughts.'

'We are discussing Lord Cliverton, are we not? That you do not love him in the way he loves you?'

'But he does not love me!' She stood up, pressed her hand to her belly where the food suddenly turned on her. 'He would not be—that is, he would—'

He would not be marrying Mildred if he did. But that was all wrong. He was marrying Mildred because he... Because he cared for her deeply, as one could care for a lifelong friend.

'Martha, he is going to propose to Mildred at the ball.'

'That is a bit of shocking news! I cannot imagine why he would. I thought he would propose to you, but I suppose I was mistaken.'

'He did propose to me.'

'And yet you say he is going to marry Mildred?'

'I turned him down because he does not love me—you are wrong to think he does.'

'Oh, my dear, I am not wrong. In fact, I see the situation clearly. Tell me if I am mistaken.' Martha stood up, took her hand and clasped it in both of hers. 'There is only reason

Lord Cliverton would consider wedding the likes of Mildred. Once she is married the Baroness no longer has reason to get you out of her daughter's way. Since you refused the Viscount's protection, this is the only way he knows will see you safe.'

'But I do not want his protection, I want his love.'

'If he is not acting out of love, I do not know what love is. But, my sweet girl, you did ask what was more important, giving love or getting it. In your case, I would say giving love.'

'But I—'

'I think you will find that that you need to act on your love for him and then see what happens.'

'But he is proposing to Mildred tonight.'

'Perhaps he will not do it.'

'He might not have a choice. They plan to trap him into a compromise.'

'Oh, my. The poor man is not as skilled as you are at avoiding their traps.' Still holding her hand, Martha tugged her towards the servants' staircase. 'There is a train leaving Woodlore Glenn on the hour. If we hurry, we might make it to London in time. Come along, we shall do what we can do.'

Chapter Fourteen

'You are a miracle worker, Martha!'

Within moments her maid had stripped her of her day dress, put her in her ball gown, then, quick as thought, arranged her hair in a simple but elegant style.

Squinting at her handiwork, Martha added a blue ribbon to Anna Liese's hair.

'You have always been the silk purse and not the sow's ear, so it was an easy feat. Now, how will we get you to the station on time with the carriage gone?'

Martha placed Anna Liese's blue slippers into a bag which she looped over her wrist. She did not dare put them on until she reached Cliverton.

It would have been prudent to wait to put on the gown, too, but every second was urgent if she hoped to warn Peter of what awaited him. Besides, where would she change into it once she arrived? It was not as if she had time to arrange to stay anywhere.

She did take a moment to twirl in front of the mirror. The

delicate gown whirled about her, revealing how wrong her black walking boots looked with it.

No help for it, though.

The gown had no sooner settled about her ankles than Martha draped her cloak of deep blue velvet about her shoulders.

'Hurry now, missy, we barely have time to make it to the station as it is.'

'You need not come with me.'

Martha shrugged into her own cloak. 'It will be odd enough that you are travelling in that gown. You shall not do it without a proper chaperon.'

Stepping outside, she grimaced at the sky. Not only did she need to beat the clock to the village, she needed to beat the weather as well. Unless she missed her guess, it was going to snow very soon. Gathering up her skirt, she would have run, but Martha was past the age for running.

'I do not suppose you know to ride a bicycle?'

'You would be surprised what I do on my day off. I am not overly skilled, but I can make it to the depot.'

Changing direction, they dashed across the bridge and collected the bicycles. Martha helped her gather up her voluminous skirt and petticoats, tucking and folding them as neatly as possible. Balancing the two-wheeled vehicle in one hand, Anna Liese carefully mounted.

'Off we go!' Mildred said with a great grin.

Unless one of them took a wicked tumble on the path, they should make it to the depot with enough time to purchase tickets and board the train.

Cold air blew past her face, tugged at her hair and billowed under her cloak. She could only imagine what a sight she and her maid looked. Hopefully, no one was peering out windows.

Oh, drat! Coming to a skidding stop in front of the ticket office, Anna Liese found someone was looking—or staring, rather—with his mouth open and his eyes blinking wide.

No doubt Hyrum Grant was stunned to see her gripping the bicycle handlebar in one hand while letting down her skirt and fluffing it with the other. He rushed forward. Oh, dear, she did not wish to have to fend him off in her gown.

'Miss Barlow,' he said, looking sheepish. 'May I store your bicycles until you return?'

She hugged her cloak tighter against the chill. In the rush she had not given thought to what she would do with the bicycles.

'We shall expect you not to sell them in the meantime,' Martha said, shooting him a reprimanding glare.

He nodded, took them both, then pushed them towards the bank. Turning, he said, 'Please give the Viscount my regards when you see him, which—' he looked quizzically at the ball gown peeking out from under her velvet cloak '—I imagine you will be doing.'

'Not that it concerns you.' Martha shooed her fingers at him.

While this was not likely to be an apology, it was a peace offering, of sorts. Not peace with her as much as Peter. His threat had been heeded. She was safe from the banker—now she must make sure Peter was safe from Mildred and Stepmama.

Boarding the train, she garnered curious glances. Ladies dressed for balls did not travel by rail. There was nothing for it but to nod, graciously smile and take a seat.

Luckily, she found one she would not need to share since

her skirt took up the whole of the bench and would have swallowed anyone sitting beside her. Martha sat across from her and folded her hands in her lap, glancing about at their fellow travellers.

'Good day,' Anna Liese said to an older lady who paused on the way to her seat looking askance at her.

'Indeed!' the woman answered, but then she smiled. 'I imagine my day will not be nearly as interesting as yours, young lady.'

No day she had ever lived was bound to be as interesting as this one. Settling back against the cushioned seatback, she let the warmth of the car wrap her up. With time to think, she realised she had failed to bring a change of clothing for the return trip.

That was a challenge for later. Now she needed to concentrate on getting to the ball before Peter proposed to, or was trapped, by her stepsister.

Glancing out the window, she saw snow beginning to drift past the glass. Hopefully, it would not be so heavy that the train would be delayed along the way.

The man she loved needed her. If she had to leave a stranded railcar and run all the way to London, that is what she would do. Which was a brave thought for all that it was impossible.

She closed her eyes, felt the weight of her slipper bag on her arm and willed the train through the snow.

'This is a beautiful ball, Peter,' Aunt Adelia said. 'Now that Lord Helm has arrived earlier than expected, I am quite enjoying it. Which, I believe, is more than you are doing.'

She was correct. He could not imagine what man in attendance would enjoy having Mildred constantly trying to draw him under one of the many sprigs of mistletoe scattered about the ballroom.

The woman seemed oblivious to the fact that he had other guests to attend to. Perhaps he ought to pull her aside and get the proposal over with. Once he did, perhaps her attention on him would not be so intense. Then again, it might be worse.

'I adore a Christmas ball. The carols and the festive decor are delightful,' his aunt remarked.

The trappings were beautiful—he must give his staff credit for their beautiful workmanship. The problem was, he did not feel festive. He felt grim.

'Aunt Adelia—' he bent his head to whisper '—have I lost my mind?'

'If you are speaking of proposing to that woman, you have lost it completely. You did not mention how calculating she is when we spoke last night—and her mother? My word, the Baroness is—but here they come again.'

'Heaven help me,' he muttered.

'You will need Heaven's help if you carry through with this madness.'

'What choice do I have?'

'Nonsense. Marry the woman you love. Do you see your cousins over there near the Christmas tree? All of them are in love. I see no reason why it should be different for you.'

'Of course you do. She has refused me. I said so last night, Aunt.'

'You must propose again now that you have realised that you love her. You—'

The rest of what might she have said was cut off by Mildred and her mother returning from the buffet room. The break in their company had been far too short.

Seeing his potential intended with a smear of something on the corner of her lip, which she wiped off with the back of her hand, he felt his stomach sink. If he did not get this proposal out of the way quickly, he would not do it.

It was a harder thing to imagine than it was last night because his aunt was correct in saying he was in love with Anna Liese. He was—desperately and completely in love with her. How big of a fool was he to have not recognised it until it was too late?

If only he had understood what was in his heart in the stable the other night, he would not be in the situation he now was. What would he not give to be announcing his engagement to Anna Liese tonight instead of the woman clinging to his arm as if she had a right to do it.

It had only been two days since he had seen Anna Liese and yet it seemed so much longer. He felt every empty second of those days beating a sad tempo in his soul.

While he imagined Anna Liese, laughing, singing and playing with her goose, Mildred nattered on. He had no idea what she was saying. She had not ceased from gossiping about the other ladies since she came down the ballroom steps, so she was probably continuing with that.

Thankfully, Aunt Adelia had not deserted him.

'Baroness,' Aunt Adelia said, cutting into Mildred's prattle. The interruption was done smoothly. No one could possibly be offended by it because of the twinkle in his aunt's blue eyes. 'When will your stepdaughter arrive?'

'Anna Liese?'

'Yes, Baron Barlow's child. It has been many years since I have seen her, but I recall how lovely she was, even as a small girl. I am anxious to see what a beauty she must have grown to be. I can only imagine how proud you must be to have raised her.'

Lady Barlow blinked in confusion. So did he. Aunt Adelia had visited the cottage when he was a boy, but did she remember Anna Liese?

Lady Barlow and Mildred spoke at the same time.

'She fell ill.'

'She is too shy to attend.'

The women cast each other matching frowns.

'That is disappointing, isn't it, Peter?' Aunt Adelia tapped her chin in thought. One could only guess what she would say next. 'But I imagine your head is spinning with the attention of all the ladies hoping to become the Viscountess, as it is. I cannot imagine how you will pick among them.'

And then—

'Miss Anna Liese Barlow,' the butler announced from the top of the stairs.

Breathing hard, as if she had been running, she stood on the landing, her gaze scanning the guests below. It was as if a spell were cast over the crowd. All eyes were turned upon her. No one spoke. No doubt they were wondering if an angel had descended among them.

An angel in an ethereal gown which shimmered about her as if she were wearing a blue cloud with stars twinkling among the gathers. An angel who, being escorted down the stairs by the grinning butler, wore black boots.

'Mother,' Mildred groaned. 'What—?'

'Indeed.' The Baroness's grin stretched tightly over her teeth. 'What a pleasure it is to see that she overcame her illness and her shyness to join us.'

'But where did she get that gown?'

'Do you not recall that I ordered it especially for her in

the hopes she would come?' the Baroness declared, although the only one not to suspect it was a lie would be Mildred.

No, he took that back. His aunt was not easily fooled and, judging by the speculation in her smile, she had not been this time either.

'Peter, my dear. You understand what you must do? Greet your guest and tell her how—' Aunt Adelia arched a brow at Mildred and her mother who had begun to whisper to each other, all the while casting frowns at Anna Liese descending the stairs '—how you feel about her being here.'

What he felt was overwhelmed with love. What had it taken for her to come here? How had she even managed it? Indeed, how was he to find his next breath when she came down the steps, her dazzling gown fluttering about her scuffed black boots?

Her smile while she glanced about the room nearly cut him off at the knees. Wait—he *was* being cut off at the knees. All of a sudden, he nearly went down. Mildred's weight sagged against him when she fainted.

'Quickly, my lord. Take her somewhere private—to your library,' the Baroness ordered. 'I will welcome Anna Liese.'

Winded, Anna Liese stood at the head of the ballroom stairs, searching the faces of the people staring up at her. What a sight she must be. The cab she had hired had got stuck in snow. She had been forced to get out and run the last street with Martha leaning out the window and cheering her on.

Her hair had suffered. She felt loose strands tickling her neck and the blue bow drooping. In the rush to get to Cliverton, she hadn't taken a second to repair it. There had been only an instant to hand off her cloak and shoe bag before she turned to the waiting butler who announced her.

But where was Peter? Glancing about below, all she saw was a sea of strangers gaping at her. And why not? She would gape at herself if she saw herself coming down the stairs with no escort but the kindly butler, clomping down in scuffed boots instead of dancing shoes!

No matter, she had come to rescue Peter. She would not let the man she loved fall victim to her stepsister's scheme because she did not look tip top. Even if he did not love her, she would love him. Martha had been right in asking her to consider which had more value—loving or being loved.

Down below she spotted Stepmama standing beside a woman near her own age. The older lady had red hair and a sparkling smile which was resting on Anna Liese as if they were already, somehow, acquainted. How odd, she was certain they were not.

The woman hurried to meet her at the foot of the steps while Stepmama rushed away in the opposite direction.

Where was Mildred? Please, oh, please, do not let Peter be proposing to her, or worse, being seduced by her.

'I knew who you were the instant I saw you, my dear.' The woman squeezed her hand in greeting. 'The look on my nephew's face gave it away.'

'It did?'

'I am Peter's Aunt Adelia and I am happier to see you than you can imagine.'

She could not imagine, since they had never met that she recalled.

'But where is Peter?'

'That awful Mildred must have overeaten because she

fainted. Peter had to tend to her, but do not fear. Now that he has seen you, he will not be proposing to the chit.'

What? How did she know? Time for that later. In the moment she felt that she was strangling on dread.

'Mildred does not faint.' She glanced about, desperate to find him before it was too late. 'Where did they go? Was he alone with her?'

'I believe so. Many people were curious about him carrying her away, but their attention was diverted by your entrance. But her mother went after her.'

'That is bad news! We must find him,' she gasped. 'They intend to compromise him.'

'The man is not easily compromised.'

As she had reason to know—however… 'My relatives are skilled at such schemes.'

Peter's aunt waved to three ladies standing near the Christmas tree, beckoning them to follow. 'Come along. He took her to the library.'

She rushed after Peter's aunt. The three ladies she had signalled to fell in line behind them.

'If the Baroness intends to bear false witness, we shall be five to witness the truth, no matter what we might see with our eyes.'

What would they witness with their own eyes? A seduction or a proposal? Either would result in a marriage which Anna Liese was determined to prevent. She would marry Peter without being loved if that was what it took because she loved him.

And loving mattered more than anything else. What a fool she was not to have realised it sooner. She only prayed Peter did not pay for her mistake.

* * *

Peter half dragged Mildred to the sofa because her weight did not allow him to carry her in his arms. He struggled to keep from dropping her while he lowered her to the cushions. The ungainly release did not wake her. He lifted her feet on to the cushions so that she lay flat.

Going to the hearth, he stood there, not seeing the woman on the sofa, but the one who had just arrived at the ball. Anna Liese was here! She had come when she said she would not.

Why?

Why did not matter! All that mattered was that she was here. If only Mildred had not fainted, he would be with her now, discovering the reason for this miracle. He would be telling her how much he loved her and hoping she believed him.

A soft moan from the sofa brought his attention to where he supposed it ought to have been. Now that Mildred was regaining consciousness, he would need to be wary. He had been warned that she and her mother were not beyond capturing a viscount by trickery.

Until ten minutes ago, there would have been no need to. He would have taken the occasion of her revival to propose. But Anna Liese was here and he had every intention of proposing to her. This time with a declaration of love. Not only love—undying, unconditional, for better or for worse—but a true love match was what he would offer.

If she turned him down after that—then he would do what he must, as distasteful as it was.

His gaze shifted to Mildred, who blinked her eyes open. Funny how they did not appear disorientated as one would expect after a faint. If it came down to it, would he really be able to spend his life with a woman like her? How could he possibly?

No, it would be a grave mistake for more than the obvious. If he married Mildred, it would mean Anna Liese would be often in his life. He could not possibly live so closely to the woman he loved and remain faithful to the one he did not.

What he needed to do was get out of the library, find Anna Liese and admit his love for her. As soon as Mildred sat up and looked the slightest bit recovered that was what he was going to do. In a moment he was going to dash out if this room and into the arms of the woman he loved.

If she would have him. He must face the fact that she might not believe him since it had only been days since he indicated he did not love her. Dash it. While he stood here waiting for Mildred to 'recover', how many gentlemen were vying for Anna Liese's attention?

'Mildred!' he said a bit more sharply than he ought to, impatience winning out over playing his part as the gracious host. Although a proper host would not be alone with a guest. He desperately wished another woman were in the room.

She blinked again, clawed at the bodice of her gown as if the low cut somehow interfered with her breathing. 'Help— air—can't breathe', yet her bosom was heaving as if it was full of air. He suspected her lungs were working rather well.

'I must go.' He stood away from the hearth, took a step towards the door. 'Just lay still for a while. You will regain your breath. I shall send your mother to you.'

Suddenly she sat up, leapt off the sofa and snagged his coat sleeve. In a move so swift and smooth it could only have been practised, she yanked her bodice down. He heard fabric rip. And then Mildred cried out.

He backed away from her, but she advanced. When one more step would have him pressed against the bookcase, the library door crashed open.

Before the Baroness could gasp in outrage, five women rushed past her.

'Oh, you poor dear,' Aunt Adelia cooed. 'How dreadful that you ripped your gown in the faint.'

'It did not rip when I fainted. He—' She wagged a finger at Peter.

'But of course it did, my dear. I saw it happen. But being unconscious as you were, you could not have known. My nephew was quite the hero of the moment, dragging you out of the ballroom as soon as he did. We can only hope his back is not strained for dancing later.'

'The rip in your bodice would have been a horrid embarrassment had he not managed!' Cornelia, the eldest of his cousins, observed.

'Such things will happen when one's bodice is stressed,' added Felicia sweetly. 'It is not uncommon.'

'This is an outrage!' The tip of the Baroness's nose pulsed red.

'Oh, I agree.' Aunt Adelia said, her smile as bright as bubbles in champagne. 'Whoever produced such inferior fabric should be held to account.'

'It is awful when a lady is not safe in a viscount's ballroom,' Mildred whimpered.

Ginny gave her a compassionate-looking smile. 'Do not worry, Miss Hooper. I carry a repair kit at all times. One never knows when one might encounter an unfortunate event.'

She did? Apparently so since she happily plucked a pouch out of a hidden pocket in her gown. From it she withdrew a needle and thread, dangling them in the air.

'We shall have you repaired in no time at all,' Felicia said.

'And do not worry.' This encouragement came from Cornelia. 'Only someone staring intently will notice that we are forced to use red thread for your green gown.'

'But it does look Christmassy, don't you agree?' Felicia clapped her hands and perhaps she meant it. Felicia adored anything that smacked of Christmas.

Apparently, Mildred began to feel a chill on her exposed bosom. She splayed her fingers over what she had intentionally exposed. One could only hope she felt some shame for what she had done. More than likely she was mortified rather than remorseful.

'Now that help has come, you may go back to your ball, Peter. And do take Anna Liese with you so that no one will think you spent undue time alone with Miss Barlow. It would not do to have her reputation soiled.' Aunt Adelia was smiling brightly at the Baroness while she spoke. 'How relieved you must be to have everything resolved so neatly.'

He did not stay long enough to hear a response. Snatching Anna Liese's hand he fled, like his dancing shoes were afire.

As Anna Liese entered the ballroom beside Peter, the only thing she wished was for a private place to speak with him. He needed to understand the grave danger he had been in and that he must be cautious. With that said, she would tell him she understood his desire to protect her, even if it meant wedding where he did not wish to.

She did not pretend to imagine that marrying either her or Mildred was his first choice. Glancing about the ballroom, seeing so many elegant ladies hoping to win his hand, she found it hard to imagine he would be happy settling for a lower-ranked lady. And yet he was determined to sacrifice himself for her.

Very well, she was determined to do no less for him. Once a private moment presented, she was going to ask him to marry her and not Mildred. She would need to be bolder than she had ever been since such a thing was not done—it was the man who proposed.

Which he had done and she had soundly rejected. There was every chance he would not wish to ask for her hand a third time. She had been firm in her refusal and a gentleman did have his pride.

But at the least she hoped to have a quiet conversation in order to convince him what a great mistake it would be to marry Mildred, in the event he was still set on making such a wretched mistake.

Having a quiet conversation did not appear to be possible. People seemed anxious to meet her. More than likely it was because she was a new face among them—clearly a bumpkin from the country. Hopefully, they would soon satisfy their curiosity about her and she would get her moment alone with Peter.

She hugged his arm, feeling awkward among the titled. Not that she, herself, was not titled, but having grown up as free as a woodland spirit, she did not feel like it.

Peter introduced her to earls and marquesses, to countesses and marchionesses. She was half dizzy with meeting aristocrats. What a lucky thing she was weighted down by heavy walking boots. Boots which had been in plain view when she made her grand decent into society. At the time it had not mattered. Finding Peter in time had been far more urgent than proper footwear was.

After seeing several ladies glancing at the hem of her gown, she decided it mattered after all.

'Peter,' she went up on her toes to whisper. 'I need to get my shoes.'

'But you look charming. Honestly, Anna Liese, the contrast between your gown and your boots is irresistible.'

'Perhaps to you, my friend. To the others I look odd.'

'Are we so stuffy as all that? Look around you. Half the gentlemen in attendance are smitten with you. Perhaps one of them will be your true love match.' He was grimacing when he said so and she hardly knew what to make of it.

'As lovely as that might be.' And it was not at all lovely. There was only one man she wished to be smitten with her and he, apparently, still was not. She stood there, putting on a smile, her heart weeping. 'I am being judged by ladies who know fashion better than you do. I need my ball slippers.'

And her hair done up properly, but no matter that.

'Take my arm before I get snatched away by a marriage hunter,' he said.

She did and unashamedly enjoyed feeling the flex of his muscles under his coat. 'You were lucky to escape the one you did, if you want to know what I think. Had your aunt and all those ladies not burst in, you would be facing a priest.'

The thought of Peter and Mildred together made her stomach churn unpleasantly.

'Which, I realise, is what you intend to do. It's only that I do not wish for you to do it because you were tricked. You are far too honourable to have your reputation soiled in that way.'

'Is that why you came? To rescue me?'

My word, but she had missed his grin in the two days since she had seen him. Rescuing him was part of the reason she had come. But not all.

'Why else?' she said. She would find a time to ask him to marry her. But this was not it. 'When one overhears a plot to trick one's friend into making a huge mistake, one does what one can to prevent it.'

Please, oh, please let him say she had prevented it, that he had not already proposed. Before he could, the attendant in the cloakroom handed out her shoe bag.

'The ladies...the ones who rescued me,' he said while escorting her towards the women's retiring room. 'They are my cousins and my aunt. Do you remember them from their visits to Woodlore Glen?'

'I wish I did. They were quite wonderful. I admired how they made it known to my relatives that their scheme was exposed and yet did it without making open accusation.'

'I hope in time you will get to know them well.'

Because she would be related to them through Mildred?

'Go back to your party, Peter.' She shooed her hand at him before she went inside the retiring room. 'I shall find you when I am finished here.'

'I'll wait.'

'You have only just avoided a scandal with my stepsister. Surely you do not wish to cause another by showing me undue favour.'

He shrugged, shot her that grin, then turned and strode towards the ballroom. He had not gone more than a dozen steps before an eager lady rushed to take Anna Liese's place on his arm.

Given that he was so set on protecting her, it was unlikely that Peter would abandon his plan to wed Mildred and choose one of the ladies attending his ball. She should not feel relieved at that, but one felt what one did.

Finding a sofa in an alcove with the curtains drawn for privacy, she sat down upon it. While she changed her shoes, she let out a long, relieved sigh. She had overcome more than a few obstacles getting here—acted boldly in taking the train in a ball gown, hired a carriage and then abandoned it to run a street with no escort. Finding the audacity to enter the mansion alone in her walking boots had been something!

For all that she might like to sit here and regather her courage, she did not dare. Now was not the time to give up on her goal. She could not carry on much longer without speaking plainly to Peter about her feelings. After taking a moment to gather her emotions, she would leave the shelter of the retiring room and, properly attired, she would look for him among his peers, find a way to get him alone and speak about her feelings.

A pair of rustling skirts passed by her alcove.

'I look ridiculous, Mother! The red stitches are so large anyone will know my bodice is ripped.'

'Were you more skilled at seduction, you would not have needed to tear your gown. The Viscount would have peeled it from you.'

'It is Anna Liese's fault, you know. She was not supposed to come. She said she would not! And where did she get that gown?'

'Somebody will be held accountable.' No one could make her voice sound as snarly as Stepmama could. 'But do not give up. There is yet time to try again.'

If there was any hope of Mildred being successful, she must not snort as she had just done.

Taking a breath, Anna Liese listened to their footsteps going out of the room. She pressed her fingers to her heart, willing courage into it. Her success was far from guaranteed. She had rebuffed Peter's proposal. There was every chance he would not wish to offer another.

Lady Someone-or-Another was speaking earnestly to him about something, but he had no idea what it was. His attention was latched on the hallway where the retiring room was located. Where, he wondered, would he take Anna Liese once she emerged? It must be a private spot where no one would find them.

He must convince her that he was in love with her although he had so recently denied it. No one would blame her for believing his change of heart was insincere. The truth was far from it—he was completely in love with his childhood friend.

The kitchen would be bustling with activity, his bedroom was out of the question. The garden? Not unless he wished for them both to become icicles. Not the library either. That space had become tainted for declarations of true love.

The Barlow women emerged from the hallway and entered the ballroom. Suddenly he was grateful for the lady chatting merrily beside him.

Three minutes into listening to a dissertation on feathered hats, he spotted Anna Liese entering the ballroom. As if they had been watching and somehow knew he needed escape, Aunt Adelia and Felicia hurried towards him.

'Lady Lindsey!' Felicia exclaimed. 'We are about to begin

carolling. You will not wish to miss it.' It would not matter if she had, his relatives were neatly drawing her away.

Hurrying towards Anna Liese, he deliberately ignored guests trying to snag his attention.

A gentleman blocked his view of Anna Liese. When he stepped around the fellow, he spotted her again. She was frowning and glancing about. She vanished from his sight yet again when a group of laughing guests got between them. Then Anna Liese turned in a half-circle, spotted him and smiled.

He had the oddest sensation of coming home—even though he was home. In that instant, he fell even more in love with her. How could he have ever doubted it?

'I've missed you, dear friend.' He held out both hands to her and she took them. A few people stared, but no matter. 'Take a carriage ride with me?'

She nodded, so he led her towards the ballroom steps, but then caught sight of Lady Barlow and Mildred rushing towards them. Changing directions, he drew Anna Liese towards the kitchens where it would be a short run from there to the stable.

The staff would be stunned to see him in their domain. Especially since he was towing an angel in blue behind him. Even so, they went about their tasks with barely a glance. The pathway to the stable was covered, but that did not prevent the snow from blowing in sideways.

While icy, it also dusted Anna Liese's face and shoulders in flakes which glittered in the lamplight illuminating the way. She looked ethereal, a snow queen. And he, a mere man, was about to try to convince her that he was in love with her.

Once inside the stable he requested the carriage to be warmed and made ready for travel.

'Come, Anna Liese. We will wait by the stove.' The spot was somewhat warmer, but not enough to keep her from visibly shivering. He wished for nothing more than to draw her to himself, warm her thoroughly. Several images of how to go about it presented in his mind, but until he had pleaded his case, he would not act upon them.

'I have something to say, Peter.' She whisked her gloved hands over her arms, chasing away the chill which he anticipated banishing in a few moments.

In the meantime, he took off his formal coat and lay it across her shoulders, tugging it under her chin.

'You look nervous. You know you can tell me anything.'

'Yes, well, I am nervous because I feel I must confess a great mistake.'

'It cannot be as bad as that frown makes it seem.'

She took a deep breath which lifted her bosom, snatched the heart out of his chest and floated it up among the rafters. 'I wish to retract my refusal of your proposal.'

'At the cost of giving up your true love match?'

Knowing she was willing to do this for him touched his soul. How, he wondered, was it possible to love another person as much as he loved her? It did seem a miracle that love could grow so quickly—but then again, it had not been quickly. It had been a lifetime growing. He had always loved her in some form or another.

'I was wrong to refuse. You must not marry Mildred.'

She shook her head, causing a curl to spring loose from her hair and tumble against the fair column of her neck. While he had always noticed how pretty her neck was, at that moment it drew him as if his lips and her skin were magnetised.

He resisted the draw—for now. But with a bit of luck and a heartfelt prayer, in a few moments she would become his lover while remaining his friend. He would be free to express his desire for her.

Please let it be so! Forced to wed Mildred, he would have neither love nor friendship.

'Honestly, Peter, you are not the only one who can give up one's dreams of a perfect future in the name of friendship.'

The last thing he wanted was for her to give up her dream. He wanted to satisfy it. He heard the creak of wheels bringing the carriage around.

'If you are willing to marry Mildred in order to keep me safe, I am willing to marry you in order for you to not ruin your life in a miserable match.'

'That is selfless of you,' he said trying not to smile at how earnest she looked. 'I appreciate your sacrifice.'

He knew what the supposed sacrifice meant to her. To him, it meant she loved him. One would not do such a thing unless it was done in the name of love. For as late as he had come to the realisation, he did now understand that his offer to marry Mildred had not been simply an obligation to protect a friend—although protecting her had been first in his mind.

It was love for Anna Liese which had spurred him to be willing to give up his happiness for hers, as she was now doing for him. Having found his true love match, he was impatient to admit it to her. If only he had recognised his true feelings earlier, they could be well on the way to being wed by now.

The carriage driver opened the door. Peter instructed the fellow to drive slowly about Hyde Park. He helped Anna Lise inside and then climbed up after her.

Only after having sat down in the seat across from her did he wonder what the driver must think of this. Taking a lady for a carriage ride at night with no chaperon was exceptionally inappropriate.

Well, let the fellow imagine what he would. Hopefully, when they emerged from the carriage, the driver would be the first to hear the news that Anna Liese would become Viscountess Cliverton. Peter would be crowing over the news to the first person he encountered. But before he could, he had some convincing to do.

The interior of the cab was dimly lit, the curtains drawn—romantic in a way he had never noticed before. Plush, warm and, with any luck, the small space was about to get heated.

'You cannot know how glad I am to have time alone with you,' he said once the carriage began to move. 'Having an important conversation back in a house full of guests is futile.'

'And are we about to have one?' She slipped his coat off her shoulders. 'It is nice in here, warm, too. I rented a hackney carriage to get here and it was not nearly as elegant—but it did nearly get me here.'

'Only nearly?'

'It got stuck in the snow, so I had to run the last little bit to Cliverton.'

'I do not believe anyone has ever run to my rescue before—but wait!' He slid out of his seat, moved across and sat down next to her. 'You did it once before—when I was sick to death and you sang to me.'

'I remember it. But your uncle and I were not sure you could hear.'

'But I did and you saved my life then, too.'

He touched the curl at her neck, sifting the strands in his fingers. Ah, good, her smile indicated he was not overstepping. Not yet, anyway.

'All I did was sing, I do not see how—'

'I meant to die. I tried to, but Uncle would not let me. And then you came and sang to me. I decided to live after all.'

'And here we are,' she said softly. 'I will save your life again if you will offer the same proposal you did in the stable.'

She really had no idea how much he loved her.

'No, Anna Liese, I will not offer that proposal.'

'And I will not allow you to wed my stepsister for my sake!'

She looked heartsick, the blue sparkle of her eyes dimmed, the happy animation that typically radiated from her soul turning sad.

He must clear things up immediately. 'I will not offer that proposal.' He took her hand, felt her fingers trembling. 'It was wrong and so I offer you another.'

'I will not become your mistress, either, if that is what you have in mind.'

The outrage on her face made him laugh aloud because it was sincere and so pretty. Keeping hold of her hand, he slipped off the bench.

On bended knee, he said, 'Anna Liese Barlow, I love you with all my heart. Will you marry me?'

'You do not need to make up affection in order to appease me, Peter.' A tear glistened in her eye, rolled down her cheek. 'I will marry you without it.'

On his knees, he leaned forward, kissing the dampness away. He stroked the wet trail from her eye to her chin. 'You are mistaken. I love you deeply.'

'All of a sudden, Peter?' She shook her head, her frown dipping her fair brows. 'How can that be? You do not need to say those words.'

'No? I suppose that leaves me with no choice but to illustrate how I feel about you, the same as you did to me.'

Chapter Fifteen

'I… Well…' The last thing she was going to do was refuse a kiss from the man she loved. Even though, in the end, what would it prove? One's heart did not change in a matter of days. 'You do not need to prove anything.'

'Not prove…' He touched her shoulders, held them gently in his hands, gently caressed her bare skin with his fingertips. 'Express.'

'Express…prove that it is all—' Any man could woo a lady with kisses.

'I love you, Anna Liese.' His breath felt warm on her face…more, it felt a miracle. *Please, oh, please, please, please let this not be impossible.* 'Do not doubt, trust me.'

'I want to—' She was simply too dizzy to reason anything through rationally.

'Anna Liese.'

He whispered her name in the half-instant before his lips settled upon hers. His large hand cupped the back of her neck, urging her to a deeper kiss.

Oh, my, she had intended to teach him what was lacking when she kissed him in the stable—right now, Peter's kiss taught her something different. Not a lesson, but a declaration.

She was beginning to believe him—that perhaps by some Christmas miracle he was pledging himself to her. No wonder he had not reacted to her in the stable. The kiss she had given had not been an expression of love, but rather a challenge to face it.

He nibbled her bottom lip, then trailed his mouth downwards to kiss her neck. It was nearly the same kiss as in the stable, but oh, so vastly different. For as impossible as it seemed, all at once she nearly believed him, that by some great wonder of love—he was in love with her.

He pulled away from her from kissing her. Covering his heart with splayed fingers, he murmured, 'Will you marry me, Anna Liese? For love only, and no other reason. Let me be your true love match, for you are mine.'

'Truly? I only ask because—' Because her heart was turning and she scarcely knew what to say. 'Only days ago you said you did not require one.'

'I have said many foolish things. You have known me long enough to know it. But this is not one of them. Anna Liese Barlow, you are my true love match and I can only pray that I am yours.'

'You have always been that to me. Peter, why do you think I never married? I loved you as a boy, but I love you more deeply as a man. The love I feel for you now was built upon the one from our childhood.'

'Yes…' He gave her a half-lidded gaze, a seductive smile that young Peter would not have known existed. 'But I wonder if we need further proof of our affections.'

'We do not need proof, but I will happily express how I feel about you.'

Rising, he sat beside her, then lifted her in a manoeuvre which had her sitting on his lap.

For the next five minutes, she kissed him, expressing her love, making sure he would never doubt it.

'May I take this as a yes to my proposal?'

No one would ever be able to convince her that miracles did not happen. Only hours ago, she had been in fear and despair, now her heart sang Christmas carols, one after another, even with no music at hand. Peter's love was her music.

'You may consider us engaged.'

'Good, I shall act accordingly—like a man smitten, for it is what I am.'

She did not know how long they kissed, touched and vowed to love one another for ever. Eventually, Peter tapped the ceiling of the carriage, which she imagined was a signal for the driver to return to Cliverton. He drew the window curtain open. Snow drifted past the glass. The cab had begun to cool, but this was the first time she noticed it.

'We shall announce our betrothal as soon as we step inside the ballroom. People will have missed us by now, so they might as well know our intentions.'

Her hair was in worse disarray than when she had come down the ballroom steps the first time—but, oh, well, what did it matter really? Her love for Lord Cliverton was going to show no matter the condition of her coiffure. People might as well know that the reason she looked flushed and happy was something to be winked at rather than condemned.

'And we shall be wed at once,' he announced, sounding lordly and in charge.

As far as she was concerned the sooner it happened, the happier she would be. Although—

'We will need a licence and I will want a proper wedding gown. There are things to be considered.'

'Do not fear, I have cousins who have experience at quick weddings. They will be thrilled to point the way.'

'Good. Then we will be wed without delay.'

The weight of the carriage shifted when the driver stepped down.

'There is one thing I wish for, my Anna Liese.'

She kissed him quickly. 'What is it you wish?'

'For you to sing to me at our wedding. I want to hear it, knowing this time we will not be saying goodbye.'

If that was not the most touching thing she had ever heard, she did not know what was.

The driver opened the door. Peter stepped out, then helped her down.

'Simons,' Peter said, his grin wide and handsome. 'I would like to introduce Anna Liese Barlow, soon to be Viscountess Cliverton.'

'May I say how delighted I am, miss? May you and my lord be blessed for ever.'

She took his greeting to her heart, cherishing those words against the moment they made their betrothal known to everyone in the ballroom. There were some present who would not think it so wonderful.

Peter had intended to make an announcement tonight. He just had not expected to be happy about it.

Now, standing at the head of the ballroom stairs with

Anna Liese beside him, he felt like singing—like tapping his toes in a happy dance and swirling his fiancée about to express his joy. He refrained from doing so because he was aware that not everyone here would be delighted. Indeed, he spotted two of them, Mildred and the Baroness, elbowing their way through the crowd.

Anna Liese's stepsister already had one foot on the stairway as if to rush to him. He had better make his announcement quickly before she somehow latched herself on to his arm.

'Friends!' he called, just in the event that someone in the room was not already looking at them. 'I would like to tell you the most excellent news. I have proposed marriage to Miss Anna Liese Barlow. She has made me the happiest man in the world by accepting.'

Applause and huzzahs erupted. The sounds of congratulations did not entirely cover a screech.

Mildred tore at her hair, then neatly fainted backwards into the stout arms of Lord Moore. Lord Moore did not appear to be dismayed. On the contrary, he was grinning.

'Oh, dear,' Anna Liese whispered. 'I think she truly has fainted this time. The poor man must be—'

'Delighted.' He caught her hand. They hurried down the grand staircase. 'He is stronger than his round stature accounts for and I suspect this is the closest he has ever come to holding a lady. Women rarely give the poor fellow a second glance even though he is titled.'

They reached the stricken Mildred at the same time Aunt Adelia and his cousins did.

The Baroness cast Anna Liese a scathing glare which his fiancée ignored. Perhaps she was used to such looks, but he was not. As soon as there was a moment he would have a word with her.

'My goodness, Felicia,' Ginny said. 'You might have done a sturdier job on that stitching. It has come apart.'

'Such things will happen.' Aunt Adelia gave the blushing young man a smile. 'Perry, do be a dear and take Miss Mildred to the library.'

'It will be my honour, of course.'

The Baroness muttered something under her breath.

'Do not fret, Lord Moore has the matter—in hand, shall we say?' Aunt Adelia smiled after him proudly carrying his burden, which Peter imagined was not burden at all to the lonely young man.

'Lord Moore?' The Baroness's brow arched, watching her daughter being carried away. Peter had to give Perry credit for strength. All Peter had managed was to half drag her.

'You have not met our dear Perry? But perhaps Mildred overlooked the Marquess, as ladies tend to do. I promise he is a pleasant fellow, despite his rather round bearing.'

'A marquess, you say?'

'Yes, for a year now. But are you not anxious to hurry after them, just to avoid the appearance of scandal?'

'But of course.'

As expected, the Baroness took her time 'hurrying' away. She paused to wish him and Anna Liese well. Perhaps she meant it, given that the Marquess who had just left the ballroom with her daughter held a higher rank than he did.

By the time the Baroness had meandered her way through the guests and went into the hallway leading to the library, quarter of an hour had passed.

'Lord Moore will have had time to revive her by now,' Cornelia said.

'People will be watching to see how long it takes for her mother to bring her back to the festivities,' Felicia said.

'I have heard that Perry—' Aunt Adelia said.

'You have heard something untoward about Perry?' Peter asked. He would rather not have a scandal attached to his engagement ball.

'Why would I have? But he is in need of a wife and no other opportunity might present.'

'One might not present for Mildred either,' Anna Liese said, her gaze soft, thoughtful. 'And I know he is bound to be a better match than the banker.'

'I cannot speak for the banker, but dear Perry has the best of hearts.' Ginny said. 'He is terribly shy because some of the ladies on the society market are rather unkind in what they say about him.'

'I only hope that he does not regret being with my stepsister.'

'He seemed more than pleased to me.' Aunt Adelia's laugh sounded like bubbles floating on the air. 'We have one engagement to celebrate and one can only guess about another.'

He did not care about the other, only his own.

He was suddenly grateful that his staff had placed so many sprigs of mistletoe about. He fully intended to take advantage of every one of them. Catching Anna Liese's hand, he hurried her towards the nearest unoccupied sprig. Not that he needed the festive excuse. He meant to kiss her fervently, with a full and grateful heart, every day for the rest of his life.

To Anna Liese's way of thinking, a Christmas miracle was happening. It was her wedding day and it was happening only three days after she had been proposed to.

She stood in the small drawing room, wearing a gown borrowed from Ginny. It could not have been a more perfect fit, or more lovely had she spent months picking it out. What a lucky thing that she and her soon-to-be cousin were the same size.

'Here you are, Cousin,' Felicia declared, handing her a beautiful bouquet of holly and berries wrapped in red and green ribbons.

Aunt Adelia sat in a chair beside the window, stitching silk flowers on the veil which the modiste had sewn in a hurry. 'Oh, look!' she exclaimed. 'It is snowing. That is such good luck, is it not?'

'I thought it was rain which was good luck,' Mildred said, coming into the drawing room. 'May I have a private word, Sister?'

'I will not listen,' Aunt Adelia declared, remaining where she was.

'Nor will we,' Cornelia agreed while Ginny nodded.

'Well, I just want to say—you were correct when you warned me about Mr Grant. I have come to see that a handsome smile can cover many flaws. And a plain face can hide many virtues.'

'Lord Moore, you mean?' Aunt Adelia asked.

'You said you were not listening.'

'Well, my dear, we are to be family and you must get used to such things.'

Mildred leaned close to whisper, 'I'm sorry I nearly cut your hair. Please forgive me.'

That said, Mildred kissed her cheek, then said to everyone, 'It will take me some time to become accustomed to the idea of family, but I do want to.'

She did not ask, nor did anyone else, what Lady Barlow

thought of Anna Liese wedding the man she had picked for her daughter, but she could only imagine she had turned her attention to capturing a marquess.

Aunt Adelia stood up, then secured the veil on Anna Liese's hair. 'It is time to become a Cliverton, my dear.'

Just at that moment the carriages Peter had hired to carry them to Woodlore Glen's intimate and charming church pulled up in front of Maplewood. One by one the cousins went out ahead of her, taking their places in the first carriage.

Last of all, Stepmama went out, but first she paused for a second, giving Anna Liese an appraising glance. 'Well played, Anna Liese.' With something resembling a smile, she walked ahead of her towards the waiting carriage.

The second carriage was decorated with red garlands and flowers. She could not imagine where Peter had come by them this time of year. Aunt Adelia, whom she had quickly come to love, went with her into this one.

It was a short but beautiful ride to the village church, with snow drifting past the windows. My word, but villagers stood on street corners merrily waving good wishes. It was not every day that one of their own wed a viscount, after all. Their greetings touched her quite deeply.

The first carriage came to a stop at the church steps. The cousins, Mildred, and Stepmama hurried inside.

Peter came outside, a great grin on his handsome face.

'I cannot believe this is happening,' she said to Aunt Adelia.

'Dreams do come true, my dear. The Penneyjons are blessed with them. Let's go and make yours come true.'

Peter escorted them inside and then went to take his place beside the minister at the front of the church. There were flowers in the church as well, white ones which looked pretty against the snow drifting past the windows.

Standing at the back of the pews, she caught her groom's eye, felt love wash over and through her. *'By yon bonnie banks and by yon bonnie braies...'* she sang while she walked towards him. *'Where the sun shines bright on Loch Lomond...'*

The sun shone bright on her even though she was inside and there was no sunshine. She and her true love were meeting at the altar and, the Good Lord willing, they would never be parted again.

Peter would never forget his wedding day. If he lived to be a hundred years old and forgot everything else, he would not forget this day. Listening to his bride singing in her clear, sweet and utterly beautiful voice, Peter was not dying, but he might have had one foot in heaven.

If he could have seen with other eyes than the ones in his head, he felt certain he would spot his family who had gone before him standing by: Mama and Papa, his aunt and uncle. Unless he was wrong, Anna Liese must have felt her parents' presence there to bless the wedding as well.

They had been bound by the minister's words, of course. Bound by sacred vows and the love behind them, but it had been her song to him that bound him as much as anything else. Her voice had brought him back from death once. Now it was a promise of a life, filled with blessed days and long, loving nights of a more intimate type of blessing.

The first of which was about to begin in his childhood bedroom. His wife awaited him there, in his small bed next to the window.

Standing outside the door, he tightened the belt of his

robe, thought again, then loosened it and let it hang. His hand felt slick, turning the knob. Why was he so nervous? He was the man, the one in charge of the direction this first night would take. Catching his runaway heart, he opened the door.

Anna Liese was already in bed. Sitting up and smiling at him, she wore some sort of sheer fabric which covered her from her chin to where the blanket pooled at her hips.

But that was not right. While the magic fabric covered her, it hid nothing. It might as well be made of water or wishes.

'Anna Liese...' Seeing her so left him breathless, lost for words.

'Pirate!' She opened her arms.

'Yo-ho, yo-ho!'

Laughing, he pounced upon the bed and sailed away with her to an enchanted place.

Epilogue

~~~~~~

One Christmas later—Cliverton Cottage

'This time last year I was lonely,' Peter said. 'Now look. I can scarcely find a moment to be alone with my wife.'

Standing on the bridge between the cottage and Maplewood Manor, Anna Liese nestled under his arm, laughing quietly. Life in London was busier than it was here and yet Peter never failed to find time to be alone with her.

'We did intend a family gathering,' she pointed out.

'There are a lot of people gathered. How many, I wonder?'

'More than you know,' she said, wondering if he picked up on her clue.

'And a dog!' He hugged her tighter, kissing the top of her head. 'It is a lucky thing the weather is mild and not snowy like last year. So much energy cannot be contained inside.'

'Fannie will be glad when it goes home. I believe she is weary of being nipped on the tail.'

'Abigail's cat will be glad to go back home.' Peter pointed to a second-storey window. 'I do not believe the creature will come down from the upstairs window until they do.'

A second later Abigail, Felicia's young sister-in-law, appeared, plucked the protesting cat off the sill and carried it away.

'Will she offer it as a plaything for the children, do you think?'

'Ginny and William's twin boys are quick, but still too short to reach it if it jumps on a table.'

'You know how it has been my dream to restore the cottage for the family, but with so many of them I'm glad they are at staying at Maplewood and we have the cottage to ourselves.'

'I have a feeling that the nights are busy with all the infants waking up.'

'How many are there, anyway?'

'At last count...' She let the statement hang for a moment to see if he would react to the vague answer. No, all he did was blink at her while waiting for her to tell him what he surely already knew. 'There are Ginny and William's boys—toddlers do wake often, I'm told—then, of course, their twin girls are only a few months old, so they wake every couple of hours. Cornelia's son is nearly a year old and has a very loud cry.'

'And that is all of them—for now?'

'For now.' She swatted his arm in playful exasperation. 'Peter Penneyjons, I cannot believe you do not know how many children your cousins have.'

'The number keeps changing.' The changing number was the reason she had brought him to the bridge this afternoon. He seemed rather dense when it came to the hints she was giving. 'It can't be long before Felicia and Isiah are parents.' He winked at her.

Mildred and Perry came out of the manor. They waved, then strolled very slowly alongside the stream path.

'With Mildred so close to her time, I am surprised the Baroness is not here. It is quite likely our baby count will have gone up by one before this visit is finished.'

'According to my sister—' Mildred was that by now. Over the past year they had become so close that one would never guess they had been at such odds growing up '—you and I are still a sore spot with her, but she is beginning to speak of us without a scowl. Perhaps next year she will leave London and join us.'

'So, after Mildred and Perry have their child, how many babies?'

'More than you can guess.'

'I suppose we cannot guess since there might be twins.' She could not imagine she would ever get tired of seeing her husband's mischievous smile. Whenever he looked at her in this way, she felt like they were carefree children again.

'And if Felicia's family, the Penfields, join us we have no idea how many there will be. They may have adopted another child by the time they arrive.'

'People do enjoy adding children to the family.'

If he had an answer to her blatant clue, he did not express it because Aunt Adelia and William's mother, Violet Townsend, came out of the house.

'May we borrow your bicycles?' Aunt Adelia asked. 'You know, my husband purchased one in the village two days ago.'

'They appear to be great fun,' Violet remarked, although she was frowning.

Anna Liese laughed. 'We would be delighted to let you use them. But be careful.'

'It cannot be all that difficult. More people are doing it every day.'

'Not people as old as we are, Adelia,' they heard Violet announce as they walked away to get the bicycles.

'Do you think they will manage without instruction?' Peter asked, watching them go.

It was a fair question, she decided, watching while they pedalled over the path. They wobbled about, wheels going every which way. Once or twice they nearly collided with each other.

'I think you should refrain from riding for a time.'

'Whatever are you talking about? You know I am an accomplished rider.'

'I am speaking of numbers, of infants to be precise. There are six of them at present and I wish for number seven to arrive safely into our arms.'

'You guessed your Christmas gift!' At long last and after many hints.

'I have been paying attention, Anna Liese.'

'To what? How could you know?'

'To you. There have been changes of late.' He drew his finger from her chin, down her neck and across her bosom.

'Now that you have finally guessed your gift, perhaps you would care to unwrap it?'

'Indeed I would, Lady Cliverton.'

He scooped her into his arms, kissed her thoroughly and she gave the love back to him.

'You know I can walk?'

'I would not wish to risk harm coming to my Christmas gift.'

'I love you, Peter.'

'Show me how much, although you have already,' he said with an enraptured glance at her belly. 'But you know... the other way. Sing to me about how the road leads home.'

And so she did, singing softly in his ear while he carried her from the bridge to the cottage.

* * * * *

Keep reading for an excerpt of
The Princess's New Year Wedding
by Rebecca Winters.
Find it in the
Midnight Wishes anthology,
out now!

CHAPTER ONE

"*MIO FIGLIO?* I know it's early, but there are things I must talk to you about. *Come to the apartment.*"

Thirty-year-old Stefano sat up in bed. It was a shock to get a phone call from his father at 5:30 a.m., but his father's entreaty shocked him even more.

"You mean now?"

"Please."

"I'll be there as soon as I can."

Stefano realized his father's broken heart wouldn't allow him to sleep, but then Stefano doubted anyone in the palace had known a moment's rest for the past week. Alberto, his adored younger brother—his parents' beloved son and heir to the throne—had just been buried yesterday at the young age of twenty-eight. There was no antidote for sorrow.

Stefano's twenty-seven-year-old sister, Carla, and her husband, Dino, and two children, were just as grief-stricken over the loss of a wonderful brother and uncle. She was now first in line to the throne and would be queen when their father died or could no longer rule. The rules of succession fell to the firstborn, then the second or the third, regardless of gender.

Stefano would never rule.

Since his eighteenth birthday when he'd prevailed on his parents to be exempt from royal duty for the rest of his life, Stefano had been granted that exemption by parliament. From that time forward, he was no longer a royal, but he loved his family and they loved him. They'd all come together for this unexpected tragedy.

With Alberto gone, his mother looked like she'd aged twenty years and had gone to bed after the interment of her second-born son. The funeral had been too much for her.

Stefano had struggled with his pain and was forced to face the fact that he was now the *only* son of King Basilio. Though his father would rely more and more on Carla, he needed Stefano, too, and would lean on him for comfort. Stefano guessed that was why his father had summoned him this early in the morning. Forcing himself to move, Stefano dragged himself out of bed to shower and dress.

Before long he entered his parents' private lounge off their bedroom in the north wing of the palace. His bereaved father turned away from the fireplace to look at him. "Thank you for coming, Stefano. Your mother is still in bed, overcome with grief."

"As *you* are, *Papà.*" Stefano gave him a soulful hug. It would be impossible to get over the reality that Alberto had been killed in a car crash a week ago.

Stefano, who'd graduated from the Colorado School of Mines in the US, had been in Canada at the time, inspecting one of the Casale gold mines. Casale being an old family name dating back to the founding of Italy. Nothing had seemed real until he'd returned home to the Kingdom of Umbriano, located in the Alps. His father had met him after the royal jet touched down and they went to identify Alberto's body.

Yesterday's state funeral in the basilica of Umbriano, presided over by the cardinal who had also delivered the eulogy, had been a great tribute to Alberto, a favorite son revered by the people. Dignitaries of many countries had attended, including of course the royal family of the Kingdom of Domodossola bordering France, Switzerland and Italy.

Stefano would never forget the vacant look on the face of Alberto's betrothed, Princess Lanza Rossiano of Domodossola, beneath her black, gauzy veil. He'd met war victims after serving a required year in the military in the Middle East who'd had that same lost, bewildered expression, their whole world wiped out.

The twenty-two-year-old daughter of King Victor Emmanuel of Domodossola had been betrothed to Alberto twelve months ago. Their marriage was supposed to take place a year from now on New Year's Day, and her family had clearly been devastated.

Stefano, who was rarely in the country because of business, hadn't met with King Victor's family since his childhood when both families got together on occasion. Meeting them again at the funeral, he was shocked to see all three of the king's daughters grown up. Not until he witnessed their bereavement did Stefano realize how terrible the news must have been for them. Stefano still couldn't believe Alberto was gone.

"Sit down. We have something vital to discuss."

By vital, his father must mean he wanted Stefano to stay around for a while, but that would be impossible because of Stefano's latest gold mining project in Kenya. He needed to fly there the day after tomorrow to oversee a whole new gold processing invention that could bring in a great deal more money. Hopefully, it would serve as a prototype for all his other gold mines throughout the world. He imagined he'd be gone six weeks at least.

With his hands clasped between his legs, Stefano closed his eyes, knowing his father was in so much pain at the moment that he needed all their support, but he was curious as to what his father wanted to talk about.

"The wedding to Princess Lanza must go on as planned. Since losing Alberto, your mother and I have talked of nothing else. It's imperative that *you* take your brother's place."

Stefano's head jerked up. "Surely, I didn't hear you correctly."

"I know this comes as a shock to you."

Stefano shot to his feet, incredulous. "Shock doesn't describe it, *Papà.*"

"Hear me out."

Stefano groaned and walked over to the mullioned windows looking out on the palatial estate with the snow-covered peaks of the Alps in the distance. An icy shiver passed through his taut body.

"Our two countries need to solidify in order to build the resources of both our kingdoms. This necessary merger can only happen by your marrying Princess Lanza."

Stefano wheeled around, gritting his teeth. "Years ago you gave me my freedom by parliamentary decree. I'm no longer a royal."

"That decree can be reversed by an emergency parliamentary edict."

"*What?*"

His father nodded. "I've already been investigating behind the scenes. Because of the enormity of this tragedy and their eagerness to see a marriage between our two countries happen, my advisors have informed me the parliament will reinstate you immediately."

Stefano couldn't believe it. "Even if it were possible, you're not seriously asking me to marry Princess Lanza, are you? I haven't been around her since she was a young girl. And I'm seven years older than she is."

"That's not a great age difference."

Stefano tried to calm down. "Alberto was the one who was attracted to her. I can't do this, *Papà.* Right now I'm doing everything in my power to develop more lucrative gold mines and invest the revenues to help our country grow richer. We don't need the timber from Domodossola!"

His father shook his head. "What I'm asking goes a great deal deeper than cementing fortunes. Victor and I have had this dream of uniting our two families in marriage since the moment we both became parents of future kings and queens."

"But it's not *my* dream, *Papà*, and never could be," Stefano said, attempting to control his anger. "I'm sorry, but I can't do what you ask."

"*Not even to honor your brother?*"

He hadn't realized his mother had come into the lounge wearing her dressing gown. The edge in her tone caught him off guard. "What do you mean, *Mamà?*"

"This has to do with keeping faith with a sacred pledge your brother made to Princess Lanza a year ago. She's been groomed to become Alberto's bride. For the past year her life has been put on hold because she wears our family betrothal ring. All this time she's been faithful to their pledge, preparing for their wedding day."

Stefano shook his head. "No one could have imagined this crisis. It changes all the rules."

"Except for one thing your father and I have never told you about because we didn't think we would have to."

Fearing what he'd hear, Stefano's heart jolted in his chest. "What do you mean?"

"On the morning you turned eighteen, your brother came to us in secret. He wanted to give you a gift he knew you wanted more than anything on earth."

His brows furrowed. "What was that?"

"What else? Your freedom."

"I don't understand, *Mamà.*"

"Then let me explain. You never wanted to be a royal. You made it clear from the time you were old enough to express your feelings. Alberto adored and worshipped you. By the time you turned eighteen, he was afraid you'd never be happy. He literally begged us to let you live a life free of royal duty.

"He loved you so much, he promised that he would fulfill all the things we would have asked of you as a royal prince who would rule one day so *you* could have the freedom to live life without the royal trappings. That was the bargain he made with us."

"A bargain? *That's* why you suddenly gave in to me?"

His father nodded solemnly. "The only reason, *figlio mio.* You two were so close, he put you before his own wants or desires. He convinced us you had to be able to go out in the world free to be your own person. Otherwise you'd die like an animal kept in a cage."

Alberto had actually told them that?

"All he asked was that we agree. Then he would do everything and more than we expected of him as a crown prince, *and*…he consented to become betrothed to Princess Lanza on whatever date we chose. He knew how much we loved her growing up. She was always a delight. In truth, he wanted his elder brother's happiness above all else, and made that request of us out of pure love."

Stefano stood there rigid as a piece of petrified wood. His parents had never lied to him. He had to believe them now. Because of his brother's love and intervention—and *not* because of his parents' understanding—Stefano had been able to escape the world he'd been born into all this time.

His mother walked over to him and put her hands on his shoulders. It pained him to see the lines of grief carved in her features.

"His only desire was that you never know how he pled for you. He worried that if you ever found out the truth, you would always feel beholden to him. That request was his unselfish gift to you."

Unselfish didn't begin to describe what Alberto had done to ensure his happiness.

In Stefano's mind and heart, it was an unheard-of gift. He'd always loved his younger brother, his buddy in childhood. Alberto's noble character made him beloved and elevated him above the ranks of ordinary people. Many times he'd heard people say that the good ones died young. His brother was the best of the best, and death had snatched him away prematurely.

Overcome with emotions assailing him, Stefano wrapped his arms around his mother until he could get a grip on them, then he let her go. He was amazed his parents had so much love for their sons that they'd gone along with both his and Alberto's wishes at the time. It was humbling and gave him new perspective.

Her eyes clung to his. "Would you be willing to do what Alberto can't do now? Take on the royal duty you were born to and marry Princess Lanza?"

He inhaled sharply. "Do you think she would consent when she'd planned to marry Alberto?"

"King Victor says his daughter will agree. You and Lanza knew each other in your youth and you have a whole year to get reacquainted."

"But that will be close to impossible, *Papà*. My schedule has been laid out with back-to-back visits of all the mines through the next eighteen months. There's no time when so many managers are depending on me, especially with the new mining process I've developed."

His father cocked his head. "After we inform her and her parents of your official proposal of marriage, surely you could find a way to visit her once and stay in touch with her the rest of the time? Both King Victor and I have already talked to the cardinal, who has given this marriage his blessing."

Stefano could see the die had been cast.

His mother eyed him through drenched eyes. "Our two countries have been looking forward to this day since you were all children. The citizens know that your business interests throughout the world have contributed to our country's economy. Umbriano will cheer your reinstatement and honor your name for stepping into your brother's shoes, believe me."

Stefano found all this difficult to fathom. There wasn't time for him to get reacquainted with Princess Lanza. Even if parliament voted to reinstate him as a royal, he had crucial business issues around the globe.

His father walked over to them. "I've never asked anything of you before, Stefano. I've allowed you to be your own person, free of all royal responsibilities, but fate stepped in and took Alberto away too early. Now is the time when your parents and Lanza's are asking this for the good of both our countries."

"Alberto told us he hoped to have a family." His mother stared at him with longing. "I'm sure Princess Lanza was planning on children, too. That dream is gone, but you could make a whole new dream begin. I've had that dream for you, too, Stefano.

"On all your travels for business and pleasure, you've never brought a woman home for us to meet, let alone marry. We were prepared that you'd eventually want marriage and have a family, but it has never come to pass. If there's a special woman, you haven't said anything."

Stefano sucked in his breath. This whole conversation was unreal, including a discussion of a woman in his life he couldn't do without. He'd met several and had enjoyed some intimate relationships, but the thought of settling down with one of them hadn't entered his mind. As Alberto had said, he liked his freedom too much.

"Have you even considered Princess Lanza's feelings?" he asked them in a grating voice, struggling to make sense of this situation.

His father nodded. "King Victor and I talked about it before the funeral. He's as anxious as I for this to happen and has probably discussed this with her already. Victor assures me it's in her nature to do what is good for both countries."

No normal woman worth her salt would agree to such a loveless marriage, but a royal princess was a different matter if she believed it was her duty. Over the phone a few months ago, Alberto had told him in private that Princess Lanza had a sweet, biddable disposition.

Maybe she did. But the many royal princesses he'd met in his early teens were very spoiled, full of themselves, impossible to please, moody and felt entitled to the point of absurdity.

His vague memory of Lanza was that she was nice, but that was years ago and she'd been so young. His brother was a kind, decent human being. Alberto always tried to find the best in everyone and had probably made up his mind to like her.

After hearing what his parents had just told him about the sacrifice he'd made for Stefano, it was possible Alberto hadn't liked Princess Lanza at all. But he would have pretended otherwise to fulfill his obligations after making the incredible bargain with their parents. It was Alberto's way.

Stefano shook his head. He wasn't born with that kind of greatness in his soul. Humbled by what he'd learned, tortured by the decision his parents were asking him to make, he started for the door. "I need to be alone to think and will be back later."

Once outside in the chilling air, he drove his Lancia into the city to talk to his best friend, Enzo Perino, who managed his own father's banking interests. Stefano found him in his office on the phone.

The second Enzo saw him in the doorway, he waved him inside. After he hung up, he lunged from the chair to hug him. "I'm so sorry about Alberto."

"So am I, Enzo."

"Chiara and I couldn't get near you at the funeral. There were too many people." Stefano nodded. "Come to our house tonight for dinner so we can really talk."

He stared at his best friend who'd recently married. They'd been friends throughout childhood and had done everything together, including military service. Stefano had been the best man at their wedding three months ago.

"I need help."

Enzo chuckled. "Since when have you ever needed a loan?"

Stefano sat down in one of the leather chairs. "I wish money were the problem, but it isn't."

As Stefano's father had emphasized, this suggested marriage had a lot more riding on it than financial considerations.

"You sound serious."

"More serious than you'll ever know."

"Go ahead. I'm listening."

"My father woke me up at the crack of dawn to have a talk." In the next few minutes he told Enzo the thrust of the conversation with his parents, including the necessary part about being reinstated by parliament.

"Our marriage will make me heir apparent to the throne of Domodossola since King Victor has no sons. He doesn't have any married daughters yet. According to their rules of succession, a woman can't become queen in their country. He'll have to rely on a son-in-law."

His friend whistled and sank down in the chair behind his desk. "I know this used to happen in the Middle Ages, but not today." He looked gutted. "Who will take over Umbriano when *your* father can no longer rule?"

"My sister, but I imagine that's many years away. Our country doesn't run by the same laws. You know that. Since I was granted my freedom, she's been raised to be second in line should anything happen to Alberto. Which it did," he said in a mournful tone.

"But if you're reinstated—"

"No—" He interrupted him. "My destiny lies with the throne of Domodossola, the only reason for reinstating me."

Enzo slapped his hands on the desk. "There goes the end of our friendship."

"Don't you ever say that!"

He smiled sadly. "How can I not? With you living in Domodossola, you'll be a prisoner running the affairs of government, hardly ever free to leave the country or have time for me. What will you do with all your mining companies?"

"I still plan to run them, of course."

"Then you'll be carrying a double load. I thought it was too good to be true when your father released you from your princely duties on your eighteenth birthday. We should have known it would all come to an early end."

Stefano closed his eyes for a minute, never imagining he'd lose his brother so young. "I haven't told my parents what I'm going to do. Not yet."

While he'd driven into town, he'd considered the huge decision his parents had made to give Stefano his freedom. In searching his soul, one thing became clear. He could solve his parents' dilemma about the marriage situation by unselfishly taking Alberto's place. How could he not when his brother had willingly done his double royal duty to make up for Stefano's absence?

"It'll happen," Enzo muttered. "I know how much you loved Alberto. You'll never let your parents down now that you know of your brother's sacrifice. As for Princess Lanza, she'll agree to marry you. After all, you are Alberto's brother and she knew you when your families got together as children."

"That's true, but I was hoping for some much-needed advice from you."

They stared at each other for a long time. "All right—there's only one way I can see this working. You need your freedom, so do her the biggest favor of her life and yours. You've got a year before the wedding. Let her know *before* you're married that you plan to be your own person and continue doing the mining work you love while you help her father govern. It'll mean you'll be apart from her for long periods. Give her time to adjust to that fact, know what I mean?"

Pain wasn't the right word to describe Lanza's feelings since returning from the funeral in Umbriano four days ago. Shock would be more precise. Prince Alberto had always been kind to her when they had met. She'd never felt uncomfortable with him.

The second-born son of her father's best friend, King Basilio of Umbriano, had been mild-mannered. Over the years and occasional family get-togethers, both families felt their two children were the perfect fit. Since they'd wanted the marriage to happen, they went ahead with the betrothal on her twenty-first birthday.

According to what her parents had told her, they'd believed that out of her two sisters, Lanza had the right temperament and disposition to be the wife for Prince Alberto, who'd shown an interest in her.

From that time on Lanza had spent several weekends a month

with Alberto, both in Domodossola and Umbriano. They'd developed a friendship that helped her to get ready for her marriage. She'd enjoyed being kissed by him, but they hadn't been lovers.

The fact that he was nice-looking had made it easier to imagine intimacy in their marriage. She'd liked him well enough and believed they could be happy. But now that he was gone, one truth stood out from everything else.

She hadn't lost the love of her life.

Furthermore, his death had made her aware of her own singlehood in a way she would never have anticipated. Since the betrothal she'd known what her future would be. For the past year she'd been planning on the intimacy of marriage and family, the kind her parents enjoyed. Yet in an instant, that future had died with him.

His life had been snuffed out in seconds because of a car crash on an icy, narrow mountain road when he'd swerved to avoid a truck. The accident had robbed her of the destiny planned out for her. But as sorry as she was for Alberto and his family, a part of her realized that she was now free to make different plans.

There was no law of succession in Domodossola since a female couldn't rule. Now her parents would have to look elsewhere for a prince who would marry one of her older sisters, either Fausta or Donetta.

The sad, legitimate release of her betrothal vows gave Lanza a sense of liberation she'd never known before. Heaven help her but the thought was exciting. So exciting, in fact, she was assailed with uncomfortable guilt considering this was a time of mourning, and she *did* mourn Alberto's death.

In an attempt to help her deal with the fact that Prince Alberto had been taken prematurely, the palace priest, Father Mario, had been summoned. He counseled her that she should be grateful Alberto hadn't been forced to live through years of suffering. If his life had been spared, he might have lost limbs or been paralyzed.

Of course she was thankful for that and appreciated the priest's coming to see her, but no one understood what was going on inside her. No longer would she be marking time, waiting for her future with Alberto to start. There was no future except the one she would make from here on out. In truth, Lanza found the thought rich with possibilities.

Since returning from the funeral, it hit her with stunning force that she was alone and dependent on herself to make her own decisions, just like her sisters had been allowed to do. This strange new experience wasn't unlike watching a balloon that had escaped a string and was left to float with no direction in mind. But she knew what she wanted to do first.

With this new sense of freedom, she planned to visit her favorite aunt, Zia Ottavia, who lived in Rome with her husband, Count Verrini. They could talk about anything and Lanza loved her.

A knock on the door of her apartment brought her back from her thoughts.

"Lanza?" Her mother's voice. "May your father and I come in?"

She assumed they wanted to comfort her and she loved them for it. Lanza hurried across the room and opened the door, giving them both a long hug. "Come in and sit in front of the fire."

They took their places on the couch. She sat in her favorite easy chair across from them where she often planted herself to read. She'd been a bookworm from an early age.

"We asked Father Mario to visit you. Did he come?"

"Yes, and he gave me encouragement."

"Oh, good," her dark-blonde mother murmured, but Lanza could tell her parents were more anxious than ever and looked positively ill from the shock they'd all lived through. "We don't think it's good for you to stay in your apartment any longer. I've asked the cook to prepare your favorite meal, and your sisters are going to join us in the dining room for an early dinner."

Her distinguished-looking father nodded. "You need to be around family. It isn't healthy for you to be alone."

"Actually, I've needed this time to myself in order to think. Please don't be offended if I tell you I'm not hungry and couldn't eat a big meal."

"But if you keep this up, you'll waste away," her mother protested.

"No, Mamà. I promise that won't happen. Right now I have important things on my mind."

"We do, too," her father broke in. "It's time we talked seriously."

She sat back. "What is it, Papà?"

He got to his feet and stoked the fire. "I've been on the phone with Basilio almost constantly for days."

"That doesn't surprise me. I'm sure Alberto's death has brought you two even closer. He and Queen Diania must be in desperate need of comfort."

Her father blinked. "You're really not all right, are you, my dear girl?"

She frowned. "What do you mean?"

"You...don't seem quite yourself," her mother blurted.

If Lanza's parents had expected her to fall apart and take to her bed, then they truly didn't understand.

"I've shed my tears, but all it has done is give me a headache. I have to pull myself together and deal with the here and now. Honestly, I'll be fine. In fact, I'm thinking of taking a trip to Rome to visit Zia Ottavia.

"She phoned me last night and asked me to stay with her for a few months. She's planning to take a long trip to the US and wants me to go with her while Zio Salvatore has to stay in Rome on business. I love being with her and told her I'd come after I talked to you."

He shook his head. "I'm afraid you can't go."

What? She sat forward. "I don't understand."

He cleared his throat. "Alberto's brother, Stefano, has asked for your hand in marriage and wishes to marry you on New Year's Day in a year as planned."

NEW NEXT MONTH!

There's much more than land at stake for two rival Montana ranching families in this exciting new book in the Powder River series from *New York Times* bestselling author B.J. Daniels.

RIVER STRONG

In-store and online January 2024.

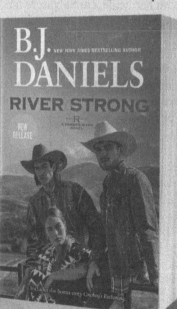

MILLS & BOON

millsandboon.com.au